P9-CCX-658

LIBERTY'S LAST STAND

STEPHEN COONTS

LIBERTY'S LAST STAND

REGNERY PUBLISHING
A Division of Salem Media Group

ISBN 978-1-62157-507-8

Cataloging-in-Publication Data on file with the Library of Congress

Published in the United States by
Regnery Publishing
A Division of Salem Media Group
300 New Jersey Ave NW
Washington, DC 20001
www.Regnery.com

Manufactured in the United States of America

10 9 8 7 6 5 4 3 2 1

Books are available in quantity for promotional or premium use. For information on discounts and terms, please visit our website: www.Regnery.com.

Distributed to the trade by
Perseus Distribution
250 West 57th Street
New York, NY 10107

ALSO BY STEPHEN COONTS

The Art of War
Saucer: Savage Planet
Saucer: The Conquest
Saucer
Pirate Alley
The Disciple
The Assassin
The Traitor
Liars & Thieves
Liberty
America
Hong Kong
Cuba
Fortunes of War
The Intruders
The Red Horseman
Under Siege
The Minotaur
Final Flight
Flight of the Intruder

WITH WILLIAM H. KEITH

Deep Black: Death Wave
Deep Black: Sea of Terror
Deep Black: Arctic Gold

WITH JIM DEFELICE

Deep Black: Conspiracy
Deep Black: Jihad
Deep Black: Payback
Deep Black: Dark Zone
Deep Black: Biowar
Deep Black

NONFICTION

The Cannibal Queen

ANTHOLOGIES

The Sea Witch
On Glorious Wings
Victory
Combat
War in the Air

WRITING AS EVE ADAMS

The Garden of Eden

To all those persons, wherever they are, who believe in Liberty.

The oath to be taken by the president on first entering office is specified in Article II, Section 1, of the United States Constitution.

"I do solemnly swear (or affirm) that I will faithfully execute the office of President of the United States, and will to the best of my ability, preserve, protect and defend the Constitution of the United States."

PROLOGUE

★

On that third Saturday in August, four separate events came together and snowballed into an avalanche that forever changed life in the United States.

The first occurred on a ranch in west Texas, a few minutes after one in the morning. There was no moon, so the night was dark, enlivened only by a million stars in the clear sky. The ranch belonged to Joseph Robert Hays, Joe Bob to his friends. For many years Joe Bob had made a modest living raising cattle on his twenty-two-thousand-acre spread, but drought and economics finally forced him out of that business. Like the very first Texans, he had no intention of giving up his land, so he decided to try something else.

Today the ranch raised African game animals, a dozen varieties of antelope, which rich sportsmen paid Joe Bob serious money to hunt. Why go to Africa to hunt, Africa with its desperate poverty and brutal Islamic terrorists? Hunt right here in Texas, in the beating heart of the good ol' US of A. That was what his brochures said that he mailed to anyone who inquired about his ranch. His youngest son was a schoolteacher and had cleaned up the message so it read smoother in the brochures, but that is the way Joe Bob wrote it.

Joe Bob also picked up a little money by hosting scout camps on weekends over the winter and making sure every camper got to see and photograph some of the exotic species.

His ranch adjoined the Rio Grande, the river that formed the boundary between the United States and Mexico, with its poverty, caste system, and systemic corruption. So the poor Mexicans migrated. Over thirteen million of them, over a fifth of the Mexican population, had crossed that border illegally in the last fifty years and were grubbing for work in the United States, usually for minimum wage, or living on welfare and food stamps. Illiterate, unskilled, and usually unable to speak English, they flooded the schools with their children, kept blue-collar wages low, and formed an underclass that resisted assimilation and required huge amounts of public assistance dollars.

American politicians had done little through the years to stem the flood. Hispanic voters wanted their kinsmen to be able to enter the United States regardless of their ability to contribute to the economy or pay their own bills, yet this wasn't the decisive factor. Farmers and small-business men wanted a source of cheap labor, and were content to pass the true costs, the social costs, on to the taxpayers. Generous public welfare programs also drew millions of Mexicans, more than small business or agriculture could possibly use. Even draining off an eighth of the population didn't really help Mexico, which found itself racked by turf wars between vicious criminal gangs that smuggled drugs into the United States to supply the richest narcotics market in the world.

Joe Bob's ranch had six miles of riverfront, and unfortunately sat astride an ancient trail up from old Mexico, one that had been used for millennia. The tread of thousands of feet for thousands of years had left their mark on the land. The trail began somewhere in the Mexican state of Coahuila, hundreds of miles to the south, but it could be accessed from a dirt road that crossed it two miles south of the river. From there it descended into an arroyo, avoiding the sandstone escarpments that the river had left in the tens of millions of years it had been eroding the land. The escarpments, cliffs of hard, dense rock from eight to twelve feet high, were vertical and formed walls that spread out from the arroyo in a fan pattern. On the north side of the river, the trail, about six feet wide and packed hard, climbed another arroyo into the scrub brush of the Hays ranch. The trail was the easiest and most direct way to get from the dirt road south of the river to the hard road on the north side of the ranch.

Drug smugglers sent the mules—men carrying drugs in backpacks—from the road on short summer nights after dark. They would wade the river, cross the Hays ranch on the north side, throw the drugs over the fence there to men waiting with a van, then walk back and be south of the river, safe in old Mexico, by dawn.

When he ran cattle, Joe Bob Hays had used a three-strand barbed wire fence across the trail about three hundred yards north of the river to keep his cattle in. Illegal immigrants and drug smugglers had to merely lift the top wire and press one down to crawl through. When he got into the hunting business, Joe Bob had to build a much better fence to hold the exotics, an eight-foot-high chain-link affair topped with a strand of barbed wire. The fence was more expensive than the animals. He borrowed money from the bank at the county seat to finance both. In addition to keeping the antelope in, the fence kept the Mexicans out, so they cut it, allowing the various species of expensive antelope to escape the ranch.

Joe Bob was nothing if not determined. After he had repaired holes in the fence a half-dozen times, he decided he had had enough. He complained to the Border Patrol, the DEA, and the county sheriff, and he wrote letters to his congressman and senators and members of the Texas legislature. All to no avail. The DEA, mysterious as always, didn't reply to his letters. Those who replied said they were sorry, but nothing could be done. Neither the Border Patrol nor the sheriff's department had the manpower to guard his fence.

The politicians pointed their fingers at the president, who, for political reasons, was in a squabble with Congress about immigration and refused to compromise. Of course, he was merely the latest president, and this was the latest Congress, to do little or nothing about the unarmed invasion from Mexico. Someday, someway, all those illegals would become American voters, and when it happened in that distant, hazy someday, both political parties would want their votes, but none more so than the Democrats, who had bet their political future on the bedrock of welfare and food stamps for the uneducated, the unskilled, the addicted, and the shiftless unable or unwilling to find work in an American economy increasingly fueled by science, technology, and government employment.

It never occurred to Joe Bob to complain to the Mexican government, which actively encouraged its citizens to migrate illegally to the United States and was infamously corrupted by criminals in the drug business.

So the last time he repaired his fence, Joe Bob put tin cans with small rocks in them on the top strand of barbed wire. The cans tinkled when the wind moved the wire, and they should tinkle when Mexicans operated on the chain links with wire cutters.

Tonight Joe Bob sat under some scrub brush on the bank of the arroyo on his side of the fence. Across his knees was an old Marlin lever action in .30-30, with a nightscope mounted on it that he had ordered from a Cabela's catalog.

He had been here for two nights, had seen and heard no one, and was tired. Yet this evening before twilight he had seen dust to the south, so he thought some Mexicans might come tonight. If they were drug smugglers, they wouldn't cut the fence by the hard road. Illegal immigrants would cut the northern fence, however, to squeeze through.

Damn them all, anyhow.

Joe Bob opened his snuff can and put a pinch in his mouth. He really wanted a cigarette, but they might see the glow or smell the smoke. He wanted to surprise them, throw some shots around, run them back across the river. The sons of bitches could find another place to cross, and no doubt would. But he was sick and tired of working on his goddamn fence.

He was thinking about a drink of water when he heard the cans rattle down in the arroyo. Someone, man or animal, was fooling with the fence.

Joe Bob lifted his rifle and began scanning with the scope, looking for people.

What he didn't know was that two Mexican gunmen on the other side of the fence were also looking for him with nightscopes, better ones than Joe Bob could afford. They had been hired to escort eight mules to the paved highway on the northern side of Joe Bob's ranch, where a vehicle would meet them to take the packages of cocaine on to Los Angeles.

The lead mule rattled the fence while the gunmen searched. One of the shooters, Jesus Morales, spotted Joe Bob Hays seated under a bush and settled the crosshairs of his scope on him. He squeezed the trigger.

The bullet smacked Joe Bob in the chest, a mortal wound, and he went over backward.

Nothing else moved on the ranch side of the fence, so after a twenty-minute wait to be sure, the fence was cut and the mules moved through the opening up the ancient trail. Morales climbed the bank of the arroyo to where Joe Bob Hays lay bleeding out. He found him with the nightscope.

To Morales' amazement, the rancher was still alive. Morales pointed his rifle at the dying man's head and pulled the trigger. His head exploded.

The Mexicans moved on, walking north with their loads. The wheels of commerce were turning, as they had to turn, for that was the way of the world.

At eleven o'clock that Saturday morning four clean-shaven, skinny young men bought tickets for the Amtrak Express to New York at the BWI Airport station between Washington and Baltimore. They had arrived in a stolen car that they parked on the upper level of the garage adjacent to the station. Carrying backpacks, they took the stairs down and into the train station and stood in line to buy tickets. When their turns came, they each paid cash for a ticket to New York, then went out onto the platform to wait for the train. There were no metal detectors to pass through; no one inspected their backpacks.

Ten minutes later the train arrived right on time. They climbed aboard, each entering a different car.

They found seats. The train was crowded, as usual. The young men looked around and were pleased to see that there were no uniformed police, no armed guards of any type, not that they expected any. This was America, the most under-policed nation on earth.

The train pulled out right on time, at twenty-two minutes after the hour. There was no clanking and jerking. Powered by electric locomotives, the train merely glided into motion.

The traveler who had boarded the last car, Salah al Semn, found that the only empty seat was in the middle of the car, facing two fit young men, one white, one black, clean-shaven, with military haircuts, wearing jeans and pull-over short-sleeve shirts. He had seen that type before in Iraq, and suspected, rightly, that they were in the American military. He ignored them. Beside him was a young person with unkempt long hair wearing ear buds and apparently listening to an iPod.

With their backpacks on their laps or in the overhead bins, all four of the men who boarded at BWI sat back in their seats, avoided eye contact with their fellow passengers, and checked their watches. They had some time to wait, so they watched the countryside pass outside the windows and thought private thoughts as the train ran along through suburbs and into downtown Baltimore.

In the Chicago suburb of Arlington Heights, a van pulled up outside a parochial school. There were three men in it, brown, clean-shaven skinny men in jeans. They sat watching as families parked their cars and took children into the school. Today was registration day for a new school year that was to begin Monday. Nuns ran the school and taught some of the classes. In the office, nuns supervised the registration process and shook hands with the parents and greeted the students, most of whom were returning for another year. The school was for children in grades one through six. It had been in operation for over a hundred years, and many of the parents were graduates.

The name of the school, Our Sisters of Mercy, was emblazoned above the main entrance, but the men in the van couldn't read the words. Not only did they not know how to read and write English, they were illiterate in all the world's languages, including their own, which was Farsi. The only education any of the three had ever received was in an Islamic school, where the sole item in the curriculum was the memorization of the Koran. The Prophet's message, their teachers knew, was all the boys really needed to know to wend their way through this vale of tears and earn their way into Paradise.

The men in the van checked their watches. As the two in the front seat scrutinized every vehicle and watched traffic on the street, the man in back began opening bags and extracting semiautomatic AR-15 assault rifles, into which he inserted magazines.

At Yankee Stadium in the Bronx the players were on the field warming up, tossing balls around, taking batting practice, and signing autographs for the kids and fans who hung over the rails. The Yanks were not having a good year; they were third in the American League East standings, ten games off the pace, so management expected that only half the seats in the stadium would have bodies in them when the game against the Detroit Tigers started at precisely one o'clock.

The jihadist, Nuri Said, sat in the top tier of seats watching the activities on the field as fans wandered in. He had attended two games in the past few weeks and had a rudimentary understanding of the game, which he thought boring. Mainly he watched the uniformed police who stood here and there at the portals that people had to pass through to get to and from the stands to the vast galleries where there were restaurants, fast food stands, and restrooms.

Nuri had chosen Yankee Stadium for his jihad strike because of the television cameras that would make him and his three mates famous and immortal. The police were a necessary evil, he thought, and would kill all four of them, but not until after the cameras had captured the naked power of Islam for all the world's infidels to see and ponder. Nuri Said and his three fellow believers would please Allah, he knew, which was more than most men accomplished in this life. That would be enough.

Salah al Semn found the waiting hard. He fidgeted. He tried to avoid eye contact with his fellow passengers on the train to New York, but found that he was watching them, sizing them up, wondering who they were as they got on and off at the depots in Baltimore and Wilmington.

He repeatedly checked his watch. He was acutely aware that the two young men opposite him were watching him. Every time he glanced their way their eyes were upon him, and they didn't look away.

He would kill them first, he thought. Infidel dogs.

The train was sliding into the station in Philadelphia when Salah al Semn checked his watch for the last time, picked up the backpack, which he had placed on the floor under his legs, and made his way toward the restroom.

Marine Sergeant Mike Ivy and Lance Corporal Scott Weidmann were from Brooklyn. They were on their way home for a week's leave before they shipped out for tours in South Korea.

"He's got a gun in that bag," Weidmann whispered to Ivy.

"Something hard, with angles," Ivy agreed. "Ain't his underwear."

As al Semn opened the door to the restroom and went inside, Ivy and Weidmann got up and went to the restroom door. Ivy put his ear to the door. The train coasted to a stop in the Philadelphia station.

The two Marines had to make way for people getting on and off the train, but in a moment the rush was over. Ivy leaned nonchalantly against the restroom door and listened while Weidmann watched the passengers in the car to see if anyone was paying attention. They weren't, he decided. Everyone was getting settled for the ride on to Newark, then Pennsylvania Station in New York.

Ivy said to Weidmann, "Bastard's putting his weapon together. Ain't nothing else sounds like that."

"What do you want to do?" Weidmann asked. He automatically deferred to the senior man.

"I figure it's a rifle or something. He'll come out of there with the thing pointing up so he can make the turn. Not much room. You slam the door on him and I'll take it away from him."

They took their positions and waited.

★

In Arlington Heights, the three men in the van inspected their weapons. Each made sure he had two extra magazines in his pocket, and pulled a ski mask down over his head. They doubted that they would survive this strike so it didn't matter if their faces were seen: they wore the masks to create terror in the heart of everyone who saw them. Terrorized people don't think or fight back, so they are easy to slaughter. Not that any of the three thought the nuns and children and suburban parents would fight back. These people were Christians, who routinely defamed and ridiculed the Prophet, may he rest in peace. They deserved what was coming.

In Yankee Stadium Nuri Said met his fellow terrorists at a trash can near a service door. One of them, from Iraq, had worked at the stadium for two weeks and had smuggled in weapons and ammunition, which were hidden in the can. As the last minutes ticked by and the national anthem played on the loudspeakers throughout the stadium, Nuri and his three jihadists reached into the can, dug out the trash that covered the weapons, and removed them. Checked that they were loaded. Pocketed spare magazines. And pulled black ski masks over their heads.

Then they walked toward the nearest portal to the stands. There was a woman policeman there, and Nuri saw her before she saw him. He shot her. Even though she was wearing a bulletproof vest, she went down from the impact. The report of the weapon seemed magnified inside that concrete gallery, like a thunderclap. It triggered screams. Or perhaps the sight of the ski masks and weapons triggered them.

People panicked and tried to run. One of the terrorists stood there methodically firing single shots as fast as he could aim his weapon. His three colleagues ran out the portal into the grandstands.

Salah al Semn stood in the tiny restroom aboard the express train with his AR-15 at port arms, loaded, with the safety off, and looked at his watch again. One minute to go. The train was accelerating out of the station. He could see the concrete and roofs moving through the little window and feel the motion of the car on the uneven rails.

He knew precisely what he had to do. Exit the restroom and start shooting people in this car, the nearest first.

When he had shot everyone in this car, he was to proceed forward to the other cars, where three other shooters were working. When everyone in all four cars was dead, he and any surviving shooters were to proceed all the way forward, executing people until they reached the engine.

Salah al Semn knew he would see Paradise soon, and he was ready. He would go with the blood of infidels on his hands, one of the holiest martyrs. The Prophet would be proud!

He took a deep breath and opened the door.

As it opened, he saw one of the American soldiers standing there, the black man, within a foot. He grabbed for Salah's weapon and jerked it toward him. Salah grabbed for the trigger, and the door slammed into him with terrific force. He lost control of the rifle.

Sergeant Mike Ivy didn't hesitate. He merely pulled the rifle toward him, then drove the butt at al Semn's Adam's apple with all the force he could muster. The blow pushed the Syrian back into the restroom. The commode caught the back of his legs, and he lost his balance and fell.

Mike Ivy was already examining the AR-15. It was loaded, with a round chambered. Ivy and Weidmann both heard muffled shots from the passenger car ahead of this one. Ivy glanced at Weidmann, nodded to the restroom, and Weidmann said, "Go."

Mike Ivy began running forward as people screamed and tried to cower behind their seats.

Lance Corporal Scott Weidmann jerked the door open and reached down for Salah al Semn, jerking him upright. The Syrian decided to fight, which was a fatal error. Weidmann's first blow was aimed at his solar plexus, which took the air out of the Syrian and doubled him up. His second blow, an elbow to the man's left ear, was delivered with so much force that the man's neck snapped. Dead on his feet, Salah al Semn collapsed…and started his journey to Paradise. Or Hell, depending on your faith.

Scott Weidmann left the Syrian sprawled half in, half out of the restroom and ran after Sergeant Ivy, toward the sound of shots.

He jerked open the door to the car ahead just in time to see Ivy shoot a terrorist and drop him in the aisle. People were sobbing and shouting; an unknown number had been shot. Ivy reached the body of the hooded man first, grabbed his weapon, and tossed it back to Weidmann, who fielded it in the air. As Ivy turned to go forward, Weidmann stomped on the terrorist's larynx, crushing it. Then the two Marines ran on, toward the next car.

The three shooters walked into the parochial school and the first person they saw was a nun, so they shot her. One of them, a Yemeni named Hassan, stopped to cut her throat with a knife as the other two shot down several families standing there, men, women, and kids.

Vinnie Latucca was in the principal's office with his granddaughter talking to Sister Mary Catherine, who had been one of his teachers when he was a pupil at Our Sisters of Mercy forty-some years ago. He heard the sound of gunfire and reached into his pocket for his .38 Smith & Wesson with a four-inch barrel. Vinnie never went anywhere without it.

Telling Sister Mary Catherine and his granddaughter to stay where they were, he opened the door a crack. One of the gunmen entered the office area with his weapon up. As the gunman fired at the ten or twelve people in the room, Vinnie Latucca cocked his revolver, steadied it on the door jam, and fired. One shot. The masked man with a rifle went down.

Gunfire continued to sound. A woman was bent over her limp child, cradling him, sobbing softly as Vinnie Latucca shot the gunman again, this time in the head, and then helped himself to the AR. He eased the outer office door open so he could see down the hallway.

No shooter in sight, so he pocketed his revolver and stepped out.

He walked toward the sound of gunfire and found the next shooter in a classroom. The fool had his back to the door and was shooting kids. Vinnie shot him twice in the back with the AR, then rolled him over and jerked the ski mask from his head. He put the barrel of the rifle in the man's mouth and pulled the trigger, exploding his head. The man might have been dead by then, but Vinnie hoped not.

The third man must have wondered why there was no more gunfire, because when Vinnie Latucca stepped out of the classroom into the corridor he fired a shot at him. Vinnie was quicker. Three fast, aimed shots dropped the man. He didn't even twitch. If he had, Vinnie would have blown his head off too. He ripped off the ski mask, saw the fixed eyes, and stood listening for shots.

What he heard was the sound of a siren. For the first time in his life, the sound filled Vinnie Latucca with relief.

Detective Victor Goldman, NYPD, was in the middle of his seating section when the gunmen who exited the portal into the grandstand area opened fire. He heard the shots and saw two of them. He didn't know there were three.

He had a .380 automatic strapped to his ankle, so he pulled it out and tried to get a shot. People were sobbing, shouting, diving for cover so he couldn't get a clear shot. And he was too far away. At least thirty feet, with a pistol with a three-inch barrel and a million people behind the gunmen, so if he missed he would hit a civilian or two.

He had to get closer. He made his two boys get down under the seats, then he started trying to crawl over people to get closer to the shooters, who were blazing away.

His chance came when the nearest gunman realized his magazine was empty and bent down to pop it out of his weapon and insert another. Vic Goldman had closed to ten feet. He took careful aim, using both hands on the hideout pistol, and shot the gunman in the chest. He half-turned and Vic shot him again.

That was when the gunman Vic hadn't seen shot him high in the back. Vic went down on his face, fatally wounded. He was dead when police shooting from the portals killed all the gunmen still standing, and still dead an hour later when a paramedic team found him with his two sons, ages seven and nine, holding his hands.

Someone pulled the emergency cord on the Amtrak train, so the brakes locked on every car and it screeched to a stop. Mike Ivy and Scott Weidmann had killed the third shooter by then.

After the train stopped, the fourth gunman leaped from the train onto the gravel beside the tracks. He was on a dead run heading for Newark when Sergeant Mike Ivy dropped him from a distance of one hundred yards with one shot between the shoulder blades.

As Ivy and Weidmann stood in front of the locomotive looking down at the terrorist, Weidmann said, "Nice shot, Sarge."

Ivy pointed the rifle at the dead man's crotch and fired a shot.

"Bastard won't be able to fuck his virgins in Paradise," he explained.

"You believe that shit?"

"Hell, no, but they do. Send them cock-less."

It was late afternoon in Arlington Heights when Assistant District Attorney Ronald Farrington walked into the room where Vinnie Latucca sat with two uniformed police officers and motioned to them. They stood and left, closing the door behind them.

The lawyer laid Vinnie's .38 on the table and nodded to it. "If we get a bullet for comparison, are we going to find any bullets from old open cases that match it?"

"Of course not," Vinnie said disgustedly. "That's a clean gun."

"Or you wouldn't have been carrying it."

Vinnie nodded and lit a cigarette.

"The nuns don't allow smoking in the building."

"I don't think they'll mind this evening," Vinnie replied, and blew smoke around.

Farrington sighed. "How many guys have you hit, anyway? Off the record."

Vinnie smoked in silence.

"We have you on a weapons charge if the DA decides to prosecute. I doubt if he will. You did good today. Saved a lot of lives."

Vinnie didn't say anything.

"Put your gun in your pocket and go home," Farrington said.

Vinnie pocketed the piece and stood.

Farrington held out his hand. "I'd like to shake your hand," the lawyer said.

Vinnie grinned, shook hands, and walked out. His daughter and granddaughter were waiting for him on the school lawn.

ONE

★

Occasionally people ask me, What were you doing that day? You know—that day, that Saturday the terrorists hit the United States hard? Again. Fifteen years after 9/11 had dropped the World Trade Center, more American blood had been spilled on the altar of global jihad.

My name is Tommy Carmellini, and the people who ask that question know that back then I worked for Jake Grafton. At the time he was the director of the CIA, the Central Intelligence Agency. Perhaps I should tell you a bit about Jake Grafton, a retired two-star navy admiral, a former attack pilot, a genuinely nice guy, and the worst enemy you could imagine in an alcohol-soaked nightmare. He was a pretty good spook too. So-so shuffling paper. He had an uncanny ability to connect the dots, not just the ones you and I could see, but the ones that only a savant could have suspected might be there.

Yet Jake Grafton was pretty closemouthed. He never talked about his boss. He took orders and gave orders and you never knew what the man who lived behind those gray eyes was really thinking. Until the shooting started. Then…well, then you found out that Jake Grafton was the perfect attack pilot. Away up there in the blue going fast, out of sight of the people on the ground, he could roll in, draw a bead with his bomb, and turn it loose. To kill you. Then he pulled out and dodged the flak and pointed his ass at the blast and left the vicinity to get on with his life.

While your doom was falling from the sky, toward you. That was Jake Grafton.

So...what was I doing that day, the day the old world came to an end? Well, I was in Colorado watching the windup to a Federal Emergency Management Agency (FEMA) exercise, Jade Helm 16.

When I got back to my hotel, the television in the lobby said over a hundred people were dead and another hundred injured, some seriously, not expected to live, after the three terror strikes. At least three of the terrorists had been Syrian refugees, and several of the others were here illegally.

Around the world, the news was all bad, but especially in the Middle East, where it looked like the Sunnis and Shiites were well on their way to a Hundred Years' War, each sect trying to exterminate the other, and any Christians who happened to be available. There were rumors of stray nuclear weapons, and there were definitely floods of refugees—and who knew, maybe terrorists among then—pouring into Turkey and Europe.

Back in the good old USA, we were already getting started on a presidential election campaign, and it was ugly. Both sides assured the voters that if the other side won, it was the end of civilization as we know it. And then there was the Soetoro government, getting ready for a civil war.

On Sunday I flew back to Washington. The airports looked like armed camps. Armed soldiers in full battle dress were everywhere, and there weren't many people volunteering to be victims of an airliner bombing. My plane was less than half full.

On Monday I finished my report on the FEMA exercise at my cubbyhole office at the CIA facility in the Langley, Virginia, neighborhood. When I ran out of words I decided to print out my opus and proof it. I stamped the report SECRET using my desk inkpad, stapled it together, and read it through. Signed it.

I had spent the two weeks of the exercise in Colorado at exercise headquarters, the buildings that the Federal Emergency Management Agency occupied on the federal reservation on West Sixth Avenue in Lakewood, a suburb of Denver. The head dog was a Homeland Security career civil servant who had obviously impressed his political bosses with his zeal and commitment to the cause of federal supremacy against all domestic foes.

When my report was ready for prime time on Monday morning, I walked it and the classified summary down the hall to the director's office. Admiral Grafton was in, the receptionist said.

I just had time to pour myself a cup of coffee before the receptionist sent me in. Grafton was sitting there behind his desk looking sour, and Sal Molina, the president's man Friday, was sitting across from him. Molina looked sour too. I guess the view from the White House wasn't much better than it was from my apartment.

Grafton motioned me to a seat. I handed him my report, with the classified summary attached, and he flipped through it. He was a tad over six feet tall, lean and ropy, with thinning, graying hair combed straight back. No one would ever call him handsome, not with a nose that was a size too large. When you looked straight at him, you forgot about the nose. It was those cold gray eyes that captured you.

Molina, on the other hand, was a middle-sized guy with a twenty-pound spare tire and a shiny dome. He looked as if he were about ten years younger than Grafton, in his mid to late fifties.

The admiral tossed the report at Molina and said to me, "Tell us about it."

"Jade Helm is an exercise about how the government will put down a right-wing uprising, or rebellion, and arrest everyone they think might be sympathetic with the rebels. They'll use these paramilitary police they have tucked into every government alphabet agency as storm troopers and SS troops—"

That was as far as I got. Molina exploded. "Comparing the federal government to Nazis is unacceptable. I am not going to sit here listening to that kind of shit, Carmellini."

I didn't say anything. Sal Molina couldn't fire me, and if Grafton did, I was ready to be on my way. Truth was, I had been in the belly of the beast for far too long.

"Go on, Tommy," Grafton prompted, ignoring Molina.

"They'll arrest every prominent Republican they can find and hold them in guarded camps, mainly at military bases. They have computer-generated lists. Gun owners, people who run their mouths on Facebook and Twitter, radio talk-show hosts, editors and publishers of Republican newspapers…you know, dangerous enemies of society."

"Who ran the exercise?"

"A senior Homeland Security dude named Zag Lambert. Wore a uniform shirt and a belt with a holstered pistol. Honest to God, all he needed was a Hitler mustache. That guy should be kept in a padded room."

Grafton sighed. Molina threw the report back onto the desk. Grafton picked it up and said to me, "I'll read this. Thanks, Tommy."

I got up and beat it.

Outside I rescued my cup, decided the coffee was still warm enough to be drinkable, punched the door code, and strolled into the executive assistants' office. I worked with and liked both of them: Max Hurley, a skinny long-distance runner, and Anastasia Roberts, a black woman with a PhD whose IQ was probably up in the stratosphere.

"Hey."

"Tommy," Hurley acknowledged. "You were just in the pit—how is it going with Molina?"

I shrugged. "Tense."

"They've been arguing for a week," Roberts said. "These agency police forces and huge ammo buys. The White House wants the CIA to establish our own paramilitary force, and Grafton has said no. He's defying the White House."

They stared at me and I stared back. That meant Grafton was on the way out, and we probably were too. The new man, or woman, would bring his or her own management team.

"They don't trust us," Anastasia Roberts remarked, quite unnecessarily. I knew whom she meant. The brain trust at the White House, hunkered down on Pennsylvania Avenue ever since the Democrats lost control of the Senate in the last off-year election, two years ago. The Republicans already had the House. This was August. The presidential election was in November, and no matter which way it went, the current president, Barry Soetoro, was leaving on January 20. The Constitution limited the president to two terms, so the end of his eight-year occupation of the White House was in sight at the end of a long, dark tunnel. Only 151 days of Soetoro left to endure, according to the countdown counter on Fox News that one of the hosts opened his show with every day.

"You know I was out in Denver last week at the Jade Helm 16 exercise," I remarked. "The National Oceanic and Atmospheric Administration, NOAA, has their own private army, and some of the troopers were at the exercise. A couple dozen of them came down from Boulder, decked out in camo clothes and helmets and armed to the teeth. They bonded with the storm troopers from other agencies. In my opinion, if the water and air gurus need paramilitary police, this agency certainly does."

"Boulder is a hotbed of sedition," Max Hurley observed. "Washington is a hotbed of sheep."

"The revolution will start there, no question," I agreed. "The faculty of the University of Colorado is packed with dangerous right-wing fanatics who will lead their students in a wild charge against the Bureau of Standards, burn it down, then attack NOAA."

"If they fire Grafton, will you stay with the agency?" Roberts asked me.

Needless to say, I hadn't thought about that possibility. I had an apartment just up the road, my car was paid for, I was single, my mom was doing okay out in California. When I didn't answer quickly enough, Roberts added, "I'm resigning. I've been offered a faculty position at the University of Chicago. If the job is still open, I can start when the new semester begins."

I grunted. The University of Chicago was notoriously left-wing, very politically correct, and Roberts was a level-headed, pragmatic genius who had worked for Republicans on the Hill early in her career. On the other hand, she was a she, and black, and consequently could get away with a lot that would sink a white male faculty member.

Hurley admitted he was on the fence. He loved the game of analyzing raw intelligence. He said so now, and expressed the hope that he could return to the Middle East Desk.

"Nothing but bad news there," I said, trying not to sound too downbeat.

"I think I can take it for a while longer," he said. The cockeyed optimist.

"Negativity is the problem with this agency," Anastasia Roberts declared. "Eventually it overwhelms you and your shit bucket overflows."

"I wouldn't express that opinion quite that bluntly in the faculty lounge in Chicago, if I were you," I told her. "Clean it up for the civilians."

We chuckled, locked up, and went to the cafeteria for lunch, where we discussed the weekend terror attacks.

I was working on a chicken salad sandwich with mustard and a slice of pickle on the side, plus a little bag of barbeque potato chips, when the televisions mounted high in the corner of the cafeteria broke away from their coverage of the investigation of the terrorist incidents to televise a live news conference with the president, Barry Soetoro. He had complete faith in the professionalism and competence of the FBI and Homeland Security Department. They were investigating. The terrorists were obviously criminals, he said, but they certainly didn't represent the vast bulk of American Muslims or the refugees who had been admitted to the United States. He and his security team were reviewing the information the crime scene investigators were producing, and when more was known, they would be taking any steps called for.

"Does that mean you will reconsider your decision to admit Muslims to America?"

"We can't classify people by their religion."

"Obviously refugee screening was inadequate. What will the administration do to find the jihadists and keep them out?"

"We are looking at that."

"A lot of people in Congress are saying your policies on illegal immigration and the admission of Middle Eastern refugees are abject failures, as proved by the events of the weekend. Would you comment on that?"

"My political enemies say a lot of things, every day. I haven't the time or inclination to listen and comment."

There was more, a lot more. The public was frightened and angry, and Barry Soetoro was defiant.

When the press conference was over, the cafeteria was quiet.

"It's a miracle someone hasn't shot at him before now," Max Hurley observed, leaning forward at the waist and speaking softly.

But why shoot him? The Democratic nominee was Cynthia Hinton, who, according to the polls, was going to be the victim of a landslide. The Republican nominee was Jerry Duchene, the Wisconsin governor, and if the polls could be believed, he was going to be elected by a landslide. And the Congress would get a veto-proof Republican majority. The country had had more than enough of Barry Soetoro, his left-wing agenda, and his political allies, and was waiting, more or less patiently, for his final day in office. Yet the terror strikes had stirred the pot.

Back upstairs after lunch things began to pop. Were there any indications among the intelligence bits trapped in the intestines of our intelligence systems that some evil foreign power or narco-criminals or terrorist groups had plotted with or funded the Saturday monsters?

We three EAs were told to contact every department head and find out.

We spent the afternoon talking to people throughout the agency who were trying their best to find a hint, a clue, a sniff. They failed. While it is theoretically impossible to prove a negative, you can often get close enough for government work. And we did. Nothing. Nada. Zilch. Of course, on television every terror organization in the Middle East was claiming credit.

I was elected to tell Grafton, and did so a bit after five p.m. He just nodded. He had spent the afternoon on the phone, presumably talking to other heads of agencies and political big shots all over town.

"Are you going home soon?" he asked. After all, five o'clock is traditionally quitting time, although not in the CIA.

"Not if you need me, sir."

"Hang around. Sal Molina is coming over again later. I may need a witness."

Oh boy. I wandered out past the receptionist and walked the halls a while with my hands in my pockets. Was Grafton going to resign? Or get fired?

People were standing in knots here and there, chewing the rag over the terrorist attacks. The news shows, they told me, said that Cynthia Hinton had scheduled a news conference for prime time this evening.

I was sitting in the director's reception area when the vice director, Harley Merritt, strode by on his way to the inner sanctum. He ignored me. He had an EA with him, and she ignored me too. It was that kind of day.

They were in there about a half hour and came marching out. Grafton stood in the doorway as they crossed the reception room. He motioned to me. I went in and he closed the door.

"Molina is on his way. Sit down."

"Is he going to ask for your resignation?" I asked. Why beat around the bush?

"I don't know," Grafton said crossly.

I also suspected he didn't give a damn, but I kept my mouth shut and seated myself on the couch. Laid my notebook on my lap, so I'd be ready to scribble down orders or telephone numbers or order flowers for funerals.

Grafton picked up something from his in-basket, glanced at it, tossed it back, then rose from his chair and stretched. He reminded me of a caged lion. Waiting. In a darkened office with the lights off. Behind him the day was slowly coming to an end.

"Nations don't just happen," he remarked, as if he were talking to himself, or perhaps composing an essay. "They are put together by groups who are convinced that the people who live within a certain area will be better off as one political entity, this thing called a nation. Nations are fragile. Homogenous nations seem to have done best through written history. Ours is anything but homogenous, a grand experiment with many people from diverse racial groups, cultures, and religious heritages, all mixed together willy-nilly and bound together politically."

Looking back, I think at that moment Jake Grafton had a glimpse of the future, a future that disturbed him profoundly.

He sat in silence for a while, then remarked, "A government that loses, or forfeits, the consent of the governed is doomed. Invariably. Inevitably. Irreversibly."

He was sitting in silence with the light from the window behind him throwing his face in shadow when the squawk box buzzed. "Mr. Molina."

"Send him in."

I went to open the door and close it behind Molina. He sat in the chair across the desk from Grafton and glanced at me. "You won't need him," he said to Grafton.

"He stays. Say what you want to say."

"You need a witness?"

"I won't know until I hear it."

"The president is declaring martial law tomorrow. He wants you standing behind him tomorrow at ten o'clock in the press room when he announces it."

Jake Grafton didn't look surprised. I was flabbergasted, but since I was sitting on the couch against the wall Sal Molina couldn't see the stunned look on my face unless he turned his head, and he didn't.

"Why?" said Grafton.

"These terrorist conspiracies need to be rooted out. We must make sure the American people are safe, and feel safe."

"Horseshit," Grafton roared, and smacked the desk with both fists. "Pure fucking horseshit! Oh, a million or two jihadists would love to murder Americans, including Soetoro, if they could get here, but if they were a credible threat we'd have heard about it. This is just an excuse for Soetoro to suspend the Constitution and declare himself dictator."

"The American people must be protected, Admiral. The president is taking no chances. No one wants to be the next victim of Islamic terrorists."

"So he is going to rule by decree."

"We face a national emergency."

"And he is going to postpone or cancel the election in November. Isn't that the real reason for martial law?"

"I'm not going to debate it, Grafton. Tomorrow at ten at the White House. Be there an hour early and we'll have a decree signed by the president detailing the actions that he wants from this agency."

"His staff can e-mail me a copy," Grafton said softly. "I am not going to be a prop in a presidential power grab. Not now, not ever."

Molina ran his hands over his face. "Jake, you don't have a choice," he said reasonably. "You'll either be there or your name will go on the list as an enemy of the president. They'll lock you up. Soetoro is playing for keeps. You can kiss your pension good-bye. Do you want to spend the rest of your life in prison?"

Molina stood, put both fists on the desk, and leaned forward. His voice dropped. "You think *I* want to be a part of this? I have a wife and two kids. I don't have a choice. By God, you don't either."

Grafton was silent, looking at nothing for a moment or two. Finally, he said, "Soetoro has been waiting for a terror strike so he could declare martial law, become a dictator, and fix all the things he doesn't like about America."

"You don't know that."

"I'll bet any sum you want to name he is going to call off the election and remain in office."

Molina straightened and made a gesture of irritation. He glanced around and saw me, which obviously startled him. Apparently he had forgotten I was in the room.

He took a step in my direction. "One word from you outside this room will put you in a cell, Carmellini." I'd had confrontations with Molina before. I wasn't stupid enough to open my mouth this time.

Molina swung back to Grafton.

"Be there tomorrow morning. If you aren't, I can't help you."

"*Me*? You can't help *me*?" Grafton was standing too, and he was beyond fury. He had a scar on his temple that was throbbing red. "That bastard is going to rip this country apart, and you worry about your family and pension? You think there's a lifeboat handy that will keep you and yours comfortably afloat in this sea of shit while the ship sinks? What the hell kind of man are you, Molina? He doesn't need *you* and he doesn't need *me*. Get a grip, fool."

Molina was holding on to the desk, as if he were trying to stay erect. "Jake..."

"You get out of my office and don't ever come back."

"It won't be your office long. That's what I'm trying to tell you."

"I don't ever want to see your face again, Molina. Get the fuck out."

Molina turned and walked from the room. Neither fast nor slow. He merely walked. The door closed behind him.

I was too stunned to open my mouth or move.

Grafton looked at me and gestured toward the door. "You too, Tommy. Out."

I got my muscles working and went.

In west Texas, Joe Bob Hays' hired man stood in the yard of the ranch house and watched the helicopter approach. It came from the east and slowed as it descended. It touched down in a cloud of dust and, after the sound of the engine subsided, the rotors slowly wound down.

A man in a suit but without a tie climbed out. A state trooper got out with him. They came walking over.

"I found him this morning, Governor, down by the arroyo trail. They killed him and cut the fence early Saturday, it looks like."

Governor Jack Hays was Joe Bob's nephew. He had grown up on the ranch back in the cattle days, and had gone on to law school, then into politics.

"The sheriff and his men are down there taking pictures and whatnot. I think the body is still there."

"Let's go. I want to see him."

"They shot him in the head, Governor. Executed him. Blew the top half of his head clean off."

"I want to see him. Let's go."

They went by jeep. In the late afternoon sun, the blood and bits of brain had turned black. Ants had gathered, and bugs…

The county sheriff was there, Manuel Tejada, and he shook hands with the governor. "I'm sorry, sir," the sheriff said. "You know about this trail. He complained for years, and I did what I could, but I only got so many men and this is a damn big county…"

"I know."

"They came up the trail, at least ten of them. Judging by their tracks, at least eight of them were carrying a heavy load going north, but not when all ten of them went back south. One man came up the hill here and executed Joe Bob. He would probably have died anyway from that bleeding hole in his chest, but...shit!"

"Yeah."

"The first bullet was fired from the other side—" the lawman pointed "—over there. We found a spent .223 cartridge. Probably one of them ARs. Tracks. The tracks went through the hole and up here to where Joe Bob is, and here's the second cartridge."

He opened his hand for the governor's inspection. Jack Hays merely glanced at the open hand, then said, "He's lain out here long enough. You got your photos?"

"Yes, sir."

"Get him out of here. Take him to the funeral home in Sanderson."

"Yes, sir," Sheriff Tejada said to the governor's back, for he was walking away, trying not to look again at his uncle's remains.

Back at the ranch there was a trim, fit man in his early forties waiting beside a large pickup. His name was Joseph Robert Hays Junior, but everyone called him JR.

"They're bringing him out of there now, JR," the governor said, after he hugged the younger man. "Better stay here. You don't want to see him like that. He wouldn't have wanted you to."

JR nodded. His eyes were dry. He had seen his share of bodies in Iraq and Afghanistan and had not the slightest desire to see his father's remains.

The governor continued, telling his cousin what he knew. JR had just retired after twenty years in the army, retired as a lieutenant colonel, and was working as a consultant for a military contractor in El Paso, one supplying state-of-the-art night-vision equipment to the army. After he got the news, JR threw some things in his pickup and drove east.

"He was trying to protect his fence," Jack Hays said. "They killed him and cut it."

"I told him to put a gate in that damn fence," JR said, "but he wouldn't."

"No..." the governor said thoughtfully. "That wasn't him. There was no backup in him." He eyed his cousin. He suspected there was no backup in Joe Bob's son, either.

"They'll be back," JR said matter-of-factly.

"You going to wait for them?"

"Hunting assholes in the desert was my business for a lot of years. I suspect I know more about it than Sheriff Tejada and his deputies do."

Jack Hays didn't try to talk him out of it. All he could hope for was that JR didn't get shot or caught. But JR was JR, and Joe Bob was his dad. And this was Texas. If JR shot some Mexican drug smugglers who had killed his dad, no Texas jury was going to convict him of anything.

"Fred coming down?" Fred was the younger brother, teaching school somewhere in the Dallas area.

"For the funeral. He and his wife can't get off just now."

"Call me when you get the funeral scheduled," the governor said. "Nadine and I will want to be there."

"I will, Jack."

Jack Hays hugged JR again, then went to the helicopter and climbed in. "Let's go," he told the pilot.

TWO

★

Martial law! Rule by decree from the White House! Barry Soetoro, emperor of the United States. People had been whispering for years about the possibility, but like most folks, I dismissed the whisperers as alarmist crackpots. Now, according to Sal Molina, the president's longtime guru, the crackpots were oracles.

I sat at my desk in my cubbyhole and thought about things. I wondered if there was any truth to Grafton's crack that Soetoro and company had been waiting for a terrorist incident so they could declare martial law. Well, why not? The nation was fed up with the Democrats. Seniors and the white middle class had deserted the party by the millions. Cynthia Hinton didn't have a chance. The Republicans were going to take over the government in November if there was an election.

I felt hot all over. Suddenly the room was stifling. It looked as if the nation I had grown up in, the crazy, diverse republic of three hundred million people all trying to make a living and raise the next generation, was going on the rocks. And all the king's horses and all the king's men weren't going to be able to put it back together again. That must have been the thrust of Grafton's remark before Molina arrived.

I felt as if I were on the edge of the abyss, like Dante's hero, staring down into the fiery pit. What next?

Grafton would be gone. Like tomorrow. The agency would become another arm of Soetoro's Gestapo. Molina had implied that much.

I opened the locked drawer where I kept my stuff. I had a shoulder holster and a little Walther in .380 ACP in there. Since I did bodyguard duty for Grafton, I had a permit for it signed by the director, who was Grafton. I took off my jacket, put on the shoulder holster, checked the pistol, and made sure I had a round in the chamber and the safety engaged. Put the pistol in the holster and put my coat back on.

I stood there looking around. There was nothing else in my office I wanted. Not the CIA coffee cup, the free pens, the photo of me and the guys on a big campout in Africa that hung on the wall...none of it. I locked the drawer and cabinets, left the room and made sure the door locked behind me, then headed for the parking lot.

Driving out of the lot was surreal. There were still some cars there, and people trickling out, just as there were every evening. The streetlights were on; traffic went up and down the streets obeying the traffic laws; news, music, sports, and talk emanated from my car radio...*and it was all coming to an end.*

As I drove I took mental inventory of my arsenal. If you live in America, you gotta have some guns, so when the political contract falls apart...yeah!

I drove over to a gun store I had had prior dealings with. A few people in the store, about as usual. I bought two more boxes of Number Four buckshot for the shotgun, another box of .380 ACP for my Walther, and four boxes of .45 ACP for my Kimber 1911, which was in my apartment. Three boxes of .30-30s for my old Model 94 Winchester.

"Expecting a war?" the clerk asked.

"Comes the revolution, I want to be ready," I replied.

I used a credit card to pay for the stuff. If the future went down the way I suspected, in a few days no one would be able to buy guns or ammo for love or money. Soetoro would shut down the gun stores. Screw the Second Amendment.

Then I drove over to Maryland to visit the lock shop I owned with my partner, Willie "the Wire" Varner. He was a black man about twenty years older than me, and had been up the river twice. Now reformed, he was my very best friend. Don't ask me why a two-time loser should be the only guy in the world I really trust—besides Jake Grafton—but he is. Maybe because he's so much like me. As I unlocked the front door and went into the shop, I realized that I couldn't tell him about the bomb Molina dropped, but I did have news.

Willie was in the back room of the shop wiring up the motherboard of an alarm system for installation in an old house. The final innings of an Orioles game were on the radio. "Hey," he said.

"Hey. Stopped by to tell you, I quit the agency this evening."

He stared. "No shit?"

"Honest injun. I am not going back."

"They give you any severance?"

"Uh, no."

He turned back to the alarm system. "They goin' to be lookin' for you, Carmellini?"

"Naw. It'll be days before they figure out that I'm gone. Maybe weeks."

"Want to tell me about it?"

"Just did. All I can."

He straightened up and gave me another look. "And I thought I had a monopoly on fuckin' up my life. If you ain't gonna tell me nothin', just why the hell did you drive over here tonight?"

I was at a loss for words. Why did I? I knew the answer, of course—because I needed some company—but I wasn't going to tell him that.

"Don't think you're gonna start workin' here on salary," Willie declared. "We ain't got barely enough work for me. We divide it up and neither one of us will be eatin'."

I nodded. Stood looking around. Maybe I should just give Willie a bill of sale for my half of the place and be done with it. He would never leave the metro area, and I wasn't staying. I didn't know where I was going, but I did know I wasn't staying in Washington.

I decided that was a problem for another day. Said good night and left.

★

I wasn't ready for my apartment. Hell, I had nothing better to do, so I headed for Jake Grafton's condo in Rosslyn. I had certainly been there often enough these last few years, so I knew the way. I was going to try to find a parking place on the street, but instead decided to cruise by the building and see who was sitting outside in cars. Sure enough, a half block from the entrance there was a parked car with two men in it. They were of a type. FBI. After a while you get a feel for them. Trim, reasonably fit, wearing sports coats to hide a concealed carry, maybe a tie. Who, besides middle-level government employees, dresses like that at ten o'clock at night?

I decided I didn't give a damn if they saw and photographed me. There were no parking places on the street, so I steered the Benz into the parking garage and found a spot on the third deck. Took the stairs down, crossed the street, and went into Grafton's building.

Grafton buzzed the door open and I went up. Knocked and he opened the door. Callie was sitting in the kitchen. The admiral led me there and asked, "Want a drink?"

"Sure. Anything with alcohol."

Callie Grafton was a tough lady, but she looked about the way I felt. Bad. "Tommy," she said, trying to smile.

I realized then that coming over to Grafton's was a really bad idea. But I couldn't just walk out. The admiral opened the fridge and handed me a bottle of beer. I unscrewed the top and sipped it. "Car out front with two men in it. Maybe FBI."

"A dirty gray sedan? They followed me home," he said.

"So are you going in tomorrow?" I asked.

"Of course," he said, scrutinizing my face.

"Not me. I'm done. Gonna hit the road tomorrow. I think the time has come for Mrs. Carmellini's boy Tommy to go on to greener pastures."

The admiral didn't say anything to that. Mrs. Grafton hid her face behind her tea cup.

On the way over here I wondered if Grafton had told his wife about the conversation with Sal Molina. From the silence and the way she sat looking at the dark window, I knew that he had.

"I shouldn't have come," I said. "I'll take this road pop with me to remember you by, Admiral. Good-bye." I stuck out my hand. He shook it.

"Mrs. Grafton." She rose from the table and hugged me. Fiercely.

Then I left. Pulled the door shut until the lock clicked. I took the elevator down, put the half-empty beer bottle in my side pocket, crossed the street, and climbed the stairs.

The next morning, Tuesday, August 23, I was wide awake at five in the morning. The sky was starting to get pink in the east. I hopped out of bed, showered, shaved, put on jeans and a golf shirt, and got busy packing. Everything had to go in my car, which was a 1975 Mercedes. Guns and ammo, of course, plus some of my clothes. No kitchen utensils, pots, pans, dishes, or coffee pot. No television or radio. I did decide to take my laptop and charger, but I left the printer.

When I had made my selections and the stuff was stacked in the middle of the little living area, I began shuttling stuff down to the car in the elevator.

When I got the car loaded, I stood in the middle of my apartment and took stock. Nothing else here I wanted.

I wrote a short letter to the landlord and enclosed my key and building pass. He could have everything left in the apartment. The stuff in the refrigerator I emptied into a garbage bag and carried down with me.

In light of what happened subsequently, perhaps I should have been worried about the country and martial law and what was to come, and perhaps I was on a subconscious level. I must have suspected the future might be grim or I wouldn't have worried about the guns and ammo. Still, after I packed the car, I was thinking about what I was going to do with the rest of my life.

It was a nice problem. I had daydreamed about *afterward* for years, after the CIA, but that eventuality was always somewhere ahead in a distant, hazy future. Now, boom, the future was unexpectedly here, and it wasn't hazy.

Of course I didn't have to plot my next fifty or sixty years today. I decided that this day would be a good one to head west, following the sun. A few weeks of backpacking in Idaho or Montana would suit me right down to the ground.

Already I was late for work—at Langley—as if I were ditching school. Feeling rather bucked with life, I drove to a breakfast place in a shopping mall and ordered an omelet and coffee. I scanned a newspaper while I waited for my omelet. The journalists had dug up a lot more on the dead terrorists. They were from Syria, Yemen, and Iraq. The experts were speculating on where and how they acquired their weapons, all of which were legally for sale in many states in America. Two more of the Saturday gunshot victims had died, bringing the grand total of deaths to 173.

At 9:45 I was standing in line in the lobby of the suburban Virginia bank where I had my accounts. When I reached the window, I wrote a check for the amount in my checking account, leaving only a thousand bucks in the account to cover outstanding checks.

"And how would you like this, Mr. Carmellini?" The teller was a cute lady wearing an engagement and wedding ring. The best ones are always snagged early.

"Cash, please. Half fifties and half hundreds."

She tittered. "Oh, good heavens. Since it's over ten thousand, we must fill out a form. Are you sure you don't want a cashier's check?"

Titterers set my teeth on edge. On the other hand, she wasn't still swimming around in the gene pool looking for a man. I silently wished her husband luck. "Pretty sure," I replied. "Cash, please. And while you are at it, I want to close out my savings account. I'll take that in cash too."

She had to go get more cash from the vault, then the paperwork took another few minutes. When I had my money, a little over twenty-two thousand monetary units—they gave me a little cloth envelope with the bank's name printed on it to carry it in—I opened my safe deposit box with the help of one of the ladies who didn't titter.

Back in my younger days, when I thought the day might come when I wanted to leave town in a hurry—like today, for instance—I had stashed thirty grand in cash in the box, along with a couple of false driver's licenses in various names, credit cards, and a genuine false passport. Getting that paper had taken time and money years ago, but I did it and kept the stuff. Of course, the credit cards had long expired, but they added heft to my wallet and looked good to anyone who happened to glance into my wallet while I had it open. Some people think that people with credit cards are more trustworthy than those without.

Under the money at the bottom of the drawer was another 1911 .45, an old Ithaca made during World War II with brown plastic handles and most of the bluing gone from the slide, plus two extra magazines and a box of cartridges. The pistol was marked "United States Property M 1911 A1 US Army." It had either been liberated from the army's clutches many years ago or sold as surplus. It was serviceable, although it didn't have the good sights and fancy grips of my Kimber.

If there is a possibility that you might get shot at, you should at least be prepared to shoot back. In this brave new world that Emperor Soetoro envisioned, I thought the odds of getting shot at would be increased for a great many people, me included. I emptied the metal box into my briefcase, then with the help of the vault lady, who had discreetly faded while I plundered my treasure box, put the box back into its slot where it would rest undisturbed, safer than a pharaoh's sarcophagus, for all eternity, or until my annual box rent was due and I wasn't around to pay it, whichever came first.

As I was leaving the lobby with my now-bulging briefcase, Barry Soetoro was on the television high in the corner, reading from a teleprompter. That was, I had long ago concluded, his one skill set. The audio on the TV was off, so I was spared his mellifluous tones. There were people standing behind him, but since I knew Jake Grafton wasn't among them, I didn't bother to check out the crowd of toadies. I walked out of the bank with my money—earned, not stolen, with taxes paid on every dime. I kinda wished I had stolen it, then I would have felt better about this whole deal. I was just too goddamn conventional.

To hell with all of it! I walked out of the bank into the rest of my life.

★

Barry Soetoro's declaration of martial law stunned the nation. His reason—the need to protect the nation from terrorism—met with widespread skepticism. After all, at least three of the Saturday jihadists had entered with Soetoro's blessing, over the objections of many politicians and the outraged cries of all those little people out there in the heartland, all those potential victims no one really gave a damn about.

His suspension of the writ of habeas corpus went over the heads of most of the millions of people in his audience, since they didn't know what the writ was or signified. He didn't stop there. He adjourned Congress until he called it back into session, and announced an indefinite stay on all cases before the courts in which the government was a defendant. His announcement of press and media censorship "until the crisis is past" met with outrage, especially among the talking heads on television, who went ballistic. Within thirty minutes, the listening audience found out what the suspension of the writ of habeas corpus meant: FBI agents arrested select television personalities, including some who were literally on camera, and took them away. Fox News went off the air. Most of the other networks contented themselves with running the tape of Soetoro behind the podium making his announcement, over and over, without comment.

During the day FBI agents arrested dozens of prominent conservative commentators and administration critics across the nation, including Rush Limbaugh, Mark Levin, Michelle Malkin, George Will, Ann Coulter, Bill O'Reilly, Glenn Beck, Ralph Peters, Judge Jeanine Pirro, Matt Drudge, Thomas Sowell, Howard Stern, and Charles Krauthammer, among others. They weren't given a chance to remain silent in the future, but were arrested and taken away to be held in an unknown location until Soetoro decided to release them.

Senators and congressmen, from both sides of the aisle, were told in no uncertain terms that they too would be arrested if they publicly questioned the administration's methods and motives.

Plainly, life in America had just been stood on its ear. All the usual suspects who had supported Barry Soetoro for seven and a half years, no matter what, through thick, thin, and transparent, rushed to find a reporter with a camera so that they could say wonderful things on television about their hero, the self-proclaimed messiah who had said when he was first elected that he would lower the level of the sea and allow the earth to heal.

While all this was going on, Jake Grafton was fired as director of the CIA. Two White House aides arrived in Langley with FBI agents in tow and delivered a letter from the president. Grafton was summarily relieved and the assistant director, Harley Merritt, was named acting director.

As Grafton departed with the FBI agents, the two White House aides remained for a talk with Merritt about what was expected of him.

The FBI took Grafton to a federal detention center that had been set up at Camp Dawson, a National Guard facility near Kingwood, West Virginia. Grafton should have been surprised to find that the holding facility had concertina wire, kitchens, latrines, and a field full of erect army tents containing a dozen cots each, but he wasn't. Obviously someone had done the staff work to have facilities ready and waiting, with only the date that they were to be used remaining to be selected.

Grafton arrived in time to shuffle through the lunch line, which contained about forty people. Most were men in their twenties and thirties, with here and there a few women salted in. The women huddled together. Everyone was in civilian clothes. He recognized several of the other detainees, or prisoners: two army four-star generals and a couple of former cabinet members. He picked up an aluminum tray from the stack, and a soldier in uniform spooned out mashed potatoes, mystery meat, and corn. At the end of the food line, he could select paper napkins and plastic tableware. No one trusted the detainees with real knives or forks.

Afterward Jake was given a plastic Walmart bag for his stay, one containing a disposable razor, soap, a towel, a toothbrush, and toothpaste. The tube of toothpaste was small, TSA size, and he hoped that was an indicator of how long he would be here. He suspected it wasn't.

He still had his cell phone, but he had no charger, so he turned it off in the car on the way here. He had managed a call to Callie before he left the Langley facilities, so she knew he wasn't coming home this evening, even if she didn't know where he was.

He sat on the side of the cot he had chosen in his assigned tent. He was the only occupant of the tent, so far, but he expected plenty of company. Finally he unrolled his sleeping bag and stretched out on it.

Barry Soetoro had just decapitated the American government in a coup d'état. Furthermore, Soetoro and his aides knew that Grafton was politically unreliable. How long they would hold him, if indeed he would ever be released, was unknowable.

Jake Grafton was a political prisoner.

The suspension of the writ of habeas corpus and declaration of martial law in the United States stunned the world. Abraham Lincoln did both during the American Civil War in the 1860s, so there was precedent. The Constitution itself, Article 1, Section 9, stated: "The privilege of the Writ of Habeas Corpus shall not be suspended, unless in Cases of Rebellion or Invasion the public Safety may require it." Clearly, this past week there had been no rebellion, as there had been during the Civil War. What there was, Soetoro declared, was an "invasion by terrorists," and in Soetoro's opinion, "public safety did indeed require martial law." During the Civil War Lincoln had also declared martial law, claiming he had a right to do so to preserve the Constitution; his actions were quickly ratified by Congress and the Supreme Court. Army officers arrested several politicians, including one prominent one, Ohioan Clement Vallandigham, and closed down several newspapers. Lincoln's generals caused him more trouble than the people they arrested; the newspaper editors were quickly freed, and Vallandigham, a copperhead Democrat, was taken south and handed over to the Confederates, who didn't want him either. He wound up in Canada, slipped back across the border, and ran for governor of Ohio. Lincoln ignored him and told his generals to do likewise. Vallandigham lost the Ohio governor's race of 1864.

The Constitution was silent on Soetoro's two other declarations: the adjournment of Congress until he recalled it and suspension of all federal cases in which the government was the defendant. There was absolutely no precedent for either action, which hadn't been attempted in the history of the republic, which spanned a civil war and two world wars. Critics immediately claimed that Soetoro had unconstitutionally attempted to seize power, subordinating the legislative and judicial power to that of the executive. Strident voices compared him to Hitler and Napoleon, both of whom took over the government and made themselves dictators. Soetoro's supporters—including ardent white leftists and more than ninety percent of black Americans, who had backed everything he had done in office since his first election and damned his critics as virulent racists—loudly supported him now. Amazingly, those who cheered his actions were given space in newspapers and time on television, while critics weren't. Those editors and producers who were not inclined to fall in line, and most of them were, were threatened with arrest. If that didn't make them behave, they were hustled away to detention camps.

Social media websites also received government attention and were told if they allowed "criticism of the government" on their websites, they would be shut down. Since they had no way to stop the wired-in public from posting anything they wanted, these websites were soon shut down by their corporate owners. Pirate social media websites quickly sprang up, but unhappy people could make little noise on them in the near future. Mouse squeaks, someone said.

The result of all this in much of America was an ominous silence that afternoon.

The news that Soetoro had declared martial law and suspended the holy writ arrived like an incoming missile in Austin, Texas. Legislators crowded the governor's office and all wanted to talk to the governor, Jack Hays. And they all wanted to talk at once.

State Senator Benny "Ben" Steiner copped a seat in a corner and listened. The consensus was that Barry Soetoro had declared himself dictator.

"Anybody have any idea of when America will get its Constitution back?" Charlie Swim asked. He was the most prominent black politician in the state, a former Dallas Cowboys star. He was, arguably, also one of the smartest and most articulate politicians in Texas.

The hubbub subsided somewhat. Everyone wanted to know what Charlie Swim thought. "The problem here is that Washington politicians haven't had the guts to impeach Soetoro. And I'll tell you why. He's black. They're afraid of being called racists. If Soetoro had been white, he'd have been thrown out of office years ago. Rewriting the immigration laws; refusing to enforce the drug laws; siccing the IRS on conservatives; having his spokespeople lie to the press, lie to Congress, lie to the UN; rewriting the healthcare law all by himself; thumbing his nose at the courts; having the EPA dump on industry regardless of the costs; admitting hordes of Middle Eastern Muslims without a clue who they were.... Race in America—it's a toxic poison that prevents any real discussion of the issues. It's the monkey wrench Soetoro and his disciples have thrown into the gears that make the republic's wheel turn. And now this! Already the liberals are screaming that if you are against martial law, you're a racist; if anyone calls *me* a racist, he's going to be spitting teeth."

Charlie Swim wasn't finished, and his voice was rising. "The black people in America were doing all right, working their way up the ladder, until drugs came along. Then welfare, and payments to single mothers—when you pay poor people not to work and not to marry they are going to take the money. Barry Soetoro had a real chance to do something about what's taken black America down—drugs, welfare rather than work, kids without wedlock—but he didn't bother." Swim's voice became sarcastic. "Climate change is his cause, and discrimination against Muslims. And expensive golf vacations." His voice rose to a roar. "I'm sick of this self-proclaimed black messiah!"

"That won't do any good, Charlie," Jack Hays said conversationally. He was standing behind his chair and now addressed the crowd. "I have no doubt we'll hear from Washington soon, and in great detail, and when we do I'll pass it on. You'll know what I know just about as fast as I get it."

"What are *you* going to do about this mess?" someone demanded.

"What am I going to do if it rains?" Hays said. "What am I going to do if it doesn't? You people go back to your chambers and make speeches, hold press conferences, tell the people of Texas what you think. That's all we can do right now. Tomorrow is another day. Now git!"

And they did. All except Ben Steiner. A lawyer from Abilene, he had tried civil and criminal cases all over Texas for forty years. Politics was his hobby. Now he closed the door behind the last of his colleagues and seated himself in one of the chairs across the desk from Hays.

"You are avoiding the issue, Jack, and you know it."

"I know a lot of things I don't talk about in public," Jack Hays replied curtly.

"Barry Soetoro is ripping up the Constitution and declaring himself dictator. All he needs is a crown. That's indisputable. This crap about terrorism—the FBI can find terrorists, and they don't have to go any farther than the nearest mosque. What's really happening here is Barry Soetoro taking out his political enemies. What are we Texans going to do about this? Are we going to knuckle under?"

Hays moved around in his chair, trying to get comfortable. He rearranged his scrotum. "You're working up to something, Ben. What?"

"We need to secede from the Union. Declare the Republic of Texas, again."

Hays made a face. "This isn't 1836. There are forty-nine other states and the U.S. Army, Navy, Air Force, and Marine Corps. The last time Texas got uppity, back in 1861, the roof caved in. It would again."

"Really?" Ben Steiner leaned forward and lowered his voice. "The roof has already caved in. Give me a better idea, Jack. Tell me what we are going to do if Soetoro calls off the election. If he declares himself president for life."

"He hasn't done that," Hays shot back.

"Not yet," Steiner admitted. "What he has done is declare martial law, adjourn Congress, shut down the courts, muzzle the press, and arrest his critics. How are we going to preserve our way of life, preserve our liberty, preserve our democracy with a dictator in the White House?"

"I don't know," Jack Hays admitted. "I need to think on it."

"Better not think too long," Ben Steiner said as he got out of his chair. "There's a lot of people in Texas who won't think long at all. They hate that son of a bitch and they won't take this lying down. While you're thinking, think about how to head them off if they get out of hand. If you don't, or won't, or can't, we're talking anarchy. No man's life or property will be safe. Think about that. Also think about what you're going to do if Soetoro sends some federal agents to drag you out of this office and throw you into a prison somewhere. Until such time, if ever, that he decides it's safe to let you out. Think about that too."

Ben Steiner walked out of the governor's office and closed the door behind him.

Jack Hays put his hands on his face and tried to force himself to relax. Various right-wing groups in Texas had argued for independence for years. They were the lunatic fringe, the village idiots. Hays had kept his distance. Now Ben Steiner had taken his turn at the independence podium, and he was no crackpot.

The way people lived in early-twenty-first-century Texas depended on the American monetary system, Social Security, military retirement, banks stuffed full of U.S. Treasury bonds as their capital, the national telephone grid, the power grid, all of that. Companies here paid wages to Texans to manufacture goods and sold them all over the United States—all over the world—and the stores in Texas that supplied the stuff of life were filled with goods manufactured all over the world; Texans used their paychecks to pay for what they needed. Independence, he thought, would take a civil war, and that would destroy the very fabric of life for a great many Texans. Cutting Texas out of the United States would be like trying to cut Mona Lisa's face out of her portrait and arguing that the operation wouldn't harm it.

Jack Hays didn't believe it could be done. In this interdependent world, Texas had to be part of the United States, a state in the Union.

Or did it?

He was thinking about his deceased uncle, Joe Bob Hays, and the drug smugglers who killed him when the phone on his desk summoned him to duty.

THREE

★

There were five people in Grafton's tent, all males, when he went in after sunset. Everyone introduced himself: three civil servants, one broadcaster, and one congressman.

"Where are the women?" Grafton asked.

"They have their own tents," he was told. "Politically incorrect, but those are army regulations."

"If Elizabeth Warren only knew."

The tentmates had just arrived, and were still outraged that they had been arrested. Being taken in handcuffs from their homes or work, with family or colleagues watching, and physically transported to Camp Dawson, a three-hour ride from Washington, had filled them with adrenaline that had to be burned off. They had been frightened, humiliated, and shamed, and now they were very angry. They told each other their stories and talked long into the night while Jake Grafton slept.

On his second evening in Camp Dawson, Jake Grafton ran into *Washington Post* columnist Jack Yocke in the chow line. Yocke was in his late thirties, lean and ropy, with shoulder-length hair and a fashionably grizzled face, the lumberjack look. His name was pronounced Yock-key.

"When did you get here, Admiral?" a plainly surprised Yocke asked.

"Yesterday at noon."

"Seems to be a lot of people here," Yocke said, looking around.

"Welcome to the American gulag archipelago. I think I was one of the first, but there were a bunch of people already here. Spies, I think. Stool pigeons. I would be careful what I said and who heard it, if I were you."

They ate together in silence, put their leftovers in a large garbage can, and stacked their trays, then went to sit under a shade tree near the wire, where they could talk privately.

Grafton managed to get the first question in, always a feat with Yocke. "Did you piss on the establishment or did they dump you here on general principles?"

"I'm an unreliable bastard. I wrote a column that was uncomplimentary to the administration, and a political apparatchik in the editor's office called the troopers. Needless to say, I don't think my column will be in tomorrow's paper."

"Brave editors."

"They were threatened with arrest, their families were also going to be arrested, their bank accounts and property seized, and the IRS would prosecute them. Not audit them, but prosecute them. The only thing they weren't threatened with was execution."

"Why did you flout them?"

"Stupid, I guess. And you?"

"The same."

"There's a lot of that around. Soetoro is going to be surprised."

"They've made their preparations. The administration didn't decide this after they got a look at Saturday's terror strikes. They've been getting ready for this for years."

"When this is over," Yocke mused, "someday, the only heroes will be the people who stood up to them and went to prison."

"Martyrs," Grafton murmured.

"Christians versus the lions."

"Martyrs don't win wars," Grafton stated. "That's a law, like gravity. So what's happening out there beyond the fence?"

"The country's falling apart. Inner-city riots: Chicago, Detroit, Saint Louis, LA. Just getting worked up, getting the car fires set. Agitators and race-baiters screaming about overturning white America once and for all. What they are going to do is loot Walmarts and Safeways and burn down the inner cities, then starve. We've got martial law, but there's no National Guard, no soldiers, no police stopping the rioters, there's no fire departments putting out the fires, and there's apparently no Border Patrol at the border. Go figure."

Grafton didn't say anything.

"The cops have got the message. Let it burn, baby."

Yocke got out his cell phone and checked his messages.

"You have a charger for that?" Jake asked.

"Yep. All I need is a place to plug it in. If cell phones go flat, civilization as we know it will be stone cold dead. Teenagers, millennials, reporters, and real estate agents will go through seismic withdrawal and drop dead left and right."

"The camp authorities will pass out chargers when they can lay hands on some," Jake said.

"Why?"

"The NSA can listen to every cell phone and telephone transmission in America. They've been working on it for over a year. Soetoro's orders. It used to be all they got was your number and the number you dialed. Now they can record the conversations digitally and mine them for key words or names. They *want* you to talk on your cell phone. That's why they didn't confiscate the things."

Jack Yocke sat with his cell phone in hand watching the shadows lengthen. Finally he put the device on the ground, took off his shoe, and pounded on it with the heel until the glass screen broke. Then he threw it over the fence.

After a while Yocke calmed down. "So when do you think we'll get out of here?"

Grafton snorted. "They didn't let me pack my crystal ball."

"A few days, months, years?"

When Grafton remained silent, Yocke decided to answer his own question. If you are going to make your living writing newspaper columns, you must have opinions, on everything. Yocke did. Almost every living human had opinions, but no one wanted to hear them. People paid to read Yocke's because his were better thought out and expressed.

"People are upset and angry right now, but few if any are willing to risk everything they own, everything they have, even their lives, to oppose Soetoro and the federal government. That will change over time. Government oppression in the short run pisses people off. In the long run it transforms them into revolutionaries."

"Conquer or die," Grafton mused. "Too bad you weren't there at the White House when the aides discussed how to keep Soetoro in office for life."

Yocke wanted to talk. Like most writers, his head buzzed with words. Sooner or later he had to spew them out so that he could have room to think about something else. "Being a revolutionary is very romantic," he said. "It isn't for everyone. The hours are brutal, you can get seriously hurt or dead, even if you win you'll be a pauper, and you'll probably wind up unhappy with whoever emerges from the chaos as the head dog. Sooner or later the optimistic revolutionary becomes the disillusioned veteran. If he is still above ground."

"Was this your column that won't get printed?"

"Yeah. Good solid stuff."

"So, Jack, are you willing to kiss your pension, 401(k), Mazda sports car, and Washington condo good-bye and sign on for the voyage? Are you ready to pledge your life, your fortune, and your sacred honor?"

"Not yet, Admiral. I'm working up to it. Soetoro is dragging me to it by the hair. He's dragging a whole lot of people there. If Soetoro doesn't stop this shit pretty soon, there is going to be a major explosion."

"He thinks not."

"Barry Soetoro is a damn fool. President of the United States, and he doesn't know Americans."

★

On Thursday, the twenty-fifth of August, Jack Hays and his wife, Nadine, rode a helicopter from Austin to Sanderson, Texas, where a funeral home had Joe Bob Hays laid out. JR and his brother, Fred, and Fred's wife and eldest son were there. The grandson was only four. JR had been divorced for the past ten years. His ex-wife had custody of their children. The wife had had an affair while her husband was in Afghanistan, and divorce followed. She didn't remarry. The kids were teenagers now and knew everything about everything. JR wrote them a note about their grandfather and mailed it, and that would have to do.

The sheriff, Manuel Tejada, was there with some of his deputies in uniform. One of them, a man with bright, garish yellow and green tattoos that started at both wrists and ran up his forearms, took the time to shake JR's hand and tell him how sorry he was. "Knew your dad," he said. "Good man." His name was Romero, according to the silver name tag he wore over his left shirt pocket.

The sheriff, his deputies, the mayor and county commissioners lined up to shake hands with Governor Jack Hays. Funerals aren't normally places to talk politics, but they were very worried about terrorism and martial law and asked Hays what it meant.

"Washington hasn't said much. We'll know more soon," was his stock answer. Actually, he was lying. Washington had sent him a directive that ran over a hundred pages. He had scanned it and turned it over to the attorney general for comment. His aides had run off some copies. He gave a copy to Ben Steiner and one to Charlie Swim, and told them to keep their mouths shut. He had taken another copy home and he and Nadine had read it.

As he stood listening to the preacher drone on, he was thinking of some of the major points in the directive. In effect, Soetoro and his administration were deputizing the state government to enforce their orders in Texas. That was Nadine's verdict as she read the thing. She was an archaeology professor at the University of Texas and considered herself middle of the road politically. In Texas, that put her a little left of center, but not much. At the university, that made her a conservative oddity among the faculty, most of whom didn't think much of her husband either.

Hays glanced around. Against the back wall stood two Texas state troopers in uniform who had flown out to Sanderson in the helicopter with him. They were now his official bodyguards. This morning he asked them point-blank: "What will you do if federal agents try to arrest me?"

"They better come a-shootin'," the little one said. He was the senior man. The other man merely nodded.

"I doubt if it will come to that," Jack Hays told them, "but it might."

"You're our elected governor. Ain't nobody in Washington gonna drag you outta the state house. Period."

"Thanks."

"Them guys and gals at the FBI office in Austin, some of them are Texans too. If they get orders to come and get you, they'll call us first. They promised."

After the service, Jack and Nadine stood on the lawn and watched the funeral home personnel load Joe Bob's coffin in a hearse. JR and Fred and his wife were going to follow the hearse to the ranch, where Joe Bob would be interred beside his wife, who had died of cancer ten or eleven years ago. No, Jack Hays thought. Twelve years ago. Damn, but time slides right along.

Before they closed the rear door of the hearse, he went over to the coffin and touched it. "Good-bye, Uncle Joe Bob." He started to say more but choked up. "Good-bye," he whispered and walked away.

"Drug smugglers," Nadine said as they walked to the helicopter, which was a block away in the courthouse square. Texas flags hung everywhere, from windows and poles mounted on buildings. "They killed him," she said, "and now their poison is ready for consumption all over."

"Ready to supply the addicts and recreational users who don't give a damn about violating the law or who gets killed," Jack Hays muttered, "as long as they are having a good time."

"Why haven't we sealed that border?" Nadine asked.

"We tried," he shot back. Nadine knew that. He had tried and the federal government sued and the judges said only the feds could control the border. We have to leave it open so the illegals can get in, Jack Hays told himself. Can't take a chance on pissing off the Latino voters. And all those illegals who Soetoro wants to turn into voters. Hays was in a foul mood. Drug smugglers, now Soetoro and his martial law. It's a hell of a world we live in.

His cell phone rang. He looked at the number. His aide.

The engine on the helicopter began to make noise.

"Yes."

"The Houston police got troubles. A riot broke out several hours ago in the projects. They are burning cars and building barricades. Doing some looting. Some black congresswoman is shouting into microphones about the racist right-wing conspiracy trying to keep people of color down."

He was tempted to order her arrested for inciting a riot, but that would only pour gasoline on a fire. "I'll be back in Austin as soon as I can," he told the aide. "Get out the riot plan and act on it."

"Yes, sir."

He got in the back of the helicopter with Nadine; the two troopers climbed aboard after them.

Jack saw JR watching as the machine lifted off.

After the interment, Fred Hays and his wife and son shook hands with JR, got into their car, and started driving back to Dallas. Fred and JR had just inherited a twenty-two-thousand-acre ranch in a very dry corner of Texas, and now didn't seem to be the time to discuss what they were going to do with it. Fred and his wife were schoolteachers, had two kids, and needed every dollar they could get. Neither wanted to live along the Rio Grande miles from civilization—if Pumpville, Texas, was civilization. Fred had grown up on that ranch and that was precisely the place he wanted away from when he went to college. He had never come back except for brief visits. And his parents' funerals.

JR, on the other hand, had spent too many years in Iraq and Afghanistan to look at desert chaparral with affection. The ranch was a big, windy, dry place, and in August hot as the doorstep of Hell with the fire doors open. His grandfather had settled here way back when because the land was cheap. It wasn't worth much now, either. His father had stayed because he loved it, and he had gone broke there. Oilmen had drilled some exploratory wells yet never found anything. Probably never would. The place was mortgaged for the fence and exotic animals. If JR and Fred didn't sell it, they'd need to find a way to make money to pay the bank. Hosting hunters was probably the only way.

Maybe, JR thought sardonically, he should sell it to the dope smugglers.

★

JR gave his father's sole employee a check worth two weeks' pay. "Take some time off. Visit your family. I'll call you when we need you. We'll probably sell the place, and while it's for sale we'll need someone to look after it and keep the fences repaired, so we don't lose the animals."

"I don't want to get shot by them dopers," the hired man said.

"I don't blame you. Just stay the hell out of their way and fix the fences in the daytime. You could do that, couldn't you?"

"I reckon."

"Two weeks. See you then."

JR went in the house and called his boss in El Paso. Quit his job on the phone. "I won't be coming back. Dad's dead and there's the ranch."

"I understand."

"I brought some of the company's stuff with me, and I'll bring it all back in a couple of weeks."

"Sure. Sorry about your dad."

JR inventoried the grub in the house and his father's meager collection of weapons. The sheriff had returned the Marlin, with its nightscope. JR looked it over. It seemed intact and should be workable if he charged the battery, but he had a much better one under the rear seat of the pickup. There was a twelve-gauge pump shotgun and an old thirty-eight revolver, a double-action Colt that his father had used to execute pigs years ago, when he kept pigs and cured his own hams and ate his own bacon.

Then JR got in his pickup and headed for Del Rio, eighty miles away. He drove fast, so he got there before the stores closed. Went into the first gun store he saw. The man behind the counter was sitting on a stool watching television. He wore a holstered pistol on his belt.

"I need to buy a couple of guns," JR said. "And some ammo."

The proprietor gestured toward the television. "Barry Soetoro says he is shutting down all the gun stores nationwide. We ain't supposed to sell guns and ammo anymore to anybody but law enforcement. *Fuck* that raghead commie son of a bitch. I ain't seen nothin' in writing from the ATF, and until I do I'm still open. Sell you ever'thing in the whole goddamn store if you got room on your credit card."

"Not that much. I'll limit myself to a small fraction of your inventory."

"Help yourself. I'm gonna sit here and watch the riots. Put what you want on the counter and we'll dicker. I'm easy, long as you're not a convict or illegal chili-picker and you've stopped beatin' your wife. Comrade Barry is gonna put me out of business pretty damn quick and I'll need some money until the welfare checks start arrivin' in the mailbox."

"You have any black powder?"

"Six or eight cans of the stuff. It's on a shelf in the back. Help yourself."

"I have a cannon. Need some fuses for it, too."

"Same place. I supply the local pyro club, you know, the nutcases that make their own fireworks. Got all the stuff to make their rockets go up and pop. Take all you want. That asshole Soetoro will probably shut them down too and I can't return that stuff or eat it. I'll probably end up piling it up and setting it afire in my backyard."

"You have a big backyard?"

"Couple hundred acres. That's where the pyro club does their thing."

An hour later when JR Hays paid for his purchases, the proprietor tossed in a couple of NRA bumper stickers into one bag and two that said "Fuck Soetoro."

"Classy," JR said.

"Yeah. Kinda to the point. I'm all outta the ones that say 'Soetoro Sucks.'"

JR Hays loaded his purchases into his pickup and visited the local hardware store. While there he purchased four five-gallon cans for gasoline, among other things. At the supermarket he stocked up on canned goods, dry beans, two cured hams, bacon, and coffee. He hit the liquor store for two big bottles of bourbon and a case of beer. As people in this sparsely populated country normally did, he stopped at the filling station on the edge of town, topped off the truck, and filled his gas cans.

He took his time getting back to the ranch. It was after eleven o'clock when he closed and locked the gate behind him, drove the half mile over the rutted dirt road to the ranch house, a low single-story with two bedrooms and a bath, with a telephone but no TV, and got busy carrying his purchases inside. After he had his food and hardware put away, he opened one of the bottles of bourbon and poured himself a drink, neat, just the way Joe Bob used to drink it. He turned out the lights and went out on the ramada to escape the heat of the house. Sitting there sipping whiskey, he could hear the whisper of the wind in the brush. Somewhere a coyote howled.

Above him, the obsidian sky was full of stars.

★

When Jack Hays got home from the state capitol, a Texas flag was stirring on the flagpole in the yard. It was always there, but tonight he paused to look at it. Inside, Nadine was watching television. He flopped on the couch and watched a little in silence. The "ghetto rats," as he called them when reporters weren't around, were burning and looting in Houston, St. Louis, Chicago, Detroit, Los Angeles, and Philadelphia. Screaming about the right-wing white conspiracy.

"How do they know it's whites?" he asked Nadine.

"All right-wingers are white Republicans. Ninety-eight percent of blacks are Soetoro Democrats. You know it, I know it, everybody knows it. Soetoro lit the fuse and it's burning."

When the television people began a commercial, Nadine killed the savage beast. In the silence that followed, he told her about more of the federal government's demands. And about his talk with Ben Steiner.

Nadine listened in silence and sipped Chardonnay. When he ran out of words, he went to the bar and poured himself a drink, vodka over ice. God knows, he needed it. What a hell of a day!

Seated again near Nadine, he sipped the liquor. "I feel like I'm chained to a railroad track with locomotives coming fast from both directions. Soetoro is ripping up the American Constitution and there are a large number of people in Texas who would rather fight than submit. Lincoln must have had similar feelings when he watched the Southern states pass secession resolutions. We're headed for a smash and I haven't a clue what to do about it."

"Maybe Ben Steiner is right. Texas should become its own country."

Jack Hays snorted. "Texas will become a nation over Barry Soetoro's dead body. If he lets Texas go, a lot of other states will follow. Why should people who work for a living pay taxes to provide welfare to all those rats in the center cities? Explain that one to me."

"Extortion?"

"Pay or we'll burn it down and live in the ashes. The only people who worry about that kind of logic are politicians."

"Texas could make it as an independent nation," Nadine said, eyeing her husband.

"Horseshit. American dollars are our currency—"

"Issue your own currency, backed by the state's full faith and credit. That's easy enough."

"Hundreds of thousands of people rely on Social Security and federal and military retirement. We can't abandon them. Without those pensions—"

"Texas can assume those obligations."

He stared at her.

Nadine took another sip of Chardonnay, then said, "If people paid income and Social Security taxes to Texas instead of the federal government, and if Texas didn't have the federal debt to service, I suspect that the finances would be pretty close to a wash. Dollar for dollar, in and out. Texas could guarantee U.S. government bonds held by Texas banks and pension funds. If you made welfare recipients who are able-bodied work for their check or forfeit it, that would help a bundle. And make welfare recipients take a drug test. You know, straight out of Charlie Swim's platform. No more money for single women to have kids."

She leaned forward, pleading her case. "Texas has energy to sell to the world, a great banking system, world-class hospitals, automobile factories, cutting-edge high-tech industries, a solid agricultural base, and we're on the Gulf Coast so we can import and export. Texas has an annual GDP of 1.6 trillion dollars. That is a larger economy than the state of New York, just a little less than California. Texas generates roughly ten percent of the economic activity in the United States. Our Texas economy is a third larger than Mexico's, just ten percent behind the United Kingdom's. If Texas were an independent nation, ours would be the twelfth-largest economy on earth, a smidgen less than Canada, but more than Australia, Spain, or Switzerland. And you think Texas couldn't go it alone?"

Jack Hays eyed his wife coldly. "I didn't know you were an independence crackpot."

"I'm not. But the people of Texas will not live in a dictatorship. *Will not.*"

"The United States won't let us go without a fight."

"We're heading for a fight regardless," Nadine said flatly. "Even if independence isn't your end game, it might give you leverage to demand a return to constitutional government on the federal level. Texas has a hell of a lot better hand than you think."

Jack Hays took a swig from his drink and sat staring at his wife. "We could seal the border," he suggested. "Demand the Mexican government stop allowing drug smugglers and illegals to cross. We could seal the border so tight a bat couldn't get across."

Nadine put her hand on his arm. "Sure you could, but you'd need to make it clear that no one is against immigration *per se*, from Mexico or anywhere else. The problem is *illegal* immigrants; they're swarming in faster than we can absorb them in the schools or in the labor force or with social services. When illegal, unskilled laborers flood the market, it's our own low-skilled citizens—black, white, brown—who pay the price. People understand that, and they understand that it's high time someone stood up for *them*. So sure, seal the border, cut off all trade to Mexico if necessary, and force Mexico to patrol its own borders and crush the drug trade that does even more harm to Mexico than it does to us. Make Mexico an offer it can't refuse. Not a single dollar, truck, railroad car, or immigrant, legal or illegal, crosses the border until Mexico cleans up its own house."

"That might precipitate a revolution in Mexico," Jack Hays said. "Or Mexico might declare war on us."

"Another Mexican revolution or another Mexican-Texas war, let it come," Nadine shot back. She had steel in her.

Jack Hays wasn't sure he bought all that. And yet, "We've been Mexico's safety valve for a long, long time," he admitted.

"Think about it," Nadine said, and finished her wine. "I'm sorry about your uncle. His was a needless, useless death. And as long as we leave that border open to drug gangs and criminals, we'll have more needless, useless deaths. I'm going to bed. I've had all I can take today."

Jack Hays was tired too, but he sat in the silent house thinking. About his uncle. About the possibilities of a free Texas, out from under the yoke of Barry Soetoro, Washington bureaucrats, and a feckless Congress stymied by cries of racism. Was freedom worth all the blood it would take to reap the benefits? No one but God knew how much blood freedom would cost.

His thoughts drifted back to the American Revolution. The revolutionaries then knew the British would fight. Great Britain had the finest navy in the world and a solid, although small, professional army. All the colonists had were farmers and a dream.

And yet, who today would argue that the lives of American patriots killed during the revolution had been squandered? Or the lives of the Texans who fought at the Alamo and at San Jacinto? Sometimes those half-seen, fog-shrouded dreams of national destiny and the unpredictable future must be anointed with blood to make them reality. Not someone else's blood, but yours. Or your son's or daughter's. Your blood is your gift to future generations.

He was thinking of the Texans at the Alamo who knew they were doomed but fought to the last man. Then the telephone rang. He looked at the number before he answered it. A 301 area code. The Maryland suburbs of Washington, D.C. There was no one in Washington he wanted to talk to at that hour of the night. After ten rings the phone fell silent.

Perhaps he should think of independence as a maneuver, not an end in itself. The name of the game is bettering the lot of your constituents. Nadine was right: in politics there is always an end game. You say you want A, the opposition offers E or F, and all of you settle for C. Or B or D. Something in the middle. The real problem, as Jack Hays saw it from Austin, was that Barry Soetoro refused to settle for anything less than the whole enchilada, everything he wanted, which in a democratic republic is simply impossible. He was the prophet, the messiah, and he was driving a stake through the heart of the Great Republic.

Jack Hays was a good working politician. All he wanted was to move the needle in his direction. He well knew that every political question is not black or white, but some shade of gray. He still believed that most Americans were well-meaning people, not ideological crazies, and that compromise was possible.

The telephone rang again. He looked at the number and saw that it was the state director of the Department of Public Safety, Colonel Frank Tenney. The man wanted to talk about the riot in Houston. Hays listened carefully, grunted twice, said yes three times, then hung up.

After he finished his drink, he turned off the lights in the living room and stretched out on the couch.

★

Jake Grafton was wide awake at four in the morning. The camp was lit only by floodlights on the perimeter fences, yet there was just enough illumination leaking through the front flap of the tent to see by. All the cots were occupied. It was August and hot and the cicadas outside, and the farting, snoring, deep-breathing sleepers inside made it anything but silent.

Grafton had spent the evening talking to his fellow detainees. They were almost all white and perhaps forty years old or older. Some had been arrested at home and allowed to bring their medications; others had been arrested at their places of business or in restaurants or golf clubs or bars. The police or federal agents knew whom they wanted, and they came and cuffed them and led them away without much fuss or bother. Several said they were pretty liquored up and loudly denouncing Soetoro and the feds, but the cops treated them decently anyway. Maybe the fact that they were spouting anti-government sentiments when arrested made a deeper impression on the witnesses.

The detainees were small-business men, middle or senior managers or officers in major enterprises, civil servants, state or county politicians, a few preachers, a lot of military and civil retirees. A couple of sheriffs. Basically, the feds had taken a large sample of white America. Apparently federal officers had taken a similar sample from the female population; the women were housed in other tents at Camp Dawson, and males and females mingled inside the compound until lights out was called. The detainees were a talkative bunch, gathering in ever-shifting groups, talking, talking, talking. They also gabbled endlessly on cell phones to the folks at home.

A lot of these people needed medications, and they didn't have them. Grafton thought this meant the detention was intended to be only for a short period, or whoever had planned it had planned it poorly. After many years spent in large bureaucracies, he suspected the latter was the case.

Grafton got up from his cot and headed for the latrine. Once outside the tent, he pulled the cell phone from his pocket and turned it on. In a moment the device locked onto the network. Still had a charge.

He pushed the buttons and held it to his ear. He could hear the ring signal.

"Jake, is that you?" Callie's voice.

"Yes. I—"

"Where are you?"

"Camp Dawson. It's a detention facility in West Virginia."

"Are you okay?"

"Oh, sure, Hon. Got a cot in a tent and they feed us three times a day, all the food anyone wants."

"Jake, your name was in the paper this morning. The government said you are being investigated to see if you were a member of the conspiracy that planned to assassinate the president."

"Who said that?"

"Some spokesperson for the FBI."

So Sal Molina was correct. Jake changed the subject. "Are you doing okay?"

"Oh, sure. Missing you and worried stiff. Why didn't you call sooner?"

"They are monitoring and recording all telephone calls. All of them."

"Oh," Callie said, and fell silent.

"Talk to me," Jake said. "I need to hear your voice. Talk about Amy and the grandbaby."

He leaned against the cinderblock latrine, closed his eyes, and listened to Callie's voice. She had been his rock for so many years. He was damned lucky to have had her to share his life with, and he knew it.

When they finally broke the connection, Jake Grafton stood looking at the ten-foot chain-link fence topped by three strands of barbed wire, with guard towers at the corners. This thing wasn't built overnight. Fence, latrines, sewage and water lines, showers, kitchens with natural gas stoves, electric refrigerators, concrete pads for the tents...construction must have taken months. The phone in his hand rang. He looked at the number. Tommy Carmellini.

"Hey, Tommy."

"I heard you are now famous, Admiral. Saw the news on television last night when I was eating dinner. Been trying to call you."

"My fifteen minutes."

"Where are you?"

"Camp Dawson, West Virginia."

"You got a charger for that phone?"

"I can get one. Why?"

"Keep it charged and on. I may want some investment advice. The stock market has the giggling shits, and you know how I am about bargains."

"Sure."

"Don't bend over to pick up the soap." And Tommy was gone.

Jake snorted, smiled, and put the phone in his pocket. Tommy Carmellini was one of the good guys he had known through the years. Amazing that there had been so many.

FOUR

★

I turned the iPhone off and looked at the ceiling in the motel room. Since I heard that news broadcast while munching a burger at the bar of a TGI Friday's at a little town in Ohio, I had tried Grafton's phone eight times before midnight, and two times since. Then, voila!, he answered.

Not that he had anything to say. I remembered that classified file that crossed his desk about the NSA going to comprehensive monitoring of all American telephone conversations. And I well knew how good they were at triangulating cell phone signals. They could put you within a few meters, whether you were using the phone or not, just as long as it was logged into a network. I was on teams that used that technique to find wanted terrorists in Pakistan and Syria and Yemen.

The way to defeat that was to wrap your phone in tinfoil. So I wrapped mine back up and put it in my pocket.

The thing that bothered me was the announcement by the FBI that former CIA director Jake Grafton—note that "former"—was being detained and investigated for a possible role in the right-wing conspiracy to assassinate the president. They could have just locked him up and thrown away the key, but no, they decided to create a conspiracy to help justify martial law. I had no doubt when the trolls in the White House were finished writing this fiction the guilty bastards would make quite a list. I might even be on one of them. Along with the many enemies of the administration who didn't believe in global warming or Soetorocare or his give-a-pass-to-terror treaty with the death-to-America regime in

Iran. Soetoro's enemies would be in deep and serious shit that no doubt would ruin them for life. Maybe they would get a show trial before a military commission. And afterward, be put against a wall in front of a firing squad, or permanently locked in a cell somewhere to figure out where they went wrong. Barry Soetoro had that in him. He was the savior of the planet, after all.

So the question became, what was Mrs. Carmellini's little boy Tommy going to do about it?

Well, at least I knew where Grafton was. Tonight. I suspected they would not keep him long at Camp Dawson. They would want him to sign a confession they were busy writing now, so I suspected they would move him soon and go to work on him with torture and drugs.

Personally, I didn't give a damn what he signed. I had to get to him before they killed him.

I crawled out of bed, took a shower, and shaved because I had no idea when I would get another chance, then loaded my stuff into my car. I paused for a good look at the Benz. What an impractical car. I needed a pickup. Tomorrow, maybe.

I filled the car at an all-night station, got a cup of coffee, and pointed the front bumper east. There wasn't much traffic. The sky lightened up and the tires hummed on the pavement and I passed some trucks. I left the radio off.

Normally I don't think much about politics. I am like most people, I suppose. I get wrapped up in the business of earning a living, giving pleasure to select members of the opposite sex, spending time with friends, and following the fortunes of my favorite sports teams. I vote for people to represent me at every little meeting from city council to Congress and the White House; they can worry about the public's business, about filling the potholes in the streets, the state of the sewage treatment plants, and how much, if any, foreign aid we should give to Egypt: I vote for them because I don't want to do that stuff, and they say they do.

And yet, they need to stay within certain boundaries. I don't want them messing with me any more than they absolutely must. I am choosing my path through life: I want to be responsible for my choices and the results.

Just like most people.

I sat there driving through America wondering about Barry Soetoro and his disciples. I have never trusted people who think they know how everyone else should live, and demand those other people obey. I am not a good follower.

Aaugh!

The highway spun along toward the horizon and the sky got lighter. Another day in America!

When Jack Hays woke up on his couch that Friday morning, Nadine was leaning over, brushing her lips on his. She liked to wake him with a kiss.

"The coffee is on," she said, and went back toward the kitchen, where the cook reigned. Jack padded along behind and found the cook wasn't in yet.

With both of them sipping coffee, Nadine said, "You are going to have a hell of a day."

He nodded. "I think it'll come to a boil today, or tonight."

"What are you going to do, Jack?"

"Ask God for the wisdom to make the right decision and for the courage to see it through."

She rested her head on his shoulder and they stood holding each other, feeling the warmth of each other's bodies.

JR put his Beretta 9-mm in his belt and went for a tour of the ranch in the pickup. He wanted to see the terrain again, to refresh his memory, to see how it had changed through the years. Joe Bob had built some shooting stands here and there, boxes for hunters to stand in fifteen or twenty feet above the ground. The sports would climb up there with their rifles, hunker down, drink beer, and wait for something wonderful to wander into range, where they would assassinate it.

JR climbed up into several of the stands just to look at the terrain. Shooting at people from one of these things, with people shooting back, would be suicidal.

So what were the possibilities? Ambush the bad guys as they exited their vans in Mexico, or on the trail to the river, or as they crossed the river, or cutting the Hays fence, or somewhere on the Hays land, or out near the highway as they threw the backpacks over the fence, or anywhere along the return journey.

He saw no people during his tour, but he did spot two kudu. Gorgeous creatures.

Any ambush site would have to allow him to shoot, move, and survive. The shooting would be easier with his state-of-the-art night-vision equipment.

What if he got two or three of them? Or five or six? Those who escaped would tell their bosses back in Mexico, and next time he would be facing a company of hired killers, perhaps as many as fifteen or twenty heavily armed gunmen with automatic weapons.

Late in the afternoon, JR got out his new AR-15, cleaned it thoroughly, and mounted a scope on it, a regular 3 by 9 variable. He suspected the battle might drag on into the morning, and he should be well armed if it did.

After fifty shots he was sure of the scope's zero and comfortable with the trigger. He took the rifle into the house and opened all the windows to let the breeze air out some of the heat. He cleaned his rifle thoroughly again. Then he got busy fixing dinner. Poured some bourbon and drank it as he ate out on the ramada with the sun setting.

While JR was scouting the ranch, Jack Hays was under political siege in Austin. The Texas independence crowd was getting really worked up, especially after they saw copies of the directives—there were four directives, so far—about life in an America ruled by martial law under Barry Soetoro. The press was to be censored; television shows preapproved; news would be government press releases, which would be read without comment; and military courts would replace civilian ones. Gun sales were forbidden, and all guns would be turned in to military arsenals that would be designated in a few weeks.

The directives said nothing about the upcoming November election, but the feds obviously were planning a long spell of martial law, so pessimists could read between the lines, and did.

Meanwhile, inner-city riots around the country were getting worse, as the civil authorities let crowds burn and loot. Any persons in the riot zones were fair game for the mobs. The military that now were under federal control, the U.S. Army and National Guard, did nothing. Government spokesmen on television blamed the right-wing conspiracy, evil men who didn't believe in progressive goals and wanted to use low-wage earners as slaves in the capitalist economy. Translated, that meant evil whites who wanted to exploit semiliterate, unskilled minorities for the minimum wage.

Jack Hays spoke to the National Guard brigadier in charge of Houston, James Conrad, three times that day. The first call went like this: "What's happening?"

"I need orders from Washington, Governor. I was told to await written orders. Until I get them, I can't do anything."

"Washington knows that people are getting murdered in Houston and having their homes and businesses destroyed, right?"

"Sir, I have sent in reports every hour. I don't know what else to do. If I go into the riot zone on my own hook in disobedience of orders, I'll be relieved and court-martialed and they will put someone else in my place, someone who will obey orders."

"Are you going to keep the mob inside the riot zone?"

"No one has said anything to me about that. Governor Hays, I'm just a soldier. I obey orders and I give orders. Right now, I am awaiting orders from the national command authority."

"That's Soetoro, right?"

"Yes, sir. The president."

"Call me when you hear something," Hays said, and General Conrad promised he would.

Jack Hays called in Colonel Frank Tenney, director of the Texas Department of Public Safety (TxDPS), who commanded the state police.

Hays told him about the call with Brigadier General Conrad of the National Guard. "We can't let those rioters burn down the city and murder people. I want you to get as many of your men as you can and encircle the area. Let the National Guard do its thing, but don't let those rioters out of the zone they are in right now. And evacuate anyone willing to leave. You have a copy of the riot plan?"

"Yes, sir."

"Then use it."

"I would, but FEMA's Texas chief told me I have no authority, except as *he* gives it to me in obedience to the president."

Jack Hays had pretty much had all he was willing to take. Without really thinking through the possible ramifications, he said, "You go get that bastard and take him with you. I want him right up front when I give the order to go in there."

"You know there will be trouble. FEMA has their own private army, armed to the teeth."

"And they aren't doing anything about this riot. Go get the bastard. Disarm and arrest anybody that gives you trouble. That office is in Texas, and in Texas we run the show. *Texas is ours.*"

"You're goddamn right it is, Governor."

"Then get ready to go into that riot zone and arrest those thugs when I give the order. Get the Houston police to help. Call me when you are ready to do it. Got that?"

"Yes, sir."

When Colonel Tenney left his office, Hays sensed he had crossed the line. He asked the Texas Ranger outside the door to come in and explained the situation. "I need your boss as soon as he can get here. We are coming to a crisis."

"Yes, sir." The ranger was on his cell phone as he walked from the room. Primarily criminal investigators, the Texas Rangers—there were only about 140 of them—were a division of the TxDPS.

The Constitution of the State of Texas required the governor to maintain public order and enforce the laws—and Jack Hays meant to do that. Under state law, he could assume command of the TxDPS during a public disaster, riot, or insurrection, "or to perform his constitutional duty to enforce the law." As Jack Hays saw it, Barry Soetoro could not relieve him of this responsibility or void the statutes or Constitution of the State of Texas for any reason whatsoever. Jack Hays had sworn to uphold the law and, by God, he was going to do it or die trying.

His decision made, he called in the leaders of the legislature to brief them.

It was three o'clock that Friday afternoon when Jake Grafton was led into an office in the admin building of Camp Dawson. He wasn't wearing handcuffs. The room looked like what it used to be, a crowded office for low-level bureaucrats and staff officers of the West Virginia National Guard. Now it appeared to be full of FBI agents.

"We want to ask you some questions," the man behind the desk said. He was a White House aide, maybe in Soetoro's inner circle, or only one level away. His name was Harlan Sweatt, known to the world as Sluggo. He was balding, with a double chin and a serious spare tire that was hidden behind the desk. Jake recognized him, although the two had never met.

Grafton dropped into the chair across from Sweatt. Scanned the other agents in the room, four men and one woman. All looked as if they hadn't had much sleep, and no wonder, busy as they must have been rousing citizens from offices, golf clubs, bars and beds, and transporting them here to this mountain concentration camp.

"Ask away," Grafton said.

"I am not going to read you your rights," Sluggo said, "because your rights have been suspended by the declaration of martial law."

"I didn't know that the president had the power to suspend the rules of criminal procedure or the presumption of innocence or the right to be represented by counsel."

"Are you a lawyer?"

"No."

"He has been advised by good lawyers, including the attorney general. He is fulfilling his constitutional duty to protect the nation."

"If you say so."

"We want to ask you about your role in the conspiracy to remove the president from office."

Jake sat silently, watching the man drone on. He had suspected this might be coming since Callie told him of the FBI's announcement to the press.

When Sluggo Sweatt paused for air, Grafton said, "I deny any involvement whatsoever."

"Four people have confessed, so far. They swear you knew about the planning for a coup d'état."

"Who?"

He named names. Two names Jake thought he recognized from the CIA, low-level staffers. The other two he didn't.

"I don't care what they signed. I deny any involvement whatsoever, nor did I know of any plot."

"You had better rethink that, Admiral. You have a daughter, a son-in-law, and a grandson. Your wife lives on your pension. You have money in the bank and property. With a stroke of a pen, all that can be taken away from you."

Grafton said nothing.

"I don't think you realize how serious the crime is that you are accused of," Sweatt explained, as if Grafton had a 75 IQ and his wife had to help him put on his pants in the morning. "The penalties are catastrophic, for you and your family. We have drafted a confession for your signature." He opened a drawer and removed the confession, tossed it on the desk. "As you will see, you are charged with nothing but failing to report treasonous activity. There is no suggestion that you committed any overt act. I suggest you read it, please."

Grafton didn't even pick it up. "Sluggo, I am not going to put my fingerprints on that. I have no doubt you can forge my signature, if you want it, and no doubt whatsoever that you have sold your soul to the devil. Currently there is nothing I can do about this situation, or you, but I'll remember you. Not fondly."

"I won't try to persuade you," Sluggo Sweatt said coolly. "But I want you to consider the fact that the world has turned, and you are in serious danger of being roadkill. There won't be another day in your life when you can do anything about it, about me, or about your situation. Not a day, not an hour, not a minute. You can only save yourself and your loved ones a great deal of grief by signing that document."

"Is that why you sold out? Saving yourself grief?" Grafton replied.

The man shrugged. "Unlike you, I have some common sense," he said, and gestured to the agents against the wall.

"I am delighted to hear that, Sweatt," Grafton shot back. "Common sense is almost as rare as hen's teeth, and equally hard to find."

The agents led Grafton back to the compound.

The members of the Texas legislature that packed into the governor's office were a mixed lot. Some were demanding that the legislature pass a declaration of independence and declare Texas a free republic. Others looked damned worried.

"Are you people out of your minds?" It was Smokey Bryan from Hall County. "I fought for the United States in the army. I am a citizen of the United States. My family have all been American citizens, and my great-great-grandparents who came to Texas when it was Comanche country and got scalped—they were Americans. I'll be goddamned if I am gonna commit treason and try to take Texas out of the Union. Again. The last time we tried that they shot a lot of Texans but didn't hang anybody. This time they might. Barry Soetoro is, no question, a would-be tin-pot dictator, but he *is* the president of the United States. And let's call a spade a spade—no pun intended—he's black. Most black people will stick to him even if he declares he is the risen Christ."

Luwanda Harris, a black woman representing a district in Houston, said, "Gangs of terrorists are running around killing people. People are plotting a coup. I don't know who, but it's probably Republicans. They hate him. You are damn fools to sit here discussing treason when the FBI hasn't finished its investigation."

Someone shouted from the back. "You don't seem very worried about your constituents who are caught in the middle of a riot."

"Fuck you," she shot over her shoulder. She was looking straight at Bryan when she said, "And you too, Smokey, you Nazi bigot. Black people have been shit on for centuries, ever since they were dragged to Texas as slaves. You people have segregated them, won't educate them, won't give them a leg up. You won't even increase the minimum wage. Let the niggers rot. That's—"

"You racist bitch!" Senator Bryan roared. "I have had—"

"Quiet," the governor shouted. "If you people are going to cuss at each other, go outside on the lawn to do it. You can use your fists, shout, pull hair, act like children, get your names and photos in the papers. Go on. Get the hell outta my office." Silence descended.

Jack Hays lowered his voice. "Ms. Harris, Mr. Bryan, you two seem to have lost sight of the fact you are on the same side. You are both against Texas independence. Yet we all share a common concern, I hope. We all care deeply about the people of Texas, all of them, and what is best for them."

"I'm concerned about what is best for *black* Americans," Ms. Harris shot back. "All you white people can worry about your own damned selves. We black people are going to stick together."

"You speak for yourself, woman," interjected Charlie Swim. "You don't represent me, and when the fires finally go out, don't come begging the legislature for money to rebuild the projects. You won't get it. You helped them burn."

That caused another frenzy of shouting.

"Shut up," Jack Hays roared. "The question is, How are we going to stop the riot? If the feds interfere, what are we going to do?"

"You're goin' to Houston and shoot a bunch of black people," Luwanda Harris said. "I know it, they know it, and the White House knows it."

"We're going to arrest rioters and hold them responsible for their crimes," the governor said in a normal voice. "Murder, rape, looting—nobody gets a free pass. Nobody. I have sworn to uphold the law and I will, whether you are white, black, brown, yellow, or green. If you want to do your community a service, Ms. Harris, you will get yourself to Houston and help stop the riot."

"Who do you think I am?" Luwanda Harris demanded. "You think I own them?"

"Anybody else?" the governor said.

A delegate from the Dallas suburbs wanted to discuss threats. Her name was Melissa McKinley. She didn't know whether Soetoro was right about a right-wing conspiracy, but her constituents were worried about security. Terrorist threats, insane people, drug violence, the list went on. "My constituents want to be free from fear, free to raise their children in a safe environment. Guns scare them, enraged homicidal maniacs that shoot kids in schools and theaters scare them, terrorists and assassins scare them. The specter of a civil war would horrify them. They don't want to live in Baghdad or Beirut or Syria. They want their children to have a chance to reach adulthood free from fear."

"How much freedom are they willing to trade for their security?" Ben Steiner asked.

"They don't want to bury their kids, Ben."

"So they would be happy in Hitler's Germany or Stalin's Russia in a comfortable little cell, just as long as their blood didn't flow?"

"I doubt it, but freedom doesn't do you a lot of good if you're dead."

"Amen to that," several of the legislators muttered.

They wanted to mention the grievances of their constituents, introduce them into the discussion, things such as EPA regulations designed to save the climate at the expense of the working men and women of Texas, even though there was no scientific evidence that the changes demanded would have any impact on the problem as defined by the EPA. And the EPA's demands to shut down coal-fired power plants, which would raise electric bills dramatically. Several wanted to talk about the financial and social burden of illegal aliens on the school districts and the education of American children, whose parents were paying the taxes to fund the schools. Others wanted to talk about federally mandated school curriculums and school lunches. Many were sick and tired of being dictated to by Washington bureaucrats who thought they knew more than the people ruled by their edicts.

Another just wanted to talk about a federal government many of her constituents perceived as an out-of-control, fire-belching, meat-eating monster that could not be tamed, controlled, or killed, a monster that increasingly stuck its nose into every facet of American life and propagandized their children every minute of the school day. A minister denounced a government that he believed was not just neutral on religion, but actively antireligious.

Charlie Swim broke in. "The bottom line is we need to stop these riots. You want to help black people?" He scowled at Luwanda Harris. "The people getting crippled and maimed and killed are black. The people doing it are black. A lot of the businessmen getting looted and burned out are black. If the federal government won't stop it, the state government must: it's that simple. A government that fails to protect its citizens from violence has forfeited its claim to legitimacy. And if bucking Soetoro and the feds leads to a confrontation, it's time for Texas to face the issue head-on and declare its independence."

Charlie Swim stood on a chair and looked around the room. "I tell you now," he continued, "I'm for independence. The people of Texas would be better off without the other forty-nine states, all the Texans, white, black, and brown, for all the reasons that have been mentioned here this morning. We would be better off without those fools in Washington.

"Luwanda, you, the Republicans, and everyone in the country with a brain know that Cynthia Hinton doesn't have a chance to win the November election. She knows it too. She has plenty of her own ghosts, but carrying the Soetoro record on your back would have defeated anybody. All Hinton is doing is jacking off the faithful.

"And as for Soetoro and his gang. You know what their motto is: Never let a crisis go to waste. I don't trust them or believe anything they say.

"I think the time has come for us to start our own country. When you don't trust your spouse, or your boss, or your government, it is time to say good-bye and go on down the road."

★

When JR Hays considered the tactical possibilities, he decided the only answer was booby traps, or mines. One man shooting wasn't going to get it done. Oh, he might get a few of the drug smugglers, but he wouldn't get them all, and if he didn't get them all, every last one, he would be signing his own death warrant.

Not that JR thought he was going to live forever, because he doubted that he would.

The problem with booby traps was that they kill anyone who trips them—illegal pregnant women trying to get across the river to have their babies in Texas, men looking for work, as well as any drug smugglers and professional killers who happened by. Anyone and anything, including kudus, elands, oryx, springbok, nyalas, impalas, whitetail deer, and coyotes.

Unless he wanted to bury a lot of relatively innocent people and very innocent animals, he needed mines he could detonate at the proper moment.

He unlocked the toolbox in the bed of his pickup. Using the truck's tailgate as a table, he laid out all the devices he had borrowed from his former employer, the defense contractor, and looked them over carefully. Nothing there was explosive. What he had was sensors, miniature control boxes, radio controllers, batteries, and the other bits and pieces of high-tech booby traps. With the black powder and fuses, he should be able to construct some seriously lethal homemade Claymore mines.

FIVE

★

After the crowd filed out of Jack Hays' office, Ben Steiner stayed behind and closed the door. He dropped into a chair and lit a foul little cigar. Jack Hays sat in his executive chair, which his wife had bought from Office Depot and he had assembled in his garage.

"Looks like you've crossed the Rubicon, Jack. Ain't no going back from here." Steiner blew smoke around, then looked for an ashtray. There wasn't one. "You're sort of in the position of the fellow that found himself astride a fence when the ladder gave way and he came down with one leg on either side."

"If you introduce a declaration of independence in the legislature," Hays asked, "will it pass?"

"That's the question, isn't it?" Ben Steiner said, puffing lazily. "And damn, I don't know. It might. Just might."

"Or it might not," Jack Hays said disgustedly. "Don't you think you ought to start counting noses? If it's DOA, I'd like to know it before I manage to piss off every federal employee from the postman to Soetoro."

"I'm all for it," Steiner declared, "but it's a big step. Soetoro is arresting everybody in Texas he can get his hands on—whoever intimated, hinted, or told his wife that he didn't like Soetoro. FEMA has a camp for them up in Hall County. They got a list and are rounding 'em up."

"How come you aren't on it?"

"Oh, I am, but my wife told them I was in Argentina fishing for a couple of weeks."

"Ben, it would be silly to introduce such a resolution, or bill, unless we knew it was going to pass."

"By how much?"

"Simple majority."

"That isn't much."

"We'll be lucky to get that," Jack Hays said. "We must have something to paper our ass with. Unlike Soetoro, I want to hear the people's representatives speak. One way or the other. Yea or nay."

"It's that 'lives, fortunes, and sacred honor' thing that has them worried."

The governor took his time answering. "I think everyone would like to wake up and find this is just a nightmare. But it's real. None of us are going to be able to bury our head in the sand and hope the wolves don't bite our asses. The revolution has started. Soetoro has suspended the United States Constitution and the Bill of Rights. Lincoln did it under his war powers. Unfortunately for Soetoro, we aren't in a war. A rebellion, or revolution, will change the life of *everyone* in America. Indeed, perhaps everyone on the planet. We can't start it—and the Texas legislature can't—because Barry Soetoro already did."

"That wasn't what you told me yesterday."

"I've changed my mind."

Ben Steiner took a deep drag on his cigar and let the smoke out slowly. "Our people need a little time," he said. "They gotta work up to being brave. They gotta examine all the options before they can screw up their courage for this one."

"How much time? The Soetoro administration has been planning martial law for years."

"Tomorrow or the next day."

"We better not have the vote if we aren't going to win. Barry Soetoro is too much of an egotist to ignore an independence vote, win or lose."

"We'll win," Steiner said grandly. In his fifties, with a booming voice, he knew how to sway people, persuade them. Jack Hays was a more difficult sell than the average juror, however.

"When you're sure you know how the vote will go, after you've talked to every member, come back and see me."

Ben Steiner leaned forward. "Jack, as we sit here Luwanda Harris and some of her friends are burning up the wires to Washington. If you don't want the capitol surrounded by tanks and army troopers from all over, you had better start talking to people, tell them what's at stake. We must get this done, and soon. If you don't, my best guess is the government of Texas is going to get arrested en masse and accused of treason. In the interim, let's cut off access to Washington."

"Can we take down the telephone system and the internet?"

"Of course. The only question is how fast."

"Let's do it," Jack Hays said. "Who do we call?"

"The state director of disaster response, Billy Rob Smith."

The governor picked up the phone and made the call.

Billy Rob Smith heard the governor out, then asked, "Are you nuts? Every business in America bigger than a lemonade stand relies on telephones, landline and cell, and the internet. Millions of people use the system to send or get business information and to buy and sell securities. Medical records are transmitted via fax or over the internet. The feds have been working like beavers to digitize every medical record in the nation—shutting off the internet may mean people can't get proper medical care. And the telephone system—you can't shut one system down without turning off the other. In a lot of places, voice and digital use the same wires. In some places the telephone system is completely digital. Turning off cellular and landline telephones will drop us right smack dab back into the nineteenth century. Shutting those systems down is insanity."

"I didn't ask for your opinion—I am giving you an order."

"And I'm telling you that you're crazy. Hell, I don't even know that you are the governor. You sound like an idiot jabbering on the telephone."

What ended the argument and decided the matter was an announcement at precisely that moment that was carried on television networks nationwide: The president had directed the military to work with civilian law enforcement agencies to confiscate all the guns in America in private hands. In the future, only the military and law enforcement officers would have guns.

Billy Rob Smith had a television in his office airing a twenty-four-hour news channel, which was limiting itself to government press releases these days, and he paused his conversation with the governor while an aide told him the news as rapidly as possible and pointed at the television set.

Smith was not stupid. "Did you hear that?" he demanded of Jack Hays.

"Yes."

"Holy damn. It's like the British marching to Lexington and Concord. This tears it. Americans won't stand for it. Hell, the people of Texas won't stand for it."

Jack Hays took a deep breath. He had other things to attend to. "Smith, I want you to shut off the telephone and internet systems in east Texas. Start right here in Austin, right now. Then Houston. Get busy."

A very subdued Billy Rob Smith said, "Yes, sir," and hung up.

Jack Hays repeated the news to Ben Steiner, who was taking a last puff of his little cigar. Steiner stared, slack-jawed. Finally he said, "Soetoro isn't just temporarily suspending the Constitution, he's tearing it up."

Jack Hays rubbed his forehead.

Steiner said, "Luwanda Harris will never change her mind, but this will get us Smokey Bryan and a whole lot of others who were on the fence. Of course, a lot of liberals will have a spontaneous orgasm when they hear Soetoro has repealed the Second Amendment, people like Melissa McKinley, but they weren't going to vote for independence no how, no way. They don't mind a dictator repealing the Second Amendment as long as they think he's on the side of social justice and the planet, like they are."

"Ben, if you are going to introduce a declaration of independence, and I don't mean an ordnance of secession, hadn't you better write one? After you count noses."

Ben Steiner rushed from the room, taking his cigar butt with him.

★

Trust Jack Yocke to know when something was going on, Jake Grafton thought. He was standing under a tree watching it rain from a low overcast sky when the *Washington Post* columnist found him.

"I saw them take you into the admin building, Admiral," Yocke said. "Rumor has it you are now part of the conspiracy that planned a coup d'état."

"Where did you hear that?"

"It's being whispered around."

"They wanted me to sign a confession."

"Did you?"

"I am not going to confess to anything I didn't do. Ever. Once you start that, there's no end to it."

"No matter how bad you think the Soetoro White House gang is," Yocke said, "you're wrong. They're worse."

"They certainly think they are on the side of righteousness and history."

"Hitler and Stalin were sure of it too—didn't work out so well for them."

"Now I feel better."

Jake Grafton had his hands in his pockets. He looked around. No place to sit that wasn't wet. He leaned against the tree trunk, which wasn't wet yet. The rain was falling in greater volume.

"So what are your politics, Admiral? In all the years I've known you, I never got an inkling."

Grafton snorted. "Long ago, when I was very young, I learned that all political points of view were valid for the people who held them, except for the fanatics on the fringes who are usually incapable of rational thought. Think about the blind men and the elephant. Honorable people can hold very different opinions because they have very different life experiences. Liberals, conservatives, middle-of-the-roaders, big-government types, libertarians, old, young, middle-aged, highly educated or average or uneducated, skilled or unskilled, stupid, average smarts, or genius, they all see a little bit of how the world works and process it into a worldview, and they are all correct. The genius of representative democracy is that it takes all these viewpoints and grinds them up and arrives at some kind of resolution, most of the time. Look at the federal tax code: government policy has tried to accommodate all major and many minor concerns and still raise revenue. Any dictator with half a brain could put a tax code together that is simpler and more efficient and raises more revenue. But the United States still has one of the highest, if not the highest, rate of voluntary tax compliance of any country in the world. So something must be working right."

"Democracy can't handle every problem; you have to admit that."

"Slavery was too big for representative government," Grafton acknowledged. "The story of this century is the haves versus the have nots, and illegal immigration is one aspect of that. Drugs are another piece of that problem. The disintegration of the black family is a piece. The desire of Barry Soetoro to drastically increase the number of non-white voters in America as quickly as possible to enhance the political power of blacks and Hispanics and Muslims and dilute the power of the whites is another. Representative democracy hasn't figured these problems out and may not be able to do so. Still, no other form of government has a better chance."

Lightning flashed, then two seconds later came the clap of thunder. The wind picked up.

"So how will the story turn out?" Yocke asked.

"I don't know, Jack. I really don't."

"I'm getting wet," the *Post*'s man complained, and brushed wind-driven raindrops from his hair.

"See you later," Grafton said.

"Good luck, Admiral."

"Thanks. You too." Grafton moved a few degrees around the tree and stood watching the rain.

I parked in front of the lock shop and went in to see Willie Varner, my partner. He knew more about locks than I ever hoped to know, and much of that knowledge was acquired in prison. They say prison will broaden a man; I couldn't testify to that, but the experience seemed to have stretched Willie's mind somewhat, even if it didn't do anything for his morals or ethics.

"Damn, Carmellini," he said, "I thought you was gone out west somewhere on the lone prairie learnin' to rope and ride and sing to the dogies, whatever they are."

"I've only been gone three days, Willie."

"Come back to reenlist in the CIA, have you?"

"Nope. Come back to break Jake Grafton out of prison."

"I saw the *Post*. And heard about him on TV. He's famous now. Arrested and all for tryin' to kick Barry Soetoro outta the White House and get him started on his way to Hell. You ain't serious about bustin' him out, are you?"

"I am."

He made a rude noise. "You are a real damn fool, Tommy. I've known some real losers in my day, people so damn stupid they needed help to pee, but you take the prize. Where they got 'im?"

"Camp Dawson."

"Never heard of it."

"It's a National Guard camp over in West Virginia."

"Ahh, the beatin' heart of civilization. I should of heard of it, cultured as I am. And after you get him outta there, where pray tell are you two gonna go? Yemen? You can share a goat herder's hut with some holy warriors. I heard the summers are kinda warm there. Maybe you can summer up at the North Pole in an igloo."

That was Willie, always asking the tough questions. "I don't know. Haven't thought that far ahead."

"Better get that figured out before you cross the line, Tommy. Send me your address in a year or two when you're settled so I can send you birthday cards."

"How do you like living in a dictatorship? Transition going okay?"

"So far so good. There's a kid down the street teachin' me the Sieg Heil salute. Want a beer?"

"Why not?"

We settled down with longnecks in the back room of the shop. That was where I broke the news that I needed some help.

"Oh, no!" Willie roared. "Forget that! Wash out your filthy mouth, Carmellini. I ain't ever goin' back to the joint, and how I know that is because I ain't ever goin' to do anythin' that would get me sent back there. Livin' in the joint with a bunch of losers who would as soon kill you as look at you, eatin' mac and cheese, no liquor or beer or women, jackin' off under the sheets...nope. Ain't gonna do it again, Tommy, so you just forget whatever shit is in your twisted head."

"I know you're a patriot."

"The hell I am! Who told you that? You go wave the fuckin' flag somewheres else."

"One of the sons of liberty."

He said a crude word that is illegal to say on the television or radio. Maybe even on the telephone. I knew I could talk him around, so we each had another beer and talked about Barry Soetoro and martial law and all that.

That evening I stopped in to see if Mrs. Grafton was home. I buzzed the door in the front lobby, told her who I was, and she let me in. Rode the elevator up.

Callie Grafton looked tired and out of sorts. She offered me something to drink and I chose bourbon. She poured me a healthy drink over ice.

She knew all about what the government spokesmen were saying to the press about her husband. "None of it is true. He has devoted his life to serving America. I can't believe that anyone could say these things about him with a straight face. Tonight on television they named two other men they said were coconspirators. I've never even heard their names before."

"They're sacrificial goats," I said, and watched her face.

She reached for my drink and took a sip. "I think so too."

"I'm thinking of busting him out of Camp Dawson, or wherever they move him. It can be done, but afterward he'll be a fugitive."

"So will you. And anyone who helps you."

"Can you go visit him? Like tomorrow?"

"I don't know. I can call him and ask."

"Please do so. Right now. Don't tell him that I'm here."

She went into the master bedroom, I suppose, and I sat at the little kitchen dining nook working on my drink and looking at the lights of

Washington. Lots of lights, all the way to the horizon. Thought about being a fugitive in Barry Soetoro's America.

I also thought about the possibility that the Grafton condo was bugged. It was a very slim chance, I thought. There hadn't been enough time, and why Grafton? Sure, they were setting him up as a human sacrifice, but why would they care what Callie Grafton said? There was nothing she could do about it.

Finally Callie returned. "I can see him tomorrow afternoon. They are still allowing visitors."

"Good," I said. "I doubt if they'll have the visitor's rooms wired up already, but they might." I handed her a watch. "Put this on and wear it. Pushing the stem in turns on a very high pitched sound, too high for human ears, but it will overpower any listening device and mask a conversation."

"Where did you get this?" she asked.

"Liberated it from the CIA. I thought that someday I might need it more than they did, and darn if that day didn't come. When your conversation is over, don't forget to push the stem again to turn the squealer off."

"How will I know it's working?"

"The second hand will cease to move when the squealer is on, and resume when it's off."

"Okay."

"You need to ask him if he wants out. That's the only question, and it's yes or no. He'll understand about being a fugitive if we get him out. Maybe they've been threatening him, maybe they haven't, but Jake Grafton will know the score. Yes or no. Can you do it?"

"Of course." She acted as if that were a silly question.

"On your way home, please call me. I'll give you my cell number. If his answer is yes, he wants out, you will tell me that he looks good. If the answer is no, tell me he looks tired."

"He said they were listening to telephone calls."

"It's worse than that," I admitted, and decided to share some classified information. "NSA is recording and data mining every telephone call in America. All of them. Have been for at least six months. Never say anything on any telephone that you don't want the government to hear."

She sniffed. "Handling that much information, they couldn't be very efficient."

"Computers are marvelous things. Never bet on bureaucratic sloth and incompetence. Just pray for it."

She stared straight into my eyes. "Tommy, how are you going to get him out?"

"I don't know just yet," I said. "I'll get some help and we'll put our heads together and see what is possible."

She started to say something, thought better of it, and examined her hands.

I hoped Jake Grafton would say yes, and I told Mrs. Grafton that.

"Why?" she said.

She was a tough broad, so I looked her straight in the eyes and explained. "Cynic that I am, I suspect if we don't spring him the Admiral is bound for a maximum security prison. Or a graveyard. Accused, convicted, and executed, he wouldn't be around to embarrass the crowd that needs him as a scapegoat."

She kept her eyes on mine. "You may be right," she said softly.

"Mrs. Grafton, if the White House didn't need some scapegoats, why did they accuse your husband of something ridiculous?"

She took a deep breath and exhaled slowly. "I'll call you tomorrow on the way home, Tommy. Thank you for coming."

"He looks good or he is tired."

I finished the drink, punched my cell number into her phone, said good-bye, and left. In the elevator down I thought about the fact that Callie Grafton didn't once mention herself, ask what she would do if her husband escaped custody. In her own way she was as tough as Jake Grafton. If I were Barry Soetoro, I wouldn't want to share an elevator with her.

When I was out of the parking garage and tooling through the city toward the lock shop, I got back onto the problem of how my helpers—they didn't yet know they were going to be my helpers—were going to snatch Grafton from the arms of the law. I had an idea or two about how we might evade afterward, for a little while at least, but first things first.

I decided to call my girlfriend, Sarah Houston. She used to be a data-miner at the NSA, with the world's biggest and best computer system to play with. It helped that she was also a genius and the most gifted hacker alive on this side of the Pacific. Hacking and selling secrets had gotten her into serious trouble a few years ago and she went to the joint, but Jake Grafton had sprung her to help him. That worked out, so her name was changed and she was given a new identity. Grafton had gotten her transferred to the CIA, and she had an office two floors below mine. I didn't know what she was doing at the agency, and I hadn't asked. Not that she would have told me anyway. If there was ever a woman who thrived on secret shit, Sarah Houston was her name.

She and I had an up-and-down relationship. Just now we were down. It was an old, old story: she wanted to get married and I didn't.

She answered the phone on the third ring. "What is it, Carmellini, you jerk?" I am not a fan of caller ID, and this is why.

"Hey, gorgeous. I was thinking of dropping by in about a half hour to run something—"

"No." She hung up.

We Carmellini men are made of stern stuff, so I went anyway. I buzzed her apartment from the lobby. No answer. Maybe she had a guy up there tonight, but I didn't think so. Men who could handle that edgy personality were rare indeed. I was one, sort of, but there is only one Tommy Carmellini.

I pushed the buzzers on three or four apartments, and was rewarded with a click. I was elevated to the fourth floor and marched purposefully to her door and rapped politely.

She must have looked through the security eye. "Get out of here, Carmellini, before I call the police."

"I'm here to talk about Jake Grafton."

Ten seconds... then she opened the door and stood there. She was wearing a robe and slippers.

"Well?"

"It would probably be better if we talked inside your place."

She pulled the door open and headed for her living room. I came in and closed the door.

"Well?" she said again.

"You have probably been reading about Jake Grafton being accused of conspiring to do a coup d'état. I need your help with a jail break."

She sat down and ran her hand through her hair. "Damn you, Tommy."

"I had nothing to do with it, and you know damn well Jake Grafton didn't. You know Jake Grafton. But Soetoro and his staff are going to frame him and either lock him up forever or execute him. If he doesn't get hanged in his cell while he is awaiting trial."

"They wouldn't do that," she whispered.

"You think?"

She put her face in her hands. Finally she whispered, "Okay. They would."

"Right now he's being held in a detention center at Camp Dawson in West Virginia. They'll move him soon to the federal holding center in Washington. We need to know when they plan to do that, and how many agents will transport him. I assume they will be FBI agents, but I don't know that for a fact. You could help with that."

She studied the carpet. After a bit she said, "You know if they catch me getting out of line they'll send me right back to the women's prison at Alderson. A knock on the door, handcuffs, and I'm gone for the rest of my life."

"If they catch me and Willie and the guys, we're going up the river too. If we're still alive."

She went into the kitchen and I heard her knocking around. In a few minutes she was back with two drinks. I sipped mine. Gin. I don't think much of gin, but I sipped along as if I drank it every day. She sipped hers too.

"So you get him out. Then what?"

I told her my idea.

"That won't work for long."

"Soetoro is lighting a fuse on a rebellion. We just need to be out of the blast zone until it blows up in his face, then he will have a great many more pressing problems than you, me, Grafton, and Willie the Wire."

"And if you are wrong?"

"If I'm wrong, I'll be dead. The rest of us too, maybe."

"You would take that chance for Jake Grafton?"

"Yes."

She took her drink and went to the window. Pulled back the drapes so she could see out. Stood there a while, taking an occasional sip of her drink. Finally she said, without turning around, "You would."

"I need your help to pull this off," I told her.

Back in his hotel that night, Ben Steiner went to the business center and used his computer to call up a copy of the U.S. Declaration of Independence of 1776 and the Texas Declaration of Independence of 1836. He printed them out, then logged off and went up to his room.

He read both documents carefully. The authors of the Texas declaration had obviously used the U.S declaration as a format. First there was a statement of their authority, then a list of grievances that justified what was to come, then the declaration itself, which severed the political ties with the mother country. The language of both was stirring, defiant, a political act that could not be undone except by military defeat by the mother country. Both were written for a wide audience, all the people in the nascent new nation and the citizens of the mother country, England and Mexico, respectively, and everyone in the world. The drafters of both knew they were writing a historical political document. They wrote for the people who would fight the battle and for all the generations yet to come.

Writing such a document would require the best that was in him.

Ben Steiner turned on his computer and began.

SIX

★

JR Hays dug his hide at noon. Before he turned over the first shovelful of earth he rigged up a listening device with an eighteen-inch parabolic dish. The dish picked up sound that was too faint for the human ear to detect, magnified it, and delivered it to the operator via earphones or on a speaker.

JR laid the dish antenna on the ground so he was listening to the sky. He heard jets come and go and birds flapping their wings. He began digging. The hide was on the side of the arroyo in hardpan. He had to use the pick to break it up enough to shovel. The dirt had to go in a wheelbarrow. He dumped the wheelbarrow fifty yards back where the dirt was fairly well concealed.

With the hide finished and bottles of water and weapons put inside, he installed a night-vision periscope. Twice he thought he heard piston engine sounds from the sky, so he quickly covered the hide with a green tarp. Then he lay on the ground and used night-vision goggles set for infrared. He saw the drone going northwest up the Rio Grande. When it was gone, he removed the tarp and got busy. An hour later the drone came back, so he did it all again.

When he had the hide finished, JR installed his homemade mines on both sides of the arroyo. He got them in by ten in the evening. He could clean up the sites in the morning, but they were concealed well enough to not be seen at night.

He went to his hide, checked that the parabolic dish antenna for the audio device was well concealed thirty feet away in a bush and aimed right where he wanted it, then climbed in and pulled the tarp over the hole. He donned the headset and scanned with the night-vision periscope he had borrowed from his employer.

He was tired. He ate a few energy bars, drank water, and waited.

He doubted they would come tonight. Or tomorrow night. But eventually they would. And he had an unlimited quantity of time. The rest of his life, actually.

Ambushes aren't for everyone. Few people have the patience to wait, and wait, and wait some more on the off chance that the opportunity you prepared for will actually happen. Snipers have that kind of patience, but most people don't. Most people want to attack right now. Or sooner. Yesterday would be preferable. Do it and get it over with.

Revenge isn't that way. The juice in revenge, JR knew, is in the anticipation. The longer you wait the sweeter it will be.

When he had repaired the fence that morning, he had attached a thin bare wire to it and run it to the hide. Now he twisted the end of the wire around one finger. Maybe he would feel it. His dad, he knew, had tried tin cans with rocks on the fence, but when the smugglers saw them, they knew he was nearby. JR doubted that they would see the wire. From his position near the fence, he should be able to count how many came through—and he could make sure that none got back.

So what could go wrong? Well, despite his precautions a drone might have spotted him digging the hide or planting the mines. Federal agents might be on their way here right now.

There was nothing he could do about that contingency, so he dismissed it. Never worry about things you cannot control. That was one of the hard lessons he had learned in the army. He had taken all the precautions he could, and that would have to do.

As he sat in the hide with the periscope, listening to the audio on the earphones, he reviewed the timetable again. If they didn't come by two hours before dawn, they weren't coming. They needed at least an hour to hike to the paved road on the north side of the ranch and an hour to get back here. He thought they would want to be back across the river in Mexico by dawn. Maybe.

But if they didn't come or he missed them, he could get them some other night. They would keep coming as long as this delivery route worked. As the hours passed he consoled himself with the thought that the smugglers were dead men walking.

By midnight he was having a devil of a time staying awake. Ten hours of hard manual labor in the heat of the west Texas summer had about done him in. That's what you get for not staying in shape, he thought, for letting yourself get soft.

He dozed off finally, wearing the earphones. Awoke with a start. Thought about giving up on tonight and heading back to the ranch house. But if he did that, they would come tonight. That was the way God rolled the dice.

JR checked his watch. Almost one in the morning. He decided he would give himself one more hour, and if they didn't come, go home to sleep. That decision made, he scanned with the periscope, saw nothing, and waited.

And dozed. When he awoke again with a start, he found that it was almost two. Something woke him up.

What?

Now he felt it again. A tug on the wire wrapped around his finger. Something was brushing against the fence. An animal? He unwrapped the wire and let it dangle.

He listened on the parabolic dish, adjusted the volume in the earphones. Looked through the periscope and saw three men operating with wire cutters on the fence.

They were here!

★

The internet and telephone service in the Austin area went down at ten that evening. Ben Steiner knew the system was dead because he saw legislators fiddling with their cell phones and pocketing them in disgust.

The legislature was in joint session, considering a declaration of independence for Texas. The balconies were packed, standing room only.

Steiner thought the declaration would pass, but figured it would take all night. Everyone, pro or con, had something to say.

Those for independence were outraged at the president's announcement that he was stopping all gun sales and confiscating firearms from Americans nationwide. Was he afraid of armed, law-biding American citizens? Hell yes. And what further destruction of the American way of life was in the works? Freedom of speech was already gone. Freedom from arbitrary arrest was gone. Was freedom of religion next? Federal officers were arresting people and incarcerating them for no crime other than the fact that they had been political opponents of the administration. That was deeply troubling. Even worse was the fact that no one had a clue when martial law would be over, when the country could get back to normal, or if it ever would.

The delegates and senators opposed to the declaration were equally passionate. A Texas declaration of independence was a declaration of war. It was a bold step into the unknown. War. With all the power and might of the federal government against them. Several delegates argued that the threat from terrorism justified martial law, and others pointed out that it was Soetoro himself who demanded that some of the terrorists be admitted as refugees. "He manufactured a bloody crisis and now he's using it to take the country where he wants it to go," a senator shouted acidly.

"Are you ready to lay down your life in opposition to the federal government?" one representative demanded. "Are you ready to lose everything, your family, your home, your savings, your means of making a living? Make no mistake; all those things are on the table. Are you ready to watch your children be killed in the violence? What will you say when your sons and daughters lie dead at your feet? Are you ready to turn your back on the American flag, the flag so many Texans have given their lives to defend? What the hell kind of people are you?"

Another representative wanted to argue about the process. "This question is so important that it should be voted on by the people of Texas, not passed here by majority vote. This isn't a convention of delegates elected to consider independence and draft a declaration—it's the state legislature, for God's sake."

"Texas voters will get their chance," someone shouted. "We're here to ensure that they do."

"Freedom isn't free," another speaker pointed out. "Freedom in America has been bought with blood. And that freedom purchased at such a precious price has been taken from us, ripped from our hands. The feds didn't declare martial law after Lincoln, Garfield, or JFK were assassinated. Are our institutions so flawed that a dictator can destroy them before our eyes, yet we lack the moral and physical courage to fight for our heritage? Mr. Speaker, if we won't fight to preserve our freedom, we don't deserve it. And Barry Soetoro will take it from us. He's trying to do that as we sit here this evening. There is only one thing for an American patriot to do, and that is vote to remove Texas from the tyranny of Barry Soetoro and the federal government." A roar went up from the audience.

Ben Steiner went into the governor's office and found him conferring with several senior National Guard officers. A glance out the window showed troops in the yard, a lot of them. Two tanks were visible, and three armored personnel carriers. Jack Hays had called out the Guard.

Finally Hays came over to Steiner and whispered, "How is it going over there?" He meant on the other side of the capitol building, in the House chamber.

"They're debating."

"Will we win?"

"I think so, but I guarantee nothing. Think of them as a large jury. Soetoro is on trial."

"They'd better get it done tonight. Federal agents are out there with some regular army troops, and they sent word in that everyone in this building is under arrest."

"Will the Guard hold?"

"I don't know, Ben." The skin of Jack Hays' face was drawn tightly over his cheekbones and his eyes seemed to have sunk back into his skull. "I suspect that if the legislature decides to surrender, the guardsmen will go back to their armory, turn in their weapons, and go home. What else is there for them to do?"

"I'll go tell the legislature," Steiner said.

Hays stopped him with a tug at his sleeve. "Make damned sure every person in that chamber understands that if they declare independence, their necks are on the line."

"I think they know that."

"If we can't win our independence, we're all dead, including you and me. Once they vote for independence, we've crossed the river of fire and burned our boats."

"Jesus carried his cross," Ben Steiner said gently. "We have to stand for something or the gift of life was wasted on us." He walked out the door and along the hallway through lines of state troopers.

The peons laden with backpacks full of narcotics trudged along in the darkness about six feet apart. There was starlight and a sliver of moon, but the old Indian trail up from Mexico would have been easy to follow regardless.

With the periscope, JR saw the lead man with a backpack and started counting. One...two...he quit at eight. Eight mules. No doubt there were armed guards, perhaps even the same ones who had killed his father, but they weren't on the trail. One was probably behind him, paralleling the trail.

JR glanced at the luminescent hands of his watch when the last man went by. At the speed the peons were walking, he thought it would take about a minute and a half for all of them to get into the kill zone. He had walked it himself that morning, timing it.

Carefully, ever so carefully, he rotated the periscope. If he hadn't already passed the hide, the man or men on this side of the arroyo guarding the column must be close. JR had to get them first.

The second hand of his watch was swinging, past forty-five seconds. Come on, man, where are you?

Ah, there, moving slowly and carefully. JR zoomed in on his head, which was partially obscured by brush. But for an instant he got a good look. Yep, he was wearing a night-vision headset. But there was only the one man. A quick sweep revealed no others.

JR lifted the edge of the tarp an inch or so, located the man. He was about forty feet away, moving right along so as to keep up with the mules. He was relying on the goggles, so he wasn't situationally alert. JR poked his AR-15 with the night-vision scope out under the tarp. He flicked off the safety, aimed it, and squeezed the trigger. The man went down.

Abandoning the rifle for a moment, JR located his lighter and the detonator cord by feel. Applied the flame. That cord burned at several thousand feet a second. It seemed to explode, dissolve into ashes. Then he heard the explosions, just one big roar. At least two screams, of men in mortal agony. The blast was followed by a patter on the ground and brush, like rain. JR knew what it was: he had used ten pounds of screws and nails in the mines.

Now for the shooter or shooters on the other side of the arroyo. JR hadn't seen any, but he knew someone was there. These guys didn't take chances.

He came out of the hide on his belly, wearing the night-vision goggles, with the AR cradled in his arms. He crawled as he scanned around. Black powder smoke oozed through the brush and acted like fog, reducing visibility. Still, the other men might have caught the muzzle flash of the AR or seen the flash of the burning det cord.

He caught a glimpse of a man, then saw the muzzle flash and heard the bullet strike brush near his head.

JR shot back, three shots as fast as he could squeeze the trigger, then he rolled sideways away from the spot where he had been.

Lay in the brush on his face, waiting.

Silence.

How much patience would these shooters have? They weren't trained soldiers and they had no idea how many opponents they faced.

Raising his head, JR scanned again with the goggles. There was a lot of brush, so he could be sure of nothing, except he didn't see anyone.

It occurred to him that the man behind him might be only wounded. So he crawled that way to check on him. The little .223-caliber slug had hit him square in the chest and killed him almost instantly.

Now for the other man. JR thought anyone on the other side of the arroyo would make for the hole in the fence as quickly as they could get there. They had heard explosions, screams, and shots from two different weapons, and had certainly gotten a good whiff of the stench of that black powder smoke. They knew they had walked into an ambush; they didn't know how many people they faced; they'd get out of there as fast as they could.

JR crawled to an old juniper, which screened him from the west side of the gully and allowed him to see where the fence crossed the arroyo. He waited, lying absolutely still.

Two minutes, and then he saw a man break from the brush and run toward the hole in the fence. JR shot him in the back. Down he went on his face, the rifle falling ten feet away. JR took careful aim and shot the prone man again.

He waited, listened, scanned with the goggles, felt his heart pounding in his chest.

He consciously willed his heart to slow, which was ridiculous, but it did, finally. Ten minutes passed…eleven. Now he heard a man. Sounded as if he were in the arroyo, moaning softly, dragging himself along.

JR tried to become one with the earth. Put his head down and listened.

Yes, the man was dragging himself along, moaning, "Madre de Dios…"

He was just to JR's right, down in the arroyo, crawling for the fence. He couldn't have been more than twenty-five feet away from where JR lay, but JR didn't move. Didn't even twitch. There might be another shooter out there, one with steel nerves, and if there were, to move was to die.

Finally the man made the gap in the fence and JR saw him with the goggles. Shot him with the rifle, twice. Now the man lay absolutely still, the stillness of death.

JR leaped to his feet and ran away from the fence, out of the area at an angle.

He loped along, turned north, and went around the kill zone and finally joined the trail. Jogging along with his rifle at port arms, wearing the goggles; he could do this for hours. Or used to be able to, anyway. Tonight, with his nostrils full of the black powder smell and his ears still ringing from the gunshots, he fell into a rhythm. Only two miles to go, two miles, run, run, run.

He wanted to see that van, get the license number.

He got to the fence, ran eastward along it fifty feet, and lay down. The road was empty. Checked his watch. Forty-five minutes had passed since he detonated the mines.

His breathing returned to normal and he waited.

Seems like he had spent the major portion of his life waiting. He tried not to think, just became one with the night. The van would come, if the driver wasn't waiting for a cell phone call to summon him. Waiting just up the road, around the bend.

He saw the glare of the headlights in the goggles before he heard the engine.

It came on, slowing. It wasn't a van; it was a car. Down to a creep as it approached the spot where the trail and fence met. No doubt the driver was looking for a signal. Didn't see it, so he began to accelerate on by.

JR got a good look as the car passed the fence. It had a bank of emergency lights on the roof and on the side it said "Sheriff of Upshur County," and under that, "To serve and protect."

Five minutes later it came slowly back. JR was tempted. Taking out the driver would be an easy shot, but then what? He let it go by. Big man driving. Maybe the sheriff himself, ol' Manuel Tejada.

Five or six minutes later the sheriff's car returned heading east. Five or six minutes after that, it passed again, westbound, and as the taillights went on along the road, JR heard the engine wind up to highway speed and saw the dimly glowing taillights fade into the darkness of the rolling plains.

★

In the House, Ben Steiner signaled to the speaker that he would like the floor. The speaker recognized him. The chamber was silent as he approached the podium.

"My fellow Texans," he said. "This building is surrounded by federal agents and regular army troops, who have sent in word that everyone in this building is under arrest. Defending us are Texans from our National Guard. There has been no shooting yet, but there might be, at any moment. Armed Texans are trying to defend this building, this seat of Texas government, and defend you, the elected representatives of the people of Texas. And some in this chamber worry that blood might be shed, so they advocate our surrender to tyranny."

Steiner paused and surveyed his audience on the chamber floor and in the balconies. "I *do not* believe—I *cannot* believe—that such sentiments are representative of the sentiments of the people of Texas, the physical and spiritual descendants of the defenders of the Alamo, those patriots who laid down their lives rather than surrender to the tyranny of the Mexican government. I say to you, Remember the Alamo! Remember those thirteen days of glory. Remember those brave men who laid down their lives so that Texans might be free."

The applause rose like thunder in the chamber. Ben Steiner mopped his brow with his handkerchief. He was on a roll now, and he knew the jury was with him. He waited until the noise died somewhat and said, "Hard, cold, and cruel will be the road ahead. Many difficult decisions will have to be made. Many will suffer, some will die. Yet I say to you, Americans everywhere will judge us by what we do here tonight. We can so conduct ourselves that future generations will glorify our deeds and honor our lives, and remember our deaths if need be...or we can surrender and throw ourselves on the mercy of a tyrant. Is life so precious that you would shame yourself to keep it? As for me, I want to repeat—and I hope someday they engrave these words upon my tombstone—the immortal words of Colonel William Barret Travis at the Alamo: 'Victory or Death.'"

The applause and cheering rose to a staggering volume. Ben Steiner turned around, leaned toward the speaker, and shouted to be heard. "Mr. Speaker, I move the question."

The Senate passed the declaration by two-thirds vote, and the majority was almost as large in the House.

Ben Steiner went back to the podium. "My fellow Texans, we are making history tonight, history that Texans will talk about as long as there are people in Texas and men yearn to be free. We cannot tell our children and our children's children that we passed this by a mere majority vote. I move that the vote be made unanimous."

The speaker called for a voice vote. The yeas had it.

Steiner was so relieved he had to hang on to the podium to stay erect as the legislators cheered wildly.

The leaders of both chambers signed the document and took it to the governor to be signed, which he did. He handed the signed document to the colonel in charge of the National Guard troops, one with the unfortunate name of Buster Bean, and said, "Get a loudspeaker and read this on the steps of the capitol."

When the crowd in the governor's office had thinned somewhat because many of them wanted to be outside to hear the declaration read, Jack Hays asked Ben Steiner, "What did you say to them?"

"I paraphrased Winston Churchill and Colonel Travis and appealed to their honor."

"I guess you convinced them."

"No. They knew the right thing to do. They just needed to hear someone say it."

The floodlights of several television stations almost blinded Colonel Bean, but at least their illumination helped him read the document.

"The unanimous Declaration of Independence made by the elected representatives of the people of Texas in General Convention in the City of Austin on the twenty-third day of August, 2016.

"When a government has ceased to protect the lives, liberty, and property of the people from whom its legitimate powers are derived, and for whose happiness it was instituted, and ceases to be a guarantor of those inalienable rights which are granted to every human by God Almighty, and becomes an instrument in the hands of evil rulers for their oppression:

"When the federal Constitution of their country, which they have sworn to support, has been declared a nullity by the leader of their country and the whole nature of their government has been forcibly changed without their consent from a limited federal republic into a military dictatorship:

"When, after the spirit of representative, constitutional government has been forcibly usurped, when the semblance of freedom has been removed and the sole power in the land is the whims of a dictator, the first law of nature, the right of self-preservation, the inherent and inalienable rights of the people to preserve their liberty, rights, and property by taking the political power into their own hands becomes a sacred obligation to their posterity to abolish such a government and create another in its stead, one calculated to rescue them from impending dangers and secure their future welfare and happiness."

Inside the governor's office the amplified voice outside was quite clear. Jack Hays said to Ben Steiner, "Good stuff, but I've read much of that before."

"I cribbed it. I couldn't do better."

Colonel Bean read a list of grievances, including Barry Soetoro's declaration of martial law, the arrest of political opponents, and the de facto repeal of the First Amendment.

He ended with this paragraph:

"It has been demanded that we deliver up our arms, which are essential to our defense, the rightful property of free men, and formidable only to tyrannical governments."

"The necessity of self-preservation therefore now demands our separation from the United States of America. We, therefore, the duly elected representatives of the people of Texas, in solemn convention assembled, do hereby resolve and declare that the political connection with the United States of America has forever ended, and the people of Texas do now constitute a free, sovereign, and independent republic, and are fully vested with all the rights and attributes that properly belong to independent nations; and conscious of the righteousness of our intentions, we fearlessly and confidently commit the issue to the decision of the Supreme arbiter of the destiny of nations and mankind."

Colonel Bean stepped away from the podium as applause and wild cheering broke out. Beyond the National Guard troops, many of the U.S. Army soldiers began leaving in twos and threes. Here and there sergeants and officers tried to stop them, but many went anyway. The regular army officer in charge, a colonel, knew when to fight and when to regroup. He ordered his soldiers to return to base. In less than fifteen minutes, only National Guard troops remained on the capitol lawn, facing a sea of cheering civilians. Thousands of them. People poured from the side streets as the news swiftly spread and soon packed the area as far as the eye could see. Texas flags were waved defiantly and proudly.

Texas was once again an independent nation. If the Texans could make it stick.

SEVEN

★

In Washington, Thurman Truax, the senior U.S. senator from Texas, was appalled at the spectacle on television that morning. He had been in politics since he was twenty-seven years old, which was thirty-five years ago, and he kept his ear close to the ground in Texas to find out what people were thinking, so close to the ground that the people said he had dirt in it. He had been worried for years about this independence movement and had talked about it at length with the governor, Jack Hays, who he thought was against it too. Apparently Jack Hays had changed his mind or found he was caught in a tide he couldn't resist.

Truax had suspected something of this sort might happen when Soetoro announced martial law, and had called the White House to tell the president so. He wound up speaking to some junior aide. The president had made his decision, Truax was told. He also shared his misgivings with the other senator from Texas and the members of the Texas congressional delegation, some of whom shared his concern, and the leadership in the Senate.

The television was still showing video of people cheering and celebrating independence in front of the capitol in Austin when Truax called his chief of staff. He had tried five times to call the governor and had sent him three e-mails during the broadcast, but had been unable to get through. Nor could he reach any of his political or social friends in Austin. Texas seemed to have dropped right out of the United States.

Not that he blamed Texas. Truax had fought the good fight against admitting Muslim refugees from the Middle East to America, many of whom, he suspected, were jihadists. Of course, despite Soetoro's and the secretary of state's bromides about security checks and vetting them, the reality was that the refugees had no identification whatsoever, a fact the president and his administration chose to ignore. And jihad had come to pass. Murder in a parochial school, on a train, in Yankee Stadium…sometimes Truax thought that the administration actually wanted some terrorist incidents. So now Texas had rebelled.

His chief of staff had watched the broadcast too. And she also had tried repeatedly to call people in Austin and had been unable to get through. Truax didn't wait to hear her take on the whole mess, but told her to make airline reservations to get the senator back to Texas as soon as she could this morning.

He heard pounding on his door. When he answered it, a television reporter and cameraman were standing there, wanting an interview.

"As you can see, I'm still in my pajamas. My office will have a statement for the press later this morning."

"Did you know this Declaration of Independence was going to happen, Senator?"

"No comment." He closed the door on the reporter, a woman with NBC, locked it, and went upstairs to dress.

The truth was, he was appalled. Those fools in Austin had smashed Pandora's box. Barry Soetoro would be outraged, and he was the commander in chief of the armed forces. No telling what that damned fool would do. The United States was tearing itself apart, and the senator felt powerless to prevent it. No one in Washington wanted to listen to reason. Truax well knew that every decision government made had consequences, intended and unintended. Barry Soetoro and Jack Hays were on a collision course.

After he was dressed, the senator went to the kitchen for coffee and a boiled egg. He ate his meager breakfast in front of the television watching national coverage of the news, whatever Soetoro's censors would permit to be aired, which was universal condemnation of the Texas political system and everyone in it. Terrorism seemed to have dropped off the news radar. Texas treason, one talking head said. Another speculated that since the president had declared martial law, the governor of Texas and members of the legislature could be tried by court-martial, and probably would be.

Truax had had his fill and turned the television off when he heard another knock on the door. He looked out the security peephole. It wasn't a reporter. He opened the door and found four FBI agents, who had orders to arrest him. As it turned out, the White House had ordered that Senator Truax and every member of the Texas delegation were to be arrested and held in a Washington prison for treason. An FBI agent accompanied him upstairs to get his medications.

As he rode away in the back of a car in handcuffs, Truax pondered on the reaction in Texas when this news got out.

One of the people who heard the Declaration of Independence read aloud heard it over the radio. As it happened, he was the captain of a tugboat in Galveston Harbor. He was always up early, planning the morning's work on the boat before it had to get under way for the day's tows or pushes. He took his cup of coffee out and climbed the ladder to his bridge.

Across the harbor he could see an attack submarine berthed, USS *Texas*, a *Virginia*-class boat, only a few years old, moored port side to a pier. She had come in yesterday for a three-day port call to show the flag, entertain visitors, and let the good people of Texas see where the navy's share of their federal taxes was being spent.

How long would she be here now? he wondered. Bet they'll get under way as soon as they hear the news.

He set his cup down and ran down the ladder to his crew berthing, where his engineer and first officer were sound asleep. Those two were all the crew he had right now. The seamen who fixed things and handled lines wouldn't come aboard until half past seven.

"Wake up," he urged as he shook them. "We're going to move the tug."

He gave hurried explanations as they pulled on jeans and tugged on shoes.

Ten minutes later, the tug, *Mabel Hardaway*, named after his wife, got under way. Captain Hardaway took it over to where the sub was berthed and maneuvered to anchor immediately behind it. To ensure the tug didn't swing on her anchor and damage the sub's screws, he dropped an anchor from the stern as he came up slowly, then a bow anchor. He backed down and killed the engines, then went down the outside ladder to the deck to help the first mate secure the anchors.

That sub isn't leaving until I say so, he thought, vastly pleased with himself.

He got on the radio to another tug, managed to wake up the skipper, and asked it to come anchor immediately beside the submarine. "As soon as you can get here," Captain Hardaway added for emphasis.

Aboard *Texas*, the watch officer awakened the captain, Commander Mike Rodriquez, who had spent the previous evening at a dinner in his honor in a hotel in Galveston, one attended by the mayor, most of the city councilmen, and everyone who was anyone in the Chamber of Commerce. He had probably had one or two too many glasses of wine, but toasts were offered right and left and he had to do it, he told himself then.

His head was a little thick as he listened to the watch officer. "We have a tugboat anchored immediately behind us."

"In the prohibited zone?"

"Yes, sir. I've notified the harbor police."

"They can probably handle it," the captain said. "Are our guards on the pier?"

"Yes, sir. And armed."

In the age of terror one can't be too careful, the captain well knew. Local jihadists would secure undying fame in Paradise if they could damage a U.S. nuclear submarine. The FBI had assured him they were keeping a close eye on the local Muslims, of whom there were only a few. Still...

The captain quickly donned his uniform, khakis because he wore camos only when under way and he hated them. He went to the control room, satisfied himself that everything was as it should be, then climbed the tiny conning tower to the miniscule bridge.

Yep, there was the tug, *Mabel Hardaway*. What in the world was that thing doing there? He picked up a loud-hailer and pointed it at the tug's bridge.

"You are in a prohibited zone. Get under way and move your boat immediately."

"Sorry," came the shouted reply, quite audible in the pre-dawn stillness.

"You will be arrested if you don't move that boat."

No reply.

"Sir," the watch officer said. "One of the sentries is running toward us. There are some civilians up there at the head of the pier." He was using his binoculars. "Looks as if some of them are carrying rifles." He handed the binoculars to the CO, who was staring through them as the sentry came halfway across the gangway and shouted, "Sir, those civilians say they have closed the pier. They say they won't let our liberty party back aboard."

"Why?" the officer of the deck asked loudly enough to be heard.

"They say Texas declared its independence an hour ago."

The captain rubbed his head. Jesus Christ, he thought. Of all the time for a port visit! He glanced back at the tug. Well, he couldn't back out of here, even if he got all the lines off the boat.

He looked to his starboard side. If he could swing the stern, perhaps he could back and forth using the rudder until he could go behind the tug, like a car getting out of a parallel parking place. He used the binoculars in the half-light and saw the line running off the stern of *Mabel Hardaway* at an angle, out into the open area he would have to use. He knew he was looking at a chain with an anchor on the end. Backing the naked screws of his boat into the chain would disable *Texas*.

"Here comes another tug, sir," the OOD said, and pointed.

Sure enough, there it was, maybe a mile away down the harbor, coming slowly. It would certainly be here before he could get *Texas* free of the pier and maneuver her out of this slip. And even if he did get *Texas* out of the slip, the tugs could ram her and make sure she didn't get out of the harbor.

Damn!

"Go below," Rodriquez told the OOD, "and get off a flash message to SUBLANT. Tell them we are blocked in by tugboats, with armed civilians on the pier. Go."

"Aye-aye, sir."

Gulls wheeled above him as he stood alone weighing his options. Half his crew was on liberty in Galveston. While he could operate the boat with the duty section, he had nowhere to go with tugs in the way. His sentries could keep the civilians off the pier, for a while, anyway, unless they started shooting.

He could scuttle the boat, sink her here in this slip. But the navy brass would have his balls if he did that and the independence news was some kind of misinformation or a political ploy to embarrass the Soetoro administration, something that could be cleared up or would go away in a few hours or days. He certainly didn't know. All he knew was what the sentry had told him. If he scuttled *Texas*, she could be raised of course, and eventually returned to seaworthy condition, after she had spent a year or so in the Electric Boat shipyard in Connecticut where she was built.

He decided to wait and see what SUBLANT said to do. He wanted someone in a much higher pay grade to point to if recriminations started. Let the admiral earn his pay, he thought as he watched the other tug ease into the slip and tie up starboard side to the pier abeam *Texas*. Now he was blocked in.

When the OOD came back up the ladder he said, "Message sent, Captain."

The skipper pointed at the tug on the starboard side. "Go send another one. Tell them we are corked good."

The OOD took a quick look and disappeared back down the ladder.

The skipper looked at the people milling on the pier. At least thirty of them, only a couple of sailors in uniform, and a police car. Maybe he should go up there and talk to the cop.

When the OOD came back, the captain gave his instructions, went below for his ball cap, then went to the forward torpedo room and climbed the ladder through the open hatch to the main deck. He paused on the gangway and saluted the flag flying on its portable flagpole on the stern, then went ashore.

★

After Colonel Curt Wriston, commander of the Texas National Guard in Abilene, saw the declaration read on TV, he tried to call his headquarters in Austin, with no success. The telephone didn't even ring.

Wriston dressed, skipped his morning coffee, and got into his car. He picked up his deputy commander. They discussed the situation and were in agreement: the Soetoro administration would use force against Texas, just as quickly as they could.

Wriston drove the county roads to a spot near the perimeter fence of Dyess Air Force Base. From there, they could see the two runways: the main runway, 13,500 feet long, and a short parallel runway, 3,500 feet long. Also visible in this flat country in the clear air of early dawn were the big hangars and flight line between the two runways. Wriston looked around. Not a cloud in the sky.

No doubt the commander of the base, Brigadier General l'Angistino, was on the wires right now with bomber headquarters in Nebraska and the air force brass in Washington, asking for instructions. Everyone in the chain of command would bump the decisions up the ladder, Wriston thought. He knew how the military bureaucracy worked these days. Initiative had been ruthlessly and remorselessly squeezed out of the system. Obey orders was the mantra, and, whatever you do, don't make your bosses look bad. General l'Angistino was a good man, but he would undoubtedly have to wait awhile for orders, which would have to come from the very top, perhaps even the White House, which would have a ton of other red-hot problems to deal with today.

The deputy commander said it first. "We need to block those runways, make sure the air force doesn't fly those bombers and Hercules transports out of there. Texas will need them."

"They'll probably sabotage them," Wriston said thoughtfully, "if they can't fly them out."

“Either way, they can’t use them to transport troops or bomb us.”

“We could use tanks, just go through the fence,” Wriston mused.

“We only have four tanks, and one of them has the fire control system disassembled for upgrade.”

“It’ll move.”

The deputy said, “That big runway is about three hundred feet wide, as I recall. Take a serious amount of iron to block it. And the Hercs can use the short runway.”

“We can get some construction equipment, road graders, and bulldozers,” Wriston suggested. “They can follow the tanks. We’ll block the long runway, and if we have any equipment left, leave it on the small one. We’ll have to block the long one in at least two places. Three would be better.” He used a small set of binoculars he kept in the car for looking at birds to examine the distant buildings, which looked like toy blocks sitting out there on the horizon.

Wriston added, “They’ve got cranes and such to handle crashed airplanes. If they can’t start the engines and drive our stuff off, they’ll drag it off.”

“We can disable everything.”

“Only delay them for a day, maybe two.”

“That might be enough. Let’s do it.”

Wriston started his car and they drove away planning where to get the yellow equipment, people to drive it, and how to summon their tankers.

At the head of the pier in Galveston where *Texas* was moored, Commander Mike Rodriquez found out that the Declaration of Independence news the sentry had given him was as real as a heart attack. Thirty or so civilians carrying rifles, some of them civilian versions of the M16, were standing there watching him. The sheriff had him sit in the right seat of his patrol car, which had its front windows down, then got behind the wheel. When he was comfortably settled, he gave the naval officer the news about the declaration.

"Texas is now a free republic," the sheriff said in summary. The captain scrutinized the lawman's face to see if he was kidding. He didn't appear to be. The fucking idiot! Secession in this day and age!

One of the civilians came over and leaned on the car to hear what was being said inside. The sheriff ran him off.

"Now, Captain, this is the way I see it," the sheriff continued. He had a serious pot gut that lapped over the buckle of his gun belt. His shirt needed pressing and he needed a shave. "I haven't talked to anybody in Austin 'cause the phones are out and, anyway, they're probably drunk and asleep, which I ought to be. When they wake up they're gonna be mighty busy. In any event this declaration thing sorta upset the applecart. Did you watch it on TV a while ago?"

No.

"County commissioners are asleep too, and even when they get up this morning, they're goin' to tell me what they always say, which is use my own judgment. That way if people start squallin' I have to take the heat and not them. Being an elected official and all, I suppose it comes with the territory. But you probably ain't interested in my problems, since you got a big one your own self."

Get on with it, you oaf, Rodriquez thought.

"Your problem is that these voters here aren't going to let your sailors get on your submarine. And it looks to me like those tugboat captains ain't goin' to move their boats to allow you to get goin', even if you had all your sailors. That's kinda it in a nutshell."

"And you aren't going to clear the pier and tell the tugboat captains to get out of the prohibited area?"

"That's about the size of it."

Rodriquez thought of a common dirty word but didn't say it. He pulled at the door handle.

The sheriff laid a hand on his arm. "You stay right here. I think this whole situation will go better if you sit right here with me. Keep the crowd calmed down. If these people start shootin' your sailors, we'll both have more problems than we do now."

"If they shot my sailors, you'd arrest them, wouldn't you? A crime committed in your presence."

"Well, I don't know. I haven't got my thinkin' that far down the road. Been my experience that problems are best headed off, if possible, rather than tackled afterward. That's what I'm tryin' to do. Now are you gonna just sit here like I told you, or do I have to handcuff you and lock you in the back?"

Rodriquez couldn't contain himself. "You son of a bitch!"

"Be that as it may, I need a yes or no."

"I'll sit."

"Fine. I'll radio for one of my deputies to stop by McDonald's and get us some McMuffins and coffee. Or do you want something else?"

"That'll do, thanks."

The sheriff picked up the dashboard mike and started talking.

Forty-five minutes later, after they had eaten, the sheriff had the deputy, with the crowd's help, disarm Rodriquez' sentries and take them to jail. "Just to hold for a little while," the sheriff told Rodriquez, "until somebody with more brains than me can figure out what we oughta do."

Five minutes after the sentries had departed with the deputy, a sailor from the sub came looking for his captain. He had a wad of paper in his hand. He spotted Rodriquez in the patrol car and came over to the open window. "Messages, Captain," he said and offered them.

"I'll take those, son," the sheriff said, holding out his right hand. When he had them, he told the sailor, "You're under arrest. Now you get in the back of the car here."

The sailor looked beseechingly at his commanding officer.

"Do as he says," Rodriquez said listlessly. Shit, he thought, I should have stayed on the boat. What a fool I was! There goes my naval career!

By ten o'clock the crowd had swelled to at least fifty people, most of them carrying rifles. They were having a high old time. Some of them had brought beer, which they shared. Sailors who were ashore and wanted back aboard their submarine were arrested and taken away.

"Crowd's gettin' a little rowdy, don't you think?" the sheriff asked Commander Rodriquez.

"Yes," he agreed.

"I kinda think it's time we put an end to this and let these folks go home or to work or to a bar someplace to tank up. Let's you and me walk down the pier and you get all your people out of that thing and bring them along. I'll get a bus to take them to a hotel."

Rodriquez felt like a cornered rat. Aboard the boat he could overpower the sheriff, scram the reactor, and order her scuttled. But should he scuttle her? If this political thing blew over.... He looked longingly at the classified messages the sheriff had read and tucked into a pocket in the driver's door. It wasn't as if these civilians knew how to operate a nuclear submarine, for Christ's sake. USS *Texas* wasn't going anywhere. And the U.S. Navy could destroy her with a Tomahawk cruise missile or two anytime they got around to it.

"Let me read those messages," he said.

"Nope. It's my way or I send you off to join your sailors in jail. Then I'll go down there with these voters and arrest all of them aboard. Your only choice is to go with me or go to jail."

"I'll go with you."

The sheriff got out of the car. He stopped the captain and pulled out handcuffs. "We'll put these on you," he said, "in case you get any big ideas. Just to protect myself, you understand."

He cuffed the captain's hands in front of him, then pulled his pistol. He waved it at the crowd. "You people back off and give me room. Don't want anyone comin' down the pier. Don't want anyone doin' anything we'll all regret. Come on, Captain."

At the gangway, the sheriff could see an officer or sailor on the bridge. He told the captain, "Tell them to turn off the reactor and come out. All of 'em."

"Aren't we going aboard?"

"No. They ain't goin' no place in that boat and you ain't neither. So get them out here."

When the remainder of the submarine's crew were on the pier, about two dozen men, the sheriff thought, although he didn't bother to count them, he asked one of the chiefs, "Did you turn that reactor off?"

"Yeah."

"Got everybody out of there?"

"Yeah."

"That's good, 'cause after you're gone, I'm goin' aboard and look around, and if I find anybody they might scare me and I'll probably have to shoot 'em. Hate to do it, but if I fear for my personal safety, and I will, there ain't nothin' else I can do. Promised my wife when I first run for sheriff that I wouldn't endanger myself."

"There's no one else aboard," the chief said sullenly.

The sheriff looked down the pier and saw that a blue bus marked SHERIFF had arrived on the quay. "There's your ride, Captain. Lead them down the pier and climb aboard."

That was how the brand spanking new Republic of Texas acquired its first warship.

EIGHT

★

In the dim light of dawn JR inspected the bodies. Some of the nails and screws in the mines had ripped open the backpacks and blasted white powder everywhere. JR didn't know if it was cocaine or heroin, and he didn't care. Only two of the mules had obviously tried to crawl away and bled to death; the others died almost instantly, perforated by the metal from the mines—four with nails and screws that had ripped into their brains, another eviscerated.

The two at the fence were well and truly dead, too. The man who had dragged himself had his gut torn open and intestines were trailing behind him. The bullet that killed him had been a mercy.

JR got his first surprise when he looked at the first man he shot, the man near his hide. The man had yellow and green tattoos that started at his wrists and ran up his forearms.

That deputy sheriff—he had tattoos like that, very distinctive. What was his name? Morales? He seemed to recall that was it.

JR didn't recognize the other man wearing night-vision goggles. JR pulled the goggles off. He looked like he might have a lot of Mexican in him, but with his face contorted in death, it was difficult to say.

Hays walked back to the ranch house and poured himself a stiff tot of bourbon. Sat on the porch with the AR across his lap sipping the whiskey as the sun poked over the horizon and sunlight began illuminating the high places in the brush. Cloudless blue sky. Another scorching hot day in the works. Those bodies were going to get ripe pretty quick.

The syndicate that sent those drugs across the border would send more men, probably pretty soon. JR had no idea how much money the drugs represented, but he knew it was a lot. Enough to buy the deaths of a thousand peons and a whole lot of Americans. Enough to buy half the sheriffs in Texas.

JR took out his cell phone and called his cousin the governor. Nothing. No ringtone on the thing. He looked at how many bars he had. Two. Well, that should be enough. But the cell didn't work. He went inside and tried the landline. No luck there either.

He was exhausted and needed sleep. Yet Manuel Tejada would be along in a little while to find out what had happened to his deputy and all the drugs he was supposed to pick up. He wouldn't phrase it quite that way, but that would be what he wanted. Mainly, however, he would want the drugs. If Tejada could show the syndicate the drugs he might get out of this with a whole skin. If he couldn't, he was going to be in trouble, although how much JR didn't know. Maybe he could dig Tejada's pit deeper.

JR placed the guns in the floor of the backseat of his pickup and drove down to the arroyo, as close as he could get. He retrieved the gear from the hide, including the periscope and parabolic antenna, stored all this stuff in the tool chest in the bed of the truck. Went to the bodies of the mules and removed the backpacks. Two were so torn up the white powder spilled all over the ground. JR thought each backpack had contained twenty-five pounds or so of the stuff.

The syndicate was going to be pissed.

JR put the six reasonably intact backpacks in the chest, locked it, and drove off. When he got to the main gate, he stopped and opened the gate, then got back in the truck.

Had the sheriff been in on it? Apparently. But JR wanted to be sure. He pulled out his cell phone and let it log on the network. Two bars. He called 911, got the sheriff's office number, then dialed it.

"Sheriff Tejada."

"JR Hays, Sheriff, out here at the Hays ranch."

A pause, then, "What can I do for you, JR?"

"Hell of a shootout last night here at the ranch, Sheriff, a little after three. Woke me up. A real firefight. Kinda scared me. I went down this morning for a look, and bodies are lying all over the place. Looks like a drug gang ambush. The dead men had about two hundred pounds of some kind of drug on them."

He paused, but the sheriff said nothing.

"It's pretty bloody, Sheriff. Goddamn mess is exactly what it is. Might have been some of the bastards who killed my dad."

"The drugs are still there?"

"Yeah."

"Huh! What kind of drugs?"

"Damn if I know. It isn't marijuana, that's for sure. Some kind of white powder. Anyway, I'm going to call the staties and DEA, but I wanted to give you a courtesy heads-up first."

"Appreciate that, JR. Much obliged. But before you call those other agencies, let me run out there for a look. I'll bring the county coroner and we'll see about the bodies."

"When can you get here?"

"Couple of hours."

"I'm pretty worried. God only knows what all that powder shit is worth. I kinda suspect somebody might come back to get it."

"This is my county, JR." Like the slob owned it.

"Yes. Yes, it is." He paused as if he hated to wait. "Okay, Sheriff, you come out and look around and call them. These guys aren't going anywhere. Gonna get hot again today and they'll get real ripe fast. Better bring some body bags."

"Two hours. I'm on my way."

"Sure."

He broke the connection. The sheriff hadn't even asked how many dead men there were.

He pulled the truck through the gate, got out, and shut it carefully. As he walked back to the truck a buzzard in the cloudless sky caught his eye, circling over the old trail. Two of them; no, three. Little dots up there riding the thermals. There would be more buzzards soon.

He remembered the bumper stickers. Got one out of the truck, peeled the paper off the back, and stuck it on the gate. Stood back and admired it. FUCK SOETORO. He liked it so much he put the other one on the truck's rear bumper.

JR got into his pickup and headed southeast toward Del Rio. He decided he owed himself a treat, so he reached across to the glove box and pulled out a pack of unfiltered Camels. Opened it and lit one.

The raw smoke tasted delicious. JR adjusted the bill of his ball cap to keep the rising sun out of his eyes and smoked in silence.

The television clip of Colonel Bean reading the Texas Declaration of Independence on the steps of the capitol in Austin, and the shots of the delirious crowd, went to television stations nationwide. Networks worldwide rebroadcast the scenes over and over. In the United States, many station managers had qualms, and at some stations federal officers demanded that the feed not be aired. Some stations caved, but most didn't. Managers argued that other stations would show it, and while they were arguing with federal censors, many staffs flipped switches and put it on the air. The scenes ran over and over again. Usually the scenes were aired without comment because the people in the stations were leery of the gun-toting bureaucratic squads who occasionally walked their halls, but the scenes spoke for themselves.

The spectacular act of defiance by the Texas legislature had immediate consequences. Here and there groups of armed citizens waylaid federal officers hauling away political prisoners, disarmed them, and released the prisoners. Several of these federal officers chose to fight it out and were shot dead. Others were taken to a county jail.

The armed federal police forces from bureaucracies nationwide became nervous. The mood of the public was turning ugly. Some of the agents stayed home and locked their doors.

Barry Soetoro nationalized the National Guard nationwide. Less than half the guardsmen reported to their armories to be inducted into federal service. Officers resigned on the spot. In two cities, small groups of guardsmen called local television stations, which sent crews to watch the guardsmen take off their uniforms in public, put them in a pile, and burn them.

In Oklahoma City a half-dozen armed officers from the FAA trying to arrest a local newspaper columnist, a conservative, panicked and opened fire on a crowd of vociferous unarmed citizens. Four people were killed and seven wounded, four of them severely. The payback came within an hour. A mob of armed civilians arrived at the FAA's basement office where the armed enforcers hung out and put it under siege. When the officers came out four hours later with their hands up, the crowd opened fire. The last one ran a block and took refuge in someone's basement; he was dragged out and executed with a shot in the head. No one knew if the four murdered officers were the ones who shot the unarmed civilians, nor did anyone really care. Civil wars are messy.

Up and down the plains, in the Rockies and the Midwest, people gathered in spontaneous groups to cheer Texas and wave homemade Texas flags.

In Austin, Jack Hays saw snatches of this activity on television before he, Charlie Swim, Luwanda Harris, and Colonel Tenney of the Department of Public Safety boarded a helicopter for a flight to Houston. They were met by the National Guard commander there, Brigadier General James Conrad, the mayor of Houston, and the chief of police.

Unfortunately they were downwind of some tire fires, and stinking, heavy smoke was almost overpowering.

"Have you got the riot area surrounded?" Hays asked.

"Yes, sir," Conrad said. The senior law officers nodded.

"Where's that FEMA dude," Jack Hays asked, "the one I wanted at the pointy end of this expedition?"

"He got cold feet and split."

Hays frowned.

"Would have had to handcuff him and put a gun in his back, Governor, to walk him into that riot."

"Obviously he didn't think his liberal credentials would protect him," Charlie Swim said, and Hays chuckled.

Hays explained to the politicians, "We want to capture the rioters and not let them rampage through the rest of the city." Luwanda Harris and Charlie Swim looked grim.

"Is everyone ready?" Hays asked the police chief, Colonel Tenney, and General Conrad.

Receiving affirmatives all around, Hays said, "Start 'em moving." Conrad spoke into his handheld radio. Hays turned back to the politicians. "Ms. Harris, Mr. Swim, will you accompany me?"

"You got a grandstand seat picked out?" Luwanda Harris asked sourly.

"Indeed I do. I am going to walk ahead of the troops and talk to anyone I meet. I would like you both to accompany me."

"They may shoot us," Charlie Swim pointed out. Even as he said this, several random gunshots could be heard.

"They might," Jack Hays agreed, grabbed two elbows, and started off with Swim on the left and Harris on the right. The troops in riot gear followed, then the state police carrying shotguns and wearing helmets.

Down the street, right into the middle of the riot zone.

When they were seen, young men threw some rocks, then turned and ran. Hays kept advancing. The three of them passed burning cars, looted stores, and melting asphalt. On they went.

Someone fired a shot at them from an upstairs window. Guardsmen fired back, and two soldiers charged into the building to find the shooter and arrest him, or kill him if need be.

Jack Hays pretended he didn't notice the shooting.

It took thirty minutes, but an ever-tightening cordon of law enforcement and guardsmen had brought the rioters, mostly young men, into the middle of a large intersection. Surrounded, and scared, they threw down guns, chains, tire irons, and knives.

Jack Hays was handed a loudspeaker. He climbed up on the hood of a fire truck that had followed the skirmish line and turned on the speaker.

"Folks, the party is over. Texas in an independent nation, and as governor I am going to enforce the law. You and the folks who live around here will be questioned. If anyone here is guilty of murder, he will stand trial. For the rest of you, I am here to tell you nothing will happen to you if you obey the law from this minute on. No more looting, no more stealing, no more fires, none of that."

Hays paused and silence reigned except for the moan of a siren a long way off.

"I know, Charlie Swim knows, and Luwanda Harris knows that you and your families have many grievances, from failing schools to horrific unemployment rates, to police harassment for the crime of being black.

"But the time has come for a new beginning for Texas and for its citizens. I swear to you that the Texas legislature and I are going to take action.

"We are going to have every complaint about police brutality investigated by the staff of a legislative committee, and both these folks standing beside me, Charlie Swim and Luwanda Harris, are going to be on that committee. If you think they will sweep harassment and brutality under the rug, you don't know them.

"We're going to set up a private-public partnership so that people in your community, people who study, can qualify for the thirty thousand new high-tech, high-paying jobs that are projected to grow in Houston in the next few years...and you are the people who are going to fill them. Industry will pay part of the cost of your training and the Republic of Texas will pay part. All you have to do to qualify is put your butt in a chair and study hard.

"Texas needs you right now. We are going to be invaded by United States forces in the near future. The Texas Guard needs recruits. You can do yourself and Texas a favor by enlisting. I am not going to pretend it will be easy or without danger. You may get wounded, maimed, or killed. But Texas needs your help. Make your life mean something. Fight for Texas.

"Folks, the riot is really over. Stay and talk to the guardsmen or go home. No more rioting. This is your city and your nation."

Jack Hays got down off the fire truck. "Charlie, get on in there and talk to them. We need all the soldiers you can get. These guys like to fight—let's point them in the right direction and give them some discipline and leadership. Hell, let's give them a country to fight *for.*"

Hays looked at Luwanda Harris and added, "You tell them I'm sincere—because I am." Then he turned and walked alone the mile and a half back to the helicopter.

★

In Abilene, Colonel Wriston had his column of tanks and construction vehicles ready to go by ten that morning. It had been hectic. He had received an unexpected assist from the president, who had announced via television that he was nationalizing the National Guard, so many of the soldiers had reported to the armory without waiting to be summoned.

Wriston and his officers explained that since Texas had declared its independence the Texas Guard was going to defend Texas and take its orders from the governor. All but four of the guardsmen—who were sent home—agreed to defend an independent Texas, and Colonel Wriston quickly had them organized into units and loaded them aboard trucks and buses pressed into service. With tanks in the lead, the column got rolling at ten o'clock.

One of the soldiers who was sent home instead drove straight to the main gate at Dyess and told the sergeant of the guard he wanted to see the commanding general. A call was made, and the sergeant climbed into his air force SUV and led the way to the headquarters building.

Within a minute the guardsman was standing in front of the commanding general, Brigadier General Lou l'Angistino, explaining what the Texas Guard was up to. "They're going to block your runway, General."

"When?"

"About as fast as they can get there, sir, I reckon."

"Do you know where they intend to breach our perimeter?"

"No, sir. I didn't hear anyone say."

The general thanked the man and watched him leave the office. He nodded to his chief of staff, who closed the door. They had been poring over a stream of classified messages that flowed into the office just as fast as the message center could get them decoded and printed.

Global Strike Command, GSC, headquarters had ordered him to get his airplanes ready to fly. They might be sent on bombing missions…or they might be sent to Offutt Air Force Base in Nebraska…or…. In the next message, GSC headquarters hedged. Belay the first message: Stand by for further orders. Let no civilians onto the base. Consult with local authorities and advise of the political situation in Abilene ASAP. Were the people loyal to the federal government or to the Texas rebels?

On it went. Action messages were interspersed with messages from Washington, from the Joint Chiefs, and every command all over. The army needed his C-130s in Colorado and Alabama. Send them immediately. No, wait. Get them ready to fly and when higher authority had sorted out the priorities, mission orders would be issued.

General l'Angistino shoved the whole pile to a corner of his desk. "Get the base security officer in here. Roust every air policeman on the base and get them suited up."

"Yes, sir."

L'Angistino had seen the morning news footage of the declaration. He had been horrified; his comfortable peacetime command had just been transformed.

He looked out his office window at the runway. Rows and rows of B-1 Lancer bombers and C-130 Hercules aircraft were parked on the ramps. He had thirty-six B-1s assigned, the only B-1 wing on active duty in the air force. Twenty-eight C-130s were assigned here, but five were flying, doing overnight training missions or hauling troops and supplies from one military installation to another, the usual peacetime flight schedule. Now this.

He had already issued orders to get all the airplanes serviced, fueled, and ready to fly. He didn't tell anyone to bring the bombs for the B-1s from the magazines, and wouldn't until they had missions assigned. Parking weapons on the ramp when they weren't needed violated air force safety regulations.

Block the runway. Was the guardsman telling the truth, or was this only a rumor? Or was he a plant to spread disinformation?

The general was consulting a map of the base with his security officer, a major, when Colonel Wriston stopped his column at the place he and his deputy commander had been that morning.

A lowboy behind the colonel's Humvee off-loaded a bulldozer, which scraped dirt to fill in the ditch between the road and the perimeter fence. The job was done in less than two minutes. More bulldozers off-loaded from lowboys. They quickly tore out fifty yards of eight-foot-high, chain-link, barbed-wire-topped fence and shoved it to one side. A tank covered with soldiers went through the gap.

Wriston watched his tanks, bulldozers, road graders, earthmovers, trucks, and buses full of guardsmen as they rolled through the gap and disappeared in a cloud of dust. Many of Wriston's men were heavy-equipment operators in civilian life, which had made commandeering so much equipment relatively easy; it was theirs, and by parking it on the Dyess runway, they'd be putting themselves out of work. Well, he suspected Jack Hays would want full-time soldiers.

The drivers of the tanks soon spread out until all four were running abreast raising dust clouds. This had the unintended consequence of blinding the drivers of the vehicles behind them, who were also trying to spread out to avoid colliding with everyone in front. Watching his column disintegrate, Colonel Wriston was reminded of his experience in tanks in the deserts of Iraq. He hated deserts. He climbed into his Humvee and headed off behind them to supervise this operation. If they didn't get the runways blocked, this whole adventure was for naught.

In the leftmost tank, the tank commander saw an air force SUV charging across the prairie toward him. There were four people in it, apparently. It came to a stop fifty yards in front of him, and the driver jumped out, holding up his right hand in the universal signal to stop.

"Shoot out his radiator," the tank commander told his machine gunner.

The burst of the .30-caliber apparently holed the SUV's radiator, because a cloud of steam shot forth from under the hood. The other three occupants of the vehicle jumped out with their hands in the air. Two guardsmen dropped off the tank, which speeded back up. The guardsmen disarmed the air police, pointed them at the hangar complex two miles away, and told them to start hiking.

"You can't do this," the air force sergeant protested.

"We already did," a soldier answered. "Git." They grabbed the guns in the SUV and on the ground, then ran to the left, the west, to get away from oncoming vehicles. Colonel Wriston saw them as he came up and stopped to give them a ride.

A small group, one bulldozer and three earthmovers, peeled off to block the short runway. The main column clanked up to the long runway, an awesome sight with more than two miles of thick concrete stretching before them, three hundred feet wide.

Wriston sped past the lead tanks and went a third of the way down the runway. He knew how far he was because he stopped just past the big "8" sign, marking eight thousand feet remaining to the end. He gestured to two of the tanks, and they came to a stop, then turned sideways. Other equipment would also park there.

Wriston got back in the Humvee and rolled on to the "4,000 feet remaining" sign. He stopped there and awaited his vehicles.

The operation went well, he thought. As some of the soldiers stood guard, the two tanks and four pieces of construction equipment were parked. Mechanics worked on the treads of the tanks, then the tanks ran off the treads. Bulldozers were similarly disabled. The tires of the earthmovers were shredded with automatic weapons fire.

While this was going on, four air police vehicles came rushing toward them, two on the runway and two on the adjacent taxiway. Machine-gun fire and automatic weapons fire over the top of the vehicles convinced the drivers to turn around and retreat.

Hand grenades were placed in engine bays, and guardsmen ran from the explosions. It was over in less than eight minutes. When all his guardsmen were on buses and trucks going back toward the hole in the fence, Colonel Wriston surveyed the blockade and followed along in his Humvee. The men and women of the Guard couldn't have done it any better if they had practiced it every day for a week, he thought proudly. Then he followed his retreating vehicles.

General l'Angistino had watched the dust cloud and activity on the runway from his office with binoculars. When the guardsmen had departed, he rode out to the mess of abandoned equipment and surveyed it with his fists on his hips.

His chief of staff rolled up in an air police sedan. "You know what to do," he said to the colonel. "Get busy and get this stuff off the runway. As quickly as possible."

Air force crash crews were still moving equipment at dark, when General l'Angistino went home. He had of course notified GSC and Washington of the runway obstructions, but other than a terse message to report when the runway was open again, nothing else was said.

NINE

★

There was an old sleeping bag in the workroom of the lock shop, and I spent the night in it. Willie had the television on when I woke up.

The news this Sunday morning was that Texas had declared its independence during the wee hours of the morning. I listened while I helped myself to a cup of coffee.

"The world is movin' right along, Tommy," Willie said. "Texas declared itself free of the US of A, and Barry Soetoro is havin' a shit fit. He says that the right-wing conspiracy was more virulent than he and his advisors suspected. This should silence any critics of martial law. And so on."

The coffee was hot and black, and strong enough to take the enamel off your teeth, but a man can't have everything. Idly, I thought about Sarah's coffee—hers was several times better than this stuff. Maybe I should have tried to wheedle her into letting me sleep on her couch last night. Or in her bed.

"Guess we're back to forty-nine states," Willie said philosophically, "if Texas can make Soetoro eat it. Kinda doubt that they can, but who knows. He was on the tube a minute ago, and was he ever pissed! Babbled about treason. Treachery. Betrayal. The malignant tumors in high offices."

"Good help is hard to find these days."

"Want an egg?"

"Yeah, that would be good."

"Well, we ain't got any, this bein' a lock shop. No pancakes or bacon or ham or toast. I brought in a half-dozen doughnuts for me this mornin'; if you want one I can spare it."

"That's mighty white of you."

"Don't get racial, dude."

"What else don't we have?"

"Lots of stuff. Got toilet paper, though. White toilet paper."

"That's the best kind."

"Can't believe that they let us black folk wipe our asses with it."

I took my coffee to the restroom and settled on the throne. I reflected that Willie Varner had reminded me once again why no female on the planet had succumbed to his charms and leaped into matrimony.

The Texas revolt was good news, I thought. The dung beetles at the White House now had something to think about besides forcing confessions from people like Grafton. Perhaps. Maybe they would decide that Grafton was partly responsible for the bad attitude in Austin.

I dressed, drank another cup of Willie's coffee-colored enamel-eater, and then headed over to McDonald's for a sausage and egg biscuit and a cup of decent coffee. I made some phone calls. Called some of the covert warriors I knew, guys I had served with in various third world shitholes. Two were at home. I asked if I could come by. They said yes.

Willis Coffee lived in Bethesda. His wife answered the door and told me he was around back in the garden. It looked more like a flower bed with vegetables, a few onions and some scraggly lettuce. He was hoeing.

"What the hell you doing in Washington? I thought you quit your job," he said.

"I did quit."

"Hell, so did I. When they arrested Jake Grafton, I turned in my building pass and drove out of there."

"I still have the building pass. Maybe I ought to mail it in. They might come looking for it."

Willis snorted and leaned on his hoe. "I doubt if anyone at Langley has the time. Ol' Harley Merritt is on the bridge now and Soetoro is cracking the whip. Merritt is looking for traitors within the agency. Maybe he'll find one, but I doubt it." He spotted a weed and attacked it.

"Maybe they'll invent some, like they did with Grafton."

Willis leaned on his hoe again. "Yeah," he said.

"I need your help, Willis, to rescue Grafton. You probably heard they accused him of conspiring to depose Soetoro. Blow him up. Try to turn America into a democracy."

"I heard." He stood there awhile, surveying the weeds in his agricultural project. Then he threw down the hoe. He dragged over a chair and sat in it. "I got a wife and two kids. The kids were on a sleepover last night. I need another job, one that will pay the mortgage and grocery bill. I can't afford to go tilting at windmills."

I played my ace. "If you were in some ISIS dungeon waiting for your appointment with the knife, you *know* that Jake Grafton would move heaven and earth to get you out. Whatever it took. Whether State gave its okay or not."

He jerked as if I had stuck the knife in him right there. He refused to meet my eyes.

After a bit he said, "Tell me about it."

The chairman of the Joint Chiefs, General Martin L. Wynette, was summoned to the White House that morning. Wynette was a sycophant, a paper-pushing soldier who had never seen combat but had kissed a thousand asses on his way up the ladder. He was known throughout the military for his role in destroying the career of a lieutenant colonel teaching a course at the Joint Forces Staff College about Islamic extremism and jihad, a course suggested and approved by the college. Some Muslims got wind of it and wrote a hot letter to Barry Soetoro, who ordered the offending officer disciplined and the course dropped. Wynette did the dirty work without protest. Of course Wynette knew that Soetoro's father was a Muslim, his chief political advisor was a Muslim, and a sizable chunk of the American population thought he was too, but after all, the American people had voted Soetoro into the White House, twice, so Wynette was certainly willing to let the prevailing wind flap his flag.

This morning the general was escorted into the presence of the anointed one, who was beyond fury. He was outraged and shaking, at times almost incoherent. Texas had to be punished, he told General Wynette. "Texas must be taught a lesson that the people there will never forget. What are you people in the Pentagon going to do to smash them?"

The truth was that the military had no contingency plans to attack Texas, or New York City or Honolulu or Des Moines or anywhere else in the United States. But General Wynette told the president, "Staff is working on it, sir. I assume you want boots on the ground."

"Boots on the ground, bombs on target, and the heads of every one of those sons of bitches in the legislature. And that governor—I want him alive. You go get them, General. Go to Texas and kick ass. Go as soon as you can get there."

"Yes, sir."

Dismissed, he marched out to the limo waiting to take him back to the Pentagon wondering if the president really meant for Martin L. Wynette to personally go to Texas to direct the invasion. Certainly not. He must have meant that figuratively, General Wynette decided. He settled back into the comfy leather seat of the limo.

Other than that, Wynette thought, the president had been specific enough. Bomb the hell out of those rebels, then invade. Air force fighter-bombers blasting refineries, factories, power plants, and oil fields would get those fools' attention. A naval blockade would stopper their ports and screw them down hard. Then the U.S. Army would go charging through Texas like Wynette's hero, George Patton, went through Germany. As Georgie used to say, "Like crap through a goose."

When he drove through the little town of Langtry, JR Hays saw Texas flags flying in front of every house and building, every business. Must have been a hundred of them. Was this Texas Independence Day? No, that was in March. He shrugged and kept driving.

Del Rio also looked as if it were having a flag festival. Texas flags were everywhere, flying, hanging, tacked to buildings, strung across the street. He pulled into a filling station and went in for a piss and a Coke.

The people inside greeted him like a long-lost cousin. "Happy Independence Day."

"I thought that was in March."

"That was then, this is now. Today. Early this morning Texas declared its independence. Haven't you heard?"

"No."

The young man behind the counter with rings in his ears and one in his nose pointed to a newspaper. "Special edition," he said. The headline took up all the space above the fold: "Texas Free, Again." The kid was wearing a pistol in a belt holster.

"How about that," JR said.

"Already we got some troubles," the kid said. "Mexicans tried to force the bridge from Ciudad Acuna this mornin', tryin' to get across. Must have figured that without the feds we'd be runnin' around with our thumbs up our asses. Some of the guys went down there with their rifles and put a stop to that shit. Shot some of 'em. They're layin' out there on the bridge bleedin' all over. The Mexicans won't expose themselves to drag them away and our guys ain't goin' to go to their rescue. They can crawl back to Mexico or lay there and die."

"Hmm."

"State trooper was in here a little bit ago and tol' me all about it. Eight or ten got across before the shootin' started. Folks are roundin' 'em up and gonna make 'em walk back over the bridge. Some other guys are goin' through the city right now roundin' up illegals to take the walk. Feds ain't protectin' them anymore."

"Where are the feds?"

"Home, I reckon. They're all Texans. They don't like that asshole Soetoro either, but it was do it his way or get fired."

After he went to the men's room, JR picked a Coke from the cooler and took it to the counter.

"American money still good?"

"The boss ain't tol' me not to take it. Reckon the politicians will have to figure all that stuff out."

"I guess so," JR said. "Happy Independence Day." He paid and walked out.

Outside, he looked around. There wasn't an American flag in sight. Just lots of Lone Star flags.

Being human, he wondered about his pension. Twenty years in the army and now no pension. He felt like one of those Mexicans bleeding to death down on the bridge over the river.

He started the truck and screwed the plastic lid off the plastic bottle and took a sip. Then the implications of independence hit him. Texas was going to need an army. Maybe he could join. Hell, soldiering was what he knew how to do; it was the only thing he knew how to do. He would ask Jack about that.

At a stoplight he lit another Camel.

Damn! *The Republic of Texas*. How about *that*!

Travis Clay had been home from the Middle East for only two days and had next week off. He was just getting out of bed when I knocked on the door of his apartment. He was in his underwear when he opened the door and motioned me in. I could hear television audio from the bedroom.

He went to the kitchen and put coffee in the basket and added water. As he did the work, I leaned on the door jam and asked, "How was Syria?"

"The fires of hell have leaked through the crust there. Never trust a man who wipes his ass with his bare hand. We thought we knew where that British dude was who likes to lop off heads with a knife, but he was gone when we hit the place. The Brits were royally pissed. Words cannot express how badly they want that murderous prick. They would sell a prince and maybe a princess or two to lay hands on him for just an hour."

"That's what they get for letting every raghead who can get there into the country."

"Don't say that aloud to them. They don't have warm fuzzies about the politicians. And Soetoro is doing it too. Welcome to diversity."

"So where's your significant other?"

"Rachel? She hit the road. I don't know the straight of it, but I think she got tired of waiting for me to come home and started picking up men in bars. Anyway, she left a note. Want to read it?"

"No."

"That's good, because I tore it up."

The coffee was dripping through, and he poured me a cup. He had to wait a minute for the pot to deliver enough for another cup.

When we were sitting in his little living room, I said, "I suppose you heard about Jake Grafton getting arrested."

"Yeah. And parochial school murders and martial law and Texas declaring independence and all of that. The whole damned country is going to hell in a wheelbarrow. I'm thinking about pulling the plug and going to Montana. You know I grew up there?"

"I didn't know that."

"Yeah. My folks are outfitters, fishing trips during the spring and summer and hunters in the fall. My dad told me last night I've got a job there if I want it. I'm sorta thinking I do. I don't want to go back to Syria. They're all pedophiles and wife-beaters. Sunnis and Shiites will be fighting each other for a century or two, and the truth is, I don't think it matters a single teeny tiny little goddamn who wins."

"Probably not," I murmured.

"The only thing I am absolutely convinced of, I don't want to die in that shithole."

"Montana would be good."

"I'm thinking about it."

"Before you run off, I need some help." I told him about Jake Grafton and my project to rescue him.

Travis Clay took it like a man and didn't cry. What he said was, "Fuck you, Carmellini."

"You aren't cute enough."

We batted it back and forth awhile, and I told him Willis Coffee was on board.

"Oh, hell," he finally said. "Why not?"

Half an hour later, after we had gone through my plan from end to end, he said, "If you have to shoot an FBI agent, can you do it?"

I answered honestly. "I don't know."

"Better get that figured out before we saddle up. I guarantee you they will shoot you and me and Willis Coffee in a heartbeat if we stop that car. That's what they train them to do at Quantico. They won't even think about it—they'll just throw lead."

"I suppose."

"What you need, Tommy, is a serious diversion. Think about that for a while. The feds will pull out all the stops if we snatch Jake Grafton, whether we shoot an agent or two or not. Barry Soetoro will turn purple. We must give Soetoro and the rest of them something else to think about, something with a higher priority."

I was in a McDonald's munching a Big Mac when the phone rang. It was Callie Grafton.

"I saw him," she said. "He looks good."

"Great. Maybe I'll stop by this evening for a beer."

"Sure," she said.

We hung up.

So it was a go.

★

JR Hays rolled into Austin late that Sunday afternoon. He was fighting to stay awake, but he parked by the state capitol and walked across the lawn. Upstairs, he told the governor's receptionist who he was and took a seat in the waiting room. Legislators came and went, striding purposefully, almost trotting. He gathered that the legislature was in session on the other side of the building, arguing about and passing the legislation needed to convert Texas from a state in the United States to an independent republic.

An hour passed. JR dozed in the chair. The governor shook him awake. "Come into my office, JR. I apologize for the wait. We're making history and trying to give every Texan a decent place to live."

He went into the office, and Jack Hays closed the door behind them. "Talk to me," the governor said, and sat down behind the desk.

JR dropped into a chair and told it. "There are ten dead men at the ranch. I ambushed them last night. They were carrying about two hundred pounds of some kind of drug, and I have about a hundred fifty pounds of it in the truck. Two of the backpacks the mules carried were too full of holes to hold the stuff. One of the guards was that deputy sheriff we met before the funeral, Morales I think his name was. There couldn't be two men in west Texas tattooed like that. After the ambush, I hot-footed it out to the highway, and who should be driving up and down but Sheriff Manuel Tejada."

"Was he in on it, you think?"

"I called him this morning, told him there had been a shootout between two drug gangs, and the stuff was lying all over. Told him I wanted to call the state police and DEA. He begged me to wait until he had come out to look the scene over. He would have probably tried to shoot me, so I boogied."

Jack Hays was a quick study. "How do you want to handle this?" he asked his cousin.

"We have to fix it so the drug syndicate guys don't come to the ranch with enough firepower to conquer Israel and whack little old me. Plugging Tejada would have felt mighty good, but it wouldn't have solved that problem. I want to take these backpacks over to DPS headquarters, and the colonel needs to have a press conference. Show the drugs to the press. He needs to thank Sheriff Manuel Tejada for his cooperation, which was an essential element in the investigation that allowed the Texas DPS to break up this gang of smugglers."

Jack Hays smiled. "The phones here are down. I'll take you over there. Let's go."

The cousins drove to the state police headquarters in JR's truck. They went in to see Colonel Frank Tenney. Fifteen minutes later two state troopers armed with the key to JR's toolbox in the bed of his truck carried the backpacks full of dope up to Tenney's office.

Tenney looked the governor in the eye. "There was a warrant issued for JR over in Upshur County today. He's wanted for murder and drug trafficking. It's signed by a justice of the peace. They radioed the news in."

"Squash it," Jack Hays said, waving the warrant away as if shooing a fly. "He was working as an undercover agent for the Department of Public Safety. I want you to hold a press conference, for the evening news if possible, and have the department take full credit for recovering a hundred and fifty pounds—or whatever it is—of narcotics and smashing a smuggling gang. And I want you to tell the world that it wouldn't have happened without the active help of the sheriff of Upshur County, Manuel Tejada, who gave you the intelligence necessary to break up this gang. It is unfortunate that the smugglers chose to fight rather than submit to arrest and trial by jury, but that was their choice. I want you to make the point that the Republic of Texas will seek out and actively hunt down narco-criminals. Tell the world that Governor Jack Hays has personally assured you the Department of Public Safety will get the funding and manpower needed to finally do the job right."

The lab did a quick check and established the drug was pure, uncut cocaine, and the cops weighed the stuff. The street value they came up with was $1,360,000 at twenty grand a kilo.

Driving back to the capitol, Jack Hays told JR, "Come on over to my place for dinner tonight. We need to talk. Washington is gearing up for a war against Texas."

"Breakfast tomorrow," JR said. "I've been up over thirty-six hours and am going to a hotel to crash."

"Breakfast at my house," Jack Hays said, shook his cousin's hand, and walked into the capitol.

JR did indeed crash, but not until after he had a shower and watched Colonel Tenney on the evening news. The camera lingered on the pile of cocaine on Tenney's desk. "Breaking this gang would not have happened without the intelligence provided by and the active cooperation of Sheriff Manuel Tejada of Upshur County," Colonel Tenney intoned, staring into the camera. "He was instrumental in helping us smash a major narcotics smuggling operation. All of Texas thanks you, Sheriff Tejada."

JR hit the bed and slept for ten hours.

The aftermath was not slow in coming. Two mornings later Mrs. Tejada found her husband wired to a tree in their backyard. He was dead, strangled with bailing wire. She was pretty broken up about it, until she found over a quarter of a million dollars in an old chest in the guest bedroom, wrapped in a quilt her mother made over a half century ago. Since no one knew where the money had come from, she kept it and lit a candle for her husband in the local church.

When the state police finally got around to visiting the Hays ranch, they found the bodies, which had been worked on by buzzards, coyotes, and feral pigs, one of which was lying dead with the mules. It had apparently ingested enough of the cocaine scattered around to kill it, so presumably it went to pig heaven happy. The only positive identification the cops made was the body of Deputy Sheriff Jesus Morales, identified by his fingerprints and distinctive tattoos, but his boss had been dead almost a week by then, so it was decided to not make a fuss and embarrass the Morales family, who were third-generation Americans, and by all accounts good people. The other dead men were apparently Mexican nationals, so their fingerprints were passed to the Mexican DEA, which didn't bother to acknowledge the receipt of them.

When the Hays' hired man returned from his two-week vacation, he repaired the ranch fence.

But all that was aftermath, and the lives of Jack and JR Hays had moved on by then.

TEN

★

On Monday morning, August 29, JR got his pickup from the hotel valet and drove to the governor's mansion. There he discovered that the governor had a maid, who admitted him and led him to the dining room, where Jack and Nadine were buried in the *Austin Statesman*. The events of the previous day and the full text of the Declaration of Independence filled the front page. Inside were interviews with legislators and quick man-in-the street quotations from celebrating citizens of the new republic. The *Statesman*, a liberal newspaper, editorialized that the governor and legislators who voted for independence were irresponsible radicals whose actions bordered on insanity.

After the trio had discussed the events of the previous day, JR remarked about the maid. Jack said he did a lot of official entertaining so the legislature paid the salaries of a maid and a cook.

"He's in the kitchen now whipping something up. You ready?"

"Sure," JR said.

"Jack, read that editorial aloud," Nadine urged. So he did.

Jack said dryly, "If the *Statesman* had editorialized that we had done the right thing, I would have been really worried."

Soon the maid served eggs Sardou with crumbled bacon, unbuttered toast, and white wine.

Jack said to his cousin, "If it's too early for you for wine, we have coffee and the juices."

JR glanced at his watch. "I have an ironclad rule that I never drink before seven in the morning," he said, "and it's ten after. I'll do the wine."

Nadine took coffee with cream.

Jack and Nadine expressed the hope that the Houston rioting was at last at an end. As they ate they discussed the new status of Texas.

"Tell us what you think," Nadine said to JR.

JR thought about his response, then said, "I'm a natural-born Texan, and I've had it with Soetoro. A few terrorist incidents don't seem to be a good reason to declare martial law. The FBI and local police can sort that stuff out. I sorta suspect Soetoro thought all that was a good enough excuse to become a dictator, but I don't know. I just caught snatches of the news, here and there."

Nadine zeroed in. "Are you happy with independence?"

"Anyone who isn't can hit the road," JR said. "I'm staying. But I hope you folks know that you have bought a ton of trouble. I doubt if all the U.S. soldiers and sailors and airmen will stick to Barry, but a lot of them will, and that'll be plenty. They can cause you lots of grief. Air strikes against concentrations of troops or civilians, against industry, refineries, armories, storage tanks, power generation facilities, everything you can think of, plus armored columns and infantry going through the towns and cities to take them house by house and block by block, seeking out and killing or defeating the rebels... it could get damned rough. The feds will ultimately lose, of course, but they will give it the old college try and kill a lot of Texans before they throw in the towel."

Nadine jumped right on it. "Why will they lose?"

"Because control of the cities is strategically worthless. Whoever controls the countryside always wins in the end, if they keep their nerve and are willing to take the casualties. People in cities have to eat, and the food comes from the countryside. Not to mention electrical power, gasoline, and every other commodity known to man. It all has to be produced in the country or transported through the country, which means it is militarily vulnerable."

"You think?"

"I know. The American Revolution, the French, Russian, Chinese, and Cuban Revolutions, Vietnam, Afghanistan, you name it. Control of the countryside was the essential element every time. And successful revolutions or rebellions are not the victory of a pissed-off majority, but the triumph of a dedicated minority who won't quit. It doesn't take many men. But the revolutionaries must be willing to suffer and be quite ruthless with the enemy."

"There will be casualties."

"A lot of them," JR agreed, and sipped his wine. "Bloodless revolutions are usually military coups—the generals win because no one else has weapons. The people of Texas are armed. Everyone has guns, and a lot of people know how to use them. More important, some of them are willing to do so. Just having a gun isn't enough. Successful rebels must be willing to fight, to kill, and if necessary, be killed. But you know all that and declared independence anyway, so I assume a lot of legislators have some guts. Or their constituents do, which is better. Whether a dedicated minority has enough guts and determination remains to be seen. Time will tell."

"We are hearing very little from Washington," Jack Hays said. "They aren't going to make idle threats. When the blow falls, it will be heavy."

"Don't wait for it," JR advised. "You must take it to them. Seize the initiative and put them on the defensive. That's the only way. The Confederates in the American Civil War were strategically hampered by the politicians' desire to take the defensive. In war the defense always loses. If you try to defend everything, you are spread so thin you end up defending nothing. If you try to defend just a few key places or installations, the attackers will bleed you to death someplace else."

Nadine had abandoned her breakfast. "So how do we prevail and make our independence stick?"

"Attack. As U. S. Grant said, find out where they are, hit 'em as soon as you can, as hard as you can, and keep moving on."

"The best defense is a good offense," Jack Hays said thoughtfully.

"Amen to that. In the military we call it seizing the initiative, forcing your enemy to react to your moves rather than you reacting to his."

"It's the same way in politics."

Nadine looked at her watch and said she had to leave for the university. Her breakfast was only half-eaten. She rose, got a kiss on the cheek from both men, grabbed her purse, and hurried for the garage.

Jack Hays leaned back in his chair. The maid came in with the coffee pot and poured.

When she had left again, Jack Hays asked JR, "If you were running the military show, how would you go about it?"

"That's a big *if*."

"A hypothetical."

"The commander must figure out what he has to fight with. That's Job One. What we have in the way of people, weapons, ammo, and transport defines our options. Our hypothetical commander must start there."

Jack Hays nodded, sipped his coffee, and nodded again. "If I offered to make you a general," he said, "and put you in charge of the Texas Armed Forces, which is the National Guard, Air National Guard, and every military unit within Texas, all you can grab, you'd be in charge of defending Texas. Would you take the job?"

JR grinned. "I came here this morning," he said, "to ask for a job in the Texas Army. Any job. Soldiering is all I know. I suspect that you are going to need an army very badly, very soon."

"General Twilley has wanted to retire for the last year, and I have been asking him to put it off and hang in there. I want you to take his place. The air guard guy is Major General Elvin Gentry. He'll answer to you."

"Okay," JR said.

"Before you go, I have to add the Texas Navy to your list of responsibilities. We got a nuke attack sub yesterday morning. USS *Texas*. She's sitting at a pier in Galveston, and we've got to do something with her quick before the U.S. Navy sinks her or steals her back."

"Is she undamaged?"

"The sheriff down there thinks she is, but his nautical experience is limited to bass boats."

"I've got an old army friend who got fed up with grunts and transferred to the navy," JR said slowly. "He's retired now. As I recall, he was in attack subs. Smart as a tack. Went to nuke power school and did well. He's a law student now at UT. I can send him down to evaluate the boat. If we can't move and hide her, Jack, we probably ought to scuttle her right where she is so the SEALs can't steal her out from under our noses."

"They could do that?"

"You can bet they're noodling on how to do it right now."

Jack Hays scooted his chair back and rose. "Sounds like you need to get busy."

"Yes, sir," JR Hays said. "I'll do my best."

"I'd like to introduce you to the press and the Guard brass hats this morning, but I've got to go to Houston again. We'll do the paperwork when I get back. I'll scribble a note to General Twilley. You run out to Camp Mabry, give it to him, and take command—and have him muster you up a major general's uniform."

"Where is Camp Mabry?"

His cousin stared at him a moment before he answered, "West Thirty-Fifth Street, west of Highway One." Then he grinned. If you don't know, ask. JR would do nicely.

The governor wrote the note in longhand, they shook hands, and JR headed for the front door and his pickup.

JR drove to the University of Texas Law School and went in. He found his friend, a muscular black man named Loren Snyder, standing in a hallway outside a classroom talking to two fellow students.

"Lorrie." JR smacked him on the shoulder.

"JR Hays, folks. Long time no see, JR. What are you doing here?"

"Thinking of getting a law degree and wanted to talk to you about that."

"Well," Loren glanced at his watch. "I have ten minutes."

"Terrific."

JR led Loren away from the other students to a quiet corner. "Weren't you in attack submarines?"

"Yep. Sixteen years of it after the army, which my wife said was plenty long enough. Now I'm going for the gold. Going to be a personal injury lawyer and screw those insurance companies down hard."

"Before you get to that, I need some help. I'm now a major general commanding all the military forces of the new Republic of Texas."

"You're *what*?"

"You heard me. We acquired a nuke attack sub yesterday morning down at Galveston, and I need a quick evaluation of the boat by someone who knows what they are talking about."

"I saw in the paper *Texas* was making a port visit there."

"Will you go to Galveston right now and evaluate the condition of the boat? Then answer some questions for me. Specifically, can we get enough ex-sailors to move her, can we hide her, or should we just sink her at the pier so the SEALs can't snatch her back?"

"You haven't even asked me if I'm a loyal Texan."

"Are you?"

"Well, I don't know. Haven't thought much about it."

"You do this, I'll give you a medal to frame and hang in your law office, when you get that office."

"You want me to go now, miss today's classes?"

"An hour ago would have been better."

"How do I get hold of you?"

"Any National Guard armory. They can radio me a message."

Loren gave him a sheet of paper from a notebook and JR wrote upon it, "Please allow Loren Snyder to inspect USS *Texas*," and signed it JR Hays, Major General, Commanding, dated it, and gave it to Loren.

"Well, *that* looks official," said Loren.

"I gotta run," JR said. "And you do too. Saddle up."

Brigadier General Lou l'Angistino was fifty years old, from Nebraska, an ROTC graduate who had worked his way up the ladder, flying and performing staff jobs. He flew F-4 Phantoms and F-16s, and considered it ironic that he now commanded a bomber wing. The Global Strike Command dudes must have been very unhappy when they heard. Of course, he had served a tour on the GSC commander's staff, and maybe that was why he was selected.

L'Angistino habitually went to bed at nine o'clock in the evening unless he had an official function to attend, and rose between four thirty and five o'clock a.m. He usually put a leash on his black Lab and then ran five miles, rain or shine.

The events of the previous week troubled him deeply. He knew all about Jade Helm, the plan of the Federal Emergency Management Agency to put Americans in concentration camps, and he also knew that liberals, minorities, and Democrats weren't the intended detainees. He had been appalled when Soetoro announced martial law and invoked Jade Helm.

The National Guard's blockade of the runway yesterday was only the first shot in the war, he told himself. Texas has a lot more bullets. Last night his staff thought that the crash crews would have the runway cleared by late this morning. Then he would fly the planes out, if he could find enough flight crews. He suspected that might be a problem. But he would worry about all that when he got to the office.

Normally the general ran on base, but this morning he put the lab in the car and headed for the main gate. He drove past the thirty aircraft that lined the boulevard to the highway, aircraft dating from World War II right up through the present day. One was a retired B-1 and another a retired C-130.

He drove the seven miles into town, marveled at the display of Texas flags, and, as the sun rose, was jogging in a park with his dog.

Two miles along he saw a man in a baseball cap sitting on a bench with a rifle across his knees. He had a golden retriever on a leash. As l'Angistino got closer, he saw the man was probably Latino and well past retirement age. He was also wearing a gun belt with a pistol in a holster.

The general stopped to talk. As the dogs sniffed each other and got acquainted, the man said, "Was you in the air force?" L'Angistino was wearing a faded air force T-shirt and red shorts. He nodded.

"I was too," the man said. The hands that caressed the worn old lever-action Winchester were the hands of a working man. "Wound up in Thailand turning wrenches on F-105s. Now them was airplanes!"

"Why the rifle?" the general asked.

"Oh, a bunch of us are going out to the base this mornin'. Going to talk to those people out there. We're gonna meet at nine o'clock. Can't sleep very well anymore, so came out here to the park to sit. Gonna get hot today"—it was already pushing 80—"but with the clear sky and still breeze, it's mighty nice right here right now. At my age, you enjoy ever' day because you don't know how many more you got."

"Think there'll be trouble at the base?"

"Hope not, but you never know about the blue suits. They's good 'uns and bad 'uns, just like ever'where. But if there's any shootin', I fully intend to shoot back until they get me."

"I see."

"My folks was in Texas before the white and black people ever showed up. One of my great-great-great-grandpappies died at the Alamo with Travis and them. His nephew rode with Terry's Texas Rangers during the Civil War and lost a leg at Shiloh. Yankee doctors cut it off for him. I've had granddaddies and uncles and men kin fight in ever' war this country ever fought. The world wars, Korea, and me in Vietnam. We're Texans."

"What kind of pistol is that in your holster?"

"It was my daddy's Colt Police Positive. He was a policeman in San Antone until he retired and moved here to Abilene to be near his daughters. I got it when he died."

"So what do you think of independence?"

"Some more of us are gonna have to fight for Texas again."

"When did you get out of the air force?"

"Seventy-five. Came back here and opened a garage. It was a close squeak at times, but we have six bays now. My two sons run it, and I sit and watch baseball on TV and drink beer."

General l'Angistino glanced at his watch. He needed to get going, but...

"Texans don't seem to like illegals. What is your opinion?"

"I'm like ever'body else. They flood in here and take jobs away from poor Texans because they'll work for the minimum wage or less. Down in Mexico the Church won't let 'em use contraceptives. Lots of kids guarantees they'll never get ahead and will always be poor. I'm Catholic, but believe me, after the two boys arrived I used rubbers back when the old lady could still get knocked up. I tol' the priest about it, and he said I had to do what God tol' me to do. I tol' him that I was gonna do what my wife tol' me to do, and if that got me sent to Hell, at least I'd know a lot of the people there." The old man chuckled. Apparently he had told this story many times before and still liked it.

"What does your wife think about you going out to the base this morning carrying a pistol and rifle?"

"She tol' me to be careful and never forget my family or Texas."

"Good luck to you," Brigadier General l'Angistino said. As he jogged back to his car, dog in tow, he thought, I'm the one who's going to need the good luck.

Newspapers all over Texas carried the news about independence in headlines in the largest type they had. The *Dallas Morning News* devoted its entire front section to the declaration and interviews with lawmakers, including a short one with the governor. Of the paper's editorials and op-ed pieces, all but one favored independence in order to preserve the freedom of the people of Texas. The lone dissenter was the paper's token liberal, whose column most *Morning News* subscribers read only for aggravation.

The publisher defied federal edicts when he published the paper. He got away with it because the federal censors spent Sunday at FEMA headquarters getting briefed on the latest orders from Washington, which was in a dither, apparently, unsure how to handle those goddamn Texans.

At eight that morning five FBI agents, two women and three men, plus a FEMA representative, showed up at the publisher's house in one of Dallas' toniest neighborhoods to arrest him.

They were met by several dozen armed civilians. In the shootout that followed, one civilian was killed and another wounded, but all six of the federal officers died on the scene. Two minutes after the shooting stopped, there was one more shot, which may have been a coup de grâce, but afterward none of the participants could recall hearing it.

Leaving the agents and their weapons where they lay, the victors of this encounter took their dead comrade to a funeral home and the wounded man to a hospital. Then they went to Dallas FBI headquarters and arrested everyone they could find, even the office help. The sheriff incarcerated all the prisoners in the Dallas County jail. He had to release some drunks and potheads to make room.

When the crowd, which had swelled to more than two hundred armed men and women, arrived at the Dallas FEMA building, they found it empty. The FEMA employees had fled: that was probably a good thing since the crowd was in an ugly mood.

Later that morning a television reporter on *Good Morning Texas* questioned the sheriff, Milo Makepeace. Milo claimed he was a direct descendant of Comanche war chief Quanah Parker, and he had enough Indian blood in him to make that plausible, even if newspaper reporters had been unable to ever prove or disprove the relationship. Not that it mattered. With his dark skin tint and Indian features, Makepeace was Texas "to the bone." The interview ran on *Good Morning Texas*, a popular morning staple for many in the Dallas area. The show ran fifteen seconds of footage of ambulance crews in front of the publisher's house loading the bodies of the FBI and FEMA agents. Then the station aired the interview. The reporter asked about the slayings of the FBI and FEMA agents.

"I don't know a solitary thing about it," Sheriff Makepeace said, "other than the fact they're dead. I also was told that they had federal credentials and weapons on them. Maybe they got in a shootout and killed each other, or maybe they tangled with persons unknown. If they had packed up and gotten out of Texas yesterday, that incident wouldn't have happened. It's very sad that they didn't."

"I understand you jailed some FBI agents this morning."

The sheriff nodded. "As of yesterday morning federal employees got no authority whatsoever in Texas. The FBI people had a lot of concealed weapons on them that they didn't have permits for, which is a violation of the laws of Texas and Dallas County. Texans are big on self-help, and the folks in the crowd that brought them in looked like voters to me. I'm holding them until Jack Hays or a Texas judge tells me what to do with them."

"How about a federal judge?"

"Federal judges have no authority in Texas. I just explained that. All their summonses, orders, warrants, and such don't mean diddly-squat.

If they want to keep drawing federal checks, they'd better get themselves back to Soetoro-land. If they want to stay here, they need to get a real job. That goes for all federal employees, from the janitor at the federal courthouse to the people at FEMA, ICE, the DEA, the FAA, the EPA, and the Federal Reserve Bank. All of 'em. Get out of Texas or get a real job."

Major General Twilley read Governor Jack Hays' note and came around his desk to shake JR's hand. "I can't tell you how relieved I am," he said. "I have a son in the U.S. Army Special Forces and a daughter in the U.S. Air Force in Germany. I couldn't fight against them under any circumstances, and you know as well as I do that Barry Soetoro won't let Texas go without a fight. I was going to write Jack Hays a letter and ask for immediate retirement. He saved me the trouble."

He called in his staff, introduced JR, and read the governor's letter aloud. "I have been relieved by Major General JR Hays." He and his staff saluted JR. JR returned the salute.

Then Twilley turned to a colonel. "Major General Hays will need a uniform. Until he can get some greens, get him some camos. I'll give him my stars." And he took them off right there and pinned them on JR's collar. Meanwhile, Major General Gentry, the officer in command of the Texas Air Guard, came into the room and was introduced. He read Governor Hays' order and saluted. JR saluted him back.

Twilley took a few moments to shake the hands of every officer on the staff, then he put a photo of his wife, son, and daughter that sat on his desk under his arm and walked out of the room.

"Let's go somewhere that we can sit down," JR said. "Do y'all have a conference room?"

"Sure do, sir. Follow me."

When everyone was sitting down with pads of paper and pens handy, JR got to it. "Ladies and gentlemen, you know all about the Declaration of Independence. The people of Texas, acting through their elected representatives, have declared themselves a free, independent republic. Our job is to build a military that can and will defend the Republic of Texas against all enemies. The governor has asked me to lead the military effort. Yes, I'm Jack Hays' cousin. I grew up in west Texas, graduated from West Point, and spent twenty years as an infantry officer in the United States Army. I fought in Kosovo, the Gulf War, Iraq, and Afghanistan before I retired from that army. I'm proud of my service, and I am very proud Jack asked me to lead Texas' military in a fight for freedom.

"I understand the emotional muddle many of you find yourselves in. Many of my closest friends still wear United States uniforms. They will do their duty as they see it, as I will mine.

"Still, I want you to understand the depth of my commitment. I am absolutely committed to the Texas cause. One of my kinsmen, Captain Jack Hays, was the very first captain of the Texas Rangers. Hays men have fought, bled, and sometimes died fighting for Texas, for the Confederacy, and for the United States in world wars and police actions. As a soldier, I was fully prepared to give my life for my country in every place I fought, just as I am now fully prepared to give my life for the Republic of Texas if God demands it of me. I expect no less from every one of you."

He surveyed the audience, tried to gauge their mood. He concluded most of them were with him, which was more than he hoped for.

"Every one of us in this room swore an oath to defend freedom. Every one of us swore to defend the United States Constitution. But our Constitution, and the United States as we knew it, no longer exist. They've been hijacked by a power-mad tyrant bent on transforming America into a socialist dictatorship. The people of Texas have chosen not to be a party to the destruction of their liberties. *And since freedom is never free, we are going to have to pay for ours.*"

A murmur of approval swept through the room.

Heartened, JR said, "Our first job is figuring out how many soldiers we have. I want the National Guard troops individually polled today. I intend to muster everyone in the Guard into full-time Texas service. I know every guardsman has agreed to that in his enlistment papers or officer's commission, but we need to be realistic. We're going to have a civil war. If you can't in good conscience defend Texas against other

Americans in Barry Soetoro's army, please excuse yourself right now and no questions will be asked. If you can't in good conscience take the risk because of your family obligations—again, fine, leave now and no questions will be asked. The rest of us need to get ready."

One captain in the rear of the room got up and left. The door closed behind him.

"Adjutant, take this down. Everyone who stays will be sworn into Texas service with this oath: 'I swear to support and defend the Constitution of the Republic of Texas against all enemies, foreign and domestic, and to obey the orders of the officers appointed over me, so help me God.' Make a lot of copies. Administer the oath before a Texas flag, with the oath-taker standing at attention with his right hand raised. Afterward, the oath-taker will sign a hard copy of the oath that will remain in his service record. Anyone accused of violating the oath will be tried by court-martial, and if found guilty, will be imprisoned or shot. Any questions?"

There were none.

"Okay, let's get at it. Chief of staff, have a list prepared of every United States military installation in the state, all of 'em. We'll divide up the list and take as many troops with us as we can find, go to the CO of every installation this afternoon or as soon as we can get there, and ask for the formal surrender of the base with all its weapons, ammo, and equipment. Prepare a short paragraph for the COs to sign.

"Our policy is this: Every person in Barry Soetoro's federal service who wishes to leave Texas will be allowed to take his family and personal possessions, no weapons or military gear of any kind, and depart Texas expeditiously. East, west, or north, no questions asked. Any man or woman in federal service, officer or enlisted, who wishes to serve the Republic of Texas will be mustered in by taking the oath and signing it. Enlisted will serve for four years, or until sooner discharged or our legislature decides otherwise. Officers serve at the pleasure of the governor. Time in service and pay grade will transfer directly. Any questions?"

"These folks who want to join us—the feds will probably list them as deserters."

"That is not a question, but I'll comment on that point anyway. The feds are going to do whatever they want, and that's sort of a fact of nature. Anyone in federal service wishing to join the Texas Guard by taking the oath will be allowed to do so; in fact, they will be encouraged to do so. We need all of the soldiers we can get. Civilian volunteers will be enlisted after a physical and an abbreviated background check. No crazy people, felons, dope addicts, or congenital idiots."

"We have our share of idiots now," someone remarked. "We don't need any more."

JR laughed and the tension was broken. He clapped his hands once and said, "Break out the sidearms and ammunition. I want every officer armed." After a few more housekeeping details, he said, "We don't know how much time Barry Soetoro will give us, so let's get at it, people."

As the staff dribbled out, JR and Elvin Gentry moved chairs together at the end of one table. "Call me JR," the newest general said. "Will the air guard stick?"

"Most of them," Gentry replied.

"What do you have in the way of airplanes, and where are they?"

Gentry told him. A reconnaissance wing equipped with Predator drones, an airlift wing flying C-130 Hercules planes, and a fighter wing flying F-16s stationed at Kelley Field at the joint base in San Antonio, Lackland. There was an air reserve C-5 outfit there too.

"We're going to need those fighters PDQ. How about you sending someone down there this morning to make sure we keep them?"

"Yes, sir. The air reserve also has a wing of F-16s at the Joint Base in Fort Worth, the old NAS Dallas."

"And doesn't the air force have a wing of B-1Bs over at Dyess in Abilene?"

"They do. Plus some more Hercs."

"We need them too. Fact is, we need every military asset we can lay hands on. We've got to grab everything we can reach before it is sabotaged or flown or driven out of state. We have to turn it over to loyal people."

Gentry nodded his understanding.

"Send the best people you can find on to Fort Worth and San Antone. The critical assets, however, are the B-1s. They compose our only real transcontinental offensive capability. I suggest you go to Abilene as fast as you can get there."

"I'm on my way, sir."

"We also need someone to invade the air traffic control facilities and shut them down. It would be nice to ground every commercial flight in Texas and scoff up all the planes."

"I'll do my best, sir."

"Thanks, Elvin."

ELEVEN

★

At Dyess Air Force Base in Abilene that morning General l'Angistino was trying to digest a message from Washington directing the Dyess B-1 wing and a B-52 outfit in Louisiana to prepare strikes against the heart of Austin. Before the Pentagon used this blunt weapon, however, an armored division from Fort Hood was ordered to surround the city to isolate it and, after the bombing, capture every politician they could find still alive.

An armored column cannot be organized and set in motion instantly, and the air force general knew that. He didn't know how long the army would need to comply with the directive, but he thought he had a couple of days before anyone would demand that Dyess bombers smite Austin.

And it was going to take a couple of days to get ready. The runway was now clear, but a hundred armed civilians were blockading the main gate and dozens of others blocked the other gates.

L'Angistino was rapidly running out of air policemen. Last night he had directed that machine-gun emplacements be dug on the edges of the ramp area.

He certainly didn't have the personnel to patrol the entire base perimeter. The base comprised more than six thousand acres, and it was surrounded only by the fence, which, as Colonel Wriston had proved, could be easily breached. L'Angistino did the best he could. He ordered the digging of three machine-gun emplacements to deter an attack from the front gate and had his air police patrol the base in six armored cars with mounted machine guns, the same kind of armored cars FEMA was distributing to police departments nationwide.

L'Angistino picked up the file he had on Colonel Wriston, the National Guard commander who opposed him. He was a warrior. A tanker who had done four tours in Iraq and Afghanistan, he left active duty after fifteen years and had taken a commission in the Texas National Guard. He was married, with three teenage daughters—undoubtedly the reason why he'd transferred to the Guard. Wriston knew all there was to know about bulldozer blades burying machine gunners alive, and had mounted them on tanks. Now he had bulldozers, if he could find some more, and l'Angistino thought he probably could. Wriston wasn't done, not by a long sight. The only question was what he would do next.

The major in charge of base security, Timothy Toone, had already had a confrontation with the people out front, who were standing around the county sheriff's car.

As the major reported it to l'Angistino, he told the Taylor County sheriff, "You need to get these people out of here."

"I ain't movin' nobody who's not on federal property. They've got ever' right to be here."

"They have no right to blockade our gates. Interference with U.S. military operations is a federal crime."

"Call the FBI and report it," the sheriff said calmly. "I'm sure they'll come roaring right out here and arrest everybody."

"These people are armed."

The sheriff looked around, acting as if he hadn't noticed the guns before. Then he told the major, "People have a right to openly carry firearms in Texas, except in places where it's prohibited, like courthouses. This isn't a courthouse, but a public road. Fact is, these streets and roads belong to the City of Abilene, Taylor County, or the Republic of Texas. These folks don't have to leave unless I tell them to."

The sheriff grinned, the major told l'Angistino, while he waited for the major to ask him to do just that, a request that he would cheerfully refuse in front of an audience of his constituents. So the major had kept his mouth shut and returned to headquarters. Now what did the general want him to do?

More than half the officers and airmen assigned to Dyess lived outside the gates, mostly senior people. Many of the pilots did too.

"Major, I want hourly reports on conditions at all seven gates of the base; I want you to double the base guards and ensure they're armed. If armed civilians are foolish enough to try to force their way onto the base, I want the guards to respond with lethal force. Do you understand?"

"Yes, sir."

"If this blockade continues, we won't have enough pilots, crew chiefs, and ordnance specialists to accomplish our missions. We have to break it."

"Yes, sir."

At noon, Major Toone estimated that the crowd on the streets had swelled to more than ten thousand civilians—including women and children. He estimated that half the men were armed. If they rushed the base, his troops would be in a hell of a fix if ordered to shoot. He wanted written orders from General l'Angistino.

Nothing in the brigadier's military education or experience readied him to meet this situation. Shooting unarmed women and children would be an atrocity, a war crime... and, he thought, a sin. His wife would never forgive him. He wondered if the air force would.

His operations officer entered with a mission assignment. As many B-1s as l'Angistino could get airborne were ordered to bomb Austin tonight. They were to use JDAMs, which were precision-guided munitions. A detailed target list would follow.

"But there is no fighter protection laid on," the ops officer said. "The Texas Air Guard has a squadron of F-16s at the joint base at Lackland. If they sortie to intercept the B-1s, the Bones will be toast. They have to have fighter protection, General. We could lose them all on the way to the target, over it, or on the way home. It's only seventy or eighty miles from San Antonio to Austin. Sending those guys without fighter protection is ridiculous. Foolhardy."

A knock on the door, and his aide appeared. "General, there are two squadron commanders and nine pilots waiting to see you."

The ops officer and the general exchanged glances. Did they know about the lack of fighter protection? Already?

"Send them in," he said. Then he turned to Major Toone and added, "Major, let's talk later." The two colonels, squadron commanders, passed Major Toone in the doorway. "We have a problem, General. Some of our pilots want to talk to you."

"Send them in."

The pilots were wearing flight suits. The first man in line stood at attention in front of the general's desk, saluted, and laid his silver wings insignia on the desk. "Sir, I wish to turn in my wings and be removed from flight status, immediately."

L'Angistino stared at the captain, who met his gaze. In the American military pilots and flight crewmen were all volunteers. No one could order an officer to be a pilot.

"Do you want to give me an explanation, Captain?"

"Sir, I find that in good conscience I cannot fight other Americans. I may be obligated to remain in the air force, but I am not going to fly again."

The next man laid his wings on the table and saluted. He repeated the formula, "I wish to turn in my wings and be removed from flight status, sir."

"Why?"

"My wife and I are from Texas. Born and raised here. I'm not going to take a chance that you want me to bomb Texas, maybe kill some of our relatives or some friends I grew up with or went to school with. Or their kids. I can live with a court-martial, but I couldn't live with that."

When the last man left, nine silver wings lay on the general's desk. The squadron commanders stood at parade rest.

"Where's the other squadron commander, Colonel Hurley?"

"Somewhere off base, sir, we think."

"How many pilots do we have available to fly the Bones?"

"Twelve, sir, including us. Nine command pilots and three copilots. Using some of the command pilots as copilots, we can launch six planes."

The general sank into his chair. A hundred twenty pilots in the wing, and he could muster just a dozen?

"A lot of them are trapped off base, sir. To get them in, we'd either have to run the civilians off or slip one of our own over the fence to find our guys and organize a mass break-in."

"That would take all night."

"Or longer. And we have enlisted manpower problems. Our muster list shows about thirty percent of our personnel are present for duty."

"I saw the morning muster rolls."

"It's a bad situation, sir."

The general dismissed the colonels and sat thinking. The bomb wing wasn't ready for combat. With only six flight crews and thirty percent of its enlisted personnel, it wasn't ready for anything. Not even morning colors.

The ops officer left, but he soon came back. "There is a turboprop inbound, sir. National Guard."

"Send them up here when they land."

He watched the turboprop taxi to base ops and shut down. One or two people in uniform got out, climbed into a waiting sedan. Ten minutes later they were in his office.

He recognized the Air National Guard general, Elvin Gentry, whom he saluted since Gentry was a two-star. The man with Gentry was a colonel. "Please be seated, gentlemen," l'Angistino said.

"This independence thing," Gentry said, "it's turned the world upside down. I've come to ask for you to surrender the base, its personnel, and all the military property on it."

"Are you kidding?"

"Lou, I wish I was. But I'm deadly serious. My boss, Major General JR Hays—do you know him?"

"Not that I can recall."

"He was army. Anyway, he sent me up here to get your surrender. If you refuse, he'll have to launch an F-16 strike on the base to take out the planes. Texas wants them or wants them in ashes."

"I'll fly them out of here," l'Angistino said stoutly. "The first ones leave in less than an hour."

"Lou, you couldn't have enough pilots to fly more than a handful of Bones and Hercs out of here, and I doubt you have the enlisted mechs and specialists it takes to even launch that many. We know the situation here. I've been on the radio with Colonel Wriston. Fact is, you could tell me to go to hell and sabotage all those planes, shoot holes in the spars, whatever, but we're going to take this base before very long, and General Hays is going to be royally pissed with you people if those airplanes are harmed. I don't know exactly what the Geneva Convention says about the treatment of prisoners of war, but this isn't a war we've declared. You are now trespassers on property owned by the Republic of Texas. Lawyers love tangles like this, but the local Texans won't. If you don't surrender they will be even more pissed than JR Hays. You know those people aren't under our control."

Lou l'Angistino's thoughts tumbled around.

"Lou, for God's sake. I am not trying to threaten you, although maybe it came out that way, and if so, I apologize. Most of your people don't want to fight other Americans, many are Texans who won't fight other Texans even at the point of a gun. You can't sit here on a base protected by nothing but a wire fence and defy the whole population of Texas! There is no realistic chance for victory. None. For God's sake, do the right thing and save some lives."

Gentry pointed to the little pile of wings on l'Angistino's desk. "Even your pilots are trying to tell you something. Your air force is disintegrating."

General l'Angistino picked up the op order directing a strike on Austin, glanced at it in disgust, then dropped it on the table. "What are your terms?"

An hour later, after the surrender document was signed and sent to be posted in barracks, ready rooms, and maintenance shops, Colonel Wriston of the National Guard was escorted into the office. He was wearing jeans and a faded Texas A&M T-shirt. Lou l'Angistino reached for his hand and perfunctorily shook it.

"Lou, here's the man responsible for the ten or so thousand people standing outside on the street," Gentry told the air force general. "Wriston and his men spent the night recruiting their friends and neighbors."

"You mean some of that crowd were National Guardsmen in civvies?"

"They were. Wriston did what he could to block your runways, but he didn't go home afterward to watch television. He knew the vast majority of the civilian community was behind him, so he used his men to mobilize them."

A loud voice interrupted them, to l'Angistino's relief. Colonel Wriston went to meet the man, who was standing in the reception area.

"Wriston, you bastard. I got back from Dallas this morning and nobody's workin' my job site. My foreman says the equipment operators stole ever'thin' that would move on your orders. Where the hell is my construction equipment?"

"Out beside the runways, Carroll. We used it yesterday to block the runways here. Did you watch the declaration read night before last?"

"Sure did! All I can say is, it's about damn time."

"I couldn't call and ask to borrow your stuff, but I thought since Carroll is a good man, he won't mind."

"By the runways, you say?"

"It's damaged and tore up some, but it kept all the planes from taking off. You should be able to repair some of it. Anyway, your project is going to go slow until you get some more equipment operators. Most of yours are in the Guard and they are now on active duty and won't be back for a while."

Carroll took a deep breath. "The yellow iron is insured, but the insurance company will lawyer up and refuse to pay unless I sue 'em, then offer ten cents on the dollar. You know that."

"Tell you what," Wriston said, and put his arm around the construction man. "If you eat the repair costs, we'll give you an airplane. Any one of those along the road into the base, your pick. You can put it in your front yard. When things calm down, we'll move it for you."

Carroll's eyes lit up. "Got pecan trees in the front yard, but I could put it in the horse pasture out back. Damn, I'd like that."

They shook hands on it.

★

It was noon when JR Hays, wearing a camo uniform and a pistol on a web belt, arrived at the front gate at Fort Hood, sixty miles north of Austin in Killeen. He was in the right seat of a sedan with Texas flags flying from the corners of the front bumper. Two guardsmen, a male captain and a female major, were with him. An enlisted woman was driving.

The soldier at the gate wanted to see ID, but the sergeant was right there immediately and said, "Sir, you can enter the base, but the carrying of firearms around the administrative and living areas is forbidden."

"Who is the commanding general?" JR asked the sergeant.

"Lieutenant General Gil Ellensberger, sir."

"Call him. Tell him Major General JR Hays of the Texas Army is sitting at his main gate and wants in to see him. You may tell him we are wearing sidearms, if you wish."

The sergeant did as he was told. When he hung up the phone, he came out and explained to the driver of the sedan how to get to the headquarters building. Then he saluted. JR returned it.

The commanding general was in a staff meeting. The receptionist had a television in her office, and JR stood in front of it a minute watching. Armed citizens were taking over federal office buildings statewide. The FBI agents in Waco had been arrested en masse, disarmed, and jailed. DEA and ICE headquarters had been occupied, the agents disarmed and sent home.

Ellensberger came striding in. He was a tall, lanky man. He didn't look happy, but he said, "Good lord, JR Hays, as I live and breathe. I haven't seen you since Afghanistan. Come on into my office." Ellensberger led the way and closed the door.

JR thought commanding generals' offices all looked alike: big desk, carpet, U.S. flags, mementos of the current occupant scattered around. Unbidden, he dropped into a chair.

"I retired from the army last year, General, and my cousin, Governor Jack Hays, just this morning put me in charge of the Texas Guard. Raw nepotism."

Ellensberger let that one go by. "All our off-base telephones are down, as well as the internet. Did you have anything to do with that?"

"Jack Hays did, not me. I am here today to accept your surrender of the base and all of its personnel and military equipment to the Republic of Texas."

Ellensberger snorted. "You know I can't do that. You can't just march in here and take over a United States military installation!"

"Gil, you don't have a choice. Texas is now an independent republic, and Fort Hood is right smack in the middle of it."

Ellensberger waved that away. "Texas is a state in the United States that has tried to secede from the Union. We settled all that back in the 1860s. Surely you read about that. It didn't work then and it isn't going to work now."

"We're not lawyers and I can't read tea leaves. We're soldiers, and you have an impossible military problem. How many of your troops reported for duty this morning?"

From the look on General Ellensberger's face, JR knew he had scored a hit.

"Half? Was it fifty percent?"

Ellensberger didn't reply.

"Last I heard, you had over forty-five thousand soldiers assigned here. If we blockade the base, how are you going to feed them? And for how long?"

Still no reply.

"Are you going to deploy your troops around your perimeter—how many miles of it do you have, anyway?—and defend it? How many U.S. Army troopers do we have to kill before you will surrender? Or are you going to defend this dirt to the last man and go down like they did at the Alamo? Tell me now so I can brief my staff and get at it."

"Pfui. All the good ol' boys in Texas aren't going to whip an armored division."

JR Hays rubbed his nose.

Ellensberger pushed the intercom button. "Bring in this morning's classified message traffic."

In a moment a soldier came in and handed Ellensberger a clipboard. He automatically said thank you, and the soldier left.

The commanding general flipped through the messages, then handed the clipboard to JR.

"It's the one on top. Op Immediate from the chairman of the JCS, Wynette. He has ordered me to take an armored column from the First Cavalry down the interstate to Austin and surround the city. The air force is going to bomb it. We will go in after the bombers are finished and capture every politician left alive."

JR took his time with the messages. He read the first one, then saw that Ellensberger was an info addee on a message to the B-1 bomber wing at Dyess and a B-52 outfit in Louisiana ordering them to prepare a strike on the Texas capitol in Austin. They were to wait to launch until First Cavalry had the city surrounded.

"This is insanity," JR said, gesturing with the clipboard. "They are going to indiscriminately slaughter everyone in central Austin."

"They're not thinking very straight," Ellensberger admitted.

"But you are willing to be a part of this? Murdering civilians from the air? Americans?"

Ellensberger sighed. After a bit he said, "If I surrender to you, Wynette will just order the bombers to obliterate Austin ASAP. A dozen B-52s should be able to convert the heart of the city to rubble and kill a whole bunch of civilians."

JR carefully placed the clipboard back on Ellensberger's desk. "Which side are you on, Gil?"

Ellensberger took his time answering. "As I see it, the governor of Texas and the president of the United States are locked in a hell of a political dispute. I wish they would settle it between themselves without dragging the American flag through the dirt and asking American soldiers to kill other Americans. Honest to God."

"It isn't the governor. It's the legislature and the people of Texas who are locked in a dispute with Soetoro. Haven't you been watching television?"

Ellensberger didn't reply to that remark, either.

"But politics isn't my business," JR murmured. "I'm a soldier."

"Soldiering *is* politics. You know that!"

"Yes or no, Gil. I have responsibilities too."

Ellensberger took in a bushel of air and sighed deeply. "What are your terms?"

It took a half hour for the surrender document to be typed and signed. Meanwhile JR sent the captain to the flight line to take a helicopter to National Guard headquarters at Camp Mabry in Austin with a message to Major General Gentry. Bombers were coming sooner or later to flatten Austin, and he'd better get fighters ready to fly with pilots willing to fight for Texas.

Lieutenant General Ellensberger signed the surrender. Then he went to the U.S. flag in the corner and carefully removed it from its display pole. He folded it reverently and put it into his briefcase.

"Two mornings ago," he said conversationally to JR, "when I heard the legislature had passed the declaration and the governor had signed it, I knew this moment was coming. And I didn't know what to do. I could have asked Washington, but all I would have gotten was bullshit. I wanted some time to see what my staff thought, what the troops thought—you can't fight if the troops aren't with you body and soul. The moment of decision just came sooner than I thought it would.

"JR, I am sick to death. You and I were both at West Point, served our country—all of it. Then along came Soetoro. A progressive fascist, if there is such a thing. I figured the country could stand eight years of even the devil's rule, but I was wrong. Race was the wild card. Everyone is scared to death of being labeled a racist. If Soetoro were white he would have been impeached years ago.... Do you mind if my wife and I stay in our quarters for a few days? I need to figure out what to do next."

"Whatever you need," JR replied. Ellensberger took a deep breath and looked around the office one more time. "I fear for my country," he said softly. "The United States may not survive this mess."

"Texas will," JR said with more confidence than he felt. He saluted, Ellensberger returned it, and then JR walked out to address the office staff.

"You folks in the United States Army who wish to leave can go. You folks who want to enlist in the Texas Guard can stay. You civilians have a job right here if you want it."

The civilians all stayed. Most of the soldiers asked permission, which was granted, to go home and discuss it with their wives or just to think about things.

★

JR's next problem was easily solved. The aide he had brought with him, Major Judy Saar, asked, "What are you going to do about Major Nasruli?"

Nasruli was an American-born jihadist who had murdered thirteen Fort Hood soldiers several years before and wounded thirty-two more.

"Is he still here?"

"So they tell me. In the jail or detention facility or whatever they call it."

"I thought he was convicted by a court-martial and sentenced to death."

"Yes, sir. But he's very much alive."

"We are not going to waste people running a jail or spend a dime of taxpayers' money feeding him," JR Hays said. "It's high time he was dead, anyway. Dictate an execution order addressed to yourself. Put in Nasruli's rank, full name, service number, and a place for my signature. Reference the death sentence. Then get a half-dozen volunteers, get them some M4s, and put him up against a wall. Make sure he's real dead. Then come back here and dictate a press release. The army and the civilians in Washington have screwed around and screwed around, and now he's history."

"And the body, sir?"

"Burn it."

"Yes, sir," Judy Saar said, came to attention, and saluted. Apparently she too thought Major Nasruli had lived long enough. In seven minutes she was back with a one-paragraph order she had apparently typed herself. JR Hays read it, signed it, handed it back to her, and went on to the next problem, which was the armored division at Fort Bliss, in El Paso.

He doubted that the commanding general there would surrender quite as quickly as Major General Ellensberger had. JR knew Major General Lee Parker, knew him to be a perfect bureaucrat who wouldn't want to buck the system. JR thought Parker personified everything wrong with the army: bureaucratic inertia, lack of initiative, a craven capitulation to political correctness, and a pathological fear of casualties. The media's fondness for trumpeting casualties meant that a career officer on the way up wanted as few as absolutely possible, so he took as few risks as possible, and accomplished very little. He also kicked difficult decisions up the line, so that he wouldn't be blamed if anything went wrong. JR thought that before he surrendered, Parker would want the blessing of higher authority, which he was unlikely to get.

Given some time, JR thought Parker could be conned into thinking his military bosses wanted him to surrender, but time was a diminishing asset for JR. He needed that armored division in his pocket right now. He was going to have to convince Parker that he was facing a mountain of casualties in a losing cause.

Major Judy Saar drove a staff car and parked at the first barracks she saw. Inside she found groups of male soldiers loafing in the lounge, loudly discussing Texas independence and the takeover of the base. She said, "Attention please."

Some of the soldiers looked around. "I am here to ask for volunteers for a firing squad."

Stunned silence greeted her. One black sergeant said, "Who do you want to shoot, Major?" His name tag read HILL.

"Major Nasruli. I have an execution order here in my hand."

Every man in the room raised his hand, including the black staff sergeant, short and wiry and buff, with close-cropped, prematurely gray hair. "One of the men he shot was my brother, who is paralyzed from the waist down."

"I need six people," she said. "Sergeant Hill, will you select five other men and follow me to the base armory?"

"Yes, ma'am."

At the armory she requisitioned six M4s and a cartridge for each of them. She passed the carbines to her volunteers and pocketed the cartridges.

"Turn these weapons in here afterward," she told them. "Now the detention facility."

She parked in front of the building and waited for the other vehicles, three private cars, to arrive. She felt as if she were watching herself outside of her body.

Her husband, a private physician, would not approve. But then he didn't approve of her service in the National Guard. He wanted her to stay home with the two children, who were now in junior high and didn't need her sitting at home. She wanted to make a larger contribution.

The cars drove up and the soldiers got out with their weapons.

Major Saar led them inside, showed the officer at the desk the execution order.

"You can't do this," he said. "The death sentence has to be approved by the president."

"You have heard that Texas has declared its independence and Lieutenant General Ellensberger has surrendered Fort Hood to the Republic of Texas, have you not?"

"Yes, but—"

"The president of the United States has no authority here. Would you care to call base headquarters and verify the order with Major General Hays?"

He would. He did so. After a moment of listening, he said, "Yes, sir," and hung up and looked askance at Judy Saar.

"Do you have an exercise area?" Major Saar asked.

"Yes, ma'am."

"Bring him out there. In handcuffs."

She had the sergeant arrange the squad in a line and handed a cartridge to each of them. Major Nasruli protested as the guards led him out. Apparently he had been told what was about to happen, because when he saw her he shouted, "I have written to President Soetoro demanding clemency. Allah protects the faithful. Allah has—"

"The post that holds up the basketball backboard," Major Saar told the guards. "Cuff his hands behind the post."

Nasruli continued to shout, to rant. Sergeant Hill asked, "Do you want him blindfolded?"

"He can take this with his eyes open," she said.

Nasruli refused to stop shouting. He was still shouting when Major Saar told the marksmen to aim at the center of the chest and gave the commands: Ready, aim, fire. The shots came as one report and Nasruli went down, held semi-erect by the pole. She heard the spent shells tinkling on the concrete. She walked over to the body. Blood stained his shirt. His eyes were open, staring at nothing.

Like an automaton, she drew her pistol, looked to ensure the safety was off, and, using both hands to steady and aim the pistol, shot Nasruli in the head from a distance of three feet. Brains and bloody tissue flew out the back of his head.

She engaged the safety of her Beretta, holstered it, and turned to the officer commanding the detention facility, who was staring slack-jawed at the remains of Major Nasruli. "Pour gasoline on the body and set it afire, Captain."

The sergeant called the firing squad to attention, turned them, and marched them back into the detention facility.

It took twenty minutes for the detention facility staff to come up with a five-gallon can of gasoline. *They are probably robbing a civilian on a lawnmower*, Judy Saar thought. She stood and looked at the sky, at the windows of the detention facility, at the body against the pole. She thought she was going to be sick, but she choked it down. *Later*, she whispered. A bird skittered along the top of the wall. A mockingbird, she noted.

After they put the body against an exterior stone wall, drenched it with gasoline, and set it ablaze, she marched back through the detention facility and vomited by her car. Then she drove back to headquarters.

The staff sergeant and the five other men from the firing squad were waiting for her in front of the building. They had apparently turned in the carbines to the base armory. All of them saluted and she returned their salute. "Major, we'd like to enlist in the Texas Guard," Sergeant Hill said.

She nodded and motioned for them to follow her inside.

There was a handwritten letter waiting for Major Judy Saar in the commanding general's office.

"You are now the CO of the base and the 1st Cavalry Division. Get as many soldiers enlisted as possible, and get the 1st Cavalry ready to fight. I am on my way to Fort Bliss to grab the 1st Armored, Old Ironsides. We'll need them too. You are a good soldier. I'll back you in every decision you make. Texas needs you." It was signed by JR Hays, Major General.

TWELVE

★

On the flight line at the base airfield, JR Hays went into a ready room full of helicopter pilots. They were gathered around a television, watching the feed from Washington. Someone saw JR enter the room and called everyone to attention. JR walked to a spot in front of the television, turned it off, and told everyone, "Please be seated."

He surveyed the faces. Most army pilots are warrant officers. He was looking at a bunch of them, with a few commissioned officers scattered among them.

"I'm JR Hays of the Texas Guard. As you know, Major General Ellensberger surrendered to the Texas Guard just an hour or so ago. You've been watching television, so you know the current political situation. Barry Soetoro declared martial law and ripped up the Constitution, and consequently Texas declared its independence. General Ellensberger surrendered Fort Hood because it is indefensible. Circling the wagons in a lost cause struck him as ridiculous unless he was prepared to cut his way out of Texas, and he wasn't.

"Which gets me down to you. Every one of you has a decision to make: you can go home, pack your family, and leave Texas, or you can join Texas in our attempt to build a free nation dedicated to the principles that the Founding Fathers laid down when they wrote the U.S. Constitution. I suspect Barry Soetoro's army will not be pleased if you choose to join Texas in its fight, and it will be a fight, a second American Civil War. Barry Soetoro is going to use the armed forces of the United States to try to conquer Texas, so if you sign on, you will be fighting U.S. forces. Americans against Americans, as if it were 1861 all over again.

"Finally, if you choose to join the Texas Guard and fight with us, you can't change your mind later. It's sort of like getting baptized down at the creek: as the preacher would say, once you're in, you're all in, and you can't wash it off.

"Any questions or comments?"

One of the warrant officers stood up and said, "Sir, Chief Warrant Officer Three Buck Johannson."

JR nodded and Johannson said, "My dad is a state representative in Wisconsin. His politics are right of center and he's loud. The feds arrested him yesterday and put him in a camp because they don't want other people to hear the opinions of a free man. Far as I'm concerned, Texas is on the side of freedom. I'd like to join the Texas Guard."

"Fine," JR said. "Anyone else?"

Another warrant said, "I think Soetoro wants to be a dictator. I don't want my kids to grow up in that kind of country. I'm from Georgia, but from now on I'm a Texan."

"Welcome to the Alamo," JR said, which drew a chuckle from his listeners.

About half the pilots volunteered to serve with Texas. JR dismissed the others, told them to go home and pack. "If, while you're doing that you decide to join us, you know where the headquarters building is."

When only his volunteers remained, JR said, "Our first priority is the First Armored in Fort Bliss. I want to go over there and capture the whole outfit. We need the tanks, helicopters, ammo, and all the rest of it. I'll need three Apaches and a Blackhawk armed to the teeth. We are going to do some violence, enough to make the CG there, Major General Lee Parker, surrender. Who wants to go?"

Specialist Fourth Class James B. Cassel, a name that he and his kin had always pronounced Castle, spoke for thousands of his fellow soldiers when he got home to the tiny apartment he shared with his wife, Linda

Sue, and their infant daughter. Jimmy Cassel was from a tiny town in the coalfields of southern West Virginia. He told Linda Sue, who was from Killeen and had married James just a year ago, about the surrender of Fort Hood to Texas forces.

"They say I can enlist in the Texas Guard, or we can pack up and get outta Texas," he said as he took off his uniform and put on his jeans and tennis shoes. "Get packed up. We're leavin'."

"I was born and raised here," Linda Sue protested. "I'm Texan clear through to my backbone. I'm not turning my back on my family."

"I joined the army to get the hell out of the coalfields," Jimmy explained as he pulled on a T-shirt that advertised the local Harley dealership, although he didn't own a motorcycle because he couldn't afford one, not even a used one. "I didn't join the army to shoot Americans. If I was willin' to do that when push come to shove, I'd have joined the police. I got no love for that son of a bitch Soetoro, but America's my country from coast to coast. I ain't goin' to shoot Texans or Hoosiers or Californians or anybody else from America. We're leavin'."

"I'm not," Linda Sue declared. "And the baby is stayin' with me. You just load your stuff in the car, Jimmy, and get the hell out. Go ahead, run off! If you won't fight to defend *us*, I don't want *you*."

"Now, hold on! You married me and I'm the man of the family. My dad was in the army and fought in Kuwait. My granddad fought in Vietnam and got shot for his troubles. Us Cassels been fightin' *for* this country since before it was a country. *I ain't turnin' traitor.*"

"Jimmy Cassel, I am not turnin' traitor neither. I want to hear exactly nothin' about your daddy and granddaddy. The baby and I are your family now. And if you won't fight for your family, then you just hit the road. I'm takin' the baby and walkin' down to Mom's place."

An hour later, sitting alone in his apartment, Jimmy Cassel started to cry.

★

Sergeant Claude Zeist handed beers to three of his sergeant friends at his house on base. The television was on: scenes of federal agents making arrests alternated with scenes of riots in Baltimore, St. Louis, LA, and Chicago.

"The Texans have bit off a big chunk, and I doubt if they can chew it," Zeist said. "But that's neither here nor there. Fact is, I took an oath to defend the United States of America, and when this is all over I want my kids and grandkids to know that I did my duty. Did what I swore I would. And there is no way in hell I am going into combat against my fellow American soldiers."

"It'll be over soon," his friend Benny Straight said. "Thing I can't figure is why everybody is so damned upset. Barry Soetoro will be gone in January. He can't run again. The next president can set things right."

"What if he doesn't?"

"That's tomorrow's problem. You don't burn the house down just because the sewer is backed up."

"So what are you going to do, Claude?"

"I'm going to pack up the wife and kids and get outta Texas and find an army base somewhere so I can be an American soldier again. That's what I always wanted to be, and if we have to kick ass again like we did during the Civil War in the 1860s, so be it. That damn General Ellensberger hasn't got enough guts to make a sausage."

"Generals get paid to decide when to fight and when not to," Benny remarked.

"One good fight and Texas will crack like a rotten egg," Claude Zeist insisted, and drained his beer. Then he reached for another. "We should have had it today. Never put off until tomorrow kicking ass today."

No one smiled; they were worried.

Benny Straight put into words a thought that all of them had and none of them had yet voiced. "After Texas folds, the U.S. Army is going to court-martial any United States soldier who did the turncoat trick. They'll be called traitors, and you know it."

"*If* Texas folds," Jeff Hanifan said.

"Oh, it will," Benny Straight scoffed. "For God's sake, one state against forty-nine? Texas against the United States Army, Navy, Air Force, and Marine Corps?"

"Well, something good came out of this shit storm, anyway," Claude Zeist said. "The Texans put Nasruli up against a wall and shot him. I would have bet my left nut that Soetoro was going to wait until his last day in office and commute the sentence to life in prison."

"This is Texas," Jeff Hanifan said, as if that explained everything. His comrades, all career soldiers, nodded knowingly and drank more beer.

Loren Snyder went down the open hatch in front of the small sail of USS *Texas* and found himself in the torpedo room. He looked around with his flashlight. The reactor was scrammed of course, and the boat was dead iron. The torpedoes in their cradles looked sleek and fat and ominous.

He wandered along, inspecting everything. The sailors hadn't even been able to take their personal gear. It seemed they would return any moment, but he knew they wouldn't.

The flashlight's beam in that dark ship was sorta spooky. The gentle, barely perceptible motion of the ship riding the little waves of the harbor made it even more so.

In the control room, the realization hit him that he was standing right dead center in a cruise missile target. Tomahawks could be climbing for their final dive right this instant. Each breath he took could be his last. He felt perspiration break out on his forehead and forced himself to concentrate on what he could see with the flashlight's beam.

In the reactor spaces, he examined everything and could find nothing amiss. The crew had simply secured the reactor and the batteries, then trooped up the forward ladder out of the ship.

Assuming he could get the reactor started again, how many men would he need to move this boat? Lorrie Snyder thought hard. No more than five, he thought.

Move her where? Satellites could see her submerged in shallow water, even if the water were muddy, using infrared. Where could he put a submarine so that the U.S. Navy couldn't find her?

Even if he could find such a place, did he really want to do it? JR Hays had asked the question point-blank: Was he willing to fight for Texas? Well, was he?

If he planned on living and practicing law in Texas, Loren Snyder thought he had better get that figured out. Along with everything else.

The easy way out of this personal nightmare would be to just scuttle the submarine right here at the pier. Then the U.S. Navy wouldn't need to sink her or send SEALs to steal her. JR Hays would tell him he had done his best, and thank him. Loren Snyder thought about that too.

That Sunday afternoon chairman of the JCS General Martin L. Wynette was back at the White House. He hadn't had a day this bad since he was a plebe at West Point, way back when. President Soetoro, Vice President John Rhodes, and their aides surrounded him at a conference table and wanted to know how and when the armed forces of the United States were going to crush the Texas rebellion. The general had two aides with him, a Major General Stone and a brigadier, but the questions were directed at him, and the politicians weren't happy. They wanted action now.

"Willy-nilly bombing and invasion without a plan will get us nowhere," the general explained. "We are working around the clock to formulate a coherent plan that will accomplish a military objective, which is the occupation of an enemy state."

"That's not it," Soetoro said, thumping the table. "The military objective is to destroy the political opposition in Texas."

"Your political opposition."

"You're damned right. Those who oppose the progressive policies of this administration, earth-friendly policies that will benefit all future generations, policies designed to take care of those today who are unable to participate in our high-tech economy, whether from institutional racism or white privilege or the circumstances of birth, are indeed *my* political opposition. They oppose America! Your job is to kill or capture them. Now—how are you going to get it done?"

"The navy will launch two Tomahawk cruise missiles at power-generating facilities in Houston later tonight, after dark in Texas. Your staff told me they want bombs falling immediately, so I gave the order. We are planning more strikes on the power plants—"

"Planning?"

"Scattering cruise missiles around like grass seed isn't going to kill or capture your political opposition, Mr. President. These strikes must be in coordination with armed invasion, or we are simply wasting missiles." Wynette felt his irritation leaking through. *He* was the military expert. None of these political types had ever spent a single day in uniform, unless they did a stint at scout camp once upon a time. Hell, they didn't even *like* soldiers, whom they often referred to as neolithics.

"So when is the invasion?"

"Sir, as I said, we are working around the clock to produce a plan. Going in half-cocked and getting our asses shot off isn't going to get us any closer to your objective. When we go in, we want to win."

"So when? Tomorrow? This week? Next week? Next month? Next year? *When*?"

"I would say next week. We must move soldiers and equipment from all over the country, figure out the logistics—"

"Bullshit," Soetoro's senior political advisor, Sulana Schanck, said acidly. "This isn't the invasion of Germany or Iraq! Your opposition is a mob of crackers with deer rifles who will shit their pants when the shooting starts and run like rabbits." She obviously was a believer in direct speech.

The thought shot through Wynette's head that British General Thomas Gage had that same opinion when he marched his troops from Boston to seize the arms and powder at Lexington and Concord, but he had the sense not to air it. He did, however, screw up the courage to say, "The Texans did a number on General Santa Ana, as I recall."

"Damn it, General," Soetoro roared. "I don't want a history lesson! I want you to take the United States armed forces down there and kick butt. If you can't do it, we'll find someone who can."

Wynette automatically dropped into his ass-kissing mode. "We'll get it done, sir."

"And how come the brass in charge of these military facilities in Texas are busy seeing how fast they can surrender? Are they a bunch of traitors?"

"Sir, I have ordered investigations. The commanders will be held responsible for their actions."

"Firing squads will stiffen some backbones. The sooner the better."

"Yes, sir."

"When the invasion starts, I want you down there in the lead tank, General. Do you understand? If you fuck this up, don't come back alive."

"Yes, sir," General Wynette said.

Late Sunday afternoon as JR Hays settled into one of the passenger seats of a U.S. Army executive jet, normally used to ferry flag officers around, he took stock of all the things he needed to get done and hadn't been able to attend to today. Everything needed to be done immediately. He hoped that Air National Guard Major General Elvin Gentry had hit the ground running. Air traffic facilities and their radars, in addition to fighter planes, bombers, helicopters, had to be seized by the Guard. Without ground control sites pinpointing incoming enemy planes, fighters were handicapped severely. Gentry also needed to ground civilian air traffic and confiscate every jetliner he could lay hands on so they could be used to ferry troops.

Just thinking of all the critical tasks and decisions that had to be attended to made JR's head throb and gave him a sense of anxiety that he was having trouble shaking off. The fact that the feds were equally inundated didn't help much to ease his frame of mind. If the feds got licked, they had forty-nine other states to play in. If Texas got licked, a whole lot of Texans were going to die in the aftermath.

The three Apaches and one Blackhawk that he had launched from Fort Hood were going to make a pit stop for fuel in Pecos. Unfortunately the weather was rotten around El Paso. Thunderstorms full of rain and lightning were drifting in from the west and southwest, bringing low ceilings and visibility in addition to their usual goodies.

He had no plan for forcing the 1st Armored to surrender. He had learned long ago the truth to the old maxim that no plan survives contact with the enemy, so he made none. First he had to learn what the situation was in El Paso and at Fort Bliss, then he could plan. The Apaches and the Blackhawk were arrows in his quiver. The National Guard commander, Wiley Fehrenbach, scion of the Hill Country Fehrenbachs, and his old civilian contractor boss, Pete Taylor, would know, so he would land at the civilian airport and seek them out.

He had been lucky to get into West Point, and soon hated the place. He decided to stick with it and do his required service afterward, then bail. Before he could get out, along came Kosovo. The experience left him with a profound respect for the men and women who served in the army. In Afghanistan, then Iraq, and two more combat tours in Afghanistan, their valor had left him humbled and awed. Leading troops had been the great experience of his life. The military bureaucracy—full of paper-pushers and desk soldiers angling for promotion—had defeated him when the Holy Warriors could not. He knew he had to get out when he hit twenty years, and he did.

Now he was on the cusp of a horrible dilemma, which he had helped bring on. It looked as if killing some American soldiers might well be on the menu. The hard fact was that if Texas was going to win its freedom, mortal combat was inevitable. If not here, then other places. And the sooner it was done, the sooner the bloodletting would be over.

Combat had taught JR to find strength in God when he doubted if he had enough, and so he prayed a little as the jet lifted off. He had long ago come to grips with his own mortality. He had once written a quotation from Stonewall Jackson in the front of his Bible: "God has fixed the time for my death. I do not concern myself about that, but to be always ready, no matter when it may overtake me. That is the way all men should live, and then all would be equally brave."

Be always ready. Go meet your maker with a clear conscience.

Another lesson he had learned in combat was to sleep whenever possible. He had done all he could, and could make no plans until he knew the situation he faced, so he reclined his seat as far as it would go, leaned his head back, and went to sleep.

THIRTEEN

★

Travis Clay, Willis Coffee, Willie Varner, and I sat in the work area behind the lock shop display room drinking beer and watching television. The front door was locked.

Barry Soetoro was on the tube breathing fire and damnation. Beside him stood General Martin L. Wynette, USA, looking every inch a soldier, with enough ribbons on his chest to decorate the Light Brigade. I had heard that Wynette had actually never heard a shot fired in anger, except for some outgoing artillery barrages fired several miles away, yet he looked fierce and determined, ready to chew nails. I thought it was his square jaw and steely eyes that created that impression, which had taken him far.

Apparently Willie the Wire was also impressed by the general, because he remarked, "He oughta be in movies. Central Casting must have sent him over to the White House."

Soetoro was reading from a teleprompter, as usual. I wondered who wrote his stuff: "...are going to crush the rebellion in Texas. The traitors who survive will be tried for treason. I appeal again to the sane people in Texas to put a stop to the foolishness of the legislature and the governor. They are the ones who will suffer, who will pay for the stupidity of their state officials. The price will be high..."

He went on, telling about the Texas press release reporting the execution of Major Nasruli, the convicted Fort Hood jihadist. To hear Soetoro tell it, the execution was a personal insult to him. "True, Major

Nasruli was awaiting execution, but the timing and manner of that execution, if I allowed it to go forward at all, was at *my* discretion. Many and diverse interests were at stake, including our relationship with many Muslim nations, and my judgment on this matter was rendered a nullity by a Texas National Guard officer who violated federal law. . . ."

He talked some more about the heavy burdens of the presidency, then got back to the sins of Texas. "I have ordered General Wynette to prepare a military response to Texas' blatantly illegal and violent act of secession. We will use the entire might of the federal government to stamp it out, to crush it. We owe the loyal citizens of the nation nothing less. One hundred fifty years ago Texas and other states tore this Union apart in a futile attempt to defend indefensible slavery. Now Texas is tearing this Union apart in order to defend an indefensible, reactionary vision of America that the rest of the country rejects. I can assure you that as president of the United States and commander in chief of the armed forces, I will do my duty as Abraham Lincoln did his, I will not let this stand. I will preserve the Union."

Wynette nodded several times during this rant, almost as if he were whispering amens.

Soetoro took no questions from the gathered reporters, but stepped aside to give Wynette the podium. "You may have heard rumors," Wynette said, "that the commanding generals of a few of the United States military installations in Texas surrendered today. Actually, the facilities were delivered to the enemy by treachery. We are investigating. I promise you that the Benedict Arnolds responsible will be court-martialed for treason. If they are found guilty and given the sentence that the law prescribes for that crime, they will be executed. You may have also heard that some of our soldiers and airmen have joined the enemy's ranks to fight against United States forces. I cannot comment on the truth of that rumor, but I will state that any American soldier, sailor, airman, or Marine who does indeed join the enemy's ranks will be charged with desertion. I remind any member of the American military listening to this broadcast to remember where their loyalty lies.

"We will soon begin military operations against the rebels in Texas. We cannot be responsible for the loss of innocent lives; that responsibility rests with those who have rebelled against the lawful government of the United States and taken up arms against it."

Wynette ducked questions too. He followed Soetoro and Vice President Rhodes back into the bowels of the White House.

"Lots of treachery down in Texas," I remarked.

The network went back to showing footage of the rioting in Baltimore.

"Those scenes were shot at the riot last year," Travis said. "I've seen those shots a dozen times. The TV people get around the censor by showing old footage."

I went over and snapped off the television. I would have used the remote but Willie had laid it somewhere, lost it I suppose.

"They're going to start killing people," Willis Coffee said bitterly. "He isn't even going to negotiate."

"I doubt if Texas would negotiate with him," I remarked. "If you were them, would you negotiate with that megalomaniac?"

"No," Willis admitted.

"I think those folks down in Texas are going to need a lot more killing than Barry Soetoro thinks they will," Travis said softly. "It's that Alamo thing. They get it with their mother's milk. Texas, Texas, Texas, like it's the promised land that God gave them."

"Maybe he did," Willie the Wire muttered. "For sho', he didn't give us anythin' to brag about here in Washington. I wouldn't risk a fingernail for the whole damn district."

We were batting things around when someone knocked on the front door of the lock shop. Willie went to see who it was, and came back with Sarah Houston. She looked particularly delicious that evening in her going-to-work outfit, a nice, knee-length dress with a belt that emphasized her figure. She was shod in a set of black pumps and had her purse over her shoulder.

I introduced her to Willis and Travis. She looked us over and said, "All the usual suspects."

"Want a beer?" Willie asked, ol' Mr. Hospitality.

"No," she said, and looked around for something to sit on. Willie took a box of junk off a chair and arranged it for her. She seated herself, arranged her legs in the required position for female television journalists, and tugged her dress down a millimeter. She placed her purse on the floor beside her. Royalty come to call on the peasants.

"So when are they going to move Jake Grafton?" I asked.

"I don't know. I doubt that it will be any time soon. They are frying other fish. They have a long list of people to arrest and incarcerate. They are working on a list of people who have shot their mouths off on Facebook and other social media."

"So there is no hurry," Travis remarked.

"I wouldn't say that," she said. "The White House classified net is full of e-mails about this right-wing conspiracy, and Jake Grafton is near the head of the list. They're manufacturing evidence, trying to decide the best way to spin it for the public. They're going to try a dozen or so people to justify Soetoro's decision to invoke martial law."

"What about terrorism? All those jihadists Soetoro let in?"

"The FBI is having some difficulty finding a sufficient number. They have their hands on a lot of Soetoro's domestic enemies, and Grafton, so..."

None of us had anything to say to that. If they got Grafton into a federal prison, not just a concentration camp, there was no way we could get him out without an army.

She let that soak into our beetle brains, and then said, "A snatch on the highway isn't going to work. That was Tommy's idea, I think."

I nodded.

"You were also talking about a diversion, Tommy, and I decided the best one was probably to kill the power grid in the northeastern United States."

Willis Coffee's eyes bulged. Travis whistled. I wasn't surprised, knowing as I did how Sarah's mind worked. This was a woman who arranged for a gang of Russian ex-sailors to steal an American attack submarine a few years ago. When Sarah Houston set out to do something, she didn't believe in half measures.

"Holy damn," Willie the Wire said.

"So how in the world are we going to do that?" Willis Coffee demanded.

"We don't have any explosives, and we can't easily lay hands on any," Travis Clay pointed out. "Even if we had a truckload, we can't run around the countryside blowing up a hundred substations."

"Maybe drop a hair dryer in the bathtub," Willie the Wire suggested.

Sarah Houston went on as if she hadn't heard them. "The power grid is stretched to the max in August in the Northeast. It operates at one hundred percent of capacity much of the time running air conditioners and the like. The power companies use computer programs to automatically feed power around problem spots to prevent taking down the net. Computers are cheaper than new power-generation plants. They have hardened that computer system somewhat over the last few years in response to the perceived terrorist threat, but it is still vulnerable. I can put some code into the programs that will make the system default into the problems, not away from them, and that will quickly overload the system and take it down. All over the Northeast. From Cleveland to Maine and down to Cincinnati and Richmond."

We sat in silence digesting that. Finally Willis asked the obvious question. "How are we going to create problems?"

"We are going to have to knock out some key transformers and sub stations. I have compiled a short list of the most critical ones."

He was a sucker. "So how are we going to do that?"

"With explosives," Sarah said matter-of-factly. "Shouldn't take a whole lot, but it will take some. As you may know, most of the federal agencies are stockpiling ammunition at warehouses in secret locations to use against the right-wing conspiracy, or if the locals get rowdy. Also in those warehouses are modest stocks of C-4 and enough tear gas to gas everyone east of the Mississippi. I made a list of the four closest warehouses. One of them is in Leesburg, a huge facility FEMA leased from Walmart."

"So you want us to start by breaking into a warehouse?"

"If you want to give Barry Soetoro a crisis to worry about besides chasing you and Jake Grafton, you are going to have to make it something that really gets his attention."

"Texas might be enough," Travis Clay opined.

"You think?"

"Uh, no."

Willis Coffee said, "Maybe killing the power grid is overkill. Modern cities can't work without electricity. Windows won't open, water pumps won't work, commodes won't flush, elevators won't work, lights won't work, medical equipment won't work, refrigerators won't work, microwaves won't work. Depending on how long the power stays off, some people could starve or die of heat exhaustion or dehydration."

That's when I got into the conversation. "Barry Soetoro has torn up the Constitution. He's going to try a dozen innocent men for a crime he's invented. He's declared war on America. Texas has taken up the gauntlet. Now we must decide if we are willing to fight for America and let the chips fall where they may, or whether we would rather just pull our heads down, tuck our tails between our legs, and let Soetoro and Martin Wynette kill anyone they want. They are going to whack Texas hard. They are going to whack Jake Grafton. And believe me, given half a chance they'll whack us."

They sat staring at each other.

"I was listening to the president on the radio while I drove down here," Sarah Houston said. "I would rather crawl into a hole out of the line of fire, but the fact is we have reached the point in America when it is time to choose a side."

"Jeez," Travis said softly. "So we have to burgle a government warehouse, blow up some power substations, and then break into Camp Dawson and snatch Grafton from under the noses of God knows how many troops and feds. You and your little projects, Tommy."

"Yep," I said heartily. "Gotta choose sides and smell armpits, guys. What say we all go to dinner and think this over before the power goes out. I'm buying."

Willie Varner nearly broke his leg hopping off his stool.

We went to a white-tablecloth restaurant, even though the only one of our group dressed for it was Sarah. She led the way inside and favored the maître d' with a smile, so we were seated in a corner.

"Sorta like the last supper," Willie opined, then asked the waiter, "What's the most expensive Scotch you have on your shelf?"

It was something I'd never heard of.

"I'll take a double of that, neat," my lock shop partner told the waiter, and smiled at me. Sarah ordered a bottle of eighty-four-dollar wine, and my two covert warriors ordered draft beers. I ordered a bourbon on the rocks.

All of us had the sense not to even whisper about our planned operation to spring Grafton, or any of the other mayhem we had planned. We talked about riots and politics and whether Texas could win.

After they had sipped their drinks and studied the menu, Willie ordered the most expensive steak, and Willis Coffee and Travis Clay did the same. I shrugged and ordered one too. Sarah took her time and ordered a piece of bare salmon with some lemon wedges and a small salad.

The bill was going to be a whopper, but I wasn't worried. I planned to use my CIA credit card to pay for it. I figured it would be a week or so until the clerks at Langley got around to turning the card off, and anyway, they could just deduct the amount from my severance pay, which I doubted I would ever get.

I was so tense the liquor hit my stomach hard. I began to feel the glow down there instantly. I sat back in my chair, smiled vacuously, and tried to relax. Some of us were almost certainly going to be dead soon. I wondered if one of them would be me.

When Willie Varner's steak came, it was still bloody. Travis pointed to it and said, "A good vet could have saved that cow."

"Thank God he didn't," Willie said, and stuffed a piece in his mouth.

The copilot woke JR somewhere over west Texas. "General, ATC is off the air. No one on any of their freqs or on El Paso Approach."

"Can you get into the civilian field?"

"We're in solid goo. If the ILS is on the air, no problem. If we have to shoot a GPS approach, we may have to go below minimums, we think."

"Get me on the ground. However you have to do it."

"Yes, sir." The copilot went back to the cockpit.

After another twenty minutes, the plane was maneuvering, answering the controls and responding to throttle input. They came out of the clouds perhaps three hundred feet above the ground, JR estimated.

"Good job," he told the pilots as he was getting out of the plane.

They saluted.

The ramp of the El Paso Fixed Base Operator's executive terminal was packed with planes, most of them jets or turboprops, yet the terminal was almost empty. The place reeked of luxury, with leather-covered sofas, ornate glass coffee tables, big flat-screen televisions, and subdued lighting—perfect for important business executives or people who wanted to think they were important. JR approached the woman standing at the desk, the only human in sight, a cute twenty-something brunette wearing stiletto heels and a little black dress that ended well above her knees.

"What's happening?"

"The airspace is closed to civilian traffic, General. These planes are stranded."

"I need a car."

"All our courtesy and rental cars are gone, sir. The passengers and crews of the planes outside took every one."

"Do you have a mechanic's van?"

"Yes, but—"

"I'll take it. Send for whoever has the keys."

"General—"

"Now."

He wanted to see his old civilian contractor boss Pete Taylor and then look up the local National Guard commander, Wiley Fehrenbach, who was probably at the National Guard armory.

On his drive to Taylor's house, a helicopter flew past. It was an Apache scooting along at perhaps two hundred feet.

He knocked on the door of the house, which was a modest rancher in a modest neighborhood, and Zoe Taylor answered it.

"Oh, JR. Come in."

"No time. Is Pete here?"

"No. The army came for him this afternoon. Arrested him."

"What for?"

"They had a list."

"I see." Lee Parker was following the Jade Helm plan, no doubt on orders from Washington. "Thank you, Zoe."

"Can you talk to them, JR, get him out? People have been talking for over a year about these Jade Helm things, saying it looks as if Soetoro was planning martial law." Tears leaked down her face. "I can't believe this is really happening. It's like a nightmare. Is this still the United States of America?"

"I understand," JR said, and against his better judgment, he added, "I'll do what I can, Zoe."

Tears burst forth and she closed the door.

JR got back in the van and headed for the armory.

The armory was a hive of activity. Bulldozers, generators, trucks, and construction equipment were swarmed by soldiers painting the Texas flag on every flat surface they could find. Plainly, these Texans were willing to fight, but they didn't have a lot of stuff to fight with: this was an engineering battalion. JR parked his mechanic's van in a handicapped spot and went inside.

Wiley Fehrenbach was delighted to see him. He wrung JR's hand and touched the stars on his camos. The pistol belt didn't escape his notice. He was wearing one too.

"I'm in command of the Texas Guard now, Wiley."

"Thank God."

"I need to know what's happening in town and at the base. Everything you know."

"When the news came out about the declaration, the town went wild. They've had it with the federal government. Martial law really ticked them off, then the gun thing. This morning civilian patrols started rounding up illegals and pushing them to the border crossings. The ICE people there tried to stop them, but they were surrounded and disarmed and told to disappear. Civilians shut down the border crossings. Only

Mexican nationals can cross going south. All the trucks waiting to cross are lined up—someone said the line is two miles long already."

"Okay."

"Our people came here as fast as they could this morning. I issued weapons, and it's a good thing I did. Some colonel and ten army troopers with weapons showed up at ten this morning and wanted to secure all the weapons and send everyone home. I refused, and since they were outnumbered twenty to one, they climbed into their car and left. They'll be back, and it's going to be bloody. My troops won't surrender. Right now, though, I think the army is out arresting civilians. They want all those Republic of Texas people who have been shouting for independence for years. They've arrested all of them they could find, plus newspaper people, the television and radio people, the sheriff, anyone who is anybody. It's all rumors, but everyone heard something and they're buzzing. Looks like they've opened the Jade Helm playbook and are going down the checklist."

"Where are they taking the prisoners?"

"They have some railroad cars equipped with shackles on base. The army got them ready during the last Jade Helm exercise." JR already knew about the railcars with shackles, which had been hot news and stoked the rumors about martial law being planned. "No one knows for certain," Wiley Fehrenbach said, "but probably there."

"Are you sure your troops will fight?"

"'I talked to them this morning. Told anyone that couldn't in good conscience fight for Texas to turn in his weapons and leave. Less than ten percent did. We're Texans and that's that."

"What's the situation out at Fort Bliss?"

"It's on lockdown. Only U.S. Army soldiers admitted. I've had people out watching the gates, and as near as we can figure, a lot of the soldiers living in town haven't gone in. Maybe a hundred went in since we started watching, all told. You know there are maybe ten thousand soldiers living in town, so that's good."

"Yes," JR agreed.

"Parker ordered the television and radio stations shut down this morning, and all the phones and the internet are off. Electricity and water are still on, but who knows for how long."

"You need to get some troopers out to the water plant as soon as possible."

"Already sent a squad."

"Good man."

"It looks as if Parker has troopers patrolling the fences around the main part of the base, but you know how big Bliss is. I doubt anyone is out on the fence in the boonies. I don't know what Parker has planned, but no one has been back to get our weapons, so maybe he has some loyalty troubles. A lot of soldiers may have refused to fire on fellow Americans."

JR Hays rubbed his head and tried to concentrate upon the problem. As he looked out the window, he realized the day was almost gone. It was twilight outside, under a gloomy sky. He heard another helicopter shoot overhead. With night-vision goggles, they could see everything that moved on the streets below.

Wiley Fehrenbach read his thoughts. "Supposed to get some thunderstorms in here soon. How soon, I don't know. Maybe that will ground the choppers. I didn't think it wise to deploy my people until they were grounded or had left."

"I have four helos coming in from Fort Hood. They're supposed to land at the civilian airfield. Send some armed troops to meet them. Do you have some handheld radios? Our pilots will need them." The truth was, he thought wryly, he should have thought of that before they left Fort Hood. Maybe he was too tired, or maybe he wasn't thinking clearly.

"Sure." They discussed frequencies and JR made notes. A female sergeant appeared, and he handed her a note that contained a freq, told her about the helos, and sent her off with five enlisted soldiers carrying M4s and four radios with fully charged batteries.

After they left, JR said, "Wiley, our long-term objective is to take that base. We need all the military equipment they have and all the people who will fight for Texas." He tried to visualize General Lee Parker's situation. A lot of his soldiers had stayed home. The base, with base housing running right up to the perimeter fence, was basically indefensible. If Parker had any sense, he would arrange his tanks and loyal troopers into a strong defensive position where the tanks could cover each other and his artillery could provide support. Parker's helicopters were already patrolling, searching for threats.

Parker must be very worried, JR thought, wondering if his troops would fight. No doubt he was sending messages as quickly as he could dictate them to Washington, requesting instructions. These messages would go out over the army communications net, which was radio. JR doubted that Parker would do anything without orders from Washington. Then he would move slowly, carefully.

He and Wiley Fehrenbach discussed the situation as night fell. JR didn't want a battle, but he suspected he was going to get one before long. Eight hundred or so National Guardsmen in this armory were the only organized military unit in the area, so Washington would eventually tell Parker to take the armory. Parker outnumbered the guardsmen at least ten to one and had enough armor and artillery to invade Mexico and take Mexico City.

"Will U.S. soldiers fight Texans?" JR whispered to the gods, who didn't answer back.

"Food?" Wiley asked.

JR hadn't eaten since breakfast, which seemed like years ago. "Hell, yes."

He was soon handed a paper plate with three hot dogs in buns smothered in chili, along with a plastic knife and spoon and a bottle of water. JR found he was ravenous.

He had just started on the first hot dog when the radio on the desk came to life. It was "Milestone One Six," the senior army aviator, who was flying a Blackhawk—CWO-4 Erik Sabiston, Sabby to his friends.

"JR, we're fueling at the FBO at El Paso International. Weather is turning to crap. We flew at a hundred feet to get in here."

JR answered, "Fort Bliss has Apaches on patrol. Be careful, but I want you to do a recon over the base. I need to know what they're up to. Can you do that?"

"Yes, sir. As soon as we finish fueling. Maybe fifteen minutes."

"I'd like to know if there are any units from Bliss out on the street. Your primary mission, though, is to shoot up everything on the flight line at Fort Bliss. Here are the coordinates. Ready to copy?"

"Go."

JR read them off, and Sabiston read them back. "We know the base," he said. "Trained there many times."

JR ended with an admonition. "Shoot and get out, Sabby. Hit them as hard as you can but don't be a hero. We need to deny them the sky."

"Yes, sir."

JR attacked the food on his plate and said to Wiley Fehrenbach, "They're going to come looking for you people sooner or later. You are going to have to abandon the armory. What do you have in the way of munitions?"

"Dynamite, of course. Locked in vaults out back. And a couple hundred AT4s. Maybe a dozen .30-caliber machine guns. Ammo and grenades."

JR felt a bit better. AT4s were handheld, single-shot anti-tank weapons. They came with the rocket pre-installed and could not be reloaded, so they were discarded after use. They weighed about five and a half pounds each and fired a rocket with a 1.6 pound HEAT warhead, HEAT standing for high explosive anti-tank. The rocket was marginal against an Abrams, which had the finest tank armor in the world, unless the rocket took a tread off or was fired into the rear, where the armor was thinnest. It was better against Bradley Infantry Fighting Vehicles and whatever other version of the armored personnel carrier 1st Armor had. It was hell on unarmored vehicles, such as trucks, or buildings.

JR said, "Get the explosives out of here. Ammo, weapons, radios, whatever you need, let's get it gone as soon as possible."

"Yes, sir."

"Get some people with AT4s out to El Paso International. Sooner or later Parker will send a tank column to occupy it. Tonight it is our airport. Let's get cracking."

FOURTEEN

★

Governor Jack Hays was in uncharted political territory. He had to deal with threats from the federal government, demands for interviews from newspaper and television reporters, and the myriad of details that had to be addressed and resolved to turn Texas from a state into a nation. He had the leaders of the legislature in his office all morning while he sought consensus on a wide range of issues: the republic's assumption of U.S. debt held by Texas banks and financial institutions; the issuance of currency by the new republic; collection of federal taxes by the republic; payment of federal pensions and closing the Mexican border; and organizing a system of civil defense that had been pretty much dormant since the end of the 1960s since the feds were threatening military action against targets in Texas. No one knew if that would entail mass bombing of cities, but it certainly might.

One other thing happened that afternoon that would have far-reaching consequences, not only in Texas and throughout America, but around the world. Barry Soetoro announced that legislation would be introduced in Congress to phase in a completely electronic currency and retire all paper money. The implications were unstated but obvious: the federal government could control or confiscate anyone's wealth, whether it was corporate, individual, or nonprofit. A more effective way of whipping people into line probably could not be devised. Instead of locking up people, the federal government could simply take their money. Part of it or all of the loot could be used to fund the federal deficit, recapitalize banks, pay off political friends, or all of the above. Passage of the legislation was a foregone conclusion because the president's bitterest political enemies were already incarcerated, which helped cow the rest.

Within seconds of the announcement, precious metals prices on the world's commodity exchanges took off like a rocket. Within a minute, trading limits had been reached and trading was suspended. Hours later, the government announced that all trading in precious metals was suspended indefinitely.

Texas was already committed to moving from U.S. currency as quickly as possible, but now the urgency became stark. It also hardened the resolve of those legislators who were still unsure they had done the right thing by declaring independence.

The legislators demanded that the governor make a televised speech to the legislature at midnight tonight, and Jack Hays agreed. When he was going to sort out his ideas on what he might say he didn't know. He assumed he was going to have to speak impromptu, which might be disastrous if he came across as tired, harassed, scared, or uncertain of the course of the new nation. He asked his speechwriters to consult with Ben Steiner and draft some talking points.

In the meantime, Jack Hays had an interview with the Mexican consul, Fernando Ferrante. They had a good working relationship, but Ferrante was not inclined to listen politely to protests of Mexican government policy, allegations of corruption, or complaints about illegal immigration and drug smuggling. His job, Ferrante said, was to smooth the flow of trade, not to advise the Mexican leadership on how to run the government.

"As you know, Señor, we are embarking on a war with the United States to win our freedom," Jack Hays began. "Unfortunately, we cannot guarantee the safety of Mexican nationals, nor the protection of civil commerce. Consequently Texas must temporarily close the border between Texas and Mexico."

Ferrante was sitting up straight. More than $90 billion in Mexican imports passed through Texas every year. A lesser amount, an estimated $60 to $70 billion, passed through Texas on the way to Mexico. In addition, Mexicans in the United States legally and illegally sent home hundreds of millions of dollars a year—for some families, it marked the difference between poverty and starvation.

Jack Hays lowered the boom. "It is very unfortunate, but for the moment we have no choice but to shut down all financial transactions transferring money into, out of, or through the new nation of Texas."

Ferrante protested. Hays cut him off. "I know this will be a severe hardship to people south of the border. It will be an even greater hardship to Texans as we sever our commercial and financial relationships with the people and businesses of the other forty-nine American states. I wouldn't even suggest such a course were it not absolutely necessary."

The Mexican consul tugged thoughtfully at his lip. "May I smoke?" he asked.

"Of course," Hays said, and produced an ashtray from a desk drawer.

When Ferrante had a cigarette alight, Hays continued. "Since we cannot guarantee anyone's safety, we're asking Mexican nationals to leave Texas as soon as possible, and I'm asking you to let Texans in Mexico return to Texas."

"What about the citizens of other American states?"

"If they cannot prove Texas residency, they will be refused entry."

Ferrante was shocked. He took a moment to organize his thoughts, then said, "Factories producing goods for export are the economic bedrock of the Mexican economy. Shutting them down for any significant period, more than a weekend, gives the drug cartels more recruits. People *must* feed their families."

"Mexico is in a hell of a hole," the Texan acknowledged, "that you folks dug for yourselves. Mexico has dumped its problems on us for a great many years."

"Mexico is a democracy," the Mexican diplomat shot back, "and elected politicians cannot ignore the will of our proud, poor people. It is in Texas' best interest that Mexico remain a democracy governed by the rule of law. A fascist dictatorship on your southern border will create many more problems in Texas than it will solve. You have a phrase: don't throw us under the bus. While you and your government are making policy, do not forget that the United States is the world's largest, richest market for recreational drugs of all kinds. Your 'War on Drugs' has been an abject failure. We are in the unfortunate position of being next-door neighbors to this hedonistic hell of addicts and abusers with too much money and not a shred of honor."

"I know, and I agree that a great many federal programs, including the 'War on Drugs' and the 'War on Poverty,' to name just two, were ill-conceived or abject failures," Jack Hays replied. "But we're going to change that. The Republic of Texas is no longer going to be a pawn for feckless politicians in Washington who play to the mobs elsewhere and ignore the real problems we face here. We hope to be a better neighbor to the Republic of Mexico, but both our nations need to get our houses in order."

"When will Texas cease to isolate itself and resume free trade with my country?"

Jack Hays engaged in a diplomatic lie. He planned on using trade as a weapon to force the Mexicans to stop illegal immigration, or at least to choke it down on their side of the border, and to crack down on the drug cartels and corrupt officials. He thought Mexico needed to clean the sty with a fire hose. Without Mexican help, the problems of the border would never be solved. Trade was the only issue that would force Mexico to change, Hays thought. At least he hoped it would, because it was the only big lever he had. He didn't voice this opinion, however, but said, "As soon as our position with the other American states stabilizes. I cannot foretell the future. A week, a month, a year..."

"Would Texas consider lifting this trade embargo if Mexico recognizes the new Republic of Texas?"

"That would certainly help," Jack Hays said warmly. "In fact, it would be a precondition."

The governor's answer committed him to nothing, a fact that did not escape the consul, who merely said, "Our conversation will be passed along to my government, of course. When I receive their instructions, I will call you to arrange an appointment to discuss matters."

Hays stood, signifying the interview was over. He escorted Ferrante out of the office and reception area, which was packed with people all wanting a few minutes of his time.

One of the people was Charlie Swim.

Swim was an ally that Jack Hays absolutely had to have, so he lightly grasped his elbow, escorted him into the office, and closed the door.

"Sit down, Charlie, please."

Charlie Swim did so and took a folded sheet of paper from an inside pocket of his jacket. "Governor, we've got a marvelous opportunity to finally do something positive for poor people in Texas." He tapped the paper and then passed it across the desk.

As the governor scanned it, Swim explained. "Liberal progressive policies for the last fifty years or so have devastated the poor people of America. Welfare; aid to dependent families; food stamps; essentially free medical care; schools that try to prepare everyone for a four-year college degree, when only a fraction of the poor people will ever want or get one; lack of technical training; the breakdown of the black family—all those things have led us to where we are.

"When Lyndon Johnson was lobbying Congress to pass his Great Society programs, he reportedly said, 'If we pass this the niggers will all vote Democratic for the next two centuries.' I don't know if he said that, but that has been the consequence. People do whatever it takes to get free money, because without an education and job opportunity they can't make it in America. We have to change that or we won't want to live in the poor socialist empire that will result."

Jack Hays sighed and pointed out, "Luwanda Harris and her Democratic allies will be outraged, accuse you and me of abandoning the poor people to exploitation and starvation, or worse."

"I know that. Medicine often tastes bad, but until we fix the government policies that breed poverty, we have condemned the poor, black, white, and brown to a life of economic slavery. Goddamn, Jack, a hundred fifty years after Lincoln and the Union Army freed the slaves, we're still enslaved! Enslaved to the government! If there is to be a new life, a better life, for the poor people of Texas it has to start here and now. We can't waste another hour."

Jack Hays read the note, which was Swim's political wish list, a libertarian charter for abolishing everything from public employee unions to welfare to the minimum wage.

"Why do you want to repeal the minimum wage?" Jack Hays asked.

"Without trade and technical training our supply of unskilled workers is limitless," Charlie Swim explained. "We are awash in illegals. Every economist I have talked to tells me that the minimum wage really means that unskilled labor cannot be hired and trained unless they can immediately contribute to their employer the minimum wage and the value of their benefits, plus an amount sufficient to pay for supervision and the expenses of doing the paperwork they require, such as payroll, deductions, and the rest of it. All that, plus a profit. The higher the minimum wage, the greater economic incentive for employers to automate or move jobs out of the country. We are *never* going to get wages up unless we let the free market determine the value of labor. Stopping the flow of illegals into Texas and getting some of them to leave will help. But as long as our schools turn out nothing but an endless supply of hamburger flippers and nail techs, industry goes begging for skilled labor and the free market can't work."

Jack Hays kept Charlie talking for another fifteen minutes, looked at his watch, and knew he had to come to a decision.

The governor looked Charlie Swim in the eye. "The legislature will never pass most of these things, and right now you and I lack the political capital to even push them hard. My suggestion is that you pick the most important thing on the list and push just that. For example, education reform. We need a public education system that trains people for the jobs we have and are going to see in the foreseeable future. That we can sell, maybe."

"We need that and a lot more."

"We can't change the world in a week, a month, or even a year. We have to convince the voters we are advocating needed change. If you draft education reform as a war measure and tell every delegate and senator I'm for it, and shepherd it through, I'll sign it if they don't committee it to death or amend it beyond recognition. Tell them Texas can't afford to waste valuable education dollars. Right now we need every able-bodied Texan without a job to enlist in the National Guard. But when our future is secure, we need an educational system in place that will prepare people for good jobs, veterans, high school kids, everyone."

Swim jumped out of his chair and shook the governor's hand. "Thanks, Jack."

"Thank me after I sign it. Now go get at it."

At ten that night the war began in earnest. Two cruise missiles smashed into one of the main power plants in the Houston area, leaving a section of the city without electrical power. No doubt similar strikes would soon be forthcoming for power generation facilities all over Texas. Hospitals and key public institutions had to have emergency generating facilities up and running as soon as possible and be prepared to handle mass casualties. The director of emergency preparedness, Billy Rob Smith, left the governor's office on the run in company with Lieutenant Governor Bullet G. Fitzroy. Jack Hays had already loaded Fitzroy with more tasks than the man could conceivably handle, but Fitzroy had a background as an executive at a large conglomerate and knew how to prioritize, delegate, and supervise.

Ben Steiner remarked to Jack Hays that they would soon find out what Texans were made of.

Sluggo Sweatt, the president's man, sent for Jake Grafton, and within a few minutes he was escorted into the office where he had been interrogated. Grafton, like all the prisoners, was now clad in a red one-piece jumpsuit. That morning all the prisoners had been lined up, required to take off their civilian clothes, and issued jumpsuits. It wasn't that the authorities thought any of them could escape; the jumpsuits were designed to lower their morale and emphasize their status as prisoners.

Sweatt addressed him. "Mr. Grafton—you notice that I don't call you Director Grafton or Admiral Grafton, because you are no longer entitled to either honorific—are you ready to talk sense and sign a confession?"

"No," Jake Grafton said and dropped into a chair.

"Stand up when I talk to you," Sweatt said sharply. Jake did so.

"Your wife, Callie, and daughter, Amy—have you heard from them?"

"Yes."

"Your cell phone, please." Sluggo held out his hand.

Jake removed it from the pocket of his jumpsuit and passed it across. Sluggo played with it a moment. He called up the numbers and jotted them down.

Allowing detainees, or prisoners, to retain their cell phones was counterintuitive, but Sluggo and his friends knew precisely what they were doing. Prisoners could make and receive calls from their friends, or anyone else. The prisoners would tell their sad tales and fear would spread like a hothouse fungus. Friends on the outside would soon cease to reach out to the prisoners, who would quickly become psychologically isolated.

Finally Sluggo slid the phone back across the desk. Jake didn't reach for it.

"Three more people have confessed their roles in the plot to kill the president and take over the government. They implicated you. Swore that you knew, that they had discussed key items of the plan with you on several occasions."

The assassination of the president was a new wrinkle on the coup, Grafton noted sourly. When he said nothing, Sweatt added, "The prosecutors are thinking of asking for the death penalty for you."

Still no response.

Sluggo Sweatt sighed. "Well, I've done all I can for you. I've told you the situation. You need to go back to your tent and think about your future. A confession would keep you alive."

Jake stood totally relaxed.

"Take the phone."

Jake pocketed it, and Sweatt nodded to the man behind Grafton, who took his arm and led him out.

He thought that the next time they brought him in the rough stuff would start, physical abuse, and threats against his family.

Jake Grafton knew that most men can be broken if the captors have the time to create enough pain. He didn't know if he was one of those rare men who could summon the inner strength to resist to the death, but he hoped—make that prayed—he was. Many years ago when he flew combat missions over enemy country in constant danger of being shot down, he had made up his mind to never surrender. Ever. Sluggo might make him prove it.

As he walked through the compound, he wondered what Sluggo Sweatt knew about the shenanigans at the White House.

The compound was crowded now. Jake estimated there were about two thousand people milling around. He recognized at least three congressmen and two senators. And then he saw someone whose face he knew well: Sal Molina, the president's right-hand political op. Now, apparently, his former political op. Wearing a red jumpsuit.

"Well, well, well," Grafton said as Molina recognized him. "Fancy meeting you here."

Molina turned his back on Grafton, who grabbed an arm and spun him around. That was when he realized tears were leaking from Molina's eyes.

"Did the hard-liners throw you out of the inner sanctum?" Grafton asked roughly. "Or did you just decide you needed a summer vacation courtesy of the taxpayers?"

Molina's Adam's apple went up and down a few times. "Texas insulted Soetoro with their Declaration of Independence. He took it real personal. Since I'm from Texas and have relatives there, he decided he didn't want me around."

"Can't say that I blame him."

"I tried to warn you, Jake."

"So you did."

After they had eaten dinner, some kind of stew with a little hamburger in it, Jake Grafton, Sal Molina, and Jack Yocke, the *Washington Post*'s erstwhile columnist, settled under Grafton's favorite tree. The ground was damp from a morning shower, but they could talk in semiprivacy here, something they couldn't do elsewhere, not even in the latrine, which consisted of rows of commodes with no stalls.

Yocke rattled off the latest news, gleaned from his cell phone; Grafton and Molina made few comments. Then Yocke asked Sal Molina point-blank, "So what's the big plan over at the White House? I'll bet they almost creamed their pants when the Saturday terrorists went hog wild."

"I don't know," Molina replied.

"You lying bastard. They've been planning martial law for years. Some people have even suggested Soetoro's boys gave the terrorists the weapons."

"That isn't true."

"But Schanck and Al Grantham jumped all over it, didn't they?"

"Is this off the record?"

"Oh, lighten up, dude. Like I'm going over the fence tonight and this interview will be in the *Post* tomorrow."

"They might eventually let you out."

"Might?"

"*Might*. Maybe after Soetoro drops dead of old age or cancer or something."

"Answer the question, Sal," Grafton prompted.

Molina took a deep breath and looked around for eavesdroppers. Finally he said in a low voice, "Yes. They told the president he had to do it. It would be unpopular, but martial law was the only way to save the progressive revolution. Soetoro loved it. This was his chance to change the course of history, to save the planet. The bastard has a messianic complex."

"He's got a lot of complexes," Jake Grafton muttered.

"More than you can imagine. For example, Barry and Mickey do S and M. She's a dominatrix. I guess he needs it, although don't ask me why. They didn't talk about that kind of stuff in psych class when I went to college."

"Hell, that's old news," Yocke scoffed. "For seven years I've heard rumors that Soetoro is gay. People have even accused him of being a gay prostitute when he was younger, servicing old queens for drugs."

Grafton asked Yocke, "So how come your fine newspaper hasn't investigated these rumors about Soetoro?"

"The editors don't think that crap is news," the *Post*'s man explained. "They're liberals. Some of them are gay, and for all I know some of them are swingers or dig S and M. Soetoro is liberal and black. He gets a pass. Now if he were some white Republican presidential candidate, they'd have had reporters investigate every day of his life from the moment his mom popped him out. You'd be reading about spitwads he threw in second grade and how many hours of detention hall he got in junior high." Yocke made a gesture dismissing the whole subject.

After a pause he asked Molina, "So why does Soetoro want to frame Grafton for plotting an assassination?"

"Spymasters are good villains," Molina explained. "They do a lot of secret shit they can never tell about, so people will believe almost any accusation. And the president doesn't like Grafton. And, of course, right-wing plots give the public something to talk about instead of terrorism and jihad in America. And S and M. Matt Drudge got the story from some Secret Service guy and was trying to get confirmation when a White House maid ratted him out. Still, Drudge might have broken the story anyway, so Soetoro had that hanging over his head when the terrorists did their thing. That helped push Soetoro to martial law now."

"He doesn't like a lot of people," Yocke replied. "Is he going to frame them all?"

"Oh no. He's just going to lock them up in concentration camps. Hitler and Stalin wrote the playbook."

"I suppose they grabbed Matt Drudge."

"He was locked up before the declaration. He's in solitary someplace. Drudge isn't the *Washington Post*; he would have run the story."

"So you're telling me that we're sitting in a concentration camp and the United States is about to bomb Texas because Soetoro is a pervert?"

"That's about the size of it. As my old Marxist professors used to say, 'The personal is the political.'"

★

We were leaving the restaurant when Sarah Houston said to me, "Are you going to sleep at the lock shop tonight?"

"Yes, unless I get a better offer."

"I feel the need for your manly presence to reassure me," she said.

"That's a better offer."

In the parking lot we agreed to meet at the lock shop tomorrow morning at eight. "This is it, guys," I told them. "Bring whatever you need for the op. I have no idea when we'll be back."

"After Barry Soetoro is dead," Travis Clay said gloomily.

"Christmas, maybe," Willis Coffee offered.

"The Fourth of July," Willie the Wire chimed in. "Bring an extra set of underwear."

On that note we parted.

Back at Sarah's place, she fixed drinks, Grand Marnier this time. "I didn't know you kept this stuff around," I remarked.

"For the road," she told me, and lifted her glass.

In bed she whispered, "You know we will probably all soon be dead."

"No one lives forever." That was a stupid remark. I sounded brave, which was a lie. Bravery is not on my short list of virtues. I'm anything but.

"I want more of this," she said.

"Me too," I agreed. The hell with it. Live today…

Wiley Fehrenbach and JR Hays decided to welcome any contingent that came to take the El Paso National Guard armory with a little ambush, then the ambushers would evade. Washington was probably lighting a fire under Lee Parker, so it was just a matter of time before he sent troops to the armory. This time it wouldn't be ten troopers and a colonel. This time he'd send the first team, some tanks, and maybe an infantry company, all with orders to shoot to kill.

Army Apache helicopters were already circling the area. Armed with Hellfire missiles and rockets, they could incinerate any vehicle, and their Gatling guns were hell on exposed troops.

The Apaches were the reason the Guard hadn't moved from the compound all day. Let the army open the ball, Wiley Fehrenbach and JR Hays reasoned, while they waited for the Fort Hood helicopters that were the equalizers. Every minute brought them closer.

JR was in Fehrenbach's office. He heard thunder and watched lightning from the window. A soldier rushed in; three colonels followed.

"Sir," the soldier blurted. "Four tanks and four Bradleys are coming out the main gate of Fort Bliss."

Wiley Fehrenbach looked at his colonels and said, "You know what to do."

The colonels saluted, "Yes, sir!"

"Wait!" JR roared. He got on a handheld radio. "Milestone One Six, this is JR."

"One Six, go ahead."

JR could hear the engine; the Blackhawk was airborne.

"At least four tanks and four Bradleys are coming from Fort Bliss, probably headed toward the armory. We need you to take out any airborne Apaches you can find, over."

"Can do."

"Leave the stuff on the ground to us. Over."

"One Six copies. Out."

"Some of those Apaches are ours, along with a Blackhawk," JR told the colonels. "Don't let your men shoot at a helicopter unless they are absolutely sure it's the enemy. Now go."

For the first time that day, JR felt optimistic. Lee Parker had dithered too long.

He got more news when a trooper announced, "We're destroying the decryption gear, sir, so the army doesn't get it." JR nodded, and the trooper handed him a batch of messages from Camp Mabry.

The first was from Loren Snyder: "She can be moved. I'm searching for men."

Another, from Elvin Gentry: "Dyess surrendered. Airplanes, weapons depot, and fuel facilities not sabotaged. Am recruiting crews. Awaiting further orders."

FIFTEEN

★

Lightning was flashing from the clouds and gusts of rain and wind were pounding on the Blackhawk as it ran at a hundred feet above the housetops toward the El Paso National Guard armory, the coordinates of which the crew had punched into their GPS systems. The Blackhawk rocked and rolled in the turbulence. Fortunately the myriad lights of the city were still on, houses alight, street lights, traffic on the boulevards, so they had a good ground reference. Two Apaches were behind the Blackhawk, one on the right, one on the left.

If the city had been blacked out, Sabiston would have kept his crews on the ground. Still, they could go into inadvertent IFR conditions at any moment if some of this cloud dripped toward the ground, or if they hit a column of rain, or if the ground rose up into a cloud. If they flew under a thunderstorm, with its river of cold air descending out the bottom, all bets would be off: It would be all the pilots could do to keep their machines from being driven into the ground. Or a house. Or a school. Or a telephone pole. Of course, the same held true for the army pilots in their Apaches. Sabiston was listening on the Fort Bliss air traffic frequencies, trying to discover how many of their Apaches were airborne.

It sounded like only one base Apache was still airborne, and the pilot was bitching about the weather. "I gotta get on the ground," he told the tower.

Sabiston keyed the intercom to talk to his copilot. "Good news. Only one enemy Apache in the air, and he wants to come down. So what do ya think?"

The copilot, who was from Albany, New York, keyed his mike and replied, "We are fucking crazy. Once more into the suck. Will Texas pay our widows death benefits?"

One of the Apaches behind him keyed the radio. "Sabby, I got him on infrared. Clear to the left."

The copilot initiated a turn. They were almost on the housetops. Flying a helicopter was an unforgiving art, and in filthy weather this close to the ground, it attained the level of black magic.

The Apache behind them came abreast, accelerating. The Apache was an attack helicopter, manned by a crew of two seated in tandem. The pilot sits in the rear seat, the copilot/weapons operator, or gunner, sits in the front. Both were usually rated pilots and both had controls to fly the machine, but in combat the front-seater operated the sensors and aimed and fired the weapons, which included a chain gun under the fuselage and whatever rockets or missiles were loaded for the mission. It was designed to provide close air support to infantry, armor, and artillery, and it did it well.

The Apache gunner had his target in sight; the chain gun sent a finger of fire shooting across the gloom.

The target absorbed two seconds' worth of 30-mm, then, with its tail rotor gone, lost control and tilted sideways, rotating viciously, then went into the ground and exploded.

Erik Sabiston saw the flash of the explosion in his night-vision goggles.

"The base," he told the copilot. "Turn toward it."

They turned right. The base was lit up with streetlights, house lights, lights in parking lots. Tanks and artillery were bunched up, parked in a large grass area behind the exchange, facing the main gate.

"Go down the flight line," Sabby said.

They got lost once, flying just over the tops of the buildings, then miraculously they saw the field dead ahead: Blackhawks, Apaches, and a few old Chinooks were lined up in rows illuminated by floodlights on poles. They should have at least turned the lights off.

"I have the controls," Sabby said. He turned the Blackhawk and pulled the nose up, bleeding off airspeed dramatically. When he was down to fifty knots, he straightened out, about fifty feet from the ground, and flew between the two rows closest to the hangar. He spoke on the intercom to the door gunners. "Shoot 'em up, guys."

The gunners fired one-second bursts at each target. One helicopter caught fire. *Brap*, *brap*, *brap*, the gunners worked methodically; the noise bursts were out of sync. Another Apache in the line caught fire.

"Some ground fire from the hangars," the copilot said, and within seconds a hole appeared in the right front quarter of their windshield. It was a strange feeling, being fired on intentionally by Americans.

When they finished the line, Sabiston accelerated and turned to fly back to El Paso International. No warning lights on the panel. All systems looked normal. "Any damage in back?" he asked his crew chief.

"Don't think so. I'll inspect." He turned the controls over to the copilot, then flipped freqs and got on the radio to JR Hays, who needed to know about the disposition of the base armor and artillery.

The Apache flown by Harvey Williston was following the Blackhawk down the line. "I have the target," his gunner said. Dustin Bonner, from Tupelo, Mississippi, was the gunner. Earlier, Dustin was wondering if he had made the right decision signing on with the Texas Guard. There was going to be a lot of flying, a lot of shooting, and a lot of dying done before this thing was over. Maybe, he thought, he should have sneaked back to Mississippi and got back to playing blues guitar and working on his uncle's catfish farm. One thing was sure, there was a future in catfish. Being a gunner on an Apache in the middle of a shooting war, not so much.

Certainly not when you were flying in a helicopter in shitty weather like this. Even if the bad guys didn't whack you, Mother Nature might. He fired rockets at the first few helicopters in the third row, which look undamaged. Three of them were obscured by the warhead's blast. Locked up a TOW wire-guided missile and launched it. Another. Then he was aiming the 30-mm M230 chain gun mounted on the fuselage between the landing gear. He pulled the trigger, moving from parked chopper to chopper.

The Apache flown by Mike Berk from Bemidji, Minnesota, followed along behind, with Mike's gunner doing the dirty work. Despite soldiers sheltered behind hangar doors taking pot shots, there was no opposition. First Armored had not yet got it into their collective heads that they were in a war. They'd figure it out pretty soon, though, so the next trip down the flight line wasn't going to be as pretty. Ahead of him he saw Williston turn left. "Follow me, Mike. Hellfires into the hangars. You have the one on the right, I'll take the left."

The two attack helicopters made a sweeping 270-degree turn as lightning flashed and rain came in waves, under that low ceiling, until they were lined up. The ramp lights were off by then—someone had gotten to the switches. It didn't matter to the Apaches, which had night-vision and infrared sensors that allowed the crew to fly and employ their weapons as if it were high noon on a cloudless day. The gunners fired the Hellfire missiles through the open hangar doors, and the explosions caused at least one fire that they could see.

Then the two Apaches swept away southward toward El Paso International.

Wiley Fehrenbach worked feverishly with his officers and NCOs to get their stuff loaded and out of the Guard's compound. When the trucks were rolling, men jumped in their cars and left as fast as they could get out of the garage. The last of the cars were still pouring from the parking lot when the tanks rolled into view.

The tanks stopped, then the Bradleys behind them. Only when the parking lot was empty did the tanks move forward again, carefully.

From his vantage down the street three blocks, JR Hays and two volunteer troopers watched the tanks and Bradleys go by. JR had an AT4 under his right arm and an M4 carbine on a sling across his back. One of the troopers was also carrying an AT4, an extra, just in case.

Before they left the armory, JR asked the young guardsmen, "Have either of you ever actually fired an AT4?"

"No, sir," each of them said.

"Then you get to watch me miss tonight. Your job is to act as lookouts, to ensure we don't get jumped by scouts."

But to JR's amazement, there were no scouts. This was *America*, for Christ's sake, not Baghdad or Mosul or some other squalid Arab town. Well, the soldiers would learn. And fast. The next time the Guard tried this, it wouldn't be so easy.

JR decided he would try for a Bradley when the troopers had reembarked and were headed back to base. Patrols looking for guerillas or hidden troops took manpower. A constant low-level threat also took a toll on morale. JR knew because he had done his tours in the Middle East.

JR found a basement stairwell to hide in, and took the extra antitank rocket.

"If you see a scout, open up, force him to take cover, then scatter to the rendezvous point. Tonight's goal is to ratchet up their fear a notch. You got that?"

"Yes, sir."

Both these young troopers looked to be about twenty years old, but they were game. Given time, they would be good soldiers. Time. That's what JR had to buy them by arranging some serious air attacks on the 1st Armored. Fuel storage tanks were probably the top priority if he could get some planes in the air carrying bombs. Without fuel, 1st Armored was going nowhere.

With just the top of his camo cap showing, JR watched the troops set up a perimeter around the armory, with tanks on the four corners. Bradleys each carried six troopers, so that meant there were twenty-four troopers out there afoot, searching and guarding and looking to shoot the first man they saw with a gun.

Time passed. Perhaps a half hour. The idling tanks were surprisingly quiet. The thunderstorm drifted off to the east and the wind was just a zephyr.

Finally JR realized they had fired the armory. Probably by pouring gasoline around. Some of the windows must have been broken or shattered on their own, because soon smoke was oozing around the lights on poles around the place and the lights illuminating the parking lot. He hoped the fire department had the sense to stay in the station tonight.

He checked his sentries, who were out of sight. Waited.

Waiting was the hardest part, he thought. You never get used to it. You wait for everything in the army, literally everything. Take a number, soldier. Or get in line. Then in combat, you wait some more. Wait to shoot and wait to die.

Finally, with visible fire coming from three of the armory windows, the Abrams tanks started snorting and moving. Two of them led off up the street.

JR Hays ignored them and watched the troopers return to the Bradleys. The Bradleys lined up; two tanks guarded the rear of the column.

Darn.

Picking up his AT4 and the spare, JR scuttled out of his hidey hole—he didn't want to be there if the tank or Bradleys cut loose. The Abrams main battle tank was a formidable foe. Equipped with a 120-mm gun, a .50-caliber machine gun, and two .30-caliber machine guns, it was a rolling sixty-ton fortress protected by massive armor. Quite simply, the M1A1 Abrams was the finest tank on planet earth.

The Bradley was also armored, more lightly than a tank, but for protection it did have a nice 25-mm gun that fired up to two hundred rounds a minute. Twenty-five millimeters meant the shells were about an inch in diameter. Throwing three of those monsters every second, the gun could shred buildings, vehicles, and people very nicely, thank you, at terrific ranges.

JR took up a new position, partially hidden by a corner of a building. He laid his spare AT4 on the ground against the building. The lead pair of tanks clattered past JR at perhaps eight to ten miles per hour. He turned on the battery in the AT4. Now the Bradleys came, in formation, at the same speed. Kneeling, JR glanced at the trailing tank, then sprinted forward to get a square shot at the rear of the last Bradley. He kneeled, pushed the safety button forward, quickly made sure he had the crosshairs where he wanted them, and pushed the fire button. The job took no more than four seconds. Just a tiny delay and the rocket shot out of the tube, leaving an enormous blast of glowing hot exhaust gases pouring from the rear of the launch tube…and almost instantly the rocket hit the end of the Bradley, punched through, and exploded. A jet of fire shot back out the entry hole.

JR had already dropped the empty tube and was running for the corner of the sheltering building when he heard the chatter of a machine gun. That was from the tank behind him, he thought. He tore around the side of the building, out of sight of the tanks, ran right by the extra loaded tube lying by the building, and ran hard. Troopers from the other Bradleys would be after him in seconds.

He quickly found himself in an old neighborhood of mature trees and lawns and iron fences. Vaulted a fence and ran as if the hounds of hell were behind him, which they were, then got into an alley and ran on the gravel.

From somewhere behind him he heard a shot. Not too loud. One of his kids, he hoped, slowing down the pursuit. He checked street signs and kept moving, now jogging.

The carbine on his back was slapping him at every step, slowing him, so he pulled it off and carried it in his hands. His pistol belt was also rubbing him with every step. Damn, he was going to be sore. He must have run three miles or more before he came to the parking lot of a Walmart. He found Wiley Fehrenbach sitting behind the wheel of his SUV; his two guardsmen were already seated in the back.

"I'm getting too old for this shit," he told Wiley as he motioned him to drive and put on his seatbelt. Then he tried to ease the pistol on his raw, aching hip.

Fehrenbach headed downtown.

JR thought about the troopers in the Bradley he'd shot. No doubt they were all dead, or wished they were. They had been American soldiers, and perhaps he had even served with them somewhere in the last twenty years. When he recovered his breath, he turned to the two soldiers in the backseat.

"I'm a soldier," he offered in way of explanation, "which is an ancient, honorable profession. I had absolutely nothing to do with independence. I wasn't even asked my opinion before the legislature did it. They did it because they thought their constituents wanted it desperately and without independence, Texas didn't have a chance. I don't know if they were right or wrong, yet I'm a Texan, and I'm all in. Do you understand?"

"Yes," the two young men murmured. They were Texans too. JR wasn't sure they did fully understand, so he continued: "Soldiers fight for their country. Ours is Texas. Freedom isn't free, and if we're going to get it, we're going to have to fight for it. We're going to have to hurt them worse than they hurt us, and we can't ever give up. You see that?"

One of the soldiers, his name tag said he was Murray, replied, "My dad is locked in a railroad car at the base. He's the president of the El Paso Rotary. Wrote some stuff for one of those independence movements. Fight for Texas? Hell yes."

The other soldier, his name tag said Tyler, nodded his head. At the wheel Wiley Fehrenbach was nodding too.

"Some of our enemies have to die and some of us will too," JR Hays said. "Blood is the fertilizer of freedom. Maybe yours and mine."

He fell silent and watched the street with old, careful eyes. Fehrenbach pulled into a McDonald's parking lot. Cars full of National Guard soldiers were waiting. "Murray, Tyler, run on over there and tell them to follow us to the airport. We have some work to do tonight." The young guardsmen trotted off, carrying their weapons.

On the way to the airport, JR said to Wiley, "Our objective is to isolate First Armored, make sure it can't be reinforced or resupplied and can't run. I want you to pull all those executive jets onto the runways and taxiways and then shoot out their tires so they can't be moved easily. We may not be able to hold the airport, but at least no airplane will land on it until the army takes it back."

"And the airport on base?"

"We'll take care of that in a day or two," JR said. "After you do the international airport, I want you to get busy blowing up railroad trestles, as far out of town as you can. No trains in or out. Then bridges on the highways."

"We can do that. We're engineers."

"Do some ambushes, one or two, after you blow a trestle or bridge and they come to look. Try to hit a patrol in town occasionally. Shoot, then skedaddle. Don't get in any stand-up fights when you're outnumbered and outgunned. Just worry them."

"Hit and run."

"Precisely. The playbook is so old the pages are crumbling, but the tactics still work."

After a moment he added, "The army will soon be trying to ambush your men and doing searches house to house looking for weapons and uniforms. You'll be amazed at how fast the army's combat veterans will catch on, even anticipate your tactics. They're pros, not twenty-year-old amateurs like the two with me tonight."

"I understand."

"You have to watch out for your boys, Wiley, or soon we won't have any soldiers to fight with, just a bunch of bodies."

JR thought about his comment to the soldiers that he had had nothing to do with independence. Perhaps Joe Bob's death at the hands of smugglers had pushed Jack toward independence. Certainly, he thought, his father's death had convinced him, when he heard about independence, that *he* was going to fight.

Not being an introspective man, he left it there and began thinking about how to win the war of independence. When Wiley Fehrenbach climbed out of the car and went inside the terminal to wait for his soldiers to assemble, JR found a notebook in the car and wrote an order to Major General Elvin Gentry.

"It is essential that we take the offensive and give Washington something to think about besides pounding Texas into submission. Have your B-1 people study up on railroad trestles and bridges out of the Powder River Basin in northeastern Wyoming and southeastern Montana. Send as many planes as possible as soon as possible to hit those trestles and bridges. I want to stop all the trains into and out of the Powder River Basin. The coal-fired power plants they service will soon run out of coal and shut down. The second-priority targets are pumping stations on natural gas delivery lines to the Upper Midwest and Northeast. If we can shut some of those gas lines down, many of the power plants there will have to shut down too."

He signed it JR Hays, Major General Commanding, Texas Guard. Then he went into the executive terminal, found the pilots of the executive jet that he had flown in on, gave them the note, and told them to fly to Dyess right away, before the runway was blocked. They were to deliver the message to Elvin Gentry.

Fehrenbach posted guards armed with rifles and AT4s on the access roads to the airport. He set the rest of his men to towing planes onto the runways with the little tractors and tow bars the FBO had parked on the ramp. "Park the crash truck out there too," he said.

Wiley Fehrenbach and JR Hays were called to the lobby television by the desk lady, who apparently had no idea that the jets on her ramp were being moved. She pointed to the television. Jack Hays was giving a speech.

★

President Jack Hays—the legislature had awarded him that new title along with declaring itself the Congress of Texas—was escorted by the leaders of the Texas House and Senate. They walked past television cameras from local stations whose feed was beamed to satellites that were broadcasting across the world. Soetoro's censors might prevent it from being aired outside of Texas, but it would circle the earth and eventually reach every person upon it.

After shaking dozens of hands on his way to the podium, Jack Hays at last took his place behind it. His writers and Ben Steiner had given him a speech, but to Steiner's dismay, he left the speech in his pocket. He was going to wing it.

In the packed gallery he saw his wife, Nadine.

"My fellow Texans," he began. Then he changed that, "My fellow Texans and American patriots everywhere. I speak to you tonight after a tumultuous few days, a historic period that marks the beginning of our fight for freedom, a fight that we hope patriots everywhere in America will join and stand shoulder to shoulder with us against tyranny."

He detailed President Soetoro's transgressions, laying special emphasis on his imposition of martial law and the jailing of political opponents. "Who would have thought that what is being done now was possible in the United States: that we live in fear of the midnight knock on the door; that many of our leading citizens are in concentration camps, where at any moment we might join them as prisoners. Let us be frank. America is now being ruled by a tyrant who has shredded the Constitution of the United States. In the last week, one man has seized all power unto himself, and the rights of no man or woman in America are safe.

"He has chosen to rip up the Bill of Rights, destroying the right of free speech, which is absolutely essential in a democracy. He has destroyed the right to bear arms, which is a free people's only defense against tyranny. He suspended the Writ of Habeas Corpus, an ancient writ created hundreds of years ago in England and brought to America by our first colonists to ensure the rule of law and protect the populace from government lawlessness. He has chosen to eliminate the currency. He has chosen to rule by fiat, dismissing Congress and flouting the courts. By his actions, he defines the word tyrant. In response to the dictates of a tyrant, we here in Texas have chosen to exercise our God-given right to self-government, our right to choose our own destiny and our own leaders, our right as a free people to resist tyranny and create a government worthy of a free people. In a sublime act of courage, the elected representatives of the people of Texas have done so. Yesterday morning in the very early hours they declared our independence. Today they established the Republic of Texas."

He paused in response to loud, sustained applause.

"We face difficult days ahead. The federal government has already fired the first shots, which were cruise missiles launched from a navy ship at sea off our coast. Today the navy has declared a blockade of our ports in an attempt to deny us freedom of the seas.

"The road ahead will not be easy. No doubt the federal government will escalate its pressure upon us. Still, precious as it is, freedom is worthless unless it is defended, and I fear blood will be required. How much, no man can say. At least a dozen people died and two dozen were wounded when a power plant in the Houston area was struck by those cruise missiles. Those Texans, *who wore no uniform*, were our first casualties. I am reminded of the words of that great American patriot Thomas Paine: 'If there must be trouble, let it be in my day, that my child may have peace.'"

The applause was thundering.

When the noise had at last subsided, he said: "Tonight we ask lovers of freedom all over America, indeed, lovers of freedom all over the world, to join us in our struggle. Let us here in Texas resolve to fight, no matter the price that may be required, for all that we loved about our country, for all that we treasured and hoped to pass on to our children, and their children, and the generations yet unborn. Let us here dedicate ourselves to enshrining freedom, justice, and the rule of law in the Republic of Texas, for ourselves and our posterity. *So help us God*."

The applause and shouting died after a while, because the hour was late and the day had been long for everyone. Still standing at the podium, Jack Hays shouted, "Ben Steiner, you wrote our Declaration of Independence, what is your favorite song?"

Texans argued for years afterward whether Steiner knew that question was coming, but his answer was quick and his voice carried throughout the chamber. "'The Eyes of Texas.'"

One of the television producers was about to send the program back to the studio for commentary by instant experts, but he now waited, sensing that the best might still be ahead.

Jack Hays started singing. He had a nice baritone. Everyone in the chamber was still on their feet, including the spectators in the gallery. Nadine's eyes were locked upon her husband as he sang, "The eyes of Texas are upon you, all the live long day. The eyes of Texas are upon you, and you cannot get away..."

When the roar died, Hays looked and gestured at the Speaker, who shouted, "'The Yellow Rose of Texas.'"

"There's a yellow rose in Texas, that I am going to see. Nobody else could miss her, not half as much as me...She's the sweetest little rosebud that Texas ever knew. Her eyes are bright as diamonds, they sparkle like the dew. You may talk about your Clementine and sing of Rosalee, but *the yellow rose of Texas* is the only girl for me...."

All over Texas, people were sitting in front of their televisions or radios, many singing at the top of their lungs, as Jack Hays thought they would.

Barry Soetoro watched the speech and singing on television in the family quarters of the White House. "That's a dangerous man," he remarked to Mickey. "He's firing up every half-wit cracker in the country."

"You'd better have someone shoot him quick," she said. "You knew those Texas bastards were going to give you trouble."

The president nodded. He knew good advice when he heard it.

Jack Hays said, "My favorite now, 'Deep In the Heart of Texas,'" and he led off.

"The stars at night ... are big and bright"—clap, clap, clap—"*deep in the heart of Texas.* The prairie bloom ... is like perfume"—clap, clap, clap—"*deep in the heart of Texas.* Reminds me of the one I love"—clap, clap, clap—"*deep in the heart of Texas....*"

The last notes had barely died when Jack said, "Let's end with the anthem of Texas, 'Texas, Our Texas.'"

The voices rose loudly, if not melodiously. "Texas, our Texas! All hail the mighty state! Texas, our Texas! So wonderful, so great...."

The last stanza was the best, and although many of the legislators didn't know the words, Jack Hays did. He sang it with every ounce of fervor that was in him. "Texas, dear Texas! From tyrant's grip now free, shines forth in splendor, our star of destiny! Mother of heroes, we come your children true, proclaiming our allegiance, our faith, our love for you.... God bless you, Texas! And keep you brave and strong, that you may grow in power and worth, throughout the ages long...."

Long after the singing had died and they turned off their televisions and radios, in cities, towns, and hamlets and at isolated homes and ranches, from the islands and low flatlands near the gulf and the thickets and pine forests of east Texas, to the prairies, plains, and semi-deserts of west Texas and the windswept tableland of the Panhandle, people hummed the tunes and thought about Jack Hays' words. In truck stops, cafes, and big rigs rolling along lonesome highways, people thought and pondered, about America and Texas and the dreams men carry for a someday that may or may not ever come.

As Jack Hays once remarked to Nadine, "Texas isn't a place; it's a religion."

At Fort Bliss, Major General Lee Parker had a nightmare on his hands. His flight line had been shot to hell, an Apache had been shot down, he had lost a Bradley and every soldier in it, and three helicopters had shot up his flight line. As Jack Hays spoke on the television, Parker's air officer was trying to get a count on how many helicopters were flyable.

In addition to these problems, the Pentagon was bombarding him with messages directing him to attack in all directions, disarm all civilians, and arrest every male Texan he could find. "What about the women?" he asked his chief of staff, who had no answers. Parker had served in Texas long enough to know that many Texas women were, if anything, made of even sterner stuff than the men. Given sufficient reason, they could and occasionally did shoot a man as dead as a man can get. On the other hand, arresting women, some of them mothers of young children, would not play well in Washington. And he had no decent facilities to hold them in.

So how was he going to do all this attacking and arresting? He huddled with his ops officer, the brigade commanders, and their ops officers trying to figure out what his objectives and priorities should be. Staff officers flitted around like moths around a flame. Given enough time, something might have come out of the blizzard of orders from headquarters and all this staff work, but time ran out for Lee Parker at about three a.m. He was whipped. He hadn't slept in eighteen hours, and was keeping himself running on strong black coffee.

"Sir," one of his aides whispered to him. "There is a delegation of NCOs in your outer office. They want to talk to you."

"A delegation?"

"Yes, sir. That's what they said."

"We don't do delegations in the army. Tell them to return to duty or their quarters."

"General, they insist on seeing you."

Parker stormed out of the conference room and down the hallway to the reception area outside his office, fully intending to blister some soldiers. A delegation! Just who did these sergeants think they were, anyway?

He faced a group of command sergeant majors. "What the hell do you want that can't go through the chain of command?"

"We wanted to bring this to your attention right now, General. The troops in the barracks are packing their duffle bags, getting in their cars, and driving out the main gate. Over in base housing, officers and men are loading their families and leaving."

"This base is on lockdown. No one in or out. You know that!"

"Yes, sir, but the gate guards have left too. Our gates are wide open and unmanned."

"Get them manned immediately. Anyone leaving this fort in violation of orders will be arrested and court-martialed."

"Sir, the soldiers we have left refuse to man the gate. The main road outside the gate is lined with armed civilians, and more are coming every minute. The sheriff's deputies are out there trying to keep them from flooding onto the base."

Lee Parker stared, his jaw agape. In all his years in the army he had never even heard of mass disobedience. "This is mutiny," he said to the top sergeants.

"Yes, sir, it is that. But we can't stop our soldiers short of shooting them, and they won't do the army any good if they are shot. What it boils down to is that less than ten percent of the troops will stick. That's just an estimate. More like a guess, maybe. The rest are scattering like leaves in the wind. Some say they are going to fight for Texas, others are going home, wherever that is for them. Bottom line, General, is *we have no one to fight with*."

On the way to headquarters, the sergeants agreed that having soldiers arrest local civilians and incarcerate them had been a major mistake. They didn't think it was Parker's fault; he was just following orders. Ill-considered orders. The men and women of the 1st Armored were soldiers, damn good ones too, not KGB or Gestapo or Brown Shirts. Or FEMA or Homeland thugs. "We're soldiers, sir," the division sergeant major told the general now by way of explanation, although without context the general thought that comment inane.

"Our troops aren't acting like soldiers," Parker shot back heatedly. "*Mutiny*! By God, when this is over I'm going to send a whole lot of people to Leavenworth. Just watch."

The command sergeant major, Alfredo Mendez, five feet, six inches of professional soldier from McAllen, Texas, said, "General, I don't think you understand the situation. Perhaps we weren't clear enough. Your troops are leaving. They will not fight Texans. They refuse to serve in Barry Soetoro's army. Your choice right now is to get in a plane as quickly as possible and fly out of here, or stay and surrender to the National Guard. When Wiley Fehrenbach figures out the situation here at Bliss, which will be sooner rather than later, he and his troops will be coming, armed, and *our people will not fight*."

The general went into his office, slammed the door, and tried to get control of himself. Never in his wildest nightmares had he ever imagined this. *Mutiny*!

After five or six deep breaths, he walked out, past the waiting NCOs, and headed for the staff conference room. He broke the news to his staff and his generals in four sentences.

One of the brigadiers exploded. "We'll get the loyal soldiers and kick the snot out of those guardsmen and civilians. Let's get at it."

"So you want to go out like Custer, eh?" another brigadier shot back. "This isn't Iraq. These civilians will shoot first, just like the Sioux did. The people of Texas are fighting for their freedom from what they believe is a tyrannical government that has suspended the United States Constitution. So far we have fifteen dead and thirty-two wounded and all we've accomplished is burning down an empty National Guard Armory. What do you plan to do, fight house to house to get the hell out of El Paso?

Make a last stand at a Walmart or on some lonesome, windswept hill in the middle of a cow pasture, if you get that far?"

"We could get our loyal troops and some of the equipment into New Mexico, and the Texans wouldn't follow us across the border."

"You think this is chess?" another officer retorted. "If I were making the decisions for them, I would follow you all the way to Hell to force you to surrender. And we're just not ready to move. It would take a couple of days to get ready, and we don't have two days."

Lee Parker made up his mind. The brass would court-martial him if he ran, and, in truth, he didn't have running in him. Nor did he want to fight for Barry Soetoro. He had been doing what he had done for the past thirty-two years: obeying orders because he was in the United States Army, serving under the Stars and Stripes. Now he lacked the means to fight. "We'll surrender," he said. He glanced at the chief of staff and told him to draft a message to all the higher headquarters telling them of his decision.

"Sir, shouldn't we disable the tanks, artillery, Bradleys?"

"If we had the people to accomplish that, we wouldn't be surrendering," Lee Parker said bitterly. "This command has just disintegrated. I didn't see it coming, and I doubt if anyone else in this room did either. If you did have an inkling, you certainly didn't do your country any favors by keeping your mouth shut." Yet, after all, in a vast bureaucracy, one didn't get ahead by pointing out statistically remote disastrous possibilities that had never occurred in the past. A mutiny! For heaven's sake, this *is* the United States Army, and 1st Armored was a hell of a good outfit!

Lee Parker went back to the NCOs who still stood in the reception area.

"Sergeant Major Mendez, will you please go to the main gate and tell the sheriff or his deputy to send for General Fehrenbach? I'll surrender Fort Bliss to him. Have the sheriff bring him here."

"Yes, sir," Mendez said, saluted, and marched from the room.

The thunderstorms were gone and it was drizzling rain when JR Hays and Wiley Fehrenbach were ushered into the commanding general's office at Fort Bliss. Seeing that JR was wearing major general's stars, Lee Parker, standing at attention beside his desk, saluted and said, "Gentlemen, my troops have mutinied and I am unable to defend the base or the military equipment here. In order not to squander lives uselessly, I wish to surrender the base and its personnel to the Texas forces."

JR and Wiley returned the salute. JR told Wiley, "You accept the surrender. Write it out on a computer." He dictated the terms: All military equipment would be surrendered along with the troops. Those soldiers who wished to leave Texas were welcome to do so, and those who wished to enlist in the Texas Guard would be encouraged to do so after they took a loyalty oath and signed it. Anyone caught sabotaging surrendered military equipment would be dealt with summarily.

"If you or your staff or senior officers wish to leave, General Parker, I suggest you get in one of your C-130s or executive transports and leave immediately. We are going to block the runway with tanks as soon as you depart."

"I'll stay," Lee Parker said. "My officers can make their own decisions."

"I understand you have some civilians locked up."

"Orders from Washington," Parker replied curtly. "FEMA has lists."

"Let them out, Wiley, and get them rides home. And haul down the American flags on base. Find some Texas flags and run them up."

"Yes, sir."

Wiley Fehrenbach unbuttoned his shirt and produced a Lone Star flag. He grinned at JR and handed it to the nearest soldier. "You heard him. Run it up the pole outside and get one for the pole at the main gate."

JR glanced at the leather couch, and asked the two generals to conduct their business in the outer office. When the door was closed behind them, he sacked out on the couch. He glanced at his watch. The Republic of Texas was just a bit less than forty-eight hours old. The window was open and the breeze felt good. He was asleep ten seconds later.

SIXTEEN

★

The riots continued in inner cities around the country. Baltimore was probably the worst: it had been racked by riots the previous year, and this time the mob at the core expanded across downtown and into the suburbs.

Police and National Guardsmen had disappeared. Much of their leadership had already been imprisoned by the feds. Many of those left on duty went home to protect or move their families. Others just threw up their hands. Why try to bring a mob under control when the physical risks were high and the politicians were frightened that they might lose some votes, so none of the political elite or police brass would back the men and women in uniform on the streets? Police and guardsmen went into bars, had a few, then found their cars and went home.

In the suburbs, people were getting into a state of near panic. Rumors were rampant. In subdivisions and neighborhoods, mothers and fathers surrounded by children met in front yards and culs-de-sac, exchanging rumors and fears. People talked about blocking off streets as they faced the prospect of having to defend their homes against marauders. It seemed as if much of America now had two ravenous domestic enemies—rioting, looting mobs, and the federal government. Many of the suburbanites had an old lever-action Winchester or Marlin, or a bolt-action Winchester, Remington, or Ruger in the closet, and a couple boxes of ammunition for it. They decided what they were going to do if the mobs invaded their neighborhoods to rob, loot, rape, and burn.

In Detroit, Chicago, Philadelphia, St. Louis, and Los Angeles, the mobs were still in the ghetto, but as in Baltimore, those who lived in the riot-torn area and were not a part of it were trying to flee. People left on foot and in cars, streams of refugees, some with the contents of looted stores on their backs, but all convinced they had had enough.

Local and network television were showing some of this, where censors would allow it, and radio stations were on the spot with breathless reporting. Social media filled in with some truth, rumor, and wild speculation. As usual on social media, budding writers of sardonic fiction posted absurd tales they thought only fools would believe; of course the fools did believe, but so did many frightened people who were definitely not foolish.

Everyone had someone they needed to talk to desperately: Telephone networks were at maximum capacity. Calls, e-mails, and text messages inundated city and state officials high and low, all those remaining after the FBI, FEMA, Homeland Security, and cooperating county sheriffs had carried off the disloyal for incarceration. Some of the less cooperative sheriffs and police chiefs had also been arrested, decapitating their law enforcement departments. The only thing observers could agree on was that the situation was getting worse. In the White House and congressional offices, staffers stopped answering telephones and e-mail servers crashed. Monday night, August 29, was another wild one in America.

They came for Jake Grafton at Camp Dawson at three in the morning, Tuesday, August 30. Four of them, in green coveralls with FEMA badges on the right shoulder. They woke him up by dragging him from his cot, slamming him to the floor, and kicking him.

Then they cuffed his hands behind his back and dragged him from the tent, across the common area, by the mess tents, to the building Sluggo Sweatt used as headquarters. Up the stairs into Sluggo's lair. He was up, with a light on, waiting. The four thugs lifted Grafton bodily from the floor and threw him into a chair. Another man came in and dropped Grafton's watch and cell phone on Sluggo's desk.

"Good morning, Grafton," Sluggo said pleasantly. "I decided it was time to take the gloves off and confront you with the reality of your situation."

Grafton tried to ease himself in the chair. It felt as if one of his ribs on the left side was broken. Sharp pain with every breath.

"My conscience requires me to tell you in advance that the road ahead for you is filled with pain. I need you to sign a confession of complicity in the attempted assassination of President Soetoro. Of course, there will be television cameras. You will need to speak slowly and coherently about your crimes."

Jake Grafton looked around the room, the same one he had visited twice before.

One of the men on his right used a fist into his side. He gasped at the blow and almost fell from the chair.

"Be polite and pay attention," Sluggo said. "I told my colleagues that you would undoubtedly need a lot of persuading, and they thought it would be fun to do it. There isn't much to do to pass the time here in the boonies." With that, Sluggo nodded.

The thugs dragged him from the chair and took him along a hallway to a jail cell, complete with bars and a cot and a honey bucket. There they started pounding on his ribs. One of them stomped on his scrotum. At some point he passed out.

When he came to, the lights were on, but he had no idea whether it was day or night or how long he had been unconscious.

Television. That was why they hadn't touched his face.

The good news was that he was still alive. The bad news was that Sluggo's men were going to beat him to death by inches.

Loren Snyder had been busy. He used the Houston telephone book to find the address of a former naval officer, Julie Aranado, also known as Jugs. Apparently the Aranado men of prior generations had favored big-bosomed women, so Julie was awesomely endowed. Lots of exercise kept the rest of her figure slim and trim, showing off the trophies. She had acquired her nickname at the Naval Academy and, although it reeked of political incorrectness and sexism, she liked it, so it stuck. "If you got 'em, be proud," she had been heard to remark when questioned about the appellation.

After eleven years of active duty, she decided the GI Bill's offer of a free advanced education beat the navy's retention bonuses. So she quit the navy and was earning a PhD in physics at the University of Houston. She returned to her apartment on Sunday evening, after watching Jack Hays' speech at a girlfriend's house, and found Loren Snyder sitting on the front stoop waiting for her.

"Hey, Jugs. You're looking good."

"Mr. Snyder! I haven't seen you in what, two or three years?"

"About that. And it's Loren. Hey, I need some help and you were the first person I thought of."

"I heard you were in law school at UT."

"Yep."

"What kind of help?" she asked as she unlocked the door. Snyder was at least ten years her senior, and she had served with him aboard an attack sub. Romance hadn't been on the agenda then, and she knew it wasn't now. The Loren Snyder she had known was all business.

"The Republic of Texas is now the proud owner of a *Virginia*-class sub, USS *Texas*. She's lying in Galveston. I'm the new skipper and you are now my XO."

She snorted. "Don't bullshit me, Snyder. School starts again next week and I need to study. What do you want?"

He told it as he had gotten it, then added, "I went aboard her yesterday evening. The crew scrammed the reactor, secured the batteries, and left, arrested by the county sheriff, who doesn't know jack about ships, boats, or submarines. I inspected everything I could see and couldn't find any sign of sabotage. All *Texas* needs is a crew."

Jugs snorted. "Where, pray tell, are you going to find sixty people to man her?"

"I'm not. I figure with five people who know what they are doing, I can get her under way. We can't leave her lying at the pier. I figure there is probably one chance in five the navy will destroy her with Tomahawks, and four chances in five the navy will send a SEAL team to take her."

"SEALs couldn't get her under way," Jugs objected with a frown. "They don't have that kind of training."

"They could if they brought five or six certified people with them. And you know they can do that." Both these former naval officers had a very healthy respect for the navy's special operations warriors, arguably the best in the world. If anyone could steal a submarine, they could.

"They're probably planning a mission right now," she said thoughtfully.

"If we are going to save that boat for Texas, we have to get in gear. Are you for independence?"

"Hell, yes. I'm from San Antone. I've had more than enough of Soetoro pissing on the Constitution. It's high time we went our own way." Although Aranado didn't say it, like many Mexican American Catholics, she was socially conservative. Same-sex marriages, she believed, were an insult to the sanctity of that institution. Abortion horrified her—especially late-term abortions, doctors sucking the brains from viable infants—and Soetoro's and his party's fervid support of the practice had cost them her vote years ago. In fact, she had sworn in church at the altar of God she would never vote for one of those baby-butchering sons of bitches as long as she lived.

Jugs always was blunt, Snyder reflected. "I need three more qualified people," he said. "Who do you know that we can get?" Then he added, "In Texas?"

★

Another group, five young men in their late twenties or early thirties, was also busy that Monday night. They were unemployed coal miners in southern West Virginia. They had been following Soetoro's declaration of martial law and Texas' reaction to it on television, in bits and pieces. They were nonpolitical high school grads who had become certified underground miners and worked in the mines since their early twenties. Their mines had laid them off some months back when demand for coal forced mines to lay off shifts. Their fathers had been miners, and their fathers before them. Underground mines were the last remaining sources of good jobs in southern West Virginia since NAFTA had sent factory jobs to Mexico twenty years before. They believed Barry Soetoro's EPA was killing coal, and with it, their way of life, and they were bitter. They still had fishing, hunting, riding their ATVs, and chasing girls, but without a decent paycheck, their futures looked bleak. None wanted to leave the hills to look for work elsewhere. Here was where they had spent their lives, here was where their friends were, here was where their relatives had been buried for over two centuries in the little graveyards surrounding the one-room white churches that dotted the hills. *This* was their place.

Now evil politicians, rich environmentalists, and Washington bureaucrats had robbed them of it, they believed. They had never thought of themselves as terrorists, but for months now they had been talking about getting even with those distant bastards who had taken everything they had. These young men despised Barry Soetoro and everything he stood for and admired the Texans. Unlike the miners in West Virginia, those Texans hadn't just hunkered down and let the big shits fuck them. They were fighting back.

Harlan Greathouse was the natural leader of this little group, and the biggest talker. Sunday, while they were fishing the eddies in a quiet little river shaded with verdant sycamores and drinking beer, Greathouse prodded them into action.

One of them still had a key to the explosives locker at the mine where he used to work. The padlocks on the locker were supposed to be changed periodically, but who knew when the mine foreman would get around to it. The key still worked, and for that they were grateful. The locker was a grounded steel building as far away from structures and dwellings as was practical. Sunday night they used that key, opened the locker, and helped themselves to three cases of dynamite, blasting caps, a roll of wire, and three detonators that passed their battery checks. The roll contained about a thousand feet of wire. They really needed three rolls, so they could plant three charges, but they decided to make do with one.

Harlan Greathouse led in his pickup, and his friends in two more pickups followed him to the interstate. They stopped at a convenience store on a freeway exit, gassed up, and bought more 3.2 percent beer, the so-called non-alcoholic beer, then got back onto the highway. As they finished each can of beer, they crushed it and with a practiced flip of the wrist, tossed it into the beds of their pickups. They drove into the great valley of Virginia and across the Blue Ridge to the rolling countryside cut by old rivers that ran into the Chesapeake.

On a two-lane asphalt road that ran through bucolic countryside they found a pumping station on one of the natural-gas trunk lines that ran from Louisiana northeastward all the way to Boston. Anyone could see it was a pipeline right-of-way because the tree-less terrain covered in low weeds ran from one horizon to another and was about a hundred feet wide. This line serviced a myriad of smaller feeder lines that supplied natural gas to factories, cities, towns, and gas-fed power plants.

None of the miners had the slightest idea how big the explosion would be when they blew the pumping station. Big, they figured, big enough to perhaps ignite this stand of dry pines that stood on either side of the right-of-way. They saw in the moonlight—it was four in the morning—that each stand consisted of about five acres of trees. A quick reconnaissance revealed that these two stands were surrounded by pastures and meadows as far as the eye could see, with here and there a modest house and its associated barn. Cattle grazed in the pastures. The nearest house was perhaps five hundred yards beyond the edge of the trees, so they figured no one there would be injured by the blast.

Harlan thought this a good place. They could set one case of dynamite, unroll perhaps four hundred feet of wire off the roll, cut it, and rig it to a detonator. The loss of line pressure after the explosion would cause emergency shutoff valves farther up and down the line to secure the flow of gas. Those power plants to the northeast that depended on this line would be down until gas from other, interconnecting lines, could be routed to them. The explosion would no doubt obliterate this pumping station, and it would eventually need to be rebuilt.

"They should have stayed with coal," one of the miners said, chuckling, just loud enough to be heard.

The pumping station, about a half-acre in size, was surrounded by a ten-foot-high chain-link fence topped with three strands of barbed wire and was lit by floodlights on poles. There was a gate, of course, and it was padlocked.

The gate wasn't a problem. The miners hooked a tow chain around one of the fence posts, hooked the other end to a tow-hitch, and pulled it down.

They all knew how to handle dynamite. In less than five minutes they had divided a case of dynamite into three charges, one of which was set on the main inlet line—about three feet in diameter—another on the line out, and one on the main pump itself. Between the pump and the charges on the lines were the safety cutoff valves, which were going to be destroyed too. One car went by without slowing while they worked. They inserted the blasting caps, wired up a harness that they mated to the caps, then unrolled an estimated four hundred feet of wire, cut it, and turned the pickups around.

Harlan Greathouse thought he should be the one to trigger the blast. The other two pickups went on west a half mile or so to the crest of a low hill as he wired up the detonator. He took cover behind his pickup and lifted the safety lever. Took a deep breath and pushed the button.

The resulting explosion wasn't really that bad. But it was followed by a hurricane of noise as natural gas under pressure hissed from the ruptured line. That lasted just long enough to register on Harlan's ears, then the gas was ignited by molten hotspots in the steel. A giant explosion resulted. Trees were flattened to the east and west. The stupendous fireball from the blast rose in a monstrous flaming mushroom cloud.

The pickup truck absorbed the peak pressure of the shockwave from the concussion of the gas explosion, thereby saving Harlan from being crushed. However, even with the dubious shelter of his shattered truck, he perished within a second or so as the pulse of superheated air scorched and fried him to blackened gristle. The heat pulse also set the ten acres of now-flattened pines instantly aflame.

Within a minute the gas flowing from the ruptured lines slowed as pressure bled off. Air rushing back into the blast area and escaping gas fed a blowtorch flame that rose at least three hundred feet in the air. The initial fireball, now expanding into a mushroom cloud and turning from yellow to red and orange, rose and rose into the sky, lighting the countryside as bright as day.

Harlan Greathouse's friends came driving madly back, but one look in the light of the burning gas told the story. They turned their pickups around in the road and roared away to the west toward the distant mountains.

As dawn was breaking Tuesday in Galveston, Snyder, Aranado, and three men, all of whom Jugs knew from her naval reserve weekends, were aboard *Texas* checking her out. Speedy Gonzales was a nuclear engineer, Mouse Moore was a first-class petty officer with twelve years in attack subs, and Junior Smith was a third-class who had served aboard Polaris boats. All Texans, all foursquare for independence, they had volunteered immediately.

Using flashlights, they inspected everything they could see, opened panels and examined wiring and fittings, checked the galley for provisions, and all came to the same conclusion. *Texas* was ready for sea. The former crew's personal effects were still aboard, uniforms, underwear, hygiene items, letters from wives and girlfriends. The batteries had a good charge on them. It was as if the crew had mustered on the pier and marched off, leaving everything. Although Snyder and his crew didn't know it, that was pretty much what had happened.

All five gathered in the control room and discussed their inspections. "She's ready to go, I believe," Speedy said. "A full load of Tomahawks and torpedoes, plenty of food and water, more than ample for five people. The batteries seem okay, the checklists are in place and apparently complete." He spoke like a judge, weighing every word before he uttered it because it would appear on the court reporter's transcript.

"Mouse?" Loren asked.

"She's ready to go, Mr. Snyder." Snyder was an officer, and under no conceivable circumstances would Mouse Moore address him familiarly. He had spent too many years in uniform. In his bunkroom he might tell his shipmates his opinion of Loren or Jugs, but he would never address either of them that way to their faces. It was a mark in his favor: Mouse was a good sailor who would always obey orders.

Junior Smith was cut from a slightly different pattern. He had been doused in naval tradition and most of it had washed off. He was a civilian at heart, and so he said, "Loren, I'm willing to go to sea in her."

"Just precisely what *do* you plan, Mr. Snyder?" Jugs asked, preferring to address Loren formally.

"I want to get the reactor cooking again, check that every system is working properly, run some drills to ensure we don't entomb ourselves, and if we're all cool, cast off and get the hell out of Dodge before the SEALs show up. They can't get at us if we're submerged."

"We have no secure way to communicate with JR Hays," Jugs objected.

"After a while we can poke up the mast, listen to the radio, and learn what's happening. Right now, I think it imperative we get gone before the SEALs come, and you all know they will."

"Sure as God made little green apples," Junior agreed.

"So let's check all the circuit breakers and emergency alarms, then fire off the tea kettle. Stations everyone."

"Your first command," Speedy said with a grin.

"And probably my last," Loren Snyder admitted. "Miz Aranado, you and Speedy bring the batteries online and let's do it."

Four minutes later the batteries brought the boat to life. Lights came on, air began circulating, computer displays came to standby. Back aft Speedy Gonzales checked the emergency alarms one by one. Loren Snyder snapped off his flashlight and smiled. It was as if he had returned to something he had loved and missed. He thought for three seconds about law school, and snorted. Someday, maybe.

General Martin L. Wynette, the Joint Chiefs, and their staff were having a terrible morning. The news of the surrender of Fort Bliss, after a mutiny, cast a pall on their planning to invade Texas. Large numbers of troops that refused to obey orders, or refused to fight, or went AWOL was a nightmare that the U.S. armed forces had never before dealt with. It raised the question of whether any troops ordered to attack Texas could actually be relied upon to do so. It seemed to the planners that the answer to that question would determine what could be done, and when. Of course, the White House staff was outraged and said the military was dragging its feet in the face of treason. That comment was grossly unfair, and even Martin Wynette was severely irritated by it. Everyone in the E-Ring offices of the Pentagon knew that imprudent action would lead to even more severe condemnation of the military.

The loss of USS *Texas* gave the navy serious heartburn. Some advocated launching Tomahawk cruise missiles at the attack submarine while she lay at the Galveston pier, but the chief of naval operations, the CNO, Admiral Cart McKiernan, was having none of it. "We spent 2.6 billion dollars for that boat that we had to squeeze out of Congress like it was blood," he roared to the Joint Staff. "I'll be damned if I'm going to order her destroyed until we've tried every other option. We may desperately need her if Iran and China get feisty. Those rodeo cowboys in Galveston are going nowhere in that boat; the very idea is ludicrous. Now you people get a SEAL team saddled up to go down there and get her. Have them take some submariners with them. I don't give a damn who the SEALs have to kill or how they do it, but I want that submarine back in one piece. Understand?"

That was yesterday. In the wee hours of this morning it looked as if the SEAL team needed at least another twenty-four hours to get ready. People and equipment had to be moved into position and it all took time, a fact that infuriated the White House staffers sitting in on the pre-dawn meeting, who knew absolutely nothing about logistics. While they ranted, the lights and computers in the Pentagon flickered and went out for a few seconds until the building's massive emergency power system automatically came online.

The sabotage of the natural gas trunk line from Louisiana had forced several natural gas power plants in the area to shut down until gas could be rerouted over the network. The shutdowns of the power plants blacked out cities in northern Virginia and Maryland. Then the problems began to cascade. The computer system that controlled the electrical grid, automatically rerouting electrical power to restore it to deprived areas, began to do precisely the opposite. It demanded power from the stricken plants, and when there was none to be had, began shutting down the grid across the northeastern United States. In seconds, the power was off from Chicago to Boston and south all the way to Richmond. Air conditioners quit, elevators jammed, computers died, the telephone system went down, water and sewage pumps failed.

I found out about the power failure about seven that morning when I sneaked from Sarah Houston's bed and padded into her kitchen to make coffee. The kitchen lights wouldn't illuminate. Suspecting the worst, I opened the door of a very quiet refrigerator. No light inside. Oh boy. I jabbed the remote to turn on the television, just in case, but no soap. I thought maybe it was the circuit breakers, but I didn't know where her panel was. I tried my cell phone: no service. So it wasn't the circuit breakers.

I went back to the bedroom, woke Sarah, and told her the news.

"Perhaps my little program worked," she chirped, pleased with herself.

"Maybe the juice is only off in this neighborhood."

"You are always so cheerful, Tommy. And at this hour of the morning."

"I'm a natural-born optimist," I objected. "In fact, I'm so optimistic that I think we should throw on some clothes and hot foot it over to the lock shop. If the outage is regional, we don't have to wait until tonight to hit that warehouse. We can do it as soon as we can get there, and should."

"But I'm not packed."

I was already dressing and didn't reply. Sure enough, forty-five minutes later we were in my car on our way. Sarah's a trooper.

And the power was off everywhere. Traffic was light. Why go to work if nothing at the office or factory will function, if the malls, grocery and convenience stores, and gas stations are closed?

The guys were waiting at the lock shop. "How'd you do it, Sarah? How did you kill the power?"

"I waved a wand," she said.

In addition to the Wire, Willis Coffee, and Travis Clay, there was one other guy there, a big black guy, really buff, who hadn't had a haircut or shaved in months. His name was Armanti Hall, and I knew him, although not very well, because he and I had done some training together a few years back. He was in a sour mood, didn't say a word.

"Armanti was waiting for me last night at my place," Travis said. "He wants to go with us, and he has a pickup with a bed cover."

"Did you brief him?"

"No. He doesn't give a damn what we're up to. I'll tell you about it later."

We unloaded the lock shop stuff from the van and began packing it with stuff we thought we might need in our war on FEMA and Barry Soetoro. Took some propane bottles and a torch, a box of tools, two crowbars, and some other things. I took my bag of cash and my weapons and ammo from the car and packed them in the van. The other guys had some small duffle bags of personal items, so we threw them in too.

Armanti and Willis muttered to each other while we loaded up. They decided to ride in Armanti's pickup together. We locked up the shop and my car and saddled up. Willie Varner and Travis rode in the back of the van and I drove, with Sarah Houston in the right seat.

After we were off the Beltway headed for Leesburg, I asked Travis what the story was on Armanti.

"He just got back from Syria a couple days ago. He thinks the agency will be looking for him soon, maybe to turn him over to civilian prosecutors."

"Lovely. Want to tell us about it?"

"They had him working with the Brits, trying to find the executioner. Last week sometime he went into a building to drag out a guy they wanted to question, guy who they thought was a big dog in ISIS. Hall is an expert in unarmed combat and he thought he could put him down quick, minimum fuss, minimum time, and carry him out."

Travis glanced at Sarah and stopped talking. I prompted him.

"Anyway, he got in okay and started searching the house. Couldn't find his guy. He went up the stairs to the third floor and walked in on the guy. The shit was trying to get his dick into a six-year-old girl. You know those guys are pedophiles, child-fuckers?"

"Yeah. I know."

"The kid was sobbing and had been hit a couple of times. Naked from the waist down. Armanti didn't hesitate, just came up behind the guy, grabbed him, and broke his neck. Crack. So with the guy there dead and the kid sobbing, Armanti castrated the corpse and stuffed his genitals into his mouth. That took just seconds.

"He had the kid under his left arm and was on his way out when a woman walked in. She took one look at the corpse and started to scream. He hit her once in the chest as hard as he could. Maybe he wasn't trying to kill her, just wind her good so she couldn't scream, but…anyway, the way he told it to me, her heart stopped dead. Probably burst like a balloon. He's a strong man and was all pumped on adrenaline…"

Travis took a few seconds, then continued, "Met a man coming up the stairs as he and the kid went down. The guy decided to shoot Armanti, but he was a hair slow. I think Armanti actually stuck his pistol in the guy's mouth and blew his head off."

We all thought about that for a moment.

Travis went on. "The Brits took the kid and said they would send her to a British charity that is trying to get orphans out of Syria and into the UK. Of course he had to tell the Brits why they didn't have a prisoner to sweat. They said to forget it, but you know how these things are. Someone will whisper about it, and when the agency gets wind of it, killing the mother and kidnapping the girl, the shit will hit the fan. Armanti just wants to be gone."

"How does he know the woman was the child's mother?" Sarah asked.

"She was. He was briefed before he went in. But when she walked into that room, she didn't care about the child—she was screaming about the holy warrior who was going to do a Muhammad on the kid. So he killed her. Instant justice, I guess."

"Can he be trusted?" I asked.

"You've trained with him, Tommy. I'd trust him with my life, but I don't do kids."

We left it there.

As we approached Leesburg I glanced to my left and saw a strip mall with one store all lit up. It was a drugstore. I wheeled the van into the parking lot. We locked it and went inside.

"How come you're open?" I asked the guy behind the counter.

"We have an emergency generator. We're open twenty-four/seven, all year around, rain, snow, or power outages. People sometimes need medications in the middle of the night. That's our edge."

We stocked up on bandages, antiseptics, needles and thread, surgical tape, aspirin, and a box of surgical gloves. "Be prepared," my scoutmaster always said.

The warehouse district is on the south side of Leesburg, in an industrial district that looked as if it contained only warehouses and light industry. Without power, there were only a few vehicles there today.

Sarah pointed out the warehouse we wanted. It was a big steel building and the sign said "Walmart. Always low prices. Always." It was locked up tight, with a steel personnel door and a code pad.

I parked the van so people down the street couldn't see what we were doing. Armanti parked a block away in the other direction.

We put on surgical gloves, and then used a propane torch and a crowbar. Took about ten minutes but we got that door open. No alarm sounded. The place was dark as King Tut's tomb. We used flashlights and right in front of us was a deuce and a half and four pickups with FEMA markings, plus a gaggle of big forklifts. I left the Wire outside to warn us if anyone came along, then, using flashlights, the rest of us explored.

The place looked like the hold of a ship heading for D-Day in Normandy. More pickups, trucks, Humvees, electrical generators on trailers, mobile kitchens, tanks for water and fuel, even some weird looking things that Travis said were microwave radar for crowd control, plus mobile radio setups and com units mounted on the backs of trucks. The stuff was painted a dark green and had a white star stenciled on each side. It wasn't marked U.S. Army. This was FEMA stuff, for Barry Soetoro's army.

That was one side of the warehouse. On the other side, arranged so there was room for forklifts to go between the stacks, were pallets of ammo, several tractor-trailer loads; more pallets with boxes full of one-piece green coveralls emblazoned with a FEMA badge on the right shoulder and an American flag on the left; tractor-trailer loads of MREs, meals ready to eat; mountains of weapons; crates of M4s, AT4s, heavy belt-fed .30-caliber machine guns and M279 light machine guns, hand grenades, belted ammo, and pistols; and even some small wooden boxes containing two sniper rifles each. There were some industrial-sized coffee pots, a truckload of first aid supplies, including anti-coagulant pads, and medical emergency kits for corpsmen. Basically, it looked to me like enough military supplies to outfit an infantry brigade for a trek across Africa even if they had to fight every step of the way.

"When the revolution comes, these folks planned to come out on the winning side," Willis Coffee remarked. The rest of us just looked around, stunned.

"Did you know all this was here, Tommy?" Armanti asked.

"Nope. But I was hopeful we'd find some weapons. Our pistols aren't going to be enough to pry Jake Grafton out of Camp Dawson."

"So that's what's going down."

"Yeah. You still want in?"

"Why not."

"Okay, people," I said. "Let's get at it. We'll load two of their pickups, the van, and Armanti's ride. Use that forklift over there to load up some pallets of MREs. Take four of those ten-gallon jerry cans full of fuel. We want a crate of AT4s, a couple of machine guns with boxes of belted 7.62 for them, a couple of light machine guns, a couple M4s for each of us, lots of ammo, and anything that looks interesting, like those boxes of hand grenades and the medical supplies. I don't want to die for lack of a Band-Aid. I'd also like a sniper rifle for my personal collection in case I decide to take up groundhog hunting. But what I'd really like to find in here is some C-4, timers, and detonators. Chop chop."

The good news was that Willis, Travis, Armanti, and I knew how to use all these weapons and keep them in good working order. Sarah didn't, of course, and neither did Willie the Wire. On one trip to the van with a crate of MREs, I asked Willie, "You want a rifle or pistol for a souvenir?"

"I'm a two-time loser, man, and you know it. If I got a pistol in my pocket when they arrest me for jaywalking while black, it's mandatory life. Thanks, but no thanks."

He was going to bet his life on our ability to rescue Grafton, but wanted to do it disarmed. Explain that logic if you can.

Since it was already ninety degrees outside, we threw our jeans and shirts in the van before we stepped into the new duds. Everyone but Willie strapped a web belt and pistol holster on, including Sarah. Beretta nines were the flavor of the day. "You know how to use that shooter?" I asked her.

"No, but it's the fashion accessory of the season, so I want one."

There were boxes of army combat boots in the warehouse, so we each took a pair. Sarah, of course, said, "I'm not wearing those."

"Find a pair that fits, try them on to make sure, then throw them in the van, just in case we have to wade a swamp."

She nodded and did it.

We spent fifteen minutes opening the overhead door so we could get the pickups out. Using the forklift, they raised me as high as possible and I unlatched it from the opening mechanism, then we used one of the door cables to pull it open. The forklift pulled and up it went. Willis and Travis climbed into the cabs of the pickups. The keys were in them, lying on the dashes.

"Look around and get all the people out of this area. You're FEMA guys, tough dudes. Government orders. Don't take any backtalk."

"You aren't going to blow this warehouse, Tommy," Willis Coffee said.

"I thought I would."

Willis lowered his head onto the steering wheel for a moment. When he raised his head, he said, "And I thought we were just going to burgle and run."

"Hey, Walmart's lawyers undoubtedly got FEMA to agree to indemnify them. The surrounding owners can sue in the sweet by and by, if the courts ever get back up and running."

"I don't care about that lawyer shit. I would prefer not to be chased. Not anytime soon, anyway."

"An opportunity like this comes along only once in a lifetime, if that," I told him.

So they drove through the open door and I walked over to the C-4 pile and got busy. I figured the C-4 would ignite all the ammo in the warehouse, so there would be a pretty good pop. Even if it didn't, the blast should wreck all this stuff, turn it into junk. Just to make sure, I poured a jerry can of gasoline on the ammo pile and opened three or four others. I gave us twenty minutes on the timer, checked my watch and saw it was two minutes after one o'clock, and pushed the button. The countdown began.

I used the forklift to lower the overhead door, then walked out of the warehouse through the buckled personnel door and pushed it shut. The three or four civilian vehicles that had been in front of other warehouses were now gone. I climbed into the van with Sarah and drove away. The pickups were waiting by the front gate. We headed west.

I was glancing at my watch when the whole thing went off. I saw the top of the mushroom cloud in my rearview mirror.

Sarah saw me looking, twisted her right side mirror, and took a squint.

"Tommy, what if some civilian was killed in that explosion?"

"We all have to die sometime. I'll pray for 'em." I wouldn't, though, if I heard they were Soetoro voters.

It took a little under half a minute for the sound of the blast to reach us. The concussion probably broke windows in Leesburg.

SEVENTEEN

★

The mushroom cloud was still hanging over Leesburg when General Martin L. Wynette and two staff officers, both generals, arrived at the Executive Office Building across from the White House. President Soetoro and thirty or so of his staff were waiting in a large conference room. The emergency generators were apparently running sweetly: the building was well lit and the air conditioners were pumping cool air.

"So what is your plan to crush Texas?" the president asked the chairman of the JCS.

"The briefer has some maps. He'll run through it and we'll answer questions."

The briefer, Major General Strong, stood in front of a huge computer screen, upon which a PowerPoint presentation was projected. "Our first problem is manpower. Given desertions, we're estimating our combat effectives are fifty percent of what they should be."

The president's chief of staff, Al Grantham, blew up. By reputation, he was one of the most aggressive leftists on the president's staff, and, although he was white, was of the opinion that white America would have to be conquered. He thought most whites were racists and Nazis. "You mean to tell me that in the armed forces only the people who want to fight have to fight?"

Wynette said flatly, "We have a volunteer army. It's hard to make someone fight if they refuse to do so."

Grantham glared. "What the hell have we been paying them for?"

"We have been paying them to defend the United States. Not to put too fine a point on it, a lot of our personnel don't think shooting their fellow Americans meets those criteria."

"Court-martial the bastards."

"Oh, we can do that, if the president orders us to do so. We can convict them of cowardice, give them bad discharges, maybe some jail time, but that still doesn't put people in ranks willing to fight."

The president gestured at the briefer to continue.

The major general nodded and said, "We will take two divisions, one armored, one infantry, from Georgia and Alabama; put them on trains, trucks, and air force transports; and assemble at Barksdale Air Force Base in Louisiana. From there we will proceed to Austin and take it, engaging any Texas military units or guerilla bands we encounter along the way. Meanwhile we will have the Fourth Infantry division at Fort Carson in Colorado proceed by road to Amarillo, and from there to Austin. So we will have three divisions in a two-pronged assault. Operating on two fronts—"

"How will they get across the rivers and all that?" Grantham interrupted, glowering.

"I was about to cover that, sir," the briefer said patiently. "We will drop paratroops to seize the key bridges and hold until relieved. Then—"

"So how are you going to get there? Across cow pastures and rice paddies?"

"We will use the interstates and other roads where possible. A division cannot move on only one road. It must move on a wide front, yet not so wide that one brigade cannot reinforce the other. Where we must cross rivers without a bridge available, we will use pontoons. We will have close air support from attack helicopters and air force fighters every foot of the way. We'll use satellite reconnaissance, aerial reconnaissance, and drones to keep us apprised of the enemy's movements."

"Those crackers are going to shoot at you," Al Grantham said. "Probably a lot. Every one of those racists has a gun, or two or three or four."

"No doubt," Martin Wynette replied. "We'll take casualties, yet we'll annihilate all opposition and proceed forward as fast as possible to our objective."

The president smiled at that comment. He apparently liked to think of his opposition being annihilated. Then the smile faded. "When?" he asked.

"It will take at least two days to get people sorted out and transferred to fill up our three assault divisions. Another four days to get our people and equipment to Barksdale, and another two days to get them under way. The Fort Carson division commander says he can get his division under way in two days, after he gets his personnel sorted out and is reinforced by willing fighters. That shuffling will take at least two days, maybe three. Then it will take another three days to get them to the Texas line. Seven days total. If anything slips, eight or nine."

"What will the rebels be doing while we are getting our show ready to go on the road?"

"Making a nuisance of themselves and getting ready to block our moves."

"How will they know what we intend?"

"Texas' commander is JR Hays, Jack Hays' cousin, and he was a career army officer, although retired now. He could probably write our op order. If he hadn't burned out in the Middle East and retired, he would have become a general. I've seen his service record. JR Hays is a soldier from head to toe, and he doesn't shrink from combat. He's seen more than his share and knows precisely how to fight. And how to win. The Taliban had a price on his head: ten thousand American dollars. No one in the Middle East was able to earn it."

"Can you whip him?"

"The United States Army can."

"Eight days to get combat troops into Texas," Al Grantham stated. "Or nine. Or ten. Or eleven. That's too long. Can't we use fewer troops and go sooner?"

"Even if we cut our invasion force to only one division, we will only save one day," Wynette said flatly. "So the tradeoff is one division that can possibly be surrounded and cut off, or a two-pronged assault that will force the Texans to divide their forces to fight them both. In my military judgment, and the judgment of the Joint Chiefs, if we are going to hit Texas with a hammer, it should be a really big hammer, as big as we can put together in a reasonable amount of time. Given a month, we could hit them with every American soldier willing to fight."

The president nodded his agreement.

Grantham asked, "And how many is that?"

"I don't know yet," Wynette said. He continued, "There are around twelve thousand fighting soldiers in a division. We'd like the divisions at full strength, if possible. In addition to their weapons, artillery, air support, food, and ammo, we must also move all the support equipment and manpower required to keep the warriors eating, sleeping, and fighting, the planes and choppers flying, the artillery supplied with ammo, and enough extra stuff to provide humanitarian relief. We are doing all we can to get this organized and moving, which is everything humanly possible."

"So we sit on our asses for eight days and wait," Al Grantham summed up.

Wynette gestured to the briefer, who went on with his presentation. JCS envisioned beginning air operations against Texas tomorrow. The targets would be all the surrendered military equipment at the military bases. Missions would be flown by B-52s escorted by F-16s during the day and B-1s at night targeting Fort Bliss, the Texas Guard armories, and other military targets. The navy can bring an aircraft carrier around Florida and begin air operations in two days against the military bases around San Antonio and Killeen. "Our goal," the briefer summed up, "is to attrite their armor and air assets by seventy-five percent by D-Day, which is the day we plan to cross the Texas border."

"Why not hammer their industry, their refineries, and factories and power plants?"

"Those are legitimate strategic military targets," Major General Strong said, "but the primary goal of the air campaign must be the destruction of the enemy's combat power—the opposition we'll face when we put boots on the ground. After we knock out their combat power and render it impotent, then we can bomb strategic targets."

"But before we do that," interjected Wynette, "you must decide how much of an economy you want standing after we take over. If everyone is destitute and starving, the assets to feed them and rebuild Texas must come from the rest of the United States."

"Just the military targets," the president said. Then he added, "Unless this invasion gets bogged down. If push comes to shove, we are going to win if we have to flatten every building and kill every cow in Texas."

"Yes, sir," General Wynette said.

Barry Soetoro leaned forward in his chair and looked straight into Wynette's eyes. "I expect you to crush the rebels, General. If you don't, don't come back alive."

It was the second time that the president had told him that, and though Wynette had kissed ass for a lot of years, he was fed up with Barry Soetoro. "Mr. President, if you don't think I can win, fire me and get a general you think can. The army has plenty of experienced combat leaders for you to pick from."

"You're the man I want," Soetoro shot back. "I *know* you'll obey orders."

"And you think these others might not? What kind of orders wouldn't they obey?"

Soetoro's eyes were locked on Martin Wynette. "We'll cross that bridge when we get to it," he said.

Wynette was the first to look away.

Back in the air-conditioned Pentagon, Wynette had another bad moment. The staff had framed the loyalty question to the troops as "Are you willing to fight for the United States of America to stamp out a rebellion?" *Yes* or *No*.

Last night on television he saw commentators talking about "Barry Soetoro's army" versus Texas. Wynette thought—and he knew many of his troops thought—there was a huge difference between "Barry Soetoro's army" and "the United States Army," and the more commentators talked like that, the more desertions he would have.

The Joint Chiefs assembled in his office. They wanted to know their role in putting down the riots that were raging in the big cities.

"Forget about that for now. That doesn't seem to be the president's priority," Wynette replied. "He seems to think that if he squashes Texas, all his other problems will go away. However, in fifteen minutes Grantham may call and want us to invade Detroit."

What he didn't say, although he thought it, was that the president and his staff were fixated on the wrong problem. In his years of service he had served on joint staffs on numerous occasions and knew it was the job of a commander to define the priorities and keep his staff focused on them. Wynette thought Barry Soetoro didn't understand what his problems were or couldn't prioritize; if either was the case, he was incompetent. As the general saw it, the primary problem in America just now was that civil authority in much of the nation was about to collapse. It wasn't just Texas that the president might lose, it was America.

When JR Hays arrived in Austin that afternoon, he headed straight for the capitol and was ushered into the governor's (now the president's) office. He waited in a corner while some politicians briefed Jack.

Several thousand people a day were pouring into Texas from other states. Many of these people said their extended families, neighbors, and coworkers were only a day or two behind them. More people were coming, a lot more, and they would need housing and jobs. After the politicians had spent ten minutes discussing how the flood of refugees might be accommodated temporarily, Hays shooed them out and locked the door. He and JR sat in chairs facing each other.

"We've had some good luck," JR said, "because a lot of the people in the army and air force refused to fight for Barry Soetoro. Any commander in that position would have had to surrender. Still, those services are going to find people who *will* fight for Soetoro, and then the shooting will begin in earnest."

"So what's your plan?"

"We can't sit here waiting for Soetoro to hammer us. I would bet my soul they are plotting to do that right now in Washington. If Soetoro lets us get away with leaving the Union and setting up as an independent nation, other states will do it too, one by one, and eventually he won't own anything but the federal district in Washington. He can't let that happen. He has to whip us, and he has to do it as soon as he can assemble the forces to do it with. Every day he doesn't win is a victory for us. If we can pile up enough little victories, we can win the war."

Jack Hays nodded. He was delighted JR was thinking about all this, because he hadn't had time. Politics was his business, not the military.

"We need to seize the initiative and force Soetoro's military forces to react to us. We need to put them on the defensive, derail *their* plans. And, if possible, we need to move the fight out of Texas; we want the front line to be somewhere else, not here."

"So how do you propose to do that?"

JR Hays began explaining his plans.

When he had finished, Jack nodded.

"We're going to have a lot of civilian problems to deal with," JR added. "Soon the enemy will target our power plants. Houston and Dallas and the high-rises all over Texas will instantly become uninhabitable. We need to get organized now to take care of what will become a huge humanitarian crisis."

"Houston and Dallas are using school buses to evacuate all the people stranded at the airports," the governor mused, "so we have a start, anyway. I'll get our emergency people involved."

"In my view, Jack, your number one job is to buck up the people of Texas with your courage and determination to see this through to the end."

"My courage? How much do you think I have?"

"Enough, or we're doomed. Leaders must lead. But the more effective you are, the more likely Soetoro will send assassins or commandos to take you out. If they kill you, the backbones of a lot of people will soften. Get some bodyguards, and good ones. Use them."

"The Texas Rangers," Jack Hays decided.

"Your call. But they must keep you alive. That said, you and the Congress need to get out of this building and set up at an undisclosed location. I suggest somewhere underground, like a parking garage under a hotel. Right now a handful of cruise missiles into the capitol would decapitate the new republic. No doubt Soetoro is thinking about that right now, trying to figure out what the repercussions of a mass assassination would be on his political base up north."

"We'll be out by five o'clock."

Jack Hays nodded, stood, and shook hands. JR left. He had a ton of things to do, all of which needed to be done at once. Or yesterday.

His jailers came in midafternoon and tossed a plastic water bottle on the cot. Jake Grafton was still on the floor. One of the jailers came in and kicked Grafton in the ribs, repeatedly.

The man who delivered the water stopped the kicker. "Don't kill him. Sluggo wants him alive."

Grafton was still conscious. His ribs were on fire. If one of the broken edges penetrated a lung, he would die quickly. If he started coughing blood, he would know.

Steeling himself, he moved. The pain was searing. He managed to reach the water bottle.

The plastic cap almost defeated him. He had to open it with his teeth. After he drained it, he lay back on the floor. And passed out.

As it happened, the White House political staff was indeed trying to estimate the damage decapitating the Republic of Texas would cause in the president's political base. Would it fuel insurrection elsewhere? There were no easy answers, so the staff was having a wonderful time wrestling with these imponderables, preparing a list of options for the chosen one.

While staff was staffing, Barry Soetoro signed an order temporarily closing all stock and commodity exchanges. Since the power was off in New York and Chicago, this order wouldn't create much of a sensation today, but it would when the power came back on. Tomorrow, perhaps. Or the next day. No one knew when the juice would again flow. The power company execs were doing all they could, they told his staff. One of them darkly hinted at sabotage, but Soetoro wasn't buying that excuse. One natural-gas trunk line in Virginia had been severed, stopping the gas flow through that line, yet that amount was only a drop in the bucket. Sheer damned incompetence, he thought angrily. One of these days he was going to have to nationalize all the public utilities, replace the executives with reliable people.

His thoughts turned back to Texas. Using cruise missiles or JDAMs on all the power plants in Texas was certainly an option. In August and September it was a lot hotter in Texas than it was in most of the Northeast. Texas was closer to Hell.

Had Soetoro been a fly on the wall in Jack Hays' office that afternoon, he would have been delighted at what he heard. A delegation of oil and gas and refinery executives had called in a body upon the new president. Many rich men and women value predictability and stability above all else, so this crowd had been cold to the idea of independence from the start, hinting strongly, as it did, of civil war. There is a lot of money to be made in war, but people with multibillion dollar capital investments in the line of fire wouldn't be making much of it. If anything, they stood to have their investments wiped out.

Jack Hays listened patiently to the executives.

"Mr. President, the fact is that any damned fool with a machine gun or a few sticks of dynamite could take down the refineries on the southeast coast of Texas." Even if that didn't happen, the feds could destroy the refineries and oil storage tanks by air attack. And the U.S. Navy could prevent tankers carrying foreign oil from discharging their cargoes, restricting supply to what Texas could produce, which in fact was a hell of a lot, since Texas was the biggest producer of hydrocarbons among the fifty states. Still, guerillas or federal forces could stop the flow of natural gas and gasoline out of Texas, destroying their markets. All together, the group spokesman said, the picture was "bleak."

"What assurances, Mr. President, can you give us that the armed forces of the Republic can protect our facilities?"

"Very few, gentlemen," Jack Hays said. "In fact, I was thinking of asking you to stop pumping oil and gas to the northeastern United States and California. That would bring a significant amount of political pressure to bear on the Soetoro administration."

The executives were horrified. Such an action would cut off their cash flow, and it would mean that many of their facilities would have to shut down, oil and gas wells would be shut in, people would be laid off, and money would cease to percolate through the economy.

"Do you realize, sir, how many people make their livings directly from the petroleum industry in Texas? And twice that many indirectly. You are talking about a depression, *millions* jobless."

Another said, "The people of Texas didn't sign up for *that*!"

Jack Hays refused to be riled. "I think the people of Texas knew that they would have to fight for their independence when the idea was first discussed. In a war one stands to lose not only his livelihood, his home, and everything he owns, but also his life and the lives of his family. Texans aren't stupid; they knew that. They were for independence anyway, if that meant they could preserve the benefits of a free society with a representative democratic government that they had enjoyed all their lives, benefits they hoped to again enjoy, benefits that would be their legacy to their children and the generations of Texans still to come. They were willing to pay the price. Or most of them were, anyway."

Everyone tried to talk at once, but Jack Hays silenced them with a gesture.

"We have taken a political step that cannot be reversed," he said.

"Of course it can be reversed," a big oil executive said loudly, to drown out other voices. "It's time to make peace with Soetoro. You've made your political points, Hays. Now let's settle this mess and get on with business."

"Talk loud, then surrender. Is that your advice?"

"Now see here. That isn't what I said. Oil and gas are the heart of Texas industry. Hell, of American industry."

"Gentlemen, thank you for your time today," Jack Hays said. "I will carefully consider all your points. For my part, I'm glad that Colonel

Travis had men with him at the Alamo who had more backbone than you have."

One of the executives—dressed in an Armani suit, hand-tooled alligator boots, and a two-hundred-dollar silk tie—snarled: "Travis didn't own a goddamn thing but his horse and some worthless scrub land. If he had owned something he'd have been a bit more careful."

And you'd be speaking Spanish and working for Petromex, Jack Hays thought savagely. He didn't say that, of course. What he did say was, "I will meditate upon that insight. Now if you ladies and gentlemen will excuse me..."

"How much time do you think we have before the electrical wizards figure out what you did to their computer, and fix it?" I asked Sarah as we rolled into the West Virginia panhandle.

"I have no idea," she said distractedly. She was looking at the huge towers carrying their high-voltage transmission wires across the countryside.

When I realized what she was looking at, I said, "Are you thinking what I'm thinking?"

"There's no power on those wires right now. If we could lay down some towers, they wouldn't know we did it until the grid came back up. People who see it fall can't even call in."

"You are a natural-born terrorist," I acknowledged.

I pulled over to the side of the road and the pickups pulled up behind me. I got out, and we all huddled over a roadmap. "Here is where we're going, Camp Dawson, near Kingwood, West Virginia, in Preston County. I thought we would stay off the interstates and do the back roads. But along the way, I'd like to take down some of these transmission towers. Two or three on each right of way, to put the wires on the ground. Use C-4, set the timers to the max on the dial."

"That's an hour," Armanti Hall said.

"You guys can drop off, do a couple of towers, then catch back up. Try to make them fall in the woods or streams, not on the road. We'll meet here." I jabbed my finger at a crossroads, near Kingwood.

"Okay by me," Travis said. The others nodded their heads.

I went back to the van and climbed in.

"I could use a bathroom," Sarah said.

"The side of the road is brushy," I pointed out. "No one will see you. Climb on down there."

"I don't have any toilet paper."

I reached around the seat to my duffle bag, extracted a roll, and passed it to her. "I stole a roll of yours this morning when we were leaving."

She scanned the roadside weeds, then observed, "There might be poison ivy or snakes."

I started the engine and got the van rolling. "Maybe we'll find an open filling station with clean restrooms," I said brightly, "or even a McDonald's."

"Jerk."

She ended up using a port-a-potty on a road bridge rebuild project. The construction crew wasn't around. After she finished, I used it too. It smelled like every port-a-potty I'd ever been in, but it was like the facilities at the Ritz compared to the places I had pooped in the Middle East, often merely a hole in the floor you squatted over. Or a patch of desert. The miracle of toilet paper has not yet been revealed to most of the sons of Islam. Muhammad never said a word about it. If you don't believe me, read your Koran.

When we were back rolling again, I told her, "There may come a day when you dream longingly of that port-a-potty."

"Did you see the graffiti in there?"

"Yes."

"Men are such pigs."

I let that one go by without comment.

A little while later Sarah began to laugh.

"What's so funny?"

"Oh, I was just thinking about the irony of it all. Jake Grafton and I have been listening to the goings-on at the White House for about six months. He knew all about Soetoro's plan to declare martial law and tear up the Constitution."

I stared at her, trying to decide if she was telling the truth. And almost ran off the road.

She chuckled. "He refused to do anything about it, of course. Said there was nothing he could do. And maybe he was right. If he told people about Soetoro's plan, they would have thought him crazy. It would have gotten back to the White House, and they would have arrested him and locked him up. So he decided to do nothing and he got blamed for a fake coup and assassination plot and he's locked up anyway. Life is crazy."

"Tell me more."

"Only Grafton and I know about it. When the Iran treaty was being negotiated in Switzerland, he asked me if we could bug the hotels where the delegates were staying. He wanted to know what the Iranians were talking about, what their negotiating strategy was. The problem was that the hotels were going to be swept repeatedly, and any bugs with transmitters would be quickly discovered. So I ginned up a program to use all the hotels' computers and security systems as listening devices and have the feed sent to me over the internet.

"But when I got into their systems, I found that the Israelis had been there first. They had a surveillance system in place using the computers and security cameras and even the personal computers that everyone brought with them and that used the hotels' Wi-Fi systems to connect with the internet. You may have heard about it last year. The Russians had the same idea, and they announced the Israelis' espionage."

"I did hear about that."

"The Israeli system was better than mine. So I got all their computer code and we just listened in."

"Jesus," I said, trying to think as I steered the vehicle. That Grafton!

"Then about six months ago, he asked if I could use the Israeli system on the White House."

"Jesus!"

"He and I have been listening for six months. All the plotting, all the plans, all the bullshit. But he wouldn't do anything about it."

"You are saying he knew about the coming of martial law?"

"Oh yes. He and I knew. They were merely waiting for an excuse. They thought the excuse would be a domestic terror incident, but if that hadn't happened, it would have been something else. Martial law was going to happen. We were the only ones who knew outside the inner circle at the White House. I demanded the admiral do something, but he just gave me those cold gray eyes and asked, 'What?'"

Indeed, I thought, what? Whom do you tell? Who will believe?

"So here we go, riding to the rescue," she said sourly, "and he knew all along."

"So did you."

"Yeah. I had to agree with Grafton. What do you do when the president is plotting to become a dictator?"

"Assassinate him," I suggested.

"Who? Me? Grafton? Or should Grafton have sent you to do the dirty deed?"

She had a point.

EIGHTEEN

★

The Blackhawk helicopter settled onto the tarmac at the Longview, Texas, airport, shut down, and JR Hays went forward to speak to the pilots. CWO4 Erik Sabiston was in the right seat.

"Wait for me," JR said. "Be back late this evening. Fuel the chopper and get something to eat."

"Yes, sir."

JR climbed out and walked across the tarmac into the FBO. "I need a car," he said to the lady on the desk.

"We have a courtesy car, sir. It's kinda old and wrinkled, like me, but it'll probably get you there and back again. Always has so far, anyway."

She handed him the keys and he made a pit stop, then went outside and climbed in. It was an old Ford with sun-scorched paint and more than a hundred fifty thousand miles on the odometer. It started on the first crank.

He had gotten the address from the Texas Department of Motor Vehicles. It took him a while to find it that afternoon. There were high cirrus clouds up there, making the afternoon light gauzy. It didn't do much to soften the heat, though.

JR found his address in a newer subdivision, parked on the street, and walked up the driveway. Inside he heard a dog barking, a little one from the sound of it. Rang the doorbell.

In a moment a man in shorts and an old army T-shirt opened the door, a man in his mid-fifties.

"JR Hays! As I live and breathe!"

"Hello, Nate. May I come in?"

"Of course." The man threw the door wide, then closed it behind JR. His name was Nathaniel Danaher, and he was a retired army colonel with thirty years service. JR had served under him on his last combat tour in Afghanistan. Danaher was from Connecticut originally, but he hadn't lived there since he went away to VMI for college. He hadn't been able to score a West Point appointment so he joined the VMI corps of cadets, got a reserve commission, which, after a few years of outstanding service, the army transformed into a regular commission.

"I like the gleam of those stars on your blouse, JR. Somehow they look exactly right on you. Want a beer?"

"Sure."

With beers in hand, they sat on the covered porch in the backyard, a *ramada* as the old Texans called it. It kept the sun off and allowed the people sheltered under it to savor any breeze. The dog, some kind of terrier, was friendly enough. He did some exploratory sniffing and then found a shady spot to lie down.

Danaher was still lean and fit. He looked, JR thought, exactly as he had when he was in Afghanistan, only a little older and grayer. JR remarked on it.

"Still get up at five o'clock every morning and run five miles," Danaher said. "Might as well; can't sleep past five anyway. Heard your cousin put you in charge. He couldn't have found a better man."

"That remains to be seen. Where do you stand on independence?"

"Well, when I first heard about it, I thought, there goes my fucking pension and health benefits unless I get the hell out of Texas. That was pretty small of me, I suppose, but then I heard on TV that Texas is taking over all the federal government's obligations to military and Social Security retirees, so that was a relief. I've got some money saved up but nowhere near enough without a pension. I despise that son of a bitch Soetoro and everything he stands for. It's a big club so I have lots of friends. Independence is great if you folks can make it stick, because the country that elected that bastard twice is going somewhere most people in Texas don't want to go."

"I need some help," JR said. "I need some civilian duds, and then if you are willing, let's the two of us drive over to Louisiana and take a look around."

"You mean it?"

"I do."

"My wife is playing bridge this afternoon. Went over after lunch. I'll leave her a note. We'll be back tonight?"

"I hope."

"I think I may have some clothes that will fit you. If you haven't had lunch, mine the refrigerator while I root around. Make yourself a sandwich or something. Last night's meat loaf was pretty good."

JR was halfway through a cold meat loaf sandwich when Nate returned with a pair of baggy shorts, an ancient VMI T-shirt, and a set of worn tennis shoes. He also handed JR a pistol, an old double-action revolver, small and trim. "If you're going to Louisiana you better take this, stick it in your pocket, just in case. It's loaded."

JR checked the cylinder, snapped it back in place. The gun was an old Smith & Wesson in .38 Special with about half its bluing remaining. "That thing's about ninety or so years old," Danaher said. "Used to carry it in my pocket when a service pistol wouldn't do. Louisiana is enemy territory for you."

Nate Danaher's car was a late model sedan. "Where are we going?"

"Barksdale Air Force Base, east of Shreveport and Bossier City."

"I know where it is. Take Gina to the doctor there on a regular basis. She's got lymphoma. It's under control now, we think, but..." he shrugged, "it's in God's hands. I shop at the PX while she's getting examined."

"Stay off the interstate tonight. Take the back roads. We don't need to run into a roadblock."

"Sure."

"Got that postcard from you a while back," JR explained. "So I knew you were in Texas. Why here?"

"Our daughter is here. Her husband is an engineer in the oil business. Gina wanted to be near the grandson, Little Nate, who just turned seven. He's a pistol."

"I seem to recall you had a son, too."

"Yep. Got on drugs in high school and dropped out. Pot at first, then crack, then heroin and meth. We put him in rehab twice, but it didn't take. Haven't seen him in... well, it's been twelve years now. A few years ago someone said they saw him in New Orleans, living on the street. For all I know he may be dead now. All those drugs—it figures he won't last too long."

JR changed the subject. "So how is Longview taking to independence?"

"Was out at Walmart today. The place was packed. People on welfare were cashing their last checks, loading up their cars, and getting out of Texas. They heard Texas isn't paying welfare anymore, so a lot of them are heading for greener pastures. Everyone else is stocking up. Everything they can get, food, toilet paper, everything. People in line said the liquor stores were mobbed. I wanted to buy a little generator—figured I could wire it into the house circuits some way—but Walmart was out of them. None in the hardware stores. People sense that times are going to get hard."

"Yeah," JR said dryly.

Sarah and I drove the van along the road by Camp Dawson and sure enough, there was the compound that held the detainees, though we didn't see any. The compound, surrounded by a chain-link fence topped by barbed wire, with guard towers about ten feet above the ground on all four corners, was about a hundred yards on each side. It was lit up in the late afternoon like Macy's on Christmas Eve, so obviously they had generators going. All the comforts...

The gate was manned by four guys in FEMA dark-green coveralls carrying carbines and wearing green caps. They weren't soldiers, lounging around like that, smoking, laughing, and grab-assing. And, I suspected, they were not well disciplined. No army sergeant I ever met would allow his troops to goof off on guard duty. They were armed thugs.

I got all this on one slow drive-by. The gate guards paid no attention to us. The guy on the last guard tower was leaning on the rails of his perch, smoking a cigarette, looking into the compound.

Which made me suspect that they weren't worried about people breaking in, but their prisoners breaking out. The thought that someone might assault them with intent to kill apparently had not entered their hard little heads. When the shooting started in earnest, many would probably boogie. No one wants to be dead any time soon, which can happen when people shoot at you.

Across the road from the compound was an up-sloping pasture, maybe fifty yards wide, with what looked to me like yearling steers in there munching grass. Maybe dreaming of the girlfriends they would never have. Perhaps those were the virgins the jihadists would find in Paradise. Beyond the pasture and higher was a strip of forest on a low ridge. Over the top of the ridge I got a glimpse of a green mountain.

I kept on driving, thinking about how we could pop Jake Grafton out of that compound. Since we had no idea where in there he was, we were going to have to ask someone. That would be my job. I am pretty good at getting answers in a hurry from people who initially thought they didn't want to be bothered.

The designated rendezvous was a crossroads about eight more miles along. I pulled over to the side of the road and turned off the engine. The sun was just setting, so we had at least another half hour of evening, then maybe another fifteen minutes of twilight.

All I needed were my troops.

"You know how to use that pistol?" I asked Sarah.

"Never fired one in my life."

I showed her how the Beretta worked, popped out the magazine, jacked out the shell from the chamber, made her dry fire it, and put everything in and reloaded. "Just disengage the safety, point, and pull the trigger. It will fire thirteen shots, one with every squeeze of the trigger. The gun will kick in your hand, so use both hands. Don't use it unless the bad guy is very close, and keep shooting until he's dead on the ground. Not wounded on the ground, but obviously dead, so he can't hurt you."

"Okay," she said, hefting the weapon.

"Never point a gun at a man unless you are willing to shoot, and never shoot unless you are willing to kill. This isn't Hollywood."

"Okay," she repeated, and holstered the weapon.

I felt better. She seemed to be getting into this warrior gig. If I could just keep finding her bathrooms or port-a-potties.

I rooted in my duffel and came up with my Kimber 1911 in a holster. I added it to my web belt and put it on the right side. On the left I put my Marine Corps fighting knife with the eight-inch blade.

The Beretta was a 9-mm: it shot a .357-caliber, 125-grain full-metal-jacket bullet since it was a weapon of war—Geneva Convention and all that—and would make nice holes in people. Magazine capacity was thirteen rounds. The .45 shot a 230-grain bullet, and I used hollow points. Under fifty feet, one of those to the body would kill King Kong. It held eight cartridges, but if eight wasn't enough, I was probably gonna soon be dead anyway.

I made sure my shooter was cocked and locked, then sat there wondering where my troops were. Civilian cars and pickups came by from time to time, and after a glimpse of my FEMA green, ignored us. Apparently the boys in Soetoro's army were not yet winning the hearts and minds of the locals. I glanced at my watch from time to time.

"Stop fidgeting," Sarah said.

I loaded up some M4s, passed one to Sarah, and laid a couple behind the passenger seat where I could reach them. Broke out some grenades and put one in each shirt pocket.

Finally I got a couple of boxes of MREs and dug through them. Sarah took a fruit cup, and I munched a cardboard cookie that had come out of the oven during the first Bush administration. We certainly weren't in danger of gaining weight on this adventure.

★

Before they went onto the base, JR Hays and Nate Danaher stopped at a beer joint, which was packed, every stool and booth full, with people standing and drinking beer. The conversations were loud. A television was on up in the corner, showing the devastating effects of the power outage in the northeastern United States. Philadelphia and Baltimore were rioting as usual.

JR kept an eye on the television as he waited for Danaher to work his way to the bar and order beers. There was a short segment about rioting in Watts in LA, then a parade of Soetoro administration officials being interviewed. JR couldn't hear the audio, but he thought he knew what the officials were saying. Everything was under control. The administration was taking steps, and so on.

Then he heard a snatch of a conversation between two men at the bar. "This place is going to be packed when those soldiers get here.... Yeah, I heard the day after tomorrow.... Someone said the Fourth Brigade.... Gonna come in dribs and drabs, I suppose.... Thirty-five hundred men and equipment is a lot to move...."

The Fourth Brigade Combat Team of the 10th Mountain Division. JR knew about them. The fact that they were being deployed from Fort Polk, the massive joint training base further south in Louisiana, to Barksdale was certainly news. There was also a brigade of airborne troops at Fort Polk, JR thought, and he listened intently to see if the garrulous bar buddies knew about them. A brigade of paratroopers dropping into Texas, or Barksdale, could cause massive problems.

He wandered on, listening. Most of the men and women in the bar were talking about the run on grocery stores and Walmarts. The lines were horrendous. One woman said she waited over an hour in line to check out. One gasoline station was completely out of gas and the clerk said they didn't know when they could get more.

After they drank some of their beer, JR and Danaher left the mugs on the bar and went outside. Their retired military ID cards got them onto the base. They drove over by the flight line and looked at the rows of B-52s parked there. Barksdale was home to the 2nd Bomb Wing, the only outfit in the air force that still had B-52 Stratofortresses.

Huge hangars, flood-lit ramps, here and there a security vehicle. Half-full parking lots. Activity at the barracks.

The parking lots at the commissary and PX were packed, with almost every space occupied. A long line waited to get to the fuel pumps at the base filling station.

JR told Danaher about the conversation he had overheard.

"That's no surprise," Nate replied.

"I want you to lead an assault team in here tomorrow morning. We need to take this base and be prepared to hold it. If we can't, we need to destroy those B-52s. Can an assault team arriving on C-130s pull it off?"

"Let's go back to the flight line and take a look," Danaher said.

"If it can't, we can do an air attack tomorrow," JR explained. "Strafe the flight lines, drop some JDAMs on the hangars and fuel farm, make a royal mess."

"Hold that thought. I have a small set of binoculars in the glove box. Let's trade places, and I'll look while you drive."

They did so. The only plane in the traffic pattern was a B-52 shooting landings, apparently on a training mission. They could hear the engines roar every time it lifted off and watch it in the pattern, a big dark-green metal cloud.

"They're not bombing up the BUFFs," Danaher said after a while. "No missile batteries or missile-control radars or AAA in sight." AAA was anti-aircraft artillery. Five more minutes of looking, then Danaher said, "Let's go home. We've seen all that there is to see."

Sluggo Sweatt had Jake Grafton brought to his office that Tuesday evening. Grafton couldn't walk, so the jailers dragged him. They didn't bother putting him in a chair. Sluggo came around his desk and rested a hip on the edge of it and looked down at Grafton lying on the floor. Sluggo had a smile on his face.

"How are your ribs?"

Grafton tried to focus. Being dragged here had made him want to scream, so he had bitten his tongue. Now blood was leaking out his lips. He could feel it, warm and slick.

"I think we'll take you back to your cell and let you sleep through the night. If tomorrow you don't sign the confession in front of a television camera and read the little script we have prepared—it's only about a hundred words—we'll beat you to death tomorrow night. The other prisoners will hear your screams. I'll be honest, Grafton, I don't like you. Still, I urge you to be tough. Don't give us an inch. Then I will have the pleasure of helping the boys work on you."

Sluggo Sweatt smiled at Grafton. He picked up a sheet of paper from his desk, fluttered it, then handed it to one of the thugs and made a gesture. They dragged Grafton back to the cell. There they threw the sheet of paper on his chest and left him lying on the floor, after one of them had kicked him in the balls.

The overhead lights were on. Although Jake Grafton didn't know it, the power for the camp was being supplied by several large emergency generators since the grid was down. With the generators snoring away, grid problems didn't really matter to Sluggo Sweatt. He was the king of his own little empire, and he liked the feeling.

Every breath Grafton drew was agony. When the fierce pain in his testicles finally subsided to a dull ache, exhaustion overcame him and he went to sleep. He dreamed of Callie.

Armanti Hall and Willie the Wire showed up first. I got out of the van and Willie started motormouthing. "Damn, Tommy, did we have fun! You should have seen those towers come down. Man, if someone would pay me for doing this, I'd give up the locksmith business in a heartbeat."

I didn't have the heart to tell the fool that he was probably permanently out of the locksmith business unless a meteor hit the White House and all its inhabitants were instantly obliterated.

"How'd it go?" I asked Armanti Hall.

"We dumped towers on two different transmission lines. Just walked up to them, rigged the charges, and went on to the next one. We watched one stretch of them go down. Some of the lines broke, and the others went on the ground."

"You two get some MREs, take a whiz, and when the other guys get here I'll brief everyone."

Ten minutes later Travis Clay rolled in, and five minutes after that Willis Coffee. They had each found a transmission line and put three towers on the ground. Travis, however, had done more. He came across a substation and used an AT4 to put it out of business. "That box blew apart into a thousand pieces, Tommy. It was kinda fun."

"I'll bet. You didn't leave the tube there, did you?"

"Oh, no. It's in the back of the truck."

"Good man."

I addressed my lock shop partner. "Tell me, Willie, now that you are back in the felony business, are you willing to pull a trigger or not?"

"Well..."

"One life sentence, two, three, what does it matter?"

"You're suckin' me into a life of crime, Carmellini. I'm not ready to give up pussy. I got a few good years left, dude, me and Viagra, and a couple of women who are countin' on me to help them find a little joy in this colorless life."

"Sarah, would you put a first aid box in each truck while I brief these guys?"

We gathered around the hood of one of the FEMA pickups. I spread out the map. "Here is where we are going to rendezvous, this bridge over the Greenbrier at Bartow. Then we'll go to the CIA's safe house near Greenbank. I want each of you to go to Bartow by a different route." We traced routes with fingers in the twilight.

Then I explained the setup at Camp Dawson, how the internment compound was laid out, where the four guard towers were.

"Now, Sarah and I are going to drive in the main gate of the internment compound in a FEMA pickup. We'll want to find out where Grafton is being held. We'll ask to see the commandant of the camp. Meanwhile Armanti and Willie Varner, you will go through the main gate of the National Guard base and come around behind the compound. That gate was open when I went by and the Guard looked like it had moved out. Set up an M279 machine gun out back. There is undoubtedly a rear gate through the compound wire, and maybe a barracks where these FEMA dudes are bunking.

"When the shooting starts up front, the guards in the rear towers are going to be trying to see what's happening, and from the way the camp is laid out, I don't think they can see. They might get interested in you. If they do, open fire. If the FEMA guys stream out the back gate after the shooting starts, let them all get out. Wait until they are out, then kill them quick and fast, including anyone left in the rear towers. If the fleeing guards go into a barracks, use an AT4 on it. If they get into vehicles, use the machine gun. It is imperative that no one follow us." I looked at Armanti and asked, "Can you do that?"

"These people aren't soldiers?"

"Some of them might have some military experience, but now they're civilians. FEMA paramilitary thugs, Barry Soetoro's army. What we have going for us is surprise. We want them dead before they can figure out that they oughta shoot back. They aren't holy warriors: being a martyr for Barry Soetoro isn't on their bucket list."

"You're asking an awful lot of one man with one gun."

"Willie will help."

Armanti looked at Willie Varner, who for once kept his mouth shut.

I explained, "I don't want the guards in the compound taking hostages, and I don't want them following us. If we can't take them down quick and fast, we're going to have to clean that camp building by building."

"Okay," Hall said, and shrugged. FEMA's reputation was going downhill fast.

"Willis and Travis, you guys are the front shooters. You are to wait one minute after Sarah and I go through the gate, exactly sixty seconds, then shoot the guys in the guard towers beside the road. They may have a machine gun in each tower, although I doubt it. But they might. Shoot each of them and toss a grenade up into the tower, then do the guys at the front gate."

"I'll take the south tower," Willis said, and Travis nodded.

"Then come into the compound. Drive through the compound and kill anyone in FEMA green. Try not to shoot any of the detainees. My idea is to let the guards get out of the compound through the back gate before we lower the boom. When the shooting starts out back, go help with the rear towers and anyone in FEMA green still standing. No FEMA people are to be left alive."

"Got it, Tommy."

"Wish I had a better plan," I admitted, "and I wish we had a few days to sniff this out, but we don't have any more time. It's tonight or never. Any questions?"

We cleaned up a few details, then mounted up.

Another half-assed plan with insufficient reconnaissance. That was a prescription to get my guys killed, as all of us knew, but it couldn't be helped. We didn't have days to set this up.

Sarah and I rolled up to the main gate of the compound in our brand-new stolen FEMA truck and I leaned out the window, which was down. I had my Kimber in my left hand, out of sight behind the door.

Three guys were lounging around, two sucking cigarettes and one arranging a pinch of Skoal in his mouth. One of the smokers looked inquisitive.

"The guy who runs this place?"

"Sluggo Sweatt." He pointed. "That building on the left."

"Thanks."

I rolled on over and parked in front. I holstered the Kimber.

"Sluggo Sweatt is on the White House staff," Sarah said.

"I've heard the name. Are you ready?"

"Let's go in."

We turned off the engine, left the keys in the ignition, walked up the three steps to the porch and went inside. The receptionist's desk was empty, but the next room had a window and a desk with Sweatt seated behind it in an executive chair that he had apparently liberated from Office Depot. Sarah and I pulled our pistols and pointed them at him.

"See who else is in here," I told Sarah. As she went down the hallway looking in offices I scanned the room.

"You have precisely ten seconds to tell me where Jake Grafton is, or I'm going to shoot you." The words were no more out of my mouth than I heard M4s begin to fire bursts.

Sweatt looked startled. His eyes went to the windows. I fired a shot into his computer, and the bits of glass flew out. "Pay attention," I said.

I heard a shot from down the hallway. Then another.

His eyes were frozen on the pistol in my hand now. One of the interesting things about a .45 is how big the muzzle looks when it is pointed right at your eyes. Only a half inch in diameter, the hole in the barrel looks like a howitzer at close range. I lined up the sights and shot his right ear off.

He jerked and blood flew all over the wall behind him as a fusillade of M4 fire behind me filled the room with noise. Then a hand grenade went off. And another.

Sluggo got the message. "He's in a cell, down the hallway."

Sarah came trotting back. I gave her the news.

"The keys?"

They were on Sluggo's desk. Sarah grabbed them and ran. "If he isn't there," I told Sweatt, "I'm going to start shooting parts off."

More M4 bursts, a cacophony. Blood ran down Sluggo's neck and his face looked pasty.

In a moment Sarah was back. "He's in terrible shape. A lot of broken ribs."

"You keep Mr. Sweatt occupied. If he twitches, empty your pistol into him."

She stood precisely in front of the desk and used both hands to steady the gun on his chest.

I ran outside, grabbed a medic's pack from the bed of the truck, glanced at the gate and saw all three guards sprawled there. I ran back inside. If anyone shot at me they missed. Still some shooting going on. It would have been nice to know how many FEMA dudes we had strapped on, but we hadn't had time for an extended recon.

I found Grafton lying on the floor in a cell, the door of which was standing open.

"Tommy," he whispered. "Lots of broken ribs on both sides, I think."

I cut his shirt off with my fighting knife. His sides were black and blue. Digging into the medic pack, I got out several rolls of gauze. "I gotta sit you up, sir."

"Do it."

I took his arms, which were bruised badly where he'd tried to cover up, and pulled him into a sitting position. He groaned. Working as quickly as possible, I wrapped him in gauze from his armpits down to his belly button. Needed three rolls to do it. Then I began wrapping him with surgical tape, as tightly as I could.

A few more shots. I was listening for the sound of a machine gun, but I hadn't heard it yet. "Who did this?" I asked.

"Sweatt had it done. Wanted a confession. Said if I didn't sign, he was going to personally help beat me to death tomorrow."

"So we're right in the nick. You lucky dog."

Now I heard the stutters of a machine gun.

★

Armanti Hall had set up the M279 beside a small wooden building with a good view of the guard towers and the barracks. The fact that the only lights were in the compound and the towers were backlit probably helped. The guards, one in each tower, were looking into the light, watching the people in the compound and smoking. Armanti got the belt arranged in the gun and chambered a cartridge. When he had that attended to, he gave Willie Varner four hand grenades.

"I want you to go around on the other side of this building," Armanti said, "where you can see the front of the barracks. Then put all four of your hand grenades on the ground. Wait until I fire, then pick up one grenade. See this pin on each one—hold the lever, pull the pin, then wind up and throw it in from the outfield. Pick up another, pull the pin, and throw it. Do it until you have thrown all four. Then lay down, right where you are, and don't move a muscle until you hear me call your name. I don't want you running around out here in the dark. I'll be shooting at everything that moves. If anyone comes up on you, play dead."

"Okay, man."

"Can you do it?"

"I guess." Willie Varner took a deep breath and exhaled explosively.

Five minutes later the shooting started, and to Armanti's amazement, the man in the north tower climbed down and ran for the barracks. The man in the south tower wasn't far behind. Thirty seconds later, as gunfire popped in the front of the compound, guards in FEMA green came running through the compound toward the back gate, jerked it open—apparently it wasn't locked—and ran for their cars or the barracks.

Armanti waited until no one wearing green wanted out of the compound, then opened fire.

I heard the M279 open up, followed by grenade blasts. I hoped that was Armanti Hall behind the compound gunning every FEMA guard who had came out the back gate and jumped in a car or pickup. Or anyone who wanted out of the barracks to join in the fray, if there was a barracks back there.

When I finished with the tape, Grafton said, "Cut this jumpsuit off. I shit in it."

I knew that by the smell, but was too polite to mention it. After I used my knife and he was naked except for the tape, I got a look at his swollen balls. They were bruised almost black. I helped Grafton to his feet. "You're going to have to walk, Admiral."

"Give me a shoulder to hang on to." I put the medic bag over my shoulder, put my left arm around Grafton, and took an experimental step. He wasn't going to go down; that was one tough man. I drew the Kimber and led him down the hall.

Silence had descended on the compound. Sweatt was still in his chair, holding his ear. Blood was oozing through his fingers and running down his neck, staining his collared shirt.

Grafton paused in front of the desk and picked up a watch, put it on. Then he reached for a cell phone and handed it to me. He put a hand on my Kimber and I gave it to him.

"Sluggo, you were born eighty years too late," Jake Grafton said as he looked down to check the safety on the .45. "You should have been an SS colonel in charge of Auschwitz or Dachau."

He pointed the pistol and shot Sluggo in the center of his forehead. The back of the man's head exploded onto the wall and his body rocked back in the chair. The corpse stayed in the chair, its arms dangling, its eyes pointed at the ceiling.

Grafton handed me back my gun.

"Let's go, Tommy. Sarah."

We both helped him down the steps and into the right seat of the pickup. Then Sarah ran around and entered through the driver's door and scooted over.

A knot of civilians was standing there. Willis and Travis were policing up weapons and tossing them into a stack in the yard.

Jack Yocke and Sal Molina came over to the right-side window, which was down. "We want to go with you, Admiral."

"Get in the back."

I addressed the crowd while Yocke and Molina climbed over the tailgate. "Folks, your guards have skedaddled or died, I am not sure which. Help yourselves to the weapons. You must decide if you wish to remain here or take your chances outside. We can't stay, and you know they'll be back, sooner or later, when they figure out what went down here. All I can tell you is, good luck."

I got in the pickup, carefully backed up, then put it in drive and steered toward the gate. I ran over a body of a FEMA warrior sprawled there because I was in no mood to get out and move the corpse or wait for someone else to do it.

"Who'd you shoot?" I asked Sarah.

"A couple of men who thought I wouldn't."

"Good."

"This pistol doesn't kick as much as I thought it would." Oh, man! I glanced at her, but she was looking straight ahead at the road.

The breeze coming in the open windows felt good.

"Where are we going, Tommy?" Grafton asked.

"A place I know. You need a vacation and Sarah needs access to a real bathroom."

"Where?" he said. That was Jake Grafton. No nonsense at all.

"The CIA safe farm near Greenbank."

He grunted. Then his head tilted back onto the headrest and he was asleep, or maybe passed out. He had had a really bad time.

NINETEEN

★

Congressman Jerry Marquart was one of the civilians who watched Tommy Carmellini and the gunmen depart through the gate and down the road into the night. He recognized Jake Grafton, former CIA director, and Sal Molina, who was presumably no longer employed at the White House. The fashionably grizzled younger man who climbed into the back of the pickup with Molina he didn't know.

Jerry was in his late thirties. He was an ROTC grad, had spent six years in the Marines, had done the Afghanistan gig twice, and then had gotten out and gone into politics in Iowa. He was in his second term in the House of Representatives when FBI agents arrested him and brought him here. He didn't even bother to ask why. He was no friend of the Soetoro administration and denounced their policies at every opportunity. He actually had a lot of opportunities, because he was one of the very few members of congress with recent military experience. Or any military experience, for that matter.

He looked at the pile of carbines the attackers had left behind, walked over, and picked one up. Worked the action, checked the magazine, then went over to one of the bodies and helped himself to several full magazines.

Another man came over and asked him, "You know anything about guns?"

"A little."

"I'm from New Jersey, and I don't know shit about guns." He was about twenty-five pounds overweight, had saggy jowls, and combed his hair over his bald spot. He picked up a carbine and hefted it. "But I don't think I want to stay here."

"Don't take one unless you're willing to use it."

"I'm getting there. Name's Evan Bjerki."

"Help yourself to some ammo," Marquart advised. "The price is right."

Jerry Marquart went into the admin building and spent two seconds looking at the remains of Sluggo Sweatt. He had seen a lot of corpses so Sluggo's didn't affect him one way or the other. Nor did the two dead men sprawled on the floor of a room with cots and porn mags scattered around. He helped himself to a pistol belt that he had to pull off one of them, strapped it around his middle. He checked the pistol, a Beretta, made sure it was loaded, then moved on. The cell gave him pause. He smelled the feces, saw the jump suit on the floor, connected it to the naked Grafton, and walked back through the building and out into the compound. Knots of people, maybe a hundred by now, were talking earnestly and loudly to each other and gesturing. Bjerki trailed along behind Marquart.

Marquart went back through the camp, taking his time. There might be some guards still around, and they would undoubtedly be in a pissy mood.

The back gate of the compound was standing open. More bodies lying round. He surmised this was from the machine-gun fire he had heard. Six more bodies lay on the porch and dirt in front of the guards' barracks. One of the men wasn't dead; he was groaning and his legs worked back and forth in the dirt. Marquart didn't get near him.

The wooden sides of the building had been raked by machine-gun fire. Maybe there were more dead or wounded in there, but Marquart wasn't curious enough to go inside to find out.

He examined the vehicles. One car with a body lying beside it seemed undamaged. As he checked the pockets of the corpse, which hadn't bled much, he noted the man had taken four rounds in the chest, any one of which would probably have been fatal. He found a set of keys. They fit in the ignition. He started the engine, which seemed to run okay. Half a tank of gas. Bjerki stood by the driver's door. Marquart ran the window down. "I'm leaving," he said. "You want to come, get in."

Bjerki walked around the front of the car and climbed into the passenger's seat. He held his M4 between his knees. "Where are you going?"

"To the revolution."

"Be a shame if they had one without us," New Jersey Bjerki said.

"Put on your seatbelt."

Marquart pulled the lever to get the car into drive, and they rolled.

On their way back to Longview, Nate Danaher said to JR Hays, "You understand that if we attack Barksdale, the gloves will be off."

"Sure."

"You've talked this over with your cousin?"

"Yes."

"He understands that this is not a declaration of independence; it's a declaration of war?"

"Nate, you and I know Barry Soetoro isn't going to let Texas go without a fight. For us, the only decision to be made is whether we let Soetoro strike the first blow. Politically, it would be wise to let him be the aggressor. Militarily, not so wise. If Texas is going to win its independence, it must seize the military initiative and *never let it go*."

Danaher nodded.

"If we let Soetoro pick and choose his points of attack, we will ultimately lose our organized military forces and be reduced to years of guerilla warfare. In the long run, I think we could win a guerilla war, but it will destroy Texas and ultimately cost more lives than an offensive that takes the fight out of Texas and into Soetoro's territory. Jack thought that a Texas offensive would, in the long run, cause Soetoro to lose political control of the country. Soetoro must show his supporters he can win the battles, or else he will lose the war. He's already on record as saying that he will crush Texas. I don't think he thought that statement through very well, because Jack can say we are responding to an imminent threat, and everyone south of Canada will believe him. Barry Soetoro doesn't want to negotiate: he wants war. We must give it to him in spades."

"An assault on the base really ought to happen at night. Tonight would have been ideal. Tomorrow night would be the next choice."

"We can't wait. By tomorrow night they may have flown those B-52s out of here or arranged AAA and SAMs, plus a reception committee on the ground. In addition to air police, they can fly some troops up from Fort Polk. By tomorrow night they might be ready to kick our butts. So we must go as soon as we can get ready. The C-130s are already at Hood, and the troops, all volunteers, are getting ready. We just need you to brief them, set it up, and go. Tomorrow morning at perhaps nine o'clock is about the earliest possible time. In my judgment, we dare not wait. *We cannot wait.*"

"What are you going to do about that brigade combat team from Fort Polk? And those paratroops? They could push us right off Barksdale and back into Texas."

"I'm going to bomb them while you are taking Barksdale."

Danaher thought for a few minutes as the miles rolled by. Finally he said, "Okay, I'll do it. Gina can stay with our daughter. Let's saddle up."

"Welcome to the Texas Guard."

"Welcome to the war, you mean."

"Yeah, that too."

"I don't know if I have another war in me, but I guess we'll all find out," Nate Danaher said softly.

The CIA safe house was in the woods of a large farm that the locals thought belonged to an eccentric novelist. That was the agency's cover story, anyway. It was midnight when we entered by a gravel driveway, passing by signs that announced "Private Property, No Trespassing" and "Trespassers Will Be Persecuted and Prosecuted, This Means You." The one-lane road led across a large meadow, passing a wooden hangar and a barn, and crossed a grass runway and then a bridge across a creek.

Security cameras were mounted unobtrusively on trees and under the eaves of the hangar and barn. I led the way.

The safe house was used for interrogating defectors, Russians and Eastern Europeans back in the day, and now Islamic jihadists. I doubted if there was anyone there just now due to the current state of national affairs, but I was ready in case we met anyone. We didn't. No one was at the guard's cottage, and the gate was locked. Willie the Wire worked on it awhile and couldn't get it open, so we used a tow chain to pull the gate down and off the road. Willie's one skill in life is opening any lock without a key, yet he had just had his first taste of combat so he was a little shook up.

There was no one at the main house. After an incident a couple years ago when some bent FBI agents and former cops burned the house down, the place had been rebuilt. I was involved in that fracas, and hadn't been here since.

Willie opened the front door for us, partially redeeming himself. While the guys fired up a gasoline generator out back, I explored the layout and found that the new building had a small medical room. It contained an X-ray machine and one that I thought was probably an EKG machine. Some other equipment that I couldn't identify. I had the guys take Jake Grafton in there and put him on the gurney.

Grafton was conscious and obviously hurting. "He needs a doctor," Sarah said with a frown.

"I'll go get one."

I drove back to the hard road and went into Greenbank, and found a small white cinderblock building that said "Clinic" on the sign. It was closed of course, but a sign by the door gave a number to call in case of medical emergencies.

Back in the FEMA truck, I fired up the GPS, played with the options, and found one labeled "phone number." I clicked on it and a prompt appeared. I put in the area code, which was 304, and the number. In about two seconds a red pin appeared. Five more seconds, and the computer filled in a map with directions from my present position to the pin.

It was eight miles away. I rolled.

The doctor's house was on a secondary road at the top of the grade, in a saddle where there was a nice view. I went up his drive and, late as it was, found a man and woman sitting beside an outdoor fireplace with drinks in their hands. I got out and went over.

"Doctor?"

"Yes. Nathan Proudfoot." He was about six feet, thin, perhaps sixty years old, with cropped hair and a mustache.

"My name is Tommy Carmellini. I'm with FEMA. We have a medical emergency down the road a little ways and could certainly use your services. Could you come with me?"

To his credit, he didn't hesitate. "I'll get my bag." He charged into the house. There was a lighted kerosene lamp on the porch and apparently at least one in the house.

"Sorry to ruin your evening, ma'am," I told the lady.

"Goes with the territory," she said. "What happened?"

"Car wreck. One hurt."

Dr. Proudfoot came trotting out with his black medical bag. He got into the passenger seat of the truck, and we headed back for the safe house. I told him about the fictitious wreck.

"How did you find me?"

I gestured to the GPS. "FEMA can find anyone," I said, which was true.

"How are you making out without electricity?" I asked.

"Fine," he said confidently. "Rural nets occasionally go down when there are thunderstorms or someone knocks down a pole with a car, but only for a few hours or overnight. That's just a nuisance. Still, a few years ago we had a blizzard that took a lot of lines down and left us without power for eight days. That was a real pain, so I'm set up now. Even have a little generator that keeps the refrigerator and water pump running. We'll be fine."

As we drove up the road I told him about the patient. "He's a little over sixty-five, I think, six feet, not obese, in fairly good health as far as I know, but he has a bunch of cracked or broken ribs on each side. I taped him up as best I could; he's in a lot of pain and needs a doctor."

"He got busted ribs in a car wreck?"

"I confess, I lied to your wife. Some men beat him badly with fists and shoes. Kicked him in the balls too."

"FEMA sounds like tough duty to me," he said acidly. I didn't argue.

If he didn't know about the safe house in the woods, he didn't show surprise. I guess in his practice he gave up surprise some years back.

Dr. Proudfoot glanced at Grafton, looked around at the equipment in the room, then went to work. He cut off the tape I put on his ribs, X-rayed the admiral, asked him about his general health and how he was feeling, checked his heart and vitals. After a careful exam and a study of the X-rays on a computer screen, he taped him again, a much better job than I did. He also gave Grafton a shot to make him sleep. "Six ribs are cracked on the right side, five on the left," he told Sarah and me, "but none are severed, as far as I can determine. I think he'll heal okay, but he should be in a hospital where he can be observed."

"We'll try to get him there as soon as possible," Sarah assured him.

"Used to be I'd give him some pain pills, but the government is so tight on pain pills now I don't carry any. The good news is that the damned pill-billies aren't tempted to rob me. It's a hell of a world."

"Isn't it though," I remarked.

"If he's hurting when he wakes up, he can have a shot of whiskey. No aspirin. Keep him as inactive as possible. Now, I need all his information so I can get paid for this house call."

"I'll give you cash. Is two hundred dollars enough?"

"That's more than the government would pay me."

I paid him on the spot.

When I was taking him home, the doctor asked, "Is that a government facility?"

"Doctor Proudfoot, you appear to be a good man, and I'd like to answer your question, or questions, because I know you have more than one. But I cannot." I smiled at him benignly. "I don't know where you stand on our current national difficulties, nor do I care. What I can say is this: I want you not to tell anyone about the facility you just visited or the patient you saw there. Or me. Or the other men there."

"It's a government secret, huh?"

"Indeed it is." We were on the secondary road by then, about a mile from his house. I stopped the truck in the middle of the road and turned in the driver's seat to face him. The panel lights made his face quite plain.

"If we get visitors of any kind, sheriff, locals, FEMA people, FBI, state police, Homeland Security, anyone at all, I'll know you told someone the secret. You won't be prosecuted because you'll be dead. I'll find you like I did tonight and kill you. Do you understand?"

He stared at me with fear in his eyes.

"I don't want to kill you, but I will if you tell anyone at all. Even your wife. Tell me that you understand."

He nodded.

I took my foot off the brake and drove him the rest of the way home. As he got out of the truck, I said, "I told your wife it was a car wreck. Make her believe it. Good night."

I felt dirty and ashamed of myself, but I had to put the fear in him. I hoped for our sakes I scared him enough.

Back at the ranch, I sent Willis and Travis to spend the night in the guard cottage by the gate. Told them to drag the gate back across the road.

I put loaded weapons around the house, with a couple of grenades at each window, just in case, checked on Grafton, who was asleep, and Sarah, who was asleep in a bedroom upstairs. Armanti and the Wire, Jack Yocke and Sal Molina were sharing bedrooms. I took off my boots and flaked out on the couch downstairs.

Early that Wednesday morning, while most Americans were in bed, the Oklahoma legislature passed a declaration of independence and the governor signed it. The news had been out all day Tuesday that the legislature had been called into special session to consider the measure. Washington had instructed the FBI and FEMA to arrest the governor and the entire legislature to ensure the declaration wasn't even debated. The commander at Fort Sill was instructed to send a thousand troops to assist the federal agents in maintaining order in Oklahoma City.

The general at Fort Sill was willing, but as the evening progressed he found he didn't have a thousand troops willing to go. He had, at the most, about a hundred, so finally he sent them, armed and wearing battle dress. They went in trucks that convoyed up I-44 from Lawton. They were rolling through the open prairie south of Chickasha when the front tires of the lead truck were shot out. As the truck rolled to the side of the road, more heavy reports were heard and the tires of several following trucks went flat. The final truck had its dual rear wheels shot out while it was almost stopped.

The soldiers piled out and took up formation around the trucks, but there were no more shots. An hour later soldiers searching the prairie found where someone had apparently fired from a low hill three hundred yards from the highway toward the convoy. Not only was dirt scraped away and grass pulled to provide a decent field of fire, a single spent .50 Browning machine-gun cartridge was found in the grass. A little more searching located another firing position about equidistant from the highway on the other side of the interstate, but there were no more cartridges. Nor, apparently, were there any shooters remaining around. Whoever the marksmen were, they had retreated into the darkness with their weapons, undoubtedly bolt-action .50-caliber rifles set up for long-distance target competition.

The officer in charge of the column had already informed his commander of his predicament by radio, so the troops sat alongside the interstate smoking and munching whatever snacks they had in their packs as civilian cars and trucks rolled by. It looked like it was going to be a long evening.

Two hours later four replacement trucks from Fort Sill were fired upon from an overpass. Each truck was hit once in the radiator. The drivers didn't even walk up onto the overpass to look around. They reported the incident on their radios and settled in to spend the night sleeping in their cabs.

The FBI agents and FEMA troops found an estimated eight hundred armed National Guardsmen in battle dress surrounding the state capitol. The federal officers were disarmed and told to go home or they would be arrested. They went home.

During the course of the night, as debate raged on in the legislative chambers, civilians crowded onto the capitol grounds. They passed through the guardsmen's lines carrying lawn chairs and picnic baskets, and many had small children asleep in strollers. The floodlights around the capitol gave the warm evening a festive air. A local band set up amplifiers and microphones and got busy jamming to entertain the crowd.

Inside the building, every member of the statehouse and senate got his or her turn at the microphone. The current national situation, and Barry Soetoro's proclamations, were discussed and dissected. Oklahoma was one of only two states in the Union where Soetoro had failed to carry a single county in the 2012 election. His popularity had continued to sink since then, and it was soon clear that he had few friends in the legislature.

One woman delegate from Norman, a university town and the state's liberal bastion, argued that Soetoro would be out of office on January 20, 2017, a mere five months away, so there was no need for drastic action. "He's not only a lame duck, he's a dead duck. Why shoot ourselves in the head when he's going to be gone in five months, regardless of what we or Texas or any other state does?"

The following speaker took issue with her. "You are the wildest optimist in the history of representative government in Oklahoma. What makes you think there will be an election? Soetoro's party will lose if there is one, so he has manufactured this crisis to give himself a plausible excuse for calling off the election. He wants to be president for life. Or maybe king. Or emperor. Emperor Barry. We need to stand up for representative government here and now, regardless of the cost. We owe it to ourselves, for our own self-respect, and we owe it to our children and grandchildren. Five years from now, how will you explain to your grandchildren what happened to Oklahoma after you refused to do what you knew to be right? And we all know the *right* thing to do. But the right thing is *hard*. Let us do it now, and someday we can all stand proudly, shoulder to shoulder, in heaven before the ruler of the universe."

There was more, lots more. One of the low points was a plea by a delegate from one of the districts encompassing the poorer section of Oklahoma City. "Nothing we can do here tonight will alter the course of our nation's history. We here in Oklahoma are a sideshow. We are a thinly populated state, with only three million nine hundred thousand people. Do you really think we can realistically defy the federal government? The decisions that matter will all be made in Washington. I urge you to not compound the president's problems by being defiant. Let us not beard the lion to see if, indeed, he will bite."

Several of the following speakers heaped scorn on her position. One speaker summed it up: "Submit, submit, submit. Don't anger the tyrant. I never thought I would hear such words from a free American."

The criticism of the Soetoro administration kept rolling, mixing with a broad criticism of liberalism and federal judges. "I am sick of federal judges deciding that the United States Constitution requires abortion and same-sex marriage," a state senator from Enid said. "I challenge you to read that document from end to end, and if you can find the word 'abortion' in it I will kiss your ass tomorrow at high noon on the capitol steps. Ditto gay marriage. What's next? Plural marriages? Legalizing infanticide? We're practically there now. I say it's time we seized control of our own lives here in Oklahoma. Anyone wanting an abortion or to marry a homosexual partner can move to California or New York. We shouldn't be forced to put up with it, and my constituents don't want to. The real problem here is federal judges who enshrine their liberal philosophies in federal decisions instead of letting individual states vote their consciences in open, fair elections. Abortions, gay marriage, legalized pot, all of that should be decided by the states. Whatever happened to the governmental powers reserved to the states? Let's declare ourselves independent, give the people of Oklahoma the right to decide which laws they want to live under, and tell Barry Soetoro where to go and what to do to himself when he gets there."

Another delegate in the House had this to say: "Oklahomans are tired of being ruled by federal bureaucrats and judges, none of them elected. They decide everything from what can be taught in the public schools to what can be served to kids for lunch and whether the kids can have a prayer. They decree that welfare recipients are entitled to a color television and cell phone, all paid for by the working families of Oklahoma, some of whom can afford neither. They claim they have the right to regulate every creek, farm pond, mudhole, and wet spot in America, including here in Oklahoma. We have to pay for their crackpot regulations based on crackpot science, or no science at all. We have to pay the salaries of the bureaucrats and put up with the endless delays and mountainous paperwork. It's high time to put a stop to bureaucrats and judges running our lives. Let's take back control. *Independence today, tomorrow, and forever.*"

The Oklahoma Senate and House passed the declaration by overwhelming majorities and made the vote unanimous by voice vote, and the governor signed it. As in Texas, the declaration, which was almost word for word identical to Texas', was read before television cameras on the statehouse steps to a wildly cheering crowd that commentators estimated at more than ten thousand people.

In New Mexico the legislature also met that evening, but decided to defer any action until Soetoro had made a definitive announcement about whether the presidential election would proceed in November. If it was canceled altogether, the New Mexico legislature agreed to revisit the issue. The governor of Arizona called the legislature to meet the following evening. The governors of Kansas, Nebraska, Arkansas, South Dakota, North Dakota, Wyoming, and Utah scheduled special sessions two days hence. The governors of Montana and Iowa called for a special session of the legislature in three days time, to give lawmakers a chance to canvass their communities. Other states, too, were mulling their options.

Although the legislatures had yet to be called, in Alaska and Hawaii the question of independence was also being weighed and debated, for different reasons. The previous year Soetoro had announced his intention to ignore the U.S. statutes and declare a huge chunk of northern Alaska off-limits to oil exploration. Many of the people of that sparsely settled state were outraged; oil development created good-paying jobs, of which Alaska had far too few, and severance taxes funded state and local governments and generated a check every year for every Alaskan. Oil development had never been the ecological disaster the save-the-earth crowd swore it would be. Soetoro's announcement would slowly upend the Alaskan economy and affect every man, woman, and child who lived there. The devil of it was that the only people who visited the undeveloped Arctic were Alaskans who went to hunt and fish; the limousine liberals in Soetoro's audience rarely if ever trekked the frozen north dribbling dollars as they went. Still, Soetoro would be gone in five months, they hoped, and his extralegal imperial declarations would then be history.

In Hawaii, independence talk had been around for years, especially among native Hawaiians, many of whom were still on the bottom rung of the economic ladder. There was also a large number of people of all races that felt the Hawaiians had gotten a raw deal in 1893 when white American businessmen played a large role in toppling Hawaii's last monarch, Queen Lili'uokalani, an overthrow that even then-president Grover Cleveland thought an illegal act of war. The current political crisis on the mainland looked to many native Hawaiians like a rare, once-in-a-lifetime opportunity: perhaps the U.S. government would be too busy chasing Texas traitors to worry about the islands in the sea's middle. On the other hand, the economic ties to the mainland were the bedrock of the economy. Could trade and tourism from Japan and China replace lost American dollars? Would the people of the islands be better or worse off as an independent nation?

General Martin L. Wynette read the news summaries of all this "grandstanding," as he called it, at seven o'clock on Wednesday morning when he got to the Pentagon, and thought if this news didn't wake up the fools in the White House, nothing short of nuclear war would. Those people in flyover land were pissed off and feisty.

One of his aides had brought him a copy of the Minerva Research Initiative, which the president had directed the armed forces to draft and study after he was elected in 2008. Minerva, the Roman goddess of wisdom and war. Idly, Wynette wondered about the subtle mind that had dreamed up that title. The Minerva Research Initiative was a military plan to put down a civil insurrection in the United States.

Wynette scanned it and tossed it aside. The plan assumed that the members of the armed forces would willingly participate in armed action against angry citizens. That was a forlorn and foolish assumption, Wynette now realized. He also had on his desk a flash message from the commanding general at Fort Sill in Lawton, Oklahoma, telling him that he had scoured his command for men and women willing to fight Oklahomans. They were willing to go to Iraq, Afghanistan, Syria, and if necessary Iran to fight for America, but only a few were willing to fight Oklahomans.

He was getting briefings on the result of other army commanders' attempts to muster soldiers who would fight for the Soetoro administration against domestic enemies when he was summoned to the White House. Wynette stuffed the messages in his briefcase along with a copy of the Minerva Research Initiative and called for his aide and his driver.

In Colorado a group of FBI agents and a sheriff's deputy searching houses to confiscate guns got into a shooting scrape with a homeowner and his son. The homeowner and son were killed, but not before they shot an FBI agent and the sheriff's deputy to death. Another agent was in the hospital. Social media was aflame, with citizens promising the agents and local law officers who cooperated with them in confiscating guns more of the same.

An FBI office in Seattle was attacked, one agent wounded: perpetrators unknown. In Idaho a county sheriff who agreed to help search the homes of citizens of his county to find and confiscate guns was ambushed, stripped naked, dipped in tar and feathers, and carried to his office on a fence rail. He was now hospitalized with burns over sixty percent of his body. A county in Utah with a significant percentage of Mormon fundamentalists declared its independence from the United States and the State of Utah. Polygamy there was now legal. Finally, a dispatch from Mexico City: the Mexican government was considering diplomatic recognition of the Republic of Texas.

In Baltimore, a suburban sporting goods warehouse had been looted overnight. The gun counters were stripped clean and the looters helped themselves to every box of cartridges on the premises, then amused themselves by shooting at stuffed animal heads displayed high on the walls. The good news was that due to the federal government's massive orders for ammunition over the last two years, and the president's oft-repeated remarks about his desire for gun control that had induced civilians to buy and hoard ammo, the sporting goods store had only a small supply of cartridges, most in unpopular hunting calibers. The bad news went unspoken: the inner-city rioters were now armed.

In other riot-plagued big cities around the country, the police and National Guard contented themselves with trying to prevent the destruction from spreading. It was a losing fight. The centers of many of America's largest cities now resembled the core of German cities after World War II.

People living in the suburbs nationwide were armed and organizing. They were also emptying the grocery and hardware stores, buying everything in sight, to the limits of their credit cards. Canned and dry food items were almost completely gone in some stores. Hardware stores sold out of emergency generators, charcoal, and gasoline cans. Gasoline stations found that many of their customers were filling up as many as ten five-gallon cans with fuel. Sporting goods stores were selling every gun on the shelf and all the ammunition in stock. In Howard County, Maryland, a bedroom suburb of Washington and Baltimore populated with a large percentage of federal civil service employees of all races, the county police and Homeland Security officers tried to search homes for guns, only to be met at four houses by armed householders who threatened to shoot to kill.

The chief of the Howard County police announced that henceforth his officers would concentrate on arresting criminals, answering domestic violence calls, and helping motorists involved in traffic accidents. The chief was quoted by a reporter as saying, "If Barry Soetoro wants to confiscate guns, he can figure out how to do it. The people here are frightened by what's going on in Baltimore and elsewhere and want to be able to protect themselves. I can't say I blame them." After the story was published, two black Maryland legislators called the police chief, who was also black, a racist.

TWENTY

★

In Galveston that morning, after the sun came up, the sheriff drove his car down the pier and parked adjacent to the gangway of USS *Texas*. He walked across the gangway and shouted down into the open hatch, "Anybody home?"

In less than a minute, a man appeared below and looked up at him. "Yep, we're home."

"Mind if I come down and visit?"

"Please do."

Speedy Gonzales escorted the sheriff to a small wardroom, where he found Loren Snyder studying several large bound volumes and sipping a cup of coffee.

"Coffee, Sheriff?"

"Don't mind if I do."

"Best coffee in the world," Loren Snyder said.

The sheriff sipped at his, which he took black. Almost as good as Dunkin' Donuts coffee, he thought, but he didn't say it. Instead, he got straight to the point. "When are y'all going to nuke yourselves out of here?"

Loren laughed. "Well, we're working on that right now. Before we go, I want my crew, all five of us, to run through every emergency procedure in the book and figure out how we're going to handle it. We don't have sixty people, just five. We don't want to die in this boat."

The sheriff looked around and nodded. "I sure understand that." Just sitting here in this steel cigar gave the sheriff a mild case of claustrophobia. What it would be like being submerged he didn't want to think about.

"How long can you guys stay submerged, anyway?" the sheriff asked.

"Until we run out of toilet paper."

The sheriff chuckled at that, thinking Loren Snyder was being facetious. He wasn't. With only five people aboard eating the stores, *Texas* could stay submerged for a long, long time.

"We're going to spend today running emergency drills," Snyder said, "making sure everyone knows what is expected of him and we are all on the same page. I hope by tonight we'll be ready to leave this pier."

"What about the U.S. Navy? I'll bet they're kinda unhappy that they lost this thing."

"They'll probably send SEALs to take it back," Lorrie admitted.

"You mean like those guys who whacked bin Laden?"

"Yep. Naval Special Warfare commandos."

"Maybe y'all oughta get outta here and do your drills someplace else."

"Sheriff, I agree one hundred percent. As soon as we feel we can safely move this submarine, we will. In the interim, it would help if you would station some officers with radios out there around the harbor to keep a lookout. I suspect the SEALs will come at night. Probably tonight. We hope to be gone when they get here, but just in case, if your lookouts see anything suspicious—anything—I would appreciate a heads-up so we can cast off and get going. Once we close the hatches, the SEALs can't get inside the boat."

The sheriff nodded reluctantly. "Today and this evening?"

"Yes, sir."

"You'll try like the devil to get this stuff done and get out of Galveston?"

"Cross my heart."

"Okay, Captain. But I ain't asking my deputies to get in a shootout with SEALs. No way. They're law enforcement officers, not soldiers."

They discussed radio frequencies for a moment, then Loren Snyder said, "Thanks for stopping by, Sheriff."

The sheriff had one last gulp of coffee, then said, "Good luck to y'all out there, Captain." After he and Loren shook hands, he followed Speedy to the forward torpedo room and the ladder topside.

Captain. Loren Snyder liked the sound of that.

Secret Service sniper Tobe Baha drove slowly around Austin looking things over. He had had a private interview with President Soetoro's chief of staff, Al Grantham, then went home and packed for a trip. He put his rifle in its aluminum airline case in the toolbox behind the cab of his pickup. He carefully locked the toolbox with the best padlocks money could buy.

The rifle wasn't his service rifle. This was his personal rifle, a Remington Model 700 in .308, or as it was known in the service, 7.62x51 NATO. It certainly wasn't the best cartridge for extreme long-range shooting, but Tobe had used it extensively while in the military and knew the ballistics cold, so he was very comfortable with it. And ammo for it was available everywhere, if need be. Tobe had loaded his own with match bullets and had two boxes in the airline case.

Under his rifle was another airline case stuffed with a quarter of a million U.S. dollars and fifty thousand dollars' worth of gold. That was his down payment on the assassination of Jack Hays.

The problem was that Tobe Baha wasn't an assassin. He was a sniper, pure and simple, so he didn't even bother trying to come up with a second method of taking out the president of Texas if setting up a snipe proved difficult. Actually, he couldn't conceive of a set of circumstances that would cause him to miss a rifle shot, if and when he got one. And he would get one, sooner or later. Everyone was vulnerable to a sniper, unless they lived in a prison, and politicians especially. They had to make public appearances, they got into and out of limos and helicopters on a routine basis, and most of them, including Jack Hays, had families.

Patience was the sniper's golden asset, and Tobe Baha had more than his share. He could and would wait until he was presented with a shot he knew he could make during one of Jack Hays' inevitable public appearances. After that, with a cool million in his jeans, he would disappear.

Of course, he worried a little about the possibility that the Soetoro administration might eventually want him permanently removed from the land of the living. If they just had him arrested, he might talk. So arrest wasn't the risk.

Tobe Baha had thought it over when approached for this shoot, and decided he could handle the risk of treachery by his employers. After all, three or four of the Secret Service people knew of the plot.

He had said as much on his last interview with Al Grantham. "If you don't pay me the money you owe or if you send people after me, I'll come after you," he told Grantham, "and I won't miss."

Austin certainly had possibilities, Tobe concluded as he drove around. The capitol was surrounded by buildings, although they were several hundred yards from the capitol itself, which sat on a small knoll surrounded by scattered large trees and lots of grass. The governor's mansion also had buildings within range of a .308. The real question was whether Jack Hays' bodyguards included snipers. Protecting a public figure from bombs and maniacs with pistols and knives was what the Secret Service did best. Snipers, however, were the worst threat, which was why Tobe Baha had been recruited by the service. It takes a sniper to kill a sniper.

If the Texas crowd didn't have snipers protecting Jack Hays, Tobe Baha's mission would be a whole lot easier. So his first task was to determine if they did.

Tobe Baha smiled. This was going to be a good hunt.

Major General JR Hays launched his first offensive that morning, the thirty-first of August. He watched Texas guardsmen file aboard six C-130 Hercules transports, four-engine turboprops, at Fort Hood, sixty-four combat-equipped soldiers to each plane. Two other C-130s were being loaded with howitzers, ammunition, rations, water, and a portable field hospital.

"I'm banking on surprise," JR told Colonel Nathaniel Danaher, who was leading the attacking force. "I think you can get on the ground and establish a perimeter before the people on the ground figure out that something is going down. I want you to clear the planes and let them take off immediately for another load. Ideally, I'd like to get a brigade on the ground over there with some artillery to give it teeth. F-16s will provide close air support and top cover. But it's up to you to stop our assault if you find you are in way over your head. You must remain in radio contact with the planes in the air at all times, keep them advised of how things are going."

Nate Danaher looked ten years younger than he did last night. The challenge of leading men in combat had always energized him.

The six transports bearing soldiers took off first, escorted by a high top cover of F-16s from Lackland. The attacking force would fly east of Barksdale, turn and approach the base from that direction, calling the control tower for landing clearance. While the panicked air controllers sorted through messages trying to find one about incoming Hercs, the Hercs would land, discharge their troops, and take off again. The C-130s bearing howitzers and ammo would land an hour later, after the soldiers of the first wave had secured the flight line.

Would they achieve surprise? JR Hays asked himself that question, but he didn't know the answer. If the bad guys had gotten wind of the invasion of Louisiana, he would be among the first to hear about it.

Maybe yes, maybe no, he decided.

Perhaps he should have given his major general stars to Nate Danaher and commissioned himself a colonel, then led the troops invading Barksdale. Jack Hays would have said okay, if that was the way he wanted it. But would Nate Danaher have laid on this attack if he had been the general in charge? That hypothetical had no possible answer, because JR had made the decision. Nate had saluted and marched off to give every ounce he had in him. That quality, JR thought, was the salvation of the professional soldier. Regardless of whether the professional thought the order wise or foolish, he said, "I will do my best, sir," and the rest of the sentence was unspoken: "Even if it kills me." So generals ordered men into combat, knowing that some of them, an unknown number, would die. Generals hoped and prayed that the objective would be worth the sacrifice, and, in the end, only they and God would know how the scales balanced.

JR thought ruefully about the old observation that doctors buried their mistakes. Truly, so did generals.

And yet, even if he lost every soldier and airplane he sent this morning, JR Hays would win a strategic victory simply by attacking. He knew that in the depths of his military soul. Soetoro would stop worrying about invading Texas and wreaking havoc and start worrying about protecting what he had. People the world over expect their government to protect them, and when it doesn't, or can't, they begin to worry.

And if Danaher was victorious and captured a fleet of intact B-52s, Barry Soetoro would start fretting about where they might be used against him. Would they bomb Washington? New York? Los Angeles? A squadron of B-52s carpet-bombing with unguided weapons could destroy a city, just as they did Hanoi. Fighters would be detailed to guard the skies over cities and military bases. Soetoro *must* commit his air force to protecting those places, and if he did, those air assets would be unavailable to attack Dallas, Houston, San Antonio, Austin, or the military bases Hays had captured.

JR walked across the tarmac when the troop-laden transports were out of sight and went into the base's air traffic control facilities. "Are the Lancers from Dyess airborne?"

"Yes, sir. Target time is less than an hour away."

The B-1s were targeted against the military equipment at Fort Polk. Many of the soldiers at Hood had trained at Polk, and they helped annotate maps. The Lancer crews knew precisely where they were going, and they had air cover, F-16s from Lackland. In and out fast like a rabbit was their credo. Leaving smoldering wreckage.

JR got a cup of coffee from the pot and sat down in front of a temporary theater map taped to the wall. He had launched his strikes; now there was nothing to do but wait.

Wait, wait, wait.

★

I found Jake Grafton alert that morning when I took a cup of coffee into the dispensary. He was still on the gurney.

"Tommy, you've got to get me off this thing and help me to the restroom."

I did that, and then I put him in a large easy chair in the main room of the facility, or lodge, or whatever they called it, with a blanket wrapped around him.

"Thanks for rescuing me, Tommy," Grafton said with coffee in hand. He sniffed it, savoring the smell before he took the first sip.

"Any old time, Admiral. The guys and I had nothing to do since you got kicked out of the agency. So we thought, let's go spring the admiral and take a nice vacation."

"And Sarah Houston?"

"She's got the hots for me something terrible. I think that's affected her brain. Whatever, she came along."

About that time all the folks upstairs came down, so I got busy fixing breakfast. Needless to say, we didn't have eggs or milk or any of that, but we had beans and MREs and a lot of canned meats and veggies. I made a stew. Tasted it and added some salt and a generous dollop of Cholula sauce.

When I brought it into the main room and put it on a table, Sal Molina and Jack Yocke were in earnest conversation with Grafton. I ladled some of the stew out for the admiral, gave it to him with a spoon, and told everyone else to help themselves.

Sarah was eating tiny little bites. "The first person who complains gets to do the cooking," I said with no-nonsense authority.

Willie Varner made a face. "Tastes like shit, Tommy, but good."

When the chuckles died, he started telling about the fare in the prisons he had resided in. According to the Wire, prisons were good feeders. He was lying, again. After he got out the second time, he told me he never wanted to see a macaroni or spaghetti noodle again as long as he lived.

I sent Willie and Armanti down to the guard shack to relieve Travis and Willis. "We're going to have visitors, probably sooner rather than later." I told them about the doctor and my threat. "I doubt if he believed me. I don't have a face that will scare anybody."

"He'll blab for sure," Willie said, nodding.

When Willis Coffee got there, he went upstairs and got an extra shirt and jeans for the admiral. He was about the same size. Travis Clay loaned Grafton his tennis shoes; he said the boots were fine for him. I left the guys to clean up, took a carbine, checked to see that the magazine was full and there was a round in the chamber. Strapped my pistol belt around my middle. It had been a few years since I was here, and I wanted to refresh my memory about how the land laid. Grafton, Molina, and Yocke were busy solving the world's problems as I left.

I walked up behind the lodge, stood for a moment listening to the muffled generator, then hiked straight up the hill to the ridge. At first the hill behind the lodge was steep, then the grade lessened and it was just a walk in the forest, which was beautiful. The chain-link fence on the ridge ran north-south, surveyor straight. The trees and brush had been cleared for ten feet on either side, and this late in the summer, the open space was full of knee-high weeds. I walked the fence for about a half mile north, going downhill when the ridge turned west. I crossed a little creek that didn't have any water in it and then followed the fence back steeply uphill.

I kept track of the security cameras mounted unobtrusively in trees on our side of the fence. The cameras were battery-operated and broadcast to a receiver in the security shack. I could just discern a trail agency people had walked through the years changing the camera batteries, and no doubt replacing cameras that broke or got water in them or someone in the National Forest on the other side of the fence shot for the hell of it.

When I had had enough I turned eastward, downhill in the general direction of the guard cabin. Ended up climbing another ridge. This ground was cut up by meandering little creeks and steep slopes, all heavily wooded.

Mainly by accident I finally found the access road and followed it to the guard cabin. I could hear the generator running a hundred feet away.

I walked in without knocking and startled Willie Varner and Armanti Hall, who were listening to a radio—police calls, or maybe FEMA calls. The digital feed from the security cameras was on a monitor beside the radio, but they weren't watching it.

"With that generator going, you dudes won't even hear them coming," I remarked.

"Sit down, Tommy," Armanti said. "You should hear some of this. People are shooting at federal officers. I don't know if they are FEMA or Homeland, and I don't guess it matters."

"Where?"

"Well, I don't recognize any of the place names, but I kinda think up in Maryland or Pennsylvania someplace. One guy was talking about getting more vehicles and agents out of Harrisburg."

Willie chimed in, "Two federal guys shot and need evacuation. They claim they killed three of the locals. Civilians. Ambushers, they called them."

"We thought we should keep an ear open for transmissions around here," Armanti explained, reading the expression on my face.

"You guys start watching the barn and hangar security cameras on the monitor. The feds won't sneak down through the woods. Someone will drive up that road sooner or later and they won't give you a heads-up call on the radio. You'll see them on the barn and hangar cameras."

"We can't stay here," Willie declared. He wasn't Einstein but he got there eventually.

I tromped out and headed up the hill to the lodge. If we didn't leave we were running the risk of being trapped. I should have stuck my pistol in that doctor's mouth and scowled until he crapped his pants. Grafton was asleep again. He was certainly in no condition to be moved, so we had to stay.

I got Willis Coffee and Travis Clay to dig a nest for two heavy machine guns across the road from the parking area where they could engage any vehicles that drove up. They were pros: they knew how to set up a machine-gun nest. They took some AT4s along, just in case, and got busy moving the guns and ammo.

Jack Yocke and Sal Molina were not thrilled when I told them they were now soldiers in the Army of the Rebellion. "I'm a reporter," Yocke said stiffly.

"I just drafted you," I replied. "When this is over, you'll probably have enough material to write a couple of books and eat on the rubber chicken circuit until you die of constipation. Right now, however, your problem is staying alive. I'm about to do you a big favor and show you how you can do that, and help the rest of us stay alive too."

"And if I say no?"

"You walk down to the hard road and hitch a ride anywhere you want to go."

"I'll stay."

"I'm so thrilled."

Molina said, "I'm fat, out of shape, and never touched a weapon in my life."

"When this is over, you'll want to join the NRA."

"What about me?" Sarah asked.

"You are my inside surprise. You can toss grenades and shoot if they come through the door in front or back. I suggest that you pick a few spots to watch the back of the building. If we get visitors with something nasty on their minds, they will drop someone off to come through the woods behind us. Your job is to guard the rear."

I showed the three of them how to operate the carbines, grenades, and AT4s. "Don't fire one of these AT4s in the house. The back blast will burn the building down."

When I thought they had the basics, I gave them a little heart-to-heart about combat. "You are going to be very scared when the shooting starts. Concentrate on making your weapon function and keep firing it at the bad guys. It's really easy to shoot the wrong people, which will not help you nor the rest of us. The main thing is to stay in the fight."

"What about prisoners?"

"What about 'em?"

"Well, what if they throw down their weapons and surrender?"

"Anybody who gets into a shooting scrape with us wants our weapons, vehicles, and food. If you surrender, they'll kill you. I suggest you do the same to them."

"I can't do that," Molina said frankly. Yocke nodded his agreement.

"Don't worry. Someone will do it for you," I said. "Just don't let 'em run off."

"Could you shoot a man with his hands up?" Yocke asked Sarah.

She looked at him as if he had asked if she were still a virgin. Women are usually tougher and more realistic than men.

One of the troopers in the back of the first C-130 in the string flying just above Louisiana was Specialist Jimmy Schaffran from Minnesota. His story was unique, as was the story of every man in the plane, but perhaps similar to many. He had been a chubby nerd in high school, addicted to video games, partly because he wished to find some way to escape a bad home situation and partly because he was unattractive to girls. He had no idea what to say to them. Certainly he wasn't a jock or rocket scientist. There was no money in the family to send him to college when he graduated from high school, a fact he didn't fret because he didn't know what he wanted to do with his life and doubted that he was smart enough for college, anyway. He got a job delivering sandwiches in his father's old work car, then pizza because the tips were better, and finally decided to join the army.

Recruit training nearly killed him. Pushed mercilessly by the sergeants, the pounds began melting off and his stamina increased dramatically. After thirty pounds of fat were gone, he began gaining muscle.

Jimmy Schaffran found a home in the army. He had some buddies and they went into town together. He met a girl, a cute waitress in Killeen with a little tattoo over her heart, which happened to put it on the top of the swell of her left breast; she loved to neck in his car, the first one he had ever owned, cherry red, only three years old, with a loud aftermarket muffler.

When this Texas thing went down, a Guard officer asked him if he wanted to go back to the U.S. Army or fight for Texas. Jimmy hadn't hesitated. "I'm from Minnesota," he said, "but now I'm a Texan." His buddies, from California, Michigan, and South Carolina, also decided they were Texans. "Be a shame to break up a good team," one of them said. So all four were in this assault on Barksdale, two on this plane and two on another.

"Hell, it's all an adventure," Jimmy Schaffran told himself, wished his stomach would stop doing flips, and squeezed his weapon a little tighter.

Nathaniel Danaher sat behind the pilots in the cockpit of the first C-130 to approach Barksdale. The planes, strung out in trail about a mile apart, had flown the entire distance from Fort Hood at a hundred feet above the ground. They had managed to avoid several radio towers, which would have made flying at this altitude suicidal at night.

As briefed, the pilot called Barksdale Approach, gave his position from the field, and asked for clearance to land. "I'm leading a flight of six. My playmates are in trail and would like to land behind me."

There was a long silence, then, "We don't have a flight plan on you. Where did you take off?"

"Fort Rucker."

Another pause, then, "Make a modified straight-in to Runway Three-Three, Altimeter two niner niner six, wind three one zero at seven. Switch to Tower and report five miles."

"Wilco."

The copilot flipped the radio freq and made the call, trying to keep his voice airline-pilot, ah-shucks cool.

"Flight of six, cleared to land."

The copilot turned to Danaher. "They'll get on the phone to Rucker, sir."

"Regardless of what they say, land. Taxi right over in front of base ops and drop the ramp."

Danaher went into the back and got his troops ready. They had been carefully briefed, and knew they were to go off running as soon as the loadmaster lowered the ramp.

In Barksdale Approach Control, confusion reigned. The only planes scheduled to arrive at noon were a flight of four F-22s. If Ops had received messages about arriving Hercs, no one had seen them, but that didn't mean they didn't exist somewhere. And there was something else. Approach Control radar showed blips without transponder codes, up high and approaching from the south. What were these airplanes? The duty ops officer called his boss, a colonel, who confessed his ignorance. Flipping madly through the messages on the message board, and calls to the message center, didn't help. Nor would calling Center do any good: Center was off the air and no one was answering the telephones.

The first Herc touched down and, ignoring orders from Ground Control, taxied to a stop in front of the Ops building; armed, helmeted troops in battle dress piled out of the plane.

An enlisted controller in the tower remarked, "Rucker must have sent an advance party to augment base security."

Very shortly, everyone in the tower was disabused of that notion and jerked headlong into the reality of war. Troopers entered the tower, pointed their guns, and waved the air force controllers away from the scopes and microphones. An NCO growled, "You people get on the floor, hands in your laps, and no one will get hurt!" Troopers bound the air controllers' wrists with plastic ties. Cell phones were confiscated. Another trooper sat at a microphone to guide approaching aircraft.

Similar scenes were enacted at the base ops center, where Colonel Danaher established his command post, and at the message center. It all happened so quickly that no message of the attack was transmitted. As far as the Pentagon knew, Barksdale was still owned by the United States Air Force.

Danaher couldn't believe his good fortune. Lady Luck had just given him a gift of a few hours.

The second C-130 taxied to the B-52 parking mat. As the troops disembarked, an air police SUV came roaring up and two armed men jumped out. When a couple of the troopers fired bursts over their heads, the air policemen jumped back into the SUV and started off, but now someone shot the tires out. It kept going anyway. Another burst into the rear of it brought it to a stop. One of the air policemen was slightly wounded. They were disarmed and led away across the mat to a holding area as the troops fanned out and the C-130 began taxiing for takeoff. There were more troops at Fort Hood that needed transport.

Two minutes after the sixth and last transport off-loaded its men, Colonel Danaher could look at the base's mechanics, officers, and pilots seated in rows, hands fastened with plastic ties, and under guard. It was a quick victory for Texas. Hearing the reports over handheld radio, Colonel Danaher breathed a sigh of relief. For the first time in his life, he understood the ennui that engulfed the military personnel in Pearl Harbor in the weeks before the Japanese attack on December 7, 1941. It is devilishly difficult to instantly transition from peace to war. Danaher knew he wasn't up to speed yet, but thought maybe he better get that way fast. No doubt all the air force personnel on the base were waking up mighty quick.

★

The B-1 Lancer surprise attack on the war materiel stockpiled at Fort Polk was a complete success. Not a SAM or artillery shell rose to meet them. Using JDAMs, the six bombers hit the large tank and artillery depots. Then the F-16s flying top cover came down and used rockets and cannons on armored vehicles and artillery pieces that appeared undamaged. Several JDAMs went into the fuel storage facilities. Post-strike photos snapped by the F-16 strike leader suggested that perhaps forty percent of the tanks and artillery were no longer serviceable. The black column of smoke rising from the fuel storage areas was visible in the sky from a distance of ninety miles.

★

While that strike was going on, General Martin L. Wynette was in his limo on his way to the Executive Office Building. When he received a call from the JCS duty officer informing him of the attack on Fort Polk, Wynette hung up the phone with a frown. The president and his disciples were going to eat him alive. He briefed his general officer aides, a male and a female, so they would know what was coming.

At the Executive Office Building, Wynette and his two aides were ushered to a conference room where Soetoro, his national security advisor, and a dozen top political aides were waiting, including Sulana Schanck, the Muslim. She had always intimidated Wynette. Those eyes, glaring at everyone who didn't share her vision of a Muslim America. Wynette thought her the most evil woman he had ever met. He thought that one of these days she might snap and start cutting off heads with a butcher knife. He hoped she would begin with Al Grantham.

Wynette opened his briefcase as the men and women in the room debated the implications of Oklahoma's rebellion and the scheduled independence votes in other plains states. Soetoro seemed to have himself under control this morning, Wynette thought, as he listened to machine-gun bursts of terrible news.

Wynette dropped into a chair and tried to keep his face deadpan. His aides sat down beside him. No one mentioned the attacks on Fort Polk in Louisiana. Maybe they don't know yet, he thought.

Finally the president addressed a question to the general, his first acknowledgment of the officer's presence. "What can the military do to put a stop to this treason?"

"Nothing," Wynette said, "except maybe bomb the statehouses involved. And I'm not sure what that would achieve."

Al Grantham let out a roar. "Goddamnit, General, it would kill some traitors."

"You folks have a red-hot political crisis on your hands and the U.S. armed forces are melting away. A couple more days of this and we won't have enough people to turn the lights on and off at the Pentagon."

Silence descended upon the room. Wynette thought about all the ways the president had disrespected the men and women in uniform during his administration, including refusing to make appearances and public statements during Armed Forces Day, and refusing to salute the flag. His contempt of the people in uniform was now being returned in spades.

"We are going to have to recruit an army of progressives who are willing to fight for America," Barry Soetoro said.

Good luck with that, Wynette thought. What he said aloud was, "By the time you get your army recruited and equipped, with enough training to teach them which end of the rifle the bullet comes out of, you are going to be out of office."

The political aides merely stared ahead silently, Schanck included. Soetoro didn't say a word. Even Grantham managed to control himself. All of which proved to the chairman of the Joint Chiefs that the White House knew there was not going to be an election in November. That was still their little secret.

Finally Grantham said, "Maybe you should start shooting some of your reluctant warriors. That would inspire the rest to do their sworn duty."

"I don't have the authority to hold drumhead courts-martial and execute soldiers."

"The president can give you that authority."

"I don't want it. If you like, I'll tender my resignation right now and you can dig down through the officer corps until you find someone willing to shoot American soldiers. There must be one or two ambitious assholes in uniform that would shoot their own mothers for a big promotion. I've never met any, but they say there are rotten apples in every barrel."

Grantham snarled, "Why don't you start saying yes, sir, and no, sir, and stop this damned insubordination?"

"I thought you wanted me here for professional advice. I just gave you some."

"Enough," Soetoro said. He rubbed his face with both hands. "We have a political crisis that is fed by social media and the press pouring gasoline on hot embers. What we need to do is shut down the power grid nationwide to stop all the bitching, plotting, and conspiracies."

Martin Wynette lost control of his face. He stared slack-jawed at the president. That had to be the most idiotic suggestion he had ever heard.

"We must do something, and that might have a good effect," Al Grantham opined.

Ironically, Martin Wynette thought that comment proof that Grantham was a total, complete flaming fool, and a world-class ass-kisser to boot! Had his senior aide only known the general's thoughts, he would have probably laughed aloud. Wynette managed to close his mouth and put on his poker face again.

The civilians around the table discussed it. Indeed, they thought that something had to be done to douse the political fires, and this was something. If those rebels were sitting in the dark without air conditioning or the internet or telephones, at least they wouldn't be damning the administration and fomenting treason before a national audience, the members of which would have their own problems to deal with. And it was the president's own idea, which was nice. No one there had to take the risk of offering a suggestion that might be rejected. It never hurts to say yes to the boss.

What wasn't addressed, Wynette noted grimly, was how cutting the juice was going to stop the social collapse that he thought almost inevitable. In fact, Wynette thought that leaving people nationwide without power to stay cool and preserve and prepare food in the dead heat of August was likely to accelerate the process, not impede it. Not to mention the havoc it would play on nursing home residents and the elderly who lacked emergency generators. Police and firefighters could not be summoned in an emergency. This callous decision would kill American citizens, whether they were progressives or conservatives, loyal or disloyal, whether they worshipped the ground Barry Soetoro walked upon or urged God every night to take the bastard quick. It would also stop the American economy dead in its tracks. Factories would be left without not only electricity but natural gas, because electricity powered the compressors needed to move it through pipelines. Without pumps, water and sewage would cease to flow. And every filling station in America would be unable to pump gasoline or diesel fuel. Truck deliveries would stop. If the power outage went on long enough, urban Americans would begin to starve or die of thirst. Cutting power might be justified as a military necessity, Wynette thought, but certainly not as a political expedient to silence dissent. He almost said aloud that JR Hays would turn off America's juice if he could, but being Martin Wynette, he kept his mouth shut.

Soetoro made the decision, as his inner circle of committed progressives knew he would. "Do it," he said, and gestured toward the door.

Some moron asked, "How?"

Grantham fielded that one. "Call the heads of the various power companies and tell them to shut off the juice, and if they don't, send the FBI around to arrest them and every officer in the company. Crack the damned whip." When you have dictatorial powers, you can iron out all the little difficulties.

"Yes, sir," they said, and scattered.

"You stay," the president said to the general and his aides.

When the room was empty, the president said, "Tell me about that attack in Louisiana."

So he had heard after all. "I got a telephone call in the car on the way over here," Wynette said, "so all I know are the basics. Apparently B-1 Lancers. They probably came from Dyess Air Force Base in Abilene."

"What can we do about those Texas traitors?"

"Sir, we are putting together an invasion, as you directed. JR Hays just made the invasion a little more difficult, but he can't stop it."

"What will he do next?"

"We need to destroy those B-1s on the ground at Dyess. I was thinking of using the B-2s at Whiteman Air Force Base in Missouri to do that as soon as possible."

"Fine," Barry Soetoro said. "We should have retired those old B-1s years ago. Instead we wasted mountains of money on them that could have been better spent elsewhere."

Wynette didn't argue that point.

"I also want you to turn off the lights in Texas, General. I don't think calling the president of the power company will do it. Do it any way you can. As soon as you can. Texas started all this trouble."

"Yes, sir."

Barry Soetoro would have been furious if he had known that JR Hays was already one jump ahead of him. Another half-dozen B-1 Lancers were already in the air on their way to Missouri to bomb Whiteman Air Force Base. An hour later, as the carcasses of the B-2s at Whiteman were still burning, he found out.

★

In the limo with his general officer aides, Martin Wynette said, "He knew about that Louisiana attack when he ordered the power turned off nationwide."

His generals both nodded.

"And he knew about the state legislatures giving him the finger."

Yes.

"Did he do it to punish the American people?" Wynette asked aloud.

"Ten to one that he blames the Texans for the loss of power," the female two-star said.

"No bet," her male colleague said.

"A hundred to one," she offered.

"No bet."

But with the power off, only a few will hear him, Wynette thought. And who will care? The one fact every American will understand is that the federal government can't keep electricity flowing through the wires.

At Barksdale Air Force Base four F-22s broke over the runway and swung into trail on the downwind. They slowed, dropped their landing gear and flaps, and the controller in the tower cleared them to land. Once down, Ground Control directed them to park on one end of the B-52 ramp.

Everything appeared normal to the pilots as they followed the directions of linesmen, parked in a row, and one by one shut down. Number Four was the last to shut down, of course, and the pilot was the last to exit his cockpit onto a boarding ladder that had been pushed to the side of his plane.

He was standing with one foot in the cockpit and one foot on the ladder when he looked around and realized that the other pilots had their hands in the air and soldiers in battle dress were pointing weapons at them.

He drew his pistol from a holster under his left armpit and began shooting into the instrument panel, which was composed of complex multifunction displays.

The air force officer had fired three shots when Specialist Jimmy Schaffran triggered a three-shot burst from his M4 carbine from a distance of eighteen feet. The pilot tumbled backward without even trying to grab the ladder and fell to the concrete.

Jimmy Schaffran, late of Minnesota and now of Texas, walked over to the body. The man's head was at an odd angle. Obviously a broken neck. If the carbine bullets didn't kill him, the fall to the concrete did.

Schaffran was still staring at the corpse when his buddy from South Carolina came running over.

One look at the dead man was enough. Carolina threw an arm over Schaffran's shoulders. He turned him away from the body and said, "You had to do it, Jimmy. We may need these planes."

"Fuckin' shit," said Jimmy Schaffran.

"Hey, man. We chose our side of the fence and he chose his. Not much any of us can do about it now. God will have to figure it out."

TWENTY-ONE

★

In Galveston, Loren Snyder had a visitor. The man shouted down the open hatch, got no answer, then climbed down and wandered aft. He found Loren in the control room.

"Hi. I'm George Ranta. The sheriff sent me to see you."

"Oh." Loren was more than a little surprised. The sheriff was supposed to be guarding the pier and preventing the locals from meandering over for a look at a real submarine.

"I used to serve in attack boats. In fact, I used to be the head sonarman on this one."

"On this boat?"

"Yes, sir. Could you guys use some help? I'd kinda like to volunteer, if you could use me."

"Volunteer for what?"

"For whatever you have in mind, Captain."

That captain thing did it for Loren. This guy could be a SEAL in civvies, he reflected, here to kung fu the whole crew, all five. On the other hand, that captain thing sounded automatic, and he didn't look like a muscle man who spent four hours a day in the gym. Maybe he was on the level. "Prove it," Loren said.

Ranta sat down at the main sonar console and began flipping switches. In less than a minute the sonar was running through built-in tests. Yep, he knew what he was doing.

"We're going to sea in a few hours. If you've served in these boats, you know what we're up against. The navy won't like us out cruising around in an armed attack submarine."

"You have torpedoes in the tubes and Tomahawks in the wells?"

"Yep."

"Going to use them?"

"We might."

"To free Texas?"

"Yep."

"I'll go if you'll have me."

"Got any stuff?"

"It's on the other side of the gangway."

"Go get it, and find yourself a bunk."

Two hours later, another person showed up, a woman. Loren heard her call and went to meet her as she came out of the torpedo room.

"I heard you guys were getting ready to go to sea, so I talked to the sheriff and he let me come down here to talk to you."

"So talk."

"Got out last year after three years aboard *Colorado*."

"Why'd you get out?"

"Oh, the usual. I had a boyfriend and he wanted me home to fuck him every night. So—"

"The navy will try to sink this boat. You understand?"

"Sure."

"And you still want to go?"

"I was born and raised in Texas." She stopped, thought about that answer, and decided it was adequate. She was of medium height, trim, with a firm mouth and thin lips. Her hair was in a ponytail. The T-shirt she was wearing had a Texas flag on the front and back.

"What was your rate?"

"Quartermaster."

"Can you handle the helm?"

"Yes, sir!"

"Get your stuff and find a bunk."

"I already dropped my bag through the hatch."

"Welcome aboard."

She stuck out her hand. "My name is Ada Fuentes."

"Loren Snyder." He grabbed her hand and pumped it.

Fifteen minutes later Jugs met Ada and shook her hand. She sent Ada aft to meet the rest of the crew, who were running engine room drills.

When they were alone, Jugs said, "Lorrie, we gotta get outta here."

"As soon as the engine room drills are complete."

"No, Loren. Now."

"Are you getting worried?"

"You are goddamn right I am. What if those SEALs come before we submerge and shoot holes in the outer casing? Or shoot out the photonics masts? Or throw a chain around the screw?"

"Well. . . ."

"For God's sake, Lorrie. We can't do Texas any good if they disable us right here at the pier."

Loren Snyder ran his hand through his short hair. He had been so worried about his ability to handle this ship, perhaps losing her at sea and killing these volunteers, that he had not sufficiently considered the risks of sitting here at the pier. At the pier, *Texas* was only a harmless steel sculpture. At sea submerged, she was a powerful warship.

"You're right, Jugs," he acknowledged. "Let's get two guys topside to dump the gangway and cast off lines, you take the conn from the bridge. I'll do the control room, and we'll get the hell out of Dodge."

★

That was the way it worked. Julie Aranado gave the orders from the tiny bridge, and using her rudder and screw in reverse, *Texas* backed out of the slip in which she was moored and began forward motion toward the mouth of Galveston Harbor. Julie had her at five knots when she saw the speedboats with machine guns on the forward deck come through the harbor entrance at high speed and turn toward the submarine.

"The SEALs are here," she shouted into her voice-activated microphone on her headset. "Give me more turns."

She felt the screw of the sub biting. Behind her a rooster tail was forming. The screw was partially out of the water and was much less efficient than it would be when fully submerged.

As the three speedboats rounded the far pier, a ragged fusillade rang out. Julie didn't hear it, but she saw the faint traces of smoke and flashes from the rifles on the shore. The sheriff must have stationed sharpshooters on the piers, she thought.

One of the boats lost way. The other two turned hard to fall in formation with the sub. Julie asked for more turns on the screw.

"We're going to have to submerge the hull," she told Loren in the control room.

"For God's sake, stay in the channel," he replied.

She looked for the buoys. Fortunately this harbor was dredged regularly for cruise ships and freighters. The wind was playing with her hair as she scanned with the binoculars.

Jugs heard the snapping of bullets passing close by. A glance aft. The machine guns on the speedboats were flashing. And the hull was settling under the surface and the submarine was accelerating. Still, the bullets from the machine guns could damage the small conning tower and the photonics masts, all that remained of the submarine above water. Without those masts, *Texas* was blind at periscope depth. The photonics masts had replaced periscopes. They contained low-light, natural-light, and infrared cameras, and their video was displayed on monitors in the control room.

She timed the turn to the outbound channel and got it right. The boat answered the rudder nicely and the bow swung, and now they were going southeast into the rollers toward the ocean.

Another glance aft. One of the speedboats was dropping back, but one was staying with *Texas*, now doing at least twenty knots.

The speedboat might have managed to come alongside in calm waters, but now that they were out of the harbor the vessels hit the swells of the sea. Except for a slight pitching motion, *Texas* was unaffected, but the speedboat began to buck, rising and falling with every down thrust raising a cloud of spray.

"Give me all you've got," Julie said to Loren on the sound-powered phone.

Incredibly, the bow wave that the tower was making became larger. She could hear and see the curl of water against the tower and feel the drops of spray. She held out her tongue and collected a few drops. They tasted salty. Riding the bridge as the sub ran on the surface was a sublime sensatory experience, just as she remembered it from her submarining days, a sensual experience that would stay with her all the days of her life.

"Twenty-two knots," Loren reported.

Julie was watching the buoys. She wanted the safety of the deepest part of the channel. She was in it now, and she needed every foot. The coastal Gulf of Mexico was a shallow sea, unsuitable for submarine operations, the seabed dropping slowly away from the land.

Finally the swells were too much for the last speedboat. A few more bursts, the spang of bullets smacking the steel conning tower, then the boat slowed. The submarine ran on into the empty ocean, past a coaster that may have been the SEALs' mother ship, into the afternoon.

Finally, an hour later, with two hundred feet of water beneath the keel, Julie Aranado said into her sound-powered mike, "Dive, dive, dive." She unplugged the headset and dropped through the hatch, then pulled the hatch down behind her. Perched on the ladder, she spun the crank to dog it down. Then she went down the ladder and lowered herself through the opening in the pressure hull. She dogged that hatch behind her too, sealing the hull.

At the helm, Ada Fuentes didn't use the planes to help drive *Texas* under because the water was so shallow. The attack submarine sank slowly as her ballast tanks filled. When the conning tower disappeared under the surface in a boil of white water, the surface of the sea became a slick as the water continued to roil. While gulls soared above the place where *Texas* submerged looking for small marine life lifted by the swirling water, *Texas* ran southeastward, toward deeper water. She was in her element now, a powerful warship hidden under the surface, in the great wide sea.

★

On Thursday morning, the first day of September, the power came back on in the Baltimore area. One power company, Potomac Electric Power, had figured out that the master computer that controlled the northeast grid had been sabotaged with bad code, so it began manually restoring power in portions of their service area. Still, restoring power to their entire service area would take a while, and restoring service to the entire northeastern United States would take days.

One of the suburban residents, Lincoln B. Greenwood, a senior executive service employee of the Department of Health and Human Services, had not gone to work that day because without power nothing could be done at the office. He was delighted when his television came back on and lights illuminated in his house. He could hear the toilet tanks filling as water once again surged through the pipes. He grabbed his car keys and opened his garage door, which rose majestically.

Greenwood was worried about the uncertainties the future held and had concluded that he and his wife didn't have sufficient food in the house that would not spoil without refrigeration. And his daughter, with the four-month-old, undoubtedly needed baby food, formula, and diapers. He called her on his cell phone, and she affirmed his shopping list. She and her husband also needed more staples, she said.

The lot at the mall in Clarksville was packed with cars when Greenwood arrived, which surprised him. All of these stores closed when the power went out because their registers and computer systems were nonfunctional. Greenwood glanced at his watch; the power had only come back on twenty minutes ago. All of these people must have been here waiting, probably for hours, hoping and praying the power would be restored.

The queue to get into the supermarket, which also had a large pharmacy department, was four deep and extended around the corner of the store into the two-acre mall lot. Lincoln Greenwood got in line, resigned himself to a long wait, and began fretting that the store shelves would be empty when he got inside. The checkout lines would fill every aisle, blocking shoppers' access to the shelves. What a nightmare!

The man in front of Greenwood said he had parked on the grass across from the main entrance, and the store was not yet open. The clerks were just coming to work, he thought.

Around the corner, out of Greenwood's sight, the manager of the store stood in front of the locked doors and spoke to the crowd. "Folks, we are going to open the doors in a few minutes and admit ten shoppers a minute from the front of the line. When two hundred are inside, we will admit one additional shopper when one customer comes out. We have to comply with the fire codes, and besides, our checkout clerks can only work so fast. Due to the number of people waiting, we are limiting each shopper to the contents of one grocery cart, so there will be items on the shelves for everyone. Thank you for your cooperation and your patience."

Then, five minutes later, as he unlocked the doors, the crowd, many of them white-collar workers from the vast bureaucracies of the federal government, scientists from the nearby Johns Hopkins Applied Physics Laboratory, or mathematicians from the National Security Agency at Fort Meade, ten miles away, rushed the door. The surge was unplanned and unstoppable. The manager was swept out of the way. The exit door, on the other end of the store, shattered, apparently broken by someone in the crowd. People surged in through that door too.

Behind the people in front shoving to get through the doors, the queue disintegrated and became a mob as people ran, shoved, pushed, and forced their way forward. Lincoln Greenwood gave way to panic. His daughter *needed* the baby supplies. He and his wife *needed* food and bottled water, and so did his daughter and her husband. Without it, *they might starve if the power went off and water once again stopped coming from the tap*

So Lincoln B. Greenwood fought his way forward. He threw several women to the ground and stepped on another who had already fallen. As he came around the corner of the building he could see the huge supermarket doorway, now standing wide open. A man took a swing at him but Greenwood parried the blow and continued his odyssey through the human sea.

His shirt was torn and his face was bleeding from a woman's finger-nails when he made it through the door. People were already pushing shopping carts containing whatever they could grab, pushing them not toward the checkout counters, but toward the doors where people were trying to get in. People coming in began looting the carts. This milling, pushing, shouting, screaming swarm of humanity was no longer a group of civilized beings who attended church, obeyed the traffic laws, and were courteous to strangers; they were a primal force, much like a herd of charging elephants, driven only by their survival instincts.

The store manager who had unlocked the doors and been swept aside ran into the parking lot and used his cell phone to call 911. Within two minutes a Howard County police car rolled to a stop with lights flashing and siren wailing. The officer killed the siren and met the manager, who ran toward him. Seemingly oblivious to the presence of the officer, the crowd surrounding the doors continued to push, shove, and fight.

The police officer stood silently, watching the melee in disbelief as the manager shouted to be heard, "You have got to stop this madness. They'll kill each other in there."

Indeed, the officer could see several people sprawled on the sidewalks and in the loading lane, apparently trampled or injured. They were being ignored by the surging mob. The officer tried to estimate how many people he could see, and concluded there were more than a thousand people outside the building.

"What the hell do you think I can do?" the officer asked the manager without taking his eyes from the panicked mob.

"Tear-gas them. My God, people are going to be *killed* in there! Can't you see that?"

"Tear gas isn't going to stop them," the cop said, and began talking to his dispatcher through the radio transmitter pinned to his lapel. He got into the patrol car and locked the door so he could hear better. The manager tried to jerk the door open, then pounded on the window with his fist.

What the dispatcher knew and the officer didn't was that this scene was being played out in supermarkets all over the county. Smaller mobs, but equally frightened, were looting hardware stores and stealing gasoline at service stations as quickly as it could be pumped.

At the police station, the chief listened to the calls describing the looting and shook his head. Nothing could be done.

Throughout the Pepco service area, similar scenes were being enacted. What the violent looting would have looked like if the crowds had known that just hours before Barry Soetoro had ordered electrical power shut off nationwide is something that defies speculation.

Inside the Clarksville supermarket, Lincoln B. Greenwood managed to fill his pockets with little jars of baby food. He grabbed one box of six-quart cartons of Similac Infant Formula from a shopping cart and made for the door. He had to fight his way out, just as he had fought his way in. Now he had to keep both hands on the box of infant formula to keep it from being torn from his grasp, hug it into his belly, and use his elbows to create a pathway. When he finally reached his car, he still had the Similac, but two of the glass jars in his pockets were broken. He was bleeding from the nose where he had been punched and his shirt was in tatters.

He got into the car, started the engine, and tried to get out of the parking lot, only to find that people trying to get in had abandoned their cars in the entranceways and ran for the store. He began bumping cars, trying to shove them out of the way. And succeeded. He got to a median, jumped it with his car, and drove away quickly. He was an animal fighting to survive, and he suspected he wasn't going to make it.

When Greenwood did get home that evening, the power was off again. Officers from the Department of Homeland Security had visited Pepco headquarters and demanded at the point of a gun that power be shut off throughout Pepco's multi-county service area. When the lights again went out across the Pepco area, they handcuffed every executive they could find and led them away. Everyone else was told to leave the building immediately. The last officer out of the building seized the keys from a terrified janitor and locked the doors behind her.

★

Oblivious to the panic that had seized suburban Maryland and was spreading like an internet virus across America, on Friday morning, the second day of September, Barry Soetoro went before the cameras in his best gray suit and blue tie, a combination that his makeup artist had once assured him was flattering.

It would take hours, probably at least twenty-four, before the power went off all across the lower forty-eight states, or forty-six since Oklahoma and Texas had tried to go their own ways, so the president and his advisors thought he should use the time to build political support for the battles yet to come. "Comfort your friends and afflict your enemies," Al Grantham advised; Soetoro thought that nugget summed up his mission. He had his best speechwriter prepare the remarks, and they were on the teleprompter, so he could look the unseen audience straight in the eyes as he delivered his truth.

"My fellow Americans. As I address you today, many of our fellow Americans sit in the dark, sweltering in the heat, with food rotting, without any access to electricity because of the violent acts of desperate and dangerous men. Our nation is at war—at war with ideological fanatics who take the slave-owning Confederate States of America as their model. They want to destroy not only our nation's electrical power grid, they want to destroy this country in pursuit of an extreme ideological vision that would deny women, minorities, and everyday Americans their basic rights. Already they have attacked United States military installations and killed brave servicemen and women who were defending freedom.

"As you know, I have said repeatedly through the years that the two greatest threats to our nation are right-wing constitutionalists and climate change. I have been ridiculed in the conservative press for those statements, but as I foretold, the threat from the Right has become a deadly peril to our national life.

"Tonight I ask all loyal Americans for their support, patience, and understanding as we fight to preserve the Union. One hundred fifty years ago, one of my predecessors had to fight the same battle against an enemy that would have kept half our nation as a haven for slavery. Today we battle a similar enemy, an embittered minority who cannot break with the past, whose political beliefs are grounded in ignorance, hate, and bigotry, and who are now in open rebellion against the United States. We face trying days ahead. But I pledge, as President Abraham Lincoln did before me, to preserve our Union and ensure that this nation shall have a new birth of freedom, and that government of the people, by the people, and for the people shall not perish from the earth. Have faith, and I will lead us through the fire to the promised land. Thank you."

Where electricity still flowed through the wires, people nationwide sat staring at their television screens as picked liberal commentators talked about the president's resolve, his vision. His forceful delivery struck just the right note, one woman said. Another commentator, a tenured university professor infamous for urging all white people to commit suicide so the nonwhites of the earth could flourish, pounded the racial drum. Only through Barry Soetoro could the promise of racial justice and equal rights be realized, and white privilege once and for all be defeated and banished from the land.

Where it was seen, the presidential speech had the opposite effect from the one he presumably intended. Panicked people quite beyond rational thought got in their cars and joined mobs looting stores.

General Martin L. Wynette watched the speech on television in his Pentagon E-Ring office and shrugged sadly. Climate change!

He asked himself, Were chaos and anarchy the president's real goals, so he could build his socialist dictatorship upon the rubble? Or had the damned fool miscalculated once again? Was he a sublime evil genius, or simply a bumbling, incompetent believer in his own bullshit that fate and poisonous racial politics had raised to a very high place? Not that it mattered—the result was the same in either case. The apocalypse had finally arrived.

A few offices down the E-Ring of the Pentagon from the office of the chairman of the JCS, the chief of naval operations, Admiral Cart

McKiernan, was staring at a hard copy of the president's order for the destruction of the power plants in Texas. The best way to do that was with Tomahawk Land Attack Missiles, the admiral thought, but he had no idea how many power plants there were in Texas.

He had a much better grasp on how many Tomahawks the navy had, which was a little less than 3,400. The Soetoro administration had ended production in Fiscal Year 2015. The missiles cost $1.4 million each and the manufacturer, Raytheon, had stated that restarting the factory and suppliers' production would take two years and increase costs. The next-generation missile was not scheduled into the fleet for ten more years.

A Tomahawk was a subsonic cruise missile that carried a one-thousand-pound conventional warhead. To put a power plant out of action, the missile would need to score a direct hit. To do that, one needed to program the precise GPS coordinates, the latitude and longitude, of each target into the missiles. On a big power plant with large generators—as many as twenty, mounted on thick, reinforced concrete—direct hits by multiple missiles would be required to do significant damage. Perhaps five missiles for each target, because inevitably, as with all complex state-of-the art weapons, Tomahawk reliability was not one hundred percent. More like ninety percent, assuming they were properly and meticulously programmed before firing.

The missile depended on an accurate satellite survey of the terrain it would fly over to ensure it didn't hit an obstacle, a system called Terrain Contour Matching. This feature allowed the missile to fly as close to the earth as possible, thereby making it difficult for defenders to acquire on radar and shoot down. GPS was used to guide it over the water to its preprogrammed coast-in point and in its terminal guidance phase. So precisely where were the power plants that Soetoro wanted destroyed? It would require several days of staff work to come up with that information from existing satellite databases and then pass it on in a targeting order to the ships selected to launch the missiles.

Cart McKiernan wasn't thrilled about using Tomahawks in this manner. Blasting the hell out of Texas could deplete the navy's inventory of Tomahawks, which might hurt America down the road, assuming that down the road there still was an America and a United States Navy that needed the weapon. The Sunnis and Shiites were fighting each other in the Middle East, North Korea's dictator was strutting as usual, China was bullying its neighbors, and Iran was once again giving the world the finger over its nuclear ambitions. Israel was worried about ISIS and Iranian attacks. And what if next week Soetoro decided to punish Oklahoma, Louisiana, or Florida?

The alternative to Tomahawks was strikes against the power plants using carrier aircraft. USS *Texas* had just escaped from Galveston, so she was at sea somewhere in the Gulf of Mexico. Giving her an aircraft carrier for a torpedo target didn't appeal to the CNO's military mind. Losing an aircraft carrier or two off the Texas coast would be a poor trade for some power plants, many of which were probably scheduled to be retired in a few years anyway and replaced with more efficient ones.

Of course, McKiernan could pass the request on to the air force and ask if they wanted a piece of this action, but that didn't strike him as a good idea, either. Funding for the next generation of Tomahawk was the stake on the table, and if the navy couldn't complete assigned missions with the missiles it had, perhaps it didn't really need those new, more expensive missiles after all. And no doubt the air force already had a full plate.

McKiernan attached a memo to the order authorizing the use of one hundred Tomahawks against Texas power plants, and he directed that the plants with the largest generating capacity be attacked first using five missiles per plant. Losing the generating capacity from twenty big power plants would play hob with the Texas grid and leave millions of treasonous Texans sweltering in the dark, which should satisfy even Barry Soetoro, Cart McKiernan thought.

With CNO's proviso, the presidential order went off to the strike planners.

★

Colonel Nathaniel Danaher spent the morning and afternoon in the B-52 hangar spaces talking to the pilots, crewmen, and ground personnel attached to the squadrons. He wanted to know if any of them would fight for Texas and Oklahoma. A few people from those two states volunteered, but the vast majority didn't want to fight for anybody. He was about to give it up as a bad job when his handheld squawked. "Major General Hays is here, sir. He came on the last C-130."

The officer on the other end was a major whom Danaher liked because he was competent and could think on his feet. "You know where to put the troops?"

"Yes, sir. Augment our people at the ammo depot and fuel farm."

"Tell General Hays I'll meet him at base operations."

Nate Danaher got into his staff car and rode across the parking mat the two miles to base ops.

JR Hays was standing there in his camos. Danaher saluted, and it was returned. It felt a little strange saluting JR, who was ten years younger than he was and had been a newly minted major when he served with him, but he did it proudly, with a grin.

"It went well, sir," he said. "Total surprise. We even got into the message center before they notified the Pentagon, which bought us a few hours, anyway." Of course, with cell phones, everyone in Bossier City and Shreveport knew the base had been taken.

They walked into base ops and headed for the planning room as Danaher reported. "The commanding general was very unhappy when we stormed into his office and captured him."

"I'll bet he was," JR said with a smile.

They stood in front of a large wall-mounted map and the two career soldiers examined it with practiced eyes.

"As you suspected," Nate Danaher said, "most of the people here don't want to fight anybody, but we have enough volunteers with the right skills to make up a couple of crews."

"Fine."

The primary reason JR had wanted Barksdale was to prevent B-52s from bombing Texas cities or military bases. Taking as many of the bombers as possible to Texas was not in the cards since the infrastructure and equipment to maintain and fly the planes, not to mention their weapons, was here. It would take weeks, if not months, to move all that to a new base.

Then there was the fact that B-52s, and B-1s for that matter, were essentially defenseless against modern jet fighters equipped with air-to-air missiles with ranges up to a hundred miles. They were dinosaurs and could only be used when one had absolute air supremacy. The B-1s had managed strikes yesterday on railroad bridges in the Powder River Basin and today on Fort Polk and Whiteman Air Force Base in Missouri because there was no air opposition. In the future, there would be. Meanwhile the U.S. Air Force would be getting its act together, and strikes against Barksdale, as long as it was occupied, and Dyess and the other air bases in Texas would soon be forthcoming.

JR Hays and Nate Danaher knew that their window of opportunity would close as soon as Soetoro's brain trust could slam it shut, so they intended to use the bombers while they still could.

"We hammered Whiteman," JR said, jabbing at the map with a finger, "but of course we didn't get all the B-2s. Expect a few to visit tonight."

"We have four F-22s," Danaher said. JR had already seen them as his ride taxied in. "But no one to fly them. One of the pilots shot up the instrument panel of his before he got off the boarding ladder. The other three aren't interested in joining Texas."

JR merely nodded. A competent F-22 pilot—if he had one, which he didn't—might have been able to find B-2s in the night sky, but F-16 pilots certainly couldn't. "At least those are four F-22s that can't be used against us," he said to Danaher.

JR went back to the map. "We are loading an armored brigade at Fort Hood onto a train. Tanks and troopers and artillery. They'll be rolling tonight. At first they said it couldn't be done. Anyway, they'll be coming through here tomorrow morning. By tomorrow night I want them here." He pointed to a position between Barksdale and Fort Polk.

"A flight of four F-16s will be along in—" he consulted his watch—"about an hour. Since we don't have aerial tankers, we'll have to refuel them, top them off. As soon as we can get some B-52s ready, assuming they aren't destroyed by B-2s from Whiteman, launch them and their fighter escorts at the bridges."

JR jabbed at the map, which only showed rivers, towns, and interstates. "They know their targets. I want every highway and railroad bridge across the Mississippi from Baton Rouge to above Memphis in the river by morning. Elvin Gentry says it can be done, and he swore he could do it."

"How many bridges is that?" Danaher asked.

"I don't know, but Elvin does. All he has to do is drop at least a span of each one into the river. He says JDAMs will do it. Any intact bridges left standing tomorrow will be attacked with F-16s, or any B-52s or B-1s we have left." JDAM was an acronym that stood for Joint Direct Attack Munition. It was a guidance package that screwed into a dumb—freefall—bomb, enabling it to make a direct hit on a preprogrammed target.

JR took a deep breath and let the air out slowly as he surveyed the map. His strategy was simple. He didn't want to fight in Texas, but Louisiana would do fine. If Soetoro's army could get across the Mississippi River to fight. An opposed crossing of a big river was the most difficult maneuver an army could undertake, the equivalent of an amphibious assault against a dug-in enemy.

They had discussed this objective before, but now that they were on the cusp of trying it, they looked at it again, discussed logistics, roads, what the enemy might do.

"I wish we could get more B-52 crews," Nate Danaher said, a tad wistfully JR thought.

"If you think we have problems getting people to fight, Soetoro's forces have them worse," JR assured him. "I suspect the U.S. Army and Air Force are on the verge of falling apart, and will unless Soetoro starts putting people against a wall and shooting them. Still, mutiny and mass desertions will certainly slow them down. Our edge is that our people are fighting *for* something, for a free and independent Republic of Texas. Soetoro is fighting to become an absolute dictator, and the people in uniform aren't stupid. They'll figure out the difference, if they don't know it already."

"You put a lot of faith in average, run-of-the mill people," Danaher murmured.

"Average, run-of-the-mill people won their independence from Great Britain," JR shot back, "and have fought in every war this country ever had. They were at Valley Forge and the Alamo, at Shiloh, Gettysburg, and the Wilderness. Not to mention Belleau Wood, Normandy, Iwo Jima, Vietnam, and Afghanistan. You and I spent our military careers leading them. They'll fight for freedom, all right, to the last drop of blood. Barry Soetoro is on the wrong damned side."

TWENTY-TWO

★

With the power out again in suburban Maryland on Friday morning, Lincoln B. Greenwood was a changed man. His adventures the previous day in the supermarket had shaken him to the core. To be in the midst of a mob of people savagely fighting for basic necessities—and fighting just as hard as anyone else—had given him a glimpse of the monster in all of us.

Eat or starve. Move or die. Kill or be killed.

Those monsters were waiting out there in the darkness now. Evil people, unrestrained by the bonds of civilization or religion. People willing to do *anything* to survive.

"We gotta get outta here," he said to his wife, Anne.

"Where will we go?" she asked reasonably as she placed candles around the house for the coming evening.

He gestured vaguely. He hadn't the foggiest idea, but here there was chaos, so instinct told him to leave. To run. To escape.

"What about Suzanne and her family?"

The daughter, the son-in-law, and the baby; Lincoln B. Greenwood hadn't thought about them all morning. He glanced guiltily at the box of Similac powder and the baby food jars still resting where he had put them on the kitchen counter.

"She married that moron; they are going to have to take care of themselves."

His wife glowered at him, but Lincoln didn't notice. He walked around the living room looking out the windows at the darkness. He could see faint light in a neighbor's window across the cul-de-sac. Candles, he figured. The other houses on the cul-de-sac appeared dark. Maybe the neighbors had already left. Maybe that was the smart thing to do. Get in the car and go. Somewhere. Escape.

He felt the urge to run, to flee. Adrenaline. He broke into a sweat.

"Get packed up," he said to his wife. "Your meds, some clothes. Some food. Nothing else. We're leaving."

"But *where* are we going?" she demanded.

"I don't know. We can't stay here. They've been rioting in Baltimore all week. They rioted at the supermarket yesterday. Power is off, phones are off, internet is off. When the inner-city thugs come to the suburbs to loot and burn and rape, we had better be gone."

"I don't want to leave."

"Dear wife, we don't even have a gun, because you wouldn't have one in *your* house." That's when Lincoln B. Greenwood lost it. "*I don't give a shit what you want*!" he roared to his shocked wife. "I am not going to sit here waiting to be murdered or die of starvation. Now get upstairs and pack what you want to take."

Greenwood ran upstairs and threw three pairs of jeans and some shirts into a bag. Some underwear and socks. He added his blood pressure medicine and his prostate pills to the bag, his toothbrush and toothpaste, his razor and shaving cream, plus some laxatives and a bottle of aspirin.

Then he went to a safe in his closet, opened it, and got out the strips of gold he had invested in when the economy was going to hell in 2008 and 2009. A few Krugerrands. It was damn little, but paper dollars weren't going to be the coin of the realm and credit cards were worthless. Not that it mattered. He had maybe fifty dollars in his wallet and, since the power was out, no prospect of getting more from his bank, even if the ATMs worked or the bank was open and willing to convert every dollar in his savings and checking accounts to cash, which they wouldn't be.

He stuffed the gold into his pocket and zipped up his bag. Carried it downstairs. Anne was still upstairs packing.

A car pulled up in the driveway and he went to the window. His daughter, Suzanne. He opened the door for her. "We're leaving, Dad. Going to Gerald's parents' place in Front Royal. We're going to ride it out there."

"Good idea. We're getting ready to leave too. I got some Similac and baby food for you. I'll put it in a bag while you go upstairs and say good-bye to Mom."

When Suzanne left, Lincoln Greenwood went upstairs to check on his wife. She was sitting on a stool in her bathroom crying.

"Are you packed?"

"Oh, Lincoln. I feel as if I am saying good-bye to my life. What is to become of us?"

"If you don't get a move on, woman, we're going to be dead." He could feel the evil out there in the night. "Pack your meds and a few clothes and let's get in the car and go while there is still time."

She sobbed, trying to pull herself together. And nodded. "You're right. Another few minutes."

So he went downstairs and put his bag in the car, which was in the garage. He would pull the handle that disconnected the door and raise it to get the car out. But not until they were ready to go.

Five long minutes later, as he threw all the dry and canned food they had in garbage bags and stuffed them in the car, he heard engine noises.

He ran to the living room window and looked out. A police car and a late-model pickup were examining the houses in the cul-de-sac. Lincoln Greenwood went back to the kitchen and helped himself to a carving knife from the block on the counter. He put it up his left sleeve, leaving only a bit of the handle sticking out.

Then he went back to the window. Four young black men were coming up the walk, and all four had pistols in their hands.

One of them pounded on the door. "Open up in there or we'll kill all of you and burn this goddamn thing down around your bodies."

Greenwood unlocked the door and they rushed in. One of them pointed a pistol in his face. "Hello, asshole. Who else is here?"

"My wife is upstairs."

He jerked his head at his compatriots and they went charging up the stairs.

"You and me are goin' to the kitchen, motha-fuck. We want the food. All of it. And anything else you got."

Greenwood led the way.

The man immediately began opening cupboards and rooting through the pantry. He turned on Greenwood and pointed the pistol in his face. "Where is the grub, honkey? Don't tell me you people ain't got no grub in the house. Cause if you do, I'll just shoot you now and be done with it."

"In the car in the garage. We were just about to leave."

"So we got here just in the nick of time. Ain't that sweet? You lead. Get it out."

He went into the garage and began emptying the garbage bags of spaghetti noodles and cans onto the floor.

"Pick it up. Take it to the front door."

Greenwood hoisted a bag in each hand and led off. The thug picked up another and followed him, gun in hand.

When the bags were at the front door, the man said, "Let's go get the rest of it. Seems like you oughta be carryin'," and he laughed.

Another trip cleaned out the car. The men who went upstairs were rooting around and shouting to each other, as if they were on an Easter egg hunt.

In the kitchen, the punk with Greenwood said, "You got any guns?"

"No."

"You better not be lying, 'cause we're gonna look. If I find you lied, I'll just shoot you like a dog and that will be that."

"I'm not lying." Lincoln Greenwood was scared and his voice was an octave high and quavered.

"Pills. We want all the pills you got, motha-fuck. And your grass and powder and smack."

"Pills are upstairs." That was a mistake, Greenwood realized. There was nothing in the medicine cabinet in his bathroom, and if the man looked, there would be hell to pay. "We don't have any dope," he added.

"Like shit! You lyin' asshole. All you white motha-fucks got shit to get high on. You buy it in Baltimore from the guys in the 'hood. Us niggers ain't got the money for nothin' but pot. It's white trash like you that buy the high-dollar shit and then convict the poor dudes sellin' it who ain't got no other way to make a livin'."

The man, who was perhaps twenty or twenty-one, looked around, surveying the crystal and kick-knacks in the kitchen. He pointed his pistol at the counter television that Anne watched every morning when she made breakfast and pulled the trigger. The shot sounded like a cannon. The front of the television showered glass on the counter.

Then the gunman turned his back on Lincoln B. Greenwood. Greenwood pulled the knife from his left sleeve and rammed it between the man's ribs on his right side up to the hilt. Gave it a savage twist and jerked the knife out. Blood squirted out, under pressure.

The young gunman turned with a funny look on his face, tried to bring the pistol around. Greenwood pushed his arm up and rammed the knife into his solar plexus, then jerked it loose. The gunman collapsed on the floor, bleeding copiously.

"Hey, Joey!" A shout from upstairs. "You havin' fun, man?"

Lincoln B. Greenwood removed the pistol from his victim's grasp and went to the hallway, with the stairs on his left. He crouched against the wall so anyone coming down the stairs wouldn't see him. He waited. When they came down each had an armload of stuff. After the first two got down the stairs and went through the front door, he shot the third one in the back from a distance of three feet. At that range he couldn't miss.

The man fell the rest of the way down the stairs and piled up on the floor. Greenwood shot him again.

He ran to the door of the house and tried to align the sights of the pistol, a black thing without a cylinder. Greenwood had just fired the first two shots of his life, and now the problem of hitting anything or anyone who wasn't five feet away became a bit much. He pulled the trigger and the gun kicked and to his amazement the closest man fell flat on his face.

He aimed as well as he could in the darkness and began firing. Missing. The pistol bucked with every shot and the muzzle flash blinded him. He kept squeezing the trigger anyway.

The fourth man jumped in the right seat of the pickup and roared off as Greenwood emptied the pistol in that general direction. The truck rocketed out of the cul-de-sac and down the street with its engine howling.

Greenwood walked over to the man lying face-down on the lawn. He had a red spot dead center in his lower back, just visible in the dim evening light. Sheer dumb luck, Greenwood thought, and helped himself to the man's pistol, which lay on the grass by his outstretched hand, along with Anne's jewelry box. Without thinking, he began scooping up the baubles and dumping them back in the box. Most of it was junk, but she had a few nice pieces.

"I can't move my legs," the man whispered.

"Tough shit," Lincoln B. Greenwood said, and began going through the man's pockets. He found an extra magazine for his pistol. A roll of bills. A pack of Marlboros with one cigarette missing and a lighter. Some more jewelry, whether Anne's or someone else's, he didn't know. He put the money and jewelry in his pocket. He almost left the cigs and lighter on the grass, and changed his mind. Someone might trade him something he needed for them.

"Don't leave me like this," the man pleaded. "Please."

"Die slow, black mother-fucker," said Lincoln B. Greenwood, lately of the U.S. Department of Health and Human Services.

Upstairs, he found someone had smacked Anne across the face with a pistol. She was half out of it, with a terrific welt, but apparently otherwise uninjured.

He threw the rest of her meds in the suitcase and looked at her stuff. Everything neatly folded, dresses and sandals like she was packing for Paris. He shoved some underwear and slacks into the suitcase and closed it. Took it downstairs, walked around the man he had knifed and the man he had shot, and loaded it into the car. Then he began the chore of reloading all the food bags. That took three minutes. He tracked in the blood on the kitchen floor, now a small lake, and began leaving footprints.

The man he had knifed was apparently dead, his eyes focused on infinity, his face a grimace. Greenwood went through his pockets and found two magazines for the pistol, a wad of bills, and a cellophane baggy that apparently contained marijuana. A lighter, keys, a pack of cigarette papers, some change.

He took the pistol and a spare magazine from the man he shot coming down the stairs and dragged him into the living room, leaving a bloody streak on the carpet. The guy was still alive, apparently, because he was still bleeding, but Greenwood didn't check. Or care.

Greenwood went back upstairs and used a wet towel to bring Anne around. Helped her downstairs and through the kitchen, trying to avoid the puddles of blood. In the garage he put her in the passenger seat and belted her in.

After he got the garage door raised manually, he backed out, put the car in park, and went over to the police car and looked in. Piles of electronic gear, some silverware, and bags of food. He pulled out two bags of canned goods and left the rest. Stowed it in his car and drove off. He didn't even look to see if the man sprawled on the lawn was still alive.

As he went through Clarksville on Route 32, Greenwood turned off the highway and threaded his way past darkened fast food joints and a closed filling station into the parking lot at the mall. Three cars sat in the huge lot.

Greenwood got out of the car, taking a pistol, car keys, and a flashlight from the glove box with him. He passed a darkened wine store with its windows smashed out. An AT&T store had received similar treatment. He adjusted the pistol in his belt as he walked around to the front of the supermarket. The doors were open, the glass smashed out, and there were no lights.

He went inside, using the flashlight. The place had been ransacked. Not a crumb was left on the shelves, not even in the candy section. No cereal boxes, bags of flour, cans, none of that. The freezers were empty and the doors standing open. The pharmacy windows were shattered and the door that led behind the counter was wide open. A glance with the flashlight was enough. The pharmacy shelves were completely empty.

Near the back of the store he found a body lying in the aisle. It was a man, in his sixties, perhaps, balding, a modest spare tire. His eyes were open, staring at nothing, and a dried trickle of blood showed on one corner of his mouth. He looked to Greenwood as if he had been trampled.

Greenwood started to turn away when he realized he recognized the man. He couldn't remember his name, but he saw him occasionally in church and they nodded to each other.

We're all going to end up like this, Greenwood thought, and used his flashlight to leave the store and walk to his car.

Anne was fully conscious. "Where were you?"

"In the supermarket. They cleaned it out." He didn't tell her about the body.

He used his flashlight to inspect the pistols. The empty one was a Glock with a fat handle. There didn't appear to be a safety. He managed to get the empty magazine out and a full one in. Pulled the slide back and let it go. He guessed it was ready to go, but he would have to try to shoot it to find out.

The other pistol was an old army .45. He tried to pull the slide back, but it wouldn't move. He found the safety. Clicked it off and now the slide came back, showing a gleam of brass. The hammer was all the way back. He carefully put the safety back on. The third pistol was similar, and also loaded.

Lincoln Greenwood started the engine of the car and steered through the empty parking lot and out onto the road that led to the highway, Route 32. Turned west and fed gas.

★

In Arizona that Thursday night, a crowd of four thousand people carrying candles marched on a Homeland Security detention facility. The facility, on an unused corner of Luke Air Force Base, was off-limits to the public, which tore down the fence with chains and trucks so the crowd could walk through.

The crowd stood in the darkness with their candles singing hymns for almost an hour. Then they walked up to the gate and went through it, even though the Homeland employees tried to stop them by threatening to arrest the whole crowd.

The officer in charge gave orders for his employees to fire upon the crowd, yet not a single shot was heard. The prisoners were released and accompanied the crowd, as did many of the Homeland Officers.

In Pittsburgh a similar crowd of peaceful protesters intent on storming a detention facility were fired upon by several guards. Two people died and three were injured. The crowd pressed in relentlessly, and when it left with the prisoners, two of the guards were dangling from light poles with barbed wire twisted around their necks.

In Michigan two people were trampled and three shot to death by guards when a crowd attempted to storm a detention facility. The crowd didn't get the prisoners, but all involved knew there would be a next time, and when it came the crowd would be armed.

The widespread power outage never became total, and neither did censorship at local radio and television stations and newspapers where federal censors had been driven out. It was small towns served by small power plants that informed the larger public about what was going on, and that became the equivalent of the colonists' committees of correspondence before the Revolutionary War.

More radio and television stations said whatever they pleased on the air. They were becoming more strident over Barry Soetoro's attempts to muzzle them or force them to report only government propaganda as contained in press releases. Of course, for every rebel radio or television station, there were three or four that obeyed the government's edicts, either because ownership or management were progressive liberals who believed wholeheartedly in Barry Soetoro or the censors had them buffaloed: it was impossible to tell which was the case by listening or watching the broadcasts.

Radio audiences were almost exclusively in automobiles and pickup trucks. People at home who had solar power or an emergency generator watched television. The satellites were on the air, and a set of rabbit ears could pull in a local television station if there was one. Some of the rabbit ears were made out of coat hangers. Television audiences tended to be large: family and neighbors gathered in a living room that had service.

And in some rural communities served by small local power plants, the electricity stayed on. Either the managers of the plants ignored federal orders or intimidated the Homeland Security or FEMA Gestapo. As long as the natural gas continued to flow through the pipe or the stockpile of coal lasted, the power plants were still in business, supplying hospitals, nursing homes, residences, and everyone else who used power, which was everyone, within their service area. In a blacked-out nation, a few islands of light continued to defy the darkness.

Dinner on Thursday evening at our hideout was another culinary masterpiece of MREs, hot sauce, and canned beans. I sat down beside Sarah with my plate. Everyone else was talking about the political situation, damning Soetoro, wondering what the tidbits meant that Willie and Armanti had gleaned from the short-wave.

Times were tough and getting tougher in Soetoro land. Power seemed to be off in all directions—and the guys weren't hearing any utility repair crews chattering back and forth.

While the others gabbed, Sarah whispered, "What is going to become of us, Tommy?"

Sarah Houston never needs an arm to lean on, but still she made the gesture, and I was touched. "Hey, babe, I wish I knew."

"When do you think Admiral Grafton will be in good enough shape to travel?"

I thought about that. I'm not a doctor or trained medic, so I didn't want to move Grafton until it became absolutely necessary. And we had no better place to go. We were in a tactical trap with only one road in and out, yet being on the dead-end of a road to nowhere meant we would have to entertain few tourists. I didn't think the feds were looking for us; I suspected they had a lot of bigger problems to keep them busy. I explained this to Sarah.

"They could find us from the air," she pointed out.

"If they are looking. In the right place, that is. They probably aren't looking for us at all."

Counting on an enemy's incompetence struck me as foolish, yet expecting efficiency from a bureaucracy was the definition of insanity.

Grafton was definitely in less pain this evening. If he had to, he could walk to the restroom. Every other minute was spent sitting or lying down, and talking. Just now he was in the corner of the living room with Jack Yocke on one side and Sal Molina on the other. They were discussing all things Soetoro.

It seemed that Grafton's adventures with Sluggo Sweatt and his friends had loosened his tongue a good deal. In my on-and-off association with Jake Grafton in the past, I never heard him express a political opinion, which was proper for a serving officer. Don't criticize your superiors in front of the troops. Aye-aye, sir, and all that. However, after his boss fired him and tried to frame him for a murder plot and coup, he probably felt he owed his former superior nothing—not deference, not respect, not silence, not the benefit of the doubt.

I suspected that deep down Grafton thought he owed Barry Soetoro a bullet, the same debt he had paid to Sluggo Sweatt.

"So explain what is happening to America," Jake Grafton asked Sal Molina, the career White House insider.

Molina took a moment to gather his thoughts. "What we are seeing," he said, "is a classic political reaction to a threatened loss of power. Politics as usual meant that the progressive liberals, who have captured the Democratic Party body and soul, were going to be voted out of office and would probably be out for decades, if they ever got back in. The world is changing quickly, which has profound implications for the Democrats' powerbase, which rests solidly on the uneducated and unskilled in the center cities who are being increasingly marginalized in a world economy that is going to grow like a mushroom on steroids in the years ahead."

Jack Yocke, *Washington Post* columnist, made a noise with his lips that sounded a bit like a Bronx cheer.

Sal Molina ignored the columnist and continued: "You remember Moore's Law and what happened to computing power in the past fifty years. Gordon Moore was a tech executive who made a prediction in nineteen sixty-five that computing power would double every two years. It was a prediction for exponential growth, and those kinds of predictions rarely come true, and if they do, the growth doesn't last long. But the growth Moore predicted has lasted for fifty years, and the end of exponential growth is not in sight. Intel's latest microprocessor is thirty-five hundred times faster and ninety thousand times more efficient than its first one, the Intel 4004, which came out in nineteen seventy-one.

"Moore's Law applies to *all* technological applications, although no other technologies grow at such a multiple of efficiency. The one that will change our world is hydraulic fracking of shale formations. Drilling a well two miles deep and running horizontal lines out as far as fifteen thousand feet in undulating formations is becoming more efficient, more technologically advanced, and cheaper. The cost for these wells keeps dropping. The ocean of oil and gas being produced drives the cost of these commodities down. Shale wells produce over half their output over their lives in the first year, so that makes the frackers the marginal producers; when the market can absorb it, they can supply vast quantities of oil and gas at lower and lower prices."

"I think I see it," Jake Grafton said. "Traditional oil-producing nations will find they get less and less for their oil and their economies will stagnate."

"Ah," Molina replied, "but as the price of oil drops, the world benefits in countless ways. Industries can develop, billions of poor people will get better-paying jobs, prosperity will lift a great many boats. America will prosper. Natural gas is so cheap and abundant that industries that need lots of feed stock are coming back onshore. Low prices for gasoline and natural gas will stimulate every industry in America."

Yocke shook his head slowly. "All that may be happening, but who can see it coming? Only fortune-tellers or readers of tea leaves."

"Barry Soetoro and the people on his staff see it coming," Sal Molina said bitterly. "Why do you think he continually says climate change is one of the worst problems facing America and the world, when in fact there is no scientific proof whatsoever that man's activities on this planet have any statistically significant effect on the climate? Because the world of cheap oil and natural gas, with frackers here and in shale formations worldwide providing more production any time it makes economic sense to do so, is a direct threat to the Democratic Party power base. Good-paying new jobs at home mean the unions lose power, which means less money for Democratic candidates. The oil and gas industry's demand for skilled workers will require the companies involved to demand the school systems be reformed to teach the skills required, or they will teach the workers themselves. That threatens the teachers' unions, who are one of the main fund-raisers for Democrats and a huge source of votes, and they indoctrinate the young. So Soetoro has been trying to slow the oil and gas tidal wave with cries of climate change, which polls say eighty percent of the public think is a hoax, and by refusing to approve pipelines or allowing the bureaucracies to issue permits, and causing the bureaucracies to issue reams of regulations that drive up the cost of production. Still, as the cost of drilling and fracking goes down, more oil and natural gas can be produced at cheaper and cheaper prices.

"In our lifetimes—indeed, in the remainder of the century—oil and natural gas, like coal, will never be scarce; these commodities will become progressively cheaper, like computing power. And as they become cheaper, the economic and technical hurdles for renewable energy, such as solar and wind, become higher and higher with every passing day. In this brave new world we live in, once you get behind the technological curve, you can never catch up. Never, because the state of the art is progressing at an exponential pace! That's a corollary of Moore's Law."

"All this will drive the leftists bonkers," Grafton said.

"Indeed," Molina agreed. "And they fund the Democratic Party."

Yocke jumped in again. "So you are saying that Soetoro understands all this and has bet everything on his ability to turn the country into a socialist dictatorship?"

Molina frowned. "I don't know that he understands what is happening. He is not a brilliant man. Average intelligence, perhaps. But he understands the political pressures he is getting from unions, from big-city Democrats, from environmentalists, and he can read polls. He hears from OPEC nations worried that their domination of the world oil industry is coming to an end, and with it their prosperity, of which, by the way, only a little trickled down. Islamic fundamentalism is on the rise, and as prosperity in the Arab world drops, it will become more virulent. Barry Soetoro understands *that*!

"The future of socialism is on display in Venezuela, which will collapse one of these days, done to death by cheap oil. Socialism depends on a huge percentage of the population being unable to survive in a changing world without government help. Entrepreneurship and technical progress promise a world with abundant cheap energy that will raise prosperity for everyone who has the education to participate. Two centuries of cheap energy have made America the most prosperous nation on earth.

"At heart Barry Soetoro is a socialist, and he loves power. Soetoro understands that in this evolving world of cheap energy, the Democratic Party as it exists will become an anachronism. So he is trying to change the game and come out on top. He and his allies are screaming about climate change and proposing regulations and taxes on energy as a way to increase the cost of energy. Regulations and taxes have devastating consequences on the poor because all those costs must be passed on. In effect, the climate changers have declared war on the poor people of the earth, and they blame the carnage on evil capitalists, banks, hedge funds, and the like: those rich bastards are the enemy."

"All this was discussed in your presence at the White House?" Jack Yocke asked.

"In and out of my presence."

"And you fought Soetoro's political vision?"

"Why do you think he threw me in a concentration camp?"

"So why did Texas secede, or declare independence, whatever you want to call it?"

"Texas is going to do well in the cheap-energy future," Sal Molina said. "The people there understand that. The legislature didn't vote for poverty. They voted for a new, better, more prosperous future for everyone in Texas that felt threatened by Barry Soetoro's vision of a socialist utopia, with himself at the helm. Socialism drives taxes up—to fund social justice, the socialists say—and that makes everyone poor. That is socialism's fatal flaw. It has others, but that one always destroys socialism eventually."

"You are implying everyone is an economist," Yocke scoffed. "They aren't."

Molina made a gesture of impatience. "Politics is about macro forces. Texas and the plains states are responding to macro forces that people feel. All thinking people do that, even the uninformed. When you fill up your car, you don't need a PhD in economics to understand that something profound is happening to the price of gasoline, and that something has huge, sublime implications.

"And you don't have to be a computer scientist to see and understand how computer technology has changed the lives of everyone on earth, except perhaps some pygmies in darkest Africa or headhunters in the Amazon. Cell phones are bringing the internet to places without electricity or running water. People in central Asia are selling goods worldwide on eBay. Computers are revolutionizing life on earth, and that revolution has just begun. Changes are going to happen faster and faster—that's Moore's Law—and change threatens politicians who are invested in the status quo."

"So Texas' actions after the declaration of martial law was the monkey wrench in Soetoro's plan," Jake Grafton said thoughtfully. "That they didn't expect."

"They didn't," Molina acknowledged. "They also thought the paramilitary police they installed in every federal bureaucracy would be able to control the population. And they thought the military would be loyal; they have been purging independent thinkers from the top ranks for years, people in whom they had political doubts."

"Civil war," Jack Yocke mused.

"Like Crackerjacks," Jake Grafton said. "Remember those, with a surprise in every box?"

TWENTY-THREE

★

After dinner Travis Clay and Willis Coffee went down to the guard cabin and in a little bit Willie Varner and Armanti Hall walked into the house. They were full of radio news, which they passed to Grafton, Yocke, and Molina.

We settled in for another night. Before we did, I took off Grafton's tape and bandages and rewrapped them. His bruises were turning yellow and green. That was good, I thought. There were no hematomas that I could see, and no bulges from busted ribs pushing against his skin. He really needed to be in a hospital, but he would never agree to that, even if there were a hospital we could get him into, which there wasn't.

"Thanks for getting me out of that camp," he said. "If it weren't for you, I'd be dead by now."

"Forget it," I replied. "But I must say, you have a real talent for getting yourself in messes."

He just grunted. I figured he must be doing some serious thinking about where we were going to go and how we were going to survive the next few days, or weeks, or years, when Yocke and Molina weren't bending his ear.

"We only have so much gasoline for the generators," I told him, "and we need to save what we have for the one in the guard shack so we can monitor the security cameras. I'm going to turn off the one here in the house. There are candles and some kerosene, and we'll cook on the outdoor fireplace. Pour water from the creek into the commodes."

"Oh boy," Jake Grafton said.

"If it's yellow, let it mellow; if it's brown, flush it down." Tomorrow, I decided, I'd dream up something to keep Yocke and Molina busy. I told him that.

"Good," he said. "Neither of them can handle being alone with their thoughts for very long. They've had no practice."

"I'll probably shoot a deer and let them butcher it. Fresh meat would be a treat."

Then, out of nowhere, Grafton said, "Molina is a cynical bastard. He's an economist, so maybe it's his training. He thinks all political behavior, or most of it, can be predicted based upon where the money is going. He's right to some extent, but life is a lot more complicated than that. He's sat over at the White House for years preaching that welfare, Social Security, disability, food stamps, and cell phones would win the hearts and minds of the low-skilled and unemployed. He knows that poor people are easily bought. It's everyone else he doesn't understand."

"How so?" I ventured.

"People are motivated by a myriad of things. Religion, tradition, a sense of service, loyalty, curiosity, challenge, accomplishment, praise, patriotism, sometimes a kick in the ass, a sense of rightness... and greed, the most basic of human emotions. Greed has built civilization; greed is the reason entrepreneurs start businesses, inventors invent, businessmen try to earn profits. Greed is the reason we aren't still living in caves. *Most* people want to earn more money so they can have a better life. Yet we could make a long list of human motivations and still not get every one on it.

"The people at the White House, including Barry Soetoro, don't understand America. None of them has ever been in the military, so they don't understand the men and women in uniform. They aren't religious, so they don't understand the deep antipathy so many feel toward abortion or gay marriage. They never worked manual labor jobs, so they don't understand those who do. They think marriage and traditional morality are old fashioned, so yesterday, so they don't understand those who believe in them. Most of them have never worked in private industry, so they think business is crooked and contemptible. Their political base is in the inner cities, yet they advocate policies that will keep people poor and fight policies that would give the poor a leg up. They are perfect hypocrites, con artists, traitors to the people who believe in them. They willingly tell lies to advance their political agenda, and are amazed when that outrages people.

"They think they can ram things down people's throats, and maybe they can, to some extent. Remember Willie Varner's comment the other night: 'Tastes like shit, but good'? No matter why you put up with something that tastes like shit, you can't get the taste out of your mouth. Shit is shit."

He paused, so I said, "Soetoro picked staffers who thought like he did."

"Indeed. Yes-men. And of course women. That may be good for one's ego, but it's a lousy way to ensure you get good advice. Only a man who never ran anything would surround himself with staff that has only one point of view. Barry Soetoro is a lousy manager and a lousy politician; we're all paying for that. And he has another fatal flaw: he doesn't want to hear anything that conflicts with his opinions, or prejudices. He refuses to listen to intelligence that might make him revise an opinion or consider other options."

"There's a lot of that going around these days, especially in the universities."

Jake Grafton nodded. "People with closed minds are always the ones who get the worst surprises," he said.

"One thing is for sure," I said. "Soetoro's managed to change the political landscape in the United States, and I doubt if he likes the changes."

I wanted to ask the admiral what he had learned from eavesdropping on the White House for the last six months, but decided not to. Sarah shouldn't have told me about it, and if I mentioned it to Grafton he would know I got it from Sarah. So I kept my mouth shut. The thought occurred to me that he had just told me his conclusions.

But I wondered. If I had listened to the conniving and plotting at the White House for six whole months, what would I have done? Whom would I have told? Who would believe me when I accused the president of the United States of plotting to subvert the Constitution, the Constitution that he was sworn to uphold, and declare himself a dictator? Who would have believed me if I accused him of waiting for a terrorist incident so he could declare martial law?

The answer of course was no one. Not a solitary soul on planet Earth. That was undoubtedly the conclusion that Jake Grafton reached.

I finished my doctoring and told the admiral he was good to go.

The attack submarine *Texas*, now the flagship of the Republic of Texas' Navy, ran just below periscope depth in the Gulf of Mexico. Loren Snyder called an all-hands conference in the control room. He would rather have convened his little congregation of seven in the wardroom, but he wanted to keep a person on the helm at all times. The water was only three hundred feet deep here, so if the sub rammed into the bottom, she might never come up again. Fortunately the floor of the gulf fell away as one proceeded away from the coast, becoming well over a mile deep in places.

Snyder checked the depth, 240 feet; the heading, 130 degrees; the boat's speed on the inertial readout, eight knots.

He surveyed the faces of his crew. Submarine duty attracted smart, technically savvy people who were interesting to be around, which was why smart, technically savvy people enjoyed it. The challenge was constant and boredom rare.

Ada Fuentes was on the helm, Jugs Aranado was sipping coffee, George Ranta, Speedy Gonzales, Mouse Moore, and Junior Smith were drinking water or eating toast from a loaf Mouse made in the galley last night.

"Okay, folks," Loren said. "We made it to sea. That was the first hurdle, and we got over it, and I thank you. I thought our chances of getting out of Galveston about fifty-fifty. In any event, we are out.

"A few words on how this Texas Navy sub is going to be run. I am the captain, and I will make all decisions and expect my orders to be obeyed. That said, I want and need advice from each and every one of you on how to run the boat and use it as a military weapon. I hope you will give me honest opinions, and I will use them to make the best decision I can. But once I have decided, that is the way it is going to be. No more debate."

He got nods from everyone standing around the plotting table in the center of the room.

"Our first problem for discussion is this: What are we going to do with this boat? Are we going to find someplace to hide and wait out the war, making the U.S. Navy worry about where we are and what we might be doing every minute of every day? Or are we going to use her as an attack boat? If we are, what are our targets? Where and how can we do the new Republic of Texas the most good? Your thoughts, please."

"If we don't do anything, the navy will stop worrying before long," Speedy Gonzales said. "They'll assume we managed to submerge forever."

"Someone put two or three Tomahawks into power plants around Houston the other night," Jugs said. "I assume they were launched from a surface ship. At least, I hope they were. If there is another attack boat out here we have major problems. They are fully manned and we aren't." She shrugged. "Anyway, I suggest we put a fish into that surface combatant, then get out of this pond and into the Atlantic, preferably the Gulf Stream, where we can go deep."

"Ranta, you've been on the sonar. Any idea where that destroyer or frigate might be?"

"No, sir."

"I've been looking at the chart," Jugs said. "If I were the skipper of that ship, I'd be in the middle of the deep water rigs off Louisiana and Texas. If I were him or her, I'd be worrying about this submarine."

"Tough operating around those rigs," Ranta said. "Sonar will be crap."

"Our main problem is another attack boat out here. It'll be just as tough for them as it will be for us." Snyder's audience liked the idea that someone might be worried about what they would do.

Snyder studied the chart. Deep down, he thought the best and safest course of action was to get out of the Gulf of Mexico and look for a warship in the Atlantic. The drawback was that choice would cede the gulf to the United States Navy.

"Can we operate among those platforms without ramming a platform leg?" he mused aloud.

Junior Smith said, "We have to threaten Soetoro's navy some way, and keeping them away from the shipping channels to Houston seems worthwhile to me. Let's make 'em sweat."

"What about torpedoing a Louisiana production platform?" Mouse Moore asked. "Or a tanker loaded with Arabian oil? Soetoro's navy has to protect those tankers and platforms or the people of Louisiana are going to get huffy. Not to mention what will happen to insurance rates if one of those crude haulers gets torpedoed."

"Let me think about this," Loren Snyder said. "We certainly can't go under a rig, but we can thread our way around them using the photonics mast. We'll have to get GPS fixes as often as possible, but let's not update the inertial until we are absolutely sure the feds haven't tinkered with the GPS satellites." He used a parallel ruler to plot a new course and gave the course to Ada Fuentes at the helm. She brought the boat around to the heading.

"And slow the boat. Five knots, I think. Ranta, we need you on the sonar for as long as you can stand it. Then I'll relieve you. I was the sonar officer on my first boat, and I think I remember most of it."

"Aye-aye, sir," they said.

"Thank you for your input," Snyder told his crew, who went off to the reactor and engineering spaces and, if they were off duty, to try to nap in a bunk. Sleep was precious.

Now on a more easterly course, *Texas* ghosted along through the heart of the sea.

Loren Snyder busied himself in the control room, checking the computers and torpedo data computer, the TDC. He and Jugs were going to have to run all this stuff. As he worked he thought about his first submarine skipper, who drilled his crew mercilessly and ended up convincing himself and everyone aboard that the crew was the best in the fleet. Incidentally, they passed their Operational Readiness Inspection (ORI) with flying colors and won the Battle Efficiency E.

Snyder picked up the intercom mike and keyed it: "This is a drill, this is a drill. Runaway torpedo in Tube Two. This is a drill."

He hung the mike in its bracket and heard a loud "Oh, shit!" and then the sound of running feet.

That first night in September, F-16 Falcons from Lackland landed at Barksdale Air Force Base in Louisiana. An hour after midnight, the F-16s were gone again, fanning out to defend the B-52 Stratofortresses, which were beginning their start rituals. They were loaded with JDAMs, two-thousand-pound dumb bombs with a GPS seeker and steering that would guide them to their targets.

JR Hays knew the GPS system was controlled by the United States government, which had the capacity to induce errors into the system, or shut it down altogether, but such an action would affect air navigation all over the earth, no doubt causing a few airliners to crash, and he doubted that the Soetoro administration was ready for the inevitable international political backlash that would cause. Not yet, anyway.

The B-52s came to life—three of them, because another crew volunteered—and slowly taxied to the takeoff end of the duty runway. The wind was still out of the northwest, so the runway was 33.

Elvin Gentry was in the lead bomber. He had flown in at dusk and had a hurried conference with JR and Nate Danaher, then went to the crew briefing.

No doubt Soetoro loyalists all over the area would have liked to alert Washington when the fighters arrived and took off, and burn up the lines when the B-52s serenaded the city on their climb-outs, but the local power company had obeyed Soetoro's orders and the electricity was off in the greater Shreveport area.

B-52s were old airplanes. The first one flew in 1952. Between 1952 and 1962, when the production line was closed, the air force bought 744 of them at a cost of a couple of million dollars each. Informally and affectionately known by their crews as BUFFs, which stood for Big Ugly Fat Fuckers, they carried up to seventy thousand pounds of bombs at high subsonic speeds and were relatively cheap to operate. The design intended to replace them, the B-70 Valkyrie, was too expensive. The variable-geometry B-1 Lancer and the stealth B-2 Spirit, both of which actually made it into service, were also too expensive to acquire in large numbers, and had high operating costs. Despite the air force's institutional predilection for faster, sexier, and newer, economics reared its ugly head; the air force continually upgraded the B-52s and planned to keep them in service until 2045, over ninety years after the first one had flown. The only version still flying was the B-52H. The air force had invested an estimated $100 million into each one, so far, mere peanuts compared with the cost of newer warplanes. Twenty B-2 stealth bombers had cost Uncle Sam $2 billion *each*.

The B-52 crews planned on delivering two JDAMs on a support for each targeted bridge. The hope was the two bombs would drop one span in the water, or at least do enough damage that the bridges would no longer support sixty-three-ton M1A2 Abrams tanks.

And if tomorrow some bridges were still standing, Gentry planned on launching F-16s carrying two one-thousand-pound JDAMs each. He was willing to trade planes for the bridges.

Gentry would have loved to have an airborne early-warning airplane in the sky tonight, but he didn't have one. His F-16s would have to make do by listening to the freqs GCI sites used to control the U.S. fighters. Gentry worried about F-22s, stealth fighters, which could detect and shoot down fighters and bombers of ranges as far as a hundred nautical miles. What he didn't know was that the F-22 wing had sent all the pilots who were willing to fight for Barry Soetoro, all four, to Barksdale. So there were not going to be F-22s in the air tonight. Had he known, he would have been much less apprehensive than he was, and he might even have stayed on the ground tonight. As it was, he thought the risks were so high that he was unwilling to send his aircrews into combat unless he shared the risks with them.

JR Hays, no man to evade risks himself, reluctantly agreed. He didn't want to lose Elvin Gentry, but he had to trust Gentry's judgment and leadership abilities or get someone else. Barry Soetoro would have never understood.

Gentry had never before ridden in a Stratofortress, so the pilot's exercise of the Crosswind Crab Control while they taxied felt spooky. The wheels continued to track the centerline of the taxiway, but the airplane turned to point up twenty degrees to the left, then swung back to point twenty degrees to right.

On the runway, the wind from the right demanded a crab in that direction, so the centerline of the runway was visible out the left side of the pilot's windshield. The BUFF accelerated with all eight engines pulling, they reached decision speed right on time for the load they were carrying, and began rotating five to ten knots before liftoff speed. It wasn't much of a rotation, a bit over five degrees. Then the giant green bomber parted company with the earth.

On climb out the pilot turned to the general, just to see how he was doing. His face was lit by the glow of the red instrument lights. Gentry was struck by his youth. Captain Rogers, flying a bomber from the 1950s, was all of twenty-seven years old. Gentry felt like a fossil.

JDAMs were units that screwed into freefall bombs. They were comprised of a GPS receiver, a small computer, and canards that steered the bomb to its target, which was a preprogrammed bulls-eye defined by GPS coordinates. Accuracy was only as good as the GPS coordinates programmed in, so satellite maps of the earth had to be consulted.

The delivery crew, in this case in a B-52, had to use the onboard weapons system to drop the bomb into an invisible cone with its tip resting on the target and the large open end up in the sky. If the bomb were placed within the cone, it could steer itself to a bulls-eye. If it were released outside the cone, the canards would not be able to get the bomb back into the cone, so it would miss. This nebulous cone was defined by the capability of the canards that steered the bomb, by the prevailing wind, and by the angular velocity imparted to the weapon by the airplane that released it.

Guided weapons were the future of aerial warfare, Elvin Gentry believed. The days of dropping huge numbers of dumb bombs in the hope that one or two would hit the target you wanted destroyed were history.

GPS-guided bombs were a technological leap into the future from laser-guided bombs, which steered themselves to a dot of laser light projecting upon the target, projected by the bombing aircraft or a spotter aircraft, occasionally a person on the ground. Unlike laser-guided systems that were useless in bad weather, GPS-guided bombs hit their bulls-eyes all the time, whether they were falling through clear air, clouds, rain, snow, blowing dust, or smoke—as long as you had the correct coordinates for your target: type in a wrong digit somewhere and you missed.

The cockpit of the B-52 was cramped, almost like a two-seat tactical jet. Gentry sat in the jump seat aft of the pilots, and he didn't have an ejection seat. After everyone else ejected, he was supposed to go to the lower level, or deck, and jump through the hole in the fuselage left by the recently departed navigator or bombardier. It sounded iffy, but if worse came to worst....

The F-16s were out there somewhere ahead on a fighter sweep, looking for bad guys, protecting the bombers from beyond the range of fighter missiles. That was the theory, which was only as good as the fighter pilots. Elvin Gentry consoled himself with the thought that we all have to die sometime. At least, he reflected, he wasn't in a B-17 on the way to Berlin, harassed every mile by flak and German fighter pilots who knew their business. Those B-17 guys had balls, he thought. This little jaunt tonight was a piece of cake.

He keyed the intercom and told the crew, "A piece of cake."

"Yeah," the copilot said. "Sir."

In minutes, as they were still climbing for altitude, the B-52s split up, each headed for its initial fix, to begin a series of bomb runs on bridges. The bombardiers had been plotting their courses and run-ins to their targets, and were now checking their ordnance panels.

Gentry heard the cryptic transmissions on the intercom of his BUFF, heard the pilot and copilot running through checklists, and heard the countdown begin to the first bomb release, on the highway bridge on I-20 at Vicksburg. And on the adjacent railroad bridge. The tops of the cones overlapped, so the BUFF would drop four one-ton weapons on this run. He saw the light on the instrument panel as the bomb bay doors came open, he heard the countdown, then the bombs released and he felt the airplane give a jump upward as it became four tons lighter in a fraction of a second. Felt the plane bank into a turn. The next targets were the bridges at Natchez.

So far, so good, Gentry thought. Then he realized he had been holding his breath. He exhaled and forced himself to breathe deeply.

Walter Ohnigian was a career F-16 pilot. Flying fighters was all he had ever wanted to do since he watched the Thunderbirds perform at an air show when he was twelve. He had attended the Air Force Academy, worked like a slave to get into flight school, and once in gave it everything he had to get fighters. He had fought in Iraq and Afghanistan, had graduated from two courses at USAF Weapons School, and had served a tour as an instructor on F-16s. Along the way he found time to serve a tour in a Navy F/A-18 squadron, which meant a nine-month cruise aboard an aircraft carrier. He had planned to stay in the air force until they forced him to retire.

The Texas Declaration of Independence changed his mind. Now he was a Texas fighter pilot. His decision had been easy; born and raised in Brady, Texas, he loathed Barry Soetoro and all he stood for.

Susie Ohnigian, from Colorado Springs, was a tougher sell. She had met Walt when he was a cadet and knew the blood, sweat, and tears he had put in to succeed at his chosen profession. Basically nonpolitical, Susie loved her husband. She knew military aviation has its risks, even in peacetime, and she consoled herself with the indisputable truth that God was in charge of our lives, and He would take Walt when it suited His purpose. He hadn't yet, and she prayed that He wouldn't until they were both old and full of years. She took her marriage vows before the altar of God, and thought it her duty to stand by her husband for as long as they both lived, so with some misgivings, she concurred with his choice.

Tonight he was over southeastern Mississippi, listening to the published approach and departure frequencies for Eglin Air Force Base in the Florida panhandle. Ohnigian thought that by the time the air force figured out that bombers were attacking the Mississippi bridges, it would be too late to launch and catch the bombers, which would be several hundred miles west. On the other hand, if Eglin had fighters on a combat air patrol, they could intercept the BUFFs. Or intercept the Texas F-16s.

So he listened on all the frequencies they might use, and he used the radar in his fighter to sweep the skies for airplanes. Targets. Bad guys. Fighters that might attack the friends in the BUFFs. Fortunately civilian traffic was prohibited by the Soetoro regime. Any targets Ohnigian and Free saw tonight on their radars were enemy airplanes. Or outlaw airplanes whose pilots had decided to roll the dice and take their chances.

The F-16s flown by Walter Ohnigian and his wingman Drew Free had two AMRAAMS (advanced medium-range air-to-air missiles) and two Sidewinders each, an internal M-61A Vulcan 20-mm cannon, and a two-thousand-pound external fuel tank. No doubt if there were Eglin F-16 fighters aloft, they were similarly armed.

The AIM-120C AMRAAM was seven inches in diameter and twelve feet long, flew at Mach four, had an active radar homing seeker, carried a forty-pound high-explosive warhead, and had a maximum range of fifty-seven miles. The AIM-9 Sidewinder was a short-range (up to twenty-two miles) missile with infrared homing; in other words, a heat seeker. It was five inches in diameter and nine feet long and carried a twenty-pound warhead. The latest versions could turn over ninety degrees to chase their targets at speeds up to 2.7 Mach, and could even lock on a target up to ninety degrees off the airplane's boresight. Sidewinder was the perfect dogfight weapon: when it locked on your quarry's tailpipe signature, the hunter squeezed it off and the Sidewinder did the rest. Sidewinder even had a limited head-on capability.

Tonight Walter Ohnigian hoped and prayed that there were no F-22 Raptors aloft. If there were, he would never see them on radar. His first indications of an F-22 would be a Raptor radar locked on him, so he kept his radar warning indicator in his instrument scan. Nothing so far.

He checked that he was on Eglin Air Force Base tower frequency. Yes, two fighters were taxiing. A flight of two. The lead had a laconic, gravelly voice.

He headed that way and eased his fighter into a climb. He wanted to be as high as possible so he would have an energy advantage. His wingman to his right and aft stepped up several hundred feet.

Now the Eglin fighters were airborne and switching to Departure Control. He pushed the button on the radio for the new frequency.

And he heard that voice again. Jesus, it sounded like Johnny O'Day! Of all people, Johnny O'Day, his roommate at the Air Force Academy, way back when.

Another transmission to Departure. Hell yes, it *was* Johnny O'Day, and he flew F-16s. Headed for the B-52s over the Mississippi.

The bombs from Gentry's BUFF smashed into the bridges at Vicksburg. They were falling supersonic, so no one on the ground had a clue except for the faint, distant rumble of jet engines way up there in the night. The explosions on each bridge were so close together they sounded like one big bang, which rolled through Vicksburg and woke up several thousand folks.

Slowly, ponderously, the weight of the now unsupported bridge spans carried them down into the dark water of the big river. There were only two trucks on the highway bridge, since traffic on the interstates these days was down to a trickle. One driver on the highway bridge managed to stop his truck; the other rode the span into the river and drowned in his cab.

The railroad bridge actually had a train on it, rumbling along at eight miles per hour. The bombs went through a railcar, penetrated the track and ballast, and detonated against the targeted abutment. The spans on either side of the abutment began sagging, dragging the train along, down, down into the river.

The scene would be repeated tonight up and down the river. America was being cut in half with surgical precision.

Victory in a modern dogfight usually goes to the pilot in the most technologically advanced fighter, who will usually detect his enemy first and shoot first. Once missiles are launched, the rest is up to the missiles, those marvels of modern weaponry, which, if fired within their operating envelope, are quite deadly.

Tonight Walter Ohnigian fired two AMRAAMs at the Eglin fighters at a distance of fifty miles, head on. They raced off downhill at their targets and had soon accelerated to four times the speed of sound, the active radar in the nose of the missiles probing the night for their targets.

"Fox Three," Walter Ohnigian said over the radio, a transmission he knew Johnny O'Day would hear. He held the transmit button on the stick down and continued, "Johnny, this is Oboe. You better eject." Johnny was married to an operating room nurse and they had two kids. Ohnigian owed him the warning.

In his fighter, climbing through ten thousand feet, Johnny O'Day's eyes automatically scanned the sky for the pinpoint exhausts of the rocket engines in missiles. Oboe—Ohnigian! After wasting several seconds, he looked at his radar screen.

And saw the tiny dots streaking toward his aircraft and that of his wingman.

He pumped off chaff and tried to turn a square corner. He was pulling eight Gs when the first missile went off just below the belly of his fighter and showered it with shrapnel that penetrated into the delicate internal organs of his steed. One second later the fighter exploded.

The second AMRAAM exploded as it went through the expanding cloud of pieces.

O'Day's wingman had also turned violently to avoid the oncoming missiles, so after he was sure they had missed him, he had to turn back into the threat to acquire a firing solution on the bogeys on his radar screen. He was turning hard when the first AMRAAM from Ohnigian's wingman actually struck his machine and exploded. Like Johnny O'Day, he died in the fireball.

TWENTY-FOUR

★

Texas Ranger Parker Konczyk went to see Colonel Tenney of the TxDPS. "We think there's a sniper casing the roofs of buildings around the capitol," he said. "He's dressed in a jumpsuit that bears the logo of an air conditioning company. We spotted him with a drone."

"What air conditioning company?"

Konczyk told him. "We talked to the owner. He had the van for sale and an Anglo came along, paid him ten grand for it. He wanted fifteen, but the most the guy would pay was ten, cash, and the owner was way behind on his child support, so he took it. He signed the title and never even got the guy's name."

Konczyk used an iPad to show Colonel Tenney video from the drone. The man in a jumpsuit on the roof of a bank three hundred yards from the capitol didn't even bother looking at the rooftop-mounted HVAC units, but inspected the roof and lased the capitol and some other buildings, including the hotel with the underground parking garage that was being used by the Texas government as a bomb-proof bunker. "That location hasn't been published, but half the people in Austin know the government is down there."

"A rangefinder?"

"It looks like a laser rangefinder, a small unit that he holds in both hands up to his eye."

The picture on the iPad went to another building and apparently the same man scouted out that roof. Finally, pictures from the drone of the van parked by the curb.

"So what is your recommendation?"

"Right now all we have this guy for is not registering the van in his own name, and a few trespass charges. If we arrest him he'll be out on bail in an hour. And he might not be a sniper; he might be a scout."

"Go on."

"Or we can wait until someone appears on the roof with a rifle."

They discussed it, and decided that the best course was to keep the van under constant surveillance, and the best way to do that and not spook the suspect was to use drones. Konczyk only had access to one.

"Get a couple more from the National Guard," Colonel Tenney said. "Let's just watch this guy for a while, find out where he is staying and who he sees, and try to figure out how big this conspiracy really is, if there is one."

Chairman of the JCS General Martin L. Wynette was working late at his office in the Pentagon. The problem he faced was the disintegration of the United States armed forces, all of them, Army, Navy, Air Force, and Marines. The reports from commanders all over the nation were appalling: huge numbers of troops were not available for duty. In some major commands the AWOL rate approached forty percent. Another thirty or forty percent refused to bear arms against Americans, or as they phrased it, to fight for that son of a bitch Soetoro. Sailors on navy ships were refusing to go to sea. Commandos and paratroopers were refusing to go to Texas, Oklahoma, or Alabama, which had just declared its independence. Pilots were refusing to fly, which made it impossible to get fighters aloft to protect military targets or to attack targets in Texas. The most powerful military force on the planet was shattering like old crystal right before his eyes.

Maybe Soetoro was right, Wynette mused. Maybe it was time to start standing some people against the wall and shooting them to inspire the rest.

Wynette and several senior members of the JCS staff were trying to figure out just how many willing fighters Barry Soetoro actually had and how to get the willing to where they could fight when the news came in that the interstate and railroad bridges over the Mississippi at Vicksburg had been bombed and were impassable. Even as he tried to digest this information, he learned that bridges were being bombed from Baton Rouge to well above Memphis. Four bridges in Memphis had gone into the river. It was thought that the bombers were B-52s from Barksdale, but of course that was merely speculation.

On top of all of this were the plights of cities such as Washington, Baltimore, Philadelphia, metropolitan New York, and Boston. And Pittsburgh, Cleveland, Chicago, Milwaukee, Detroit, St. Louis, and Los Angeles. For seventy-five years architects had created urban buildings that were sealed units and uninhabitable without electrical power. Millions of city dwellers were abandoning the cities for the supposedly better life in the countryside, where some planned to throw themselves on the mercy of the rustics while others planned to rob, steal, and kill their way to a better life.

Wynette wondered what the heck was going to come of all this. According to radio reports, they were partying in Montgomery tonight. The governor had made a speech, a "rant" according to the reporter on the radio, in which he told Barry Soetoro to go to hell and do something anatomically impossible to himself when he got there. The lights were back on in most of Alabama, and the governor vowed they were going to stay on even if the Alabama National Guard had to defend the plants against Soetoro's troops and thugs. He also vowed that a copy of the Ten Commandments were going up in every courtroom and classroom in Alabama; if the justices of the United States Supreme Court didn't like it, he said, they could come to Alabama and take them down, if they could.

It was obvious to Martin Wynette that Soetoro's propaganda campaign to blame the electrical outages on Texans and right-wing fanatics hadn't moved the needle. Barry Soetoro and his minions were taking the blame.

Wynette was trying to put this mess into perspective when the assistant chairman, a four-star admiral, knocked on the sill of the open door and, when Wynette glanced up, strolled into his office and closed the door behind him. He was the only officer in the navy that outranked the chief of naval operations, Admiral Cart McKiernan.

His name was Hiram Gregory Ray. He was a feisty little cuss, a fighter pilot, and somewhere along the line he had acquired the nickname of Sugar. He was anything but sweet, but the people who worked for him regarded him in awe. Brilliant, technically savvy, aggressive, and competent, he could fire up a room full of sailors and he could kiss a congressman's ass so subtly and perfectly that the bastard would fart red, white, and blue for months.

Sugar Ray knew Wynette's peccadillos and usually tried not to fret the boss unnecessarily. After a day spent watching the United States and the armed forces come apart at the seams, he was in no mood tonight to stroke the chairman.

"I think we can wave good-bye to America," he said, "unless that damned fool in the White House turns the juice back on. New York, Chicago, and LA are in meltdown. Soldiers, sailors, and Marines deserting in droves, refusing to enforce Jade Helm mandates, refusing to fight, refusing to back up the police.... Why in the name of God did that idiot turn off the power?"

"He blamed it on the Texans," Wynette said sourly. "He's a disciple of Joseph Goebbels. The truth will never catch up to a lie. 'If you like your doctor, you can keep him. If you like your health insurance, you can keep it.' He's that kind of guy."

Sugar Ray tossed a message on the desk. "Here's a tidbit that will make your evening. Soldiers at Fort Benning are deserting and taking their weapons with them. They are driving out of the base in trucks. The CG there says all order and discipline are lost. If he tries to arrest people, he is afraid that the MPs will refuse to obey, and if they do obey, he's afraid the people he wants to arrest will shoot back. He asked the chief of staff for guidance."

Wynette picked up the message and read it. "A complete breakdown of order and discipline," he muttered.

"I think it's high time we arrest Soetoro and take over the government."

Martin L. Wynette stared at Sugar Ray for several seconds, took a deep breath, and said, "I'll pretend you didn't say that."

"Oh, shove it, Marty! Soetoro is attempting to become a dictator, and he has got to be stopped. We should arrest him or shoot him. Personally, I'd like to shoot him, and I volunteer to pull the trigger, but I'll settle for arrest and solitary confinement."

Wynette shook the message at Ray. "And just who the hell do you think we're going to lead over to Pennsylvania Avenue to do all this arresting? Or will it be just you and me with a couple of pistols and any beggars with signs that we can pick up on street corners along the way?"

Sugar Ray cocked his head as he looked at his boss. "Have you sent any of these numbers—" he gestured at the messages on Wynette's desk "—over to the White House?"

"Not yet. Tomorrow morning is soon enough."

"What do you think the reaction will be?"

"By God, I don't—"

Sugar Ray interrupted and finished the sentence for him. "You don't know. Civil society in this country is coming apart in the large cities. Old people and babies are dying like flies in un-air-conditioned apartments and tenements; people are fighting for food, looting grocery stores, banks, liquor, and jewelry stores; breaking into ATMs; shooting at police at every opportunity...and the military is collapsing. Man, we went back to the stone age in less than ten days! I hope you appreciate the delicious irony of the fact that Soetoro fucked the very people who voted for him."

Wynette grunted. He thought political loyalty was an oxymoron.

Sugar Ray wasn't done. He said to the general, "Tomorrow morning Soetoro will probably want some heads, and yours is first on the block."

Wynette didn't reply to that comment.

"But that's in the short term," the admiral said, dismissed that little problem with a flip of his hand. "Eventually Soetoro is going down hard, and anyone who saluted and said, 'Yes, sir,' may go on the gallows with him. Hitler's and Mussolini's generals didn't fare so well."

Admiral Ray stood and leaned toward Wynette, braced himself with his fingertips on the general's desk, and said, "My assessment is that this situation is completely out of Soetoro's control. If we lock up Soetoro and everyone else in the White House we can lay hands on, maybe we can stop a humanitarian disaster and save millions of lives. Maybe we can even save our miserable country and some of those morons who voted for Soetoro... *twice*."

Wynette looked at Sugar Ray for a long moment, then asked softly, "Who have you talked to about this?"

Ray straightened up and took a deep breath. "All the other chiefs. I was hoping it would be unanimous, but it isn't. The commandant and army chief are with me, but CNO and the air force want to think about things."

"Well," Wynette said dryly, "treason *is* a big step."

"Yeah—and Barry Soetoro is striding out. How long are we going to wait, Marty, before we call him on it? In a better day to come, Americans are going to ask that question of us."

Wynette sat stolidly, eyes focused on infinity.

Sugar Ray shrugged, then headed for the door. "I'm going home and getting some sleep," he tossed over his shoulder, and pulled the door shut behind him.

Walter Ohnigian actually flew two flights that night, and landed as dawn streaked the eastern sky. The B-52s were safely back on the ground at Barksdale and the Mississippi bridges all had at least one span in the river, from Baton Rouge to Memphis.

Ohnigian was numb. He let his wingman do the debrief while he stretched out on a couch in the ops building.

So Johnny O'Day was dead and he had killed him. Holy mother...

What was he going to say to Johnny's wife, Ruby? Two little kids...

How was he going to tell Susie, his wife, about this? She and Ruby had double-dated the roommates. The marriages were just a year apart.

Staring at the ceiling, he decided that Ruby and Susie might forgive him, someday. The real problem was how he was going to forgive himself.

At Fort Carson in Colorado Springs, Major General Douglas Seuss was trying to figure out how to comply with Pentagon demands that he send an armored column from the 4th Infantry Division to fight the rebels in Texas. Most of his soldiers were refusing to fight fellow Americans, and Washington was demanding court-martials. That didn't strike Doug Seuss as a productive idea. He needed soldiers who would fight, not people looking for an opportunity to desert to avoid a combat they thought morally wrong.

Seuss had been trading messages with the Pentagon. West Texas was the finest terrain on this side of the Atlantic for tank operations, but he was unwilling to commit his tanks without air protection. There was no place on the naked plains for tanks to hide if they were attacked from the air. Seuss told the generals in the Pentagon that he was unwilling to sacrifice his troops needlessly to make political points. "You must guarantee me air cover for my tanks or they will not be committed," he said flatly. His worry was that he would get the promise of air cover, commit the tanks, and friendly fighters would never appear while Texas fighters would. That, he thought, was the way the wind was blowing.

Sifting through the readiness reports and the results of interviews with his soldiers, he found a company of the 10th Special Forces Group had sixty percent of their troops willing to fight. He called the colonel in command of the group, Colonel Kevin Crislip, into his office. After a heart-to-heart talk, he decided to send the colonel and his volunteers to Texas to blow up some highway and railroad bridges.

"We've got to do something," Seuss said. They looked at maps and decided to blow some bridges on U.S. Route 287 north of Amarillo and several bridges on the nearby railroad. Route 287 was a major truck route between the Pacific Northwest via Denver and Dallas and east Texas. The railroad carried a lot of freight. Bridges were good targets for tactical air, yet the Pentagon was demanding action from the Carson troops, so the ball was in Seuss' court.

Crislip wanted to use CH-47 Chinooks to insert and extract his men, and Seuss agreed. In at dusk, out at dawn was a tactic that would minimize the chance of air attack while the commandos were on the ground. Both officers thought the chances of the Special Forces troopers running into Texas ground forces were slim or none at all, but just to be sure Predators would be launched tomorrow at dawn and reconnoiter. Tomorrow the Green Berets would ride Chinooks to the Army's Pinon Canyon Maneuver Site on the Purgatoire River, and launch from there for Texas at dusk.

As Colonel Crislip was leaving, Seuss said, "And colonel—I never dreamed I'd have to say this—make sure the men you take are politically reliable." That was the jargon of the latest Pentagon directive. General Seuss found that phrase offensive in the extreme, smacking as it did of the old soviet military and their political commissars, but what could one do?

General Martin L. Wynette was a worried man when he rode to the White House that Friday morning, the second day of September, in his limousine. Arizona had declared its independence, the fourth state to do so, along with Texas, Oklahoma, and Alabama. Other states were meeting this afternoon and tonight and no doubt some of them would pass declarations of independence.

The people of the big cities from coast to coast were about out of endurance. Without electricity, there was no way to escape the summer heat, no running water, no way to flush toilets, no way to preserve food. Soon there would be no food to preserve, since trucks couldn't deliver without fuel, and even if they could, they wouldn't deliver to looted stores. Calls to police, fire departments, and paramedics went unanswered. Houses burned down with no one there to rescue the kids or fight the blaze. People died from heart attacks because they couldn't get to the hospital. People ran out of medications and couldn't get more. Given time, people would learn to cope, those who survived, but in the interim a lot of people were going to die.

In Chicago, the Black Panthers had attacked a police station. It looked as if a race war was about to explode in the city. The mayor was begging the governor for National Guard troops.

Wynette's aide, Major General Stout, wisely kept his mouth firmly shut that morning as the limo carried them through the streets of the nation's capital.

Inside the executive mansion, the soldiers found the president flanked by his chief of staff, Al Grantham, and his senior political advisor, Sulana Schanck.

"The Texans bombed the bridges across the lower Mississippi last night, Mr. President," Wynette said. "The reports we received at the Pentagon said all the highway and rail bridges were down from Baton Rouge to above Memphis. It's going to take at least a month, perhaps six weeks, before we are ready to mount an invasion."

"Why not drop paratroopers?"

Wynette explained that lightly armed paratroopers didn't have the combat power to hold out long without relief. They were shock troops and not equipped to invade and conquer enemy territory.

"And then there is the problem of numbers. We are having extreme difficulty keeping people who will fight. About half the army and air force is AWOL. The navy's numbers are better only because they have ships at sea. There are dozens of ships on the east coast that are unable to get under way because the crews have abandoned the ships."

Sulana Schanck's eyes narrowed and her voice was hard. "It is time you shot some people, General. I think perhaps ten people from every unit, while the rest of them watch."

Al Grantham seemed inspired. "You've got to teach those damned kids that they have no choice. They are in the United States armed forces, and by God, they'll fight or die."

"As I've said before, I don't have the authority to issue such an order," Wynette objected. Indeed he didn't. The Uniform Code of Military Justice didn't provide for summary executions. Islamic militaries might do them, Wynette knew, but those of civilized nations didn't.

"You do now," Grantham said. "The president has declared martial law and he is the commander in chief."

Wynette recognized that he was being made the fall guy. "I'll need a direct order signed by the president," he insisted.

"No, by God, you won't," Grantham roared. "You are going to take the responsibility, General. *You*! *You* will write the order and sign it. *You* will have it transmitted to every major command and ship. *You* will demand that the commanding generals or officers or whoever is in charge find ten people who refuse to fight and have them executed. The names will be reported to *you*. Have I made myself clear?"

"Write it out, Grantham."

"No," Barry Soetoro said in his coldest voice. "You'll do it, General. That's a direct order from me. And summary justice for those who disobey orders applies to the Pentagon too, to the E-Ring."

So there it was. Shoot people or we shoot you.

While Martin Wynette was swallowing that, Sulana Schanck started in. "We hear that there is some talk in the E-Ring about a coup. What have you heard about that, General?"

Wynette's first impulse was to deny he had heard anything, but under the stares of Soetoro, Grantham, and the bitch Schanck, he decided that answer might get him shot. There was no telling what they had heard, who had whispered, if anyone had. Schanck was probably just shooting in the dark. Perhaps. Or perhaps not.

Soetoro smacked the table with his open palm. "Answer, damn it. Don't sit there thinking up a lie."

"The assistant chairman, Admiral Sugar Ray, told me that he, the army chief of staff, and the air force chief of staff did discuss a coup. That is all I know."

"Did you put him under arrest?"

"No."

"Ray discusses treason with you and you do not arrest him? Whose side are you on, General?"

For the first time in many years, Martin Wynette felt the cold hand of fear grip him with paralyzing fierceness. He had a powerful urge to urinate and somehow managed to hold it in. But he lost control of his face, and knew it.

Soetoro took obvious pleasure at Wynette's discomfort. He glanced at Schanck and made a little motion with his head. She got up and left the room.

"Did you order the Tomahawks launched?" Al Grantham demanded.

"Yes. We should have waited for night, but the missiles will be on their way momentarily, as soon as they can be programmed. Two destroyers will shoot fifty each. They will take out the twenty largest power plants in Texas."

Grantham nodded. Once.

Wynette said, "All of the missiles won't get through. In the daytime fighters can find cruise missiles and shoot them down."

"They might get a few," Barry Soetoro said, "and the people of Texas will hear and see them flying over, on their way to cause havoc." He smiled. "The missiles will deliver an unmistakable message that we are in charge and that disobedience has its price."

Martin Wynette was enough of a soldier to know that using military weapons to deliver political messages was a good way to lose a war, but he held his tongue. Hitler had tried delivering messages with V-1 and V-2 rockets and that hadn't worked so well. Lyndon Johnson tried to send explosive messages to the North Vietnamese and failed rather dismally. Truly, Wynette thought, Soetoro was a fool.

Armanti Hall and I were exploring the roads in his pickup truck when we saw a little house fifty yards or so from the road, a strip of twelve-foot-wide asphalt that wound around over the hills following the contours. It was a nice enough little clapboard house, but the reason it attracted my attention was the large garden beside it. The flora it contained was big and tall.

We parked and strolled over. We didn't get very far before we realized that lying near the garden gate was a body.

As we walked up I could see it was a man. He had that totally collapsed look of the dead that are in the process of returning to the earth. From ten feet away, I could see the dark mottled color of his skin and the bloating of his abdominal cavity, so I guessed he had been dead at least a day, and perhaps two.

"Don't go any closer to that gate," a woman's voice said.

We turned to face the house. A small old woman with iron-gray hair was sitting in a rocking chair under a roof on a flagstone patio that was just inches above ground level. Across her knees was a lever-action rifle. Her right hand rested on the stock above the trigger.

"Looks like this gent expired suddenly," I said conversationally.

"It come on him quick," she acknowledged. "I gave him fair warnin' and he decided he needed my tomatoes and beans more than I did. Didn't think I would shoot, I suspect."

"Did you know him?"

"Not by name. Seems like I seen him across the mountain at Walmart from time to time, but only to nod to. He was one of the hollow rats, I'm thinkin', used to sittin' on his porch drinkin' beer, waitin' for the welfare check. That and huntin' and fishin' all year 'round. Doubt if he had a garden or much food laid by."

"So he wanted yours."

"So he did. He don't need it now."

"Where's his ride? How did he get here?"

"The people he was with drove off after the shot like the hounds of hell were chasin' them. I thought they'd go get the sheriff, but I ain't seen hide nor hair of a lawman, unless you're lawmen."

"We aren't. My name is Tommy Carmellini. My friend is Armanti Hall."

"My name is Angelica Price," she said. "I see you're wearing pistols. Are you with the gover'ment?"

"No," I said. "The pistols are just fashion statements in these troubled times, strictly for social purposes. I'm a peaceful man, myself."

"We don't see many black folks up this way. Wasn't ever ver' many in these mountains, and after the Civil War most of those few traipsed off for the big cities and bright lights." She said that as if she could remember it. "Mr. Hall, you're the first black man I've seen in years."

"I don't know whether that's good or bad," Armanti told her. "If I stay I'll have to find me a white girl, I suppose."

Angelica Price supposed so too.

The garden didn't have a weed in it. Rich dark earth was heaped up along several rows of plants that I thought were probably potatoes. There were several rows of tall plants tied up with strips of rag loaded with green tomatoes, and row after row of beans climbing poles, with cucumbers growing among them. A fence surrounded the whole thing, which was perhaps forty yards wide and sixty or seventy yards long. Above the fence were a couple strands of wire that raised the fence too high for a deer to jump. Just to make sure, strands of wire ran across the top of the garden festooned with strips of cloth that flapped in the breeze. Over it all was fishing line strung from pole to pole to discourage birds.

Beyond the garden was a pasture. Up higher on the hill, right on top, I could see a few headstones sticking up inside a wooden fence, which apparently had been erected to keep cattle away from the stones. Three black cattle grazed on the hillside. To the right, almost behind the house, was a three-sided pole shed containing piles of loose hay inside a fence with an open gate. Chickens and a rooster or two wandered around inside and outside the fence.

"If you'd like, Mrs. Price, we'll tuck this gent under the sod for you. Say... up there on the hill in that cemetery."

She turned that offer over, then said, "No. I think we'll leave him lay right there as a warnin' to any other fool that happens by. He's already startin' to get ripe and I figure he'll get riper, but I can put up with it. And I don't want him up there on the hill with my folks and my man."

"He *is* getting a little strong," Armanti remarked, and headed back down the hill toward his truck.

I liked the old lady, who looked to be in her mid-seventies. She was spry and lean, so it wouldn't have surprised me to learn she was ten years older. It's a wonder some lonely man didn't try to marry her years ago. Maybe some did and were refused.

"After he gets rotted down some, I'll put him on the compost pile," Angelica Price said.

It took me a moment to get my head around that. Then I asked, "So how are you getting along without electricity?"

"Just fine. Only used it for lights. Got candles and a kerosene lantern, a wood stove and an outhouse, so life is goin' just the way it has for years, twenty-two since my man died. I got ever'thin' I need right here, young man. I was born in this house and hope to live out the rest of my days here, on this piece of earth. This is a good place."

I had to agree. Across the valley I could see clouds building. The breeze, smelling of the land as summer came to an end, was rippling the leaves of the distant trees, making the forest look like the surface of the sea. And it was quiet; the only sound was the whisper of the wind.

"Good luck to you, Mrs. Price," I said, and walked down the hill to where Armanti was waiting in the pickup.

As we drove off, I told Armanti about Mrs. Price's remark about the compost pile.

All he said was, "I saw plenty of 'em in Afghanistan and Syria that I would have enjoyed tossing on a compost pile. Killed a few of 'em myself. God bless her."

TWENTY-FIVE

★

Aboard the flagship of the Texas Navy, George Ranta, sitting at the sonar console, removed his headset. The boat was at periscope depth amid a large area of drilling and production rigs. "It's like listening to a mechanical orchestra warm up," he told Loren Snyder. "Machinery noises transferred into the water, drill strings going up and down, hammering, clanking, sucking, gurgling..."

The photonics mast was out of the water and the video was on the scope. Loren rotated it slowly around the horizon, stopping every few seconds to make a note on the chart he used to back up the computer plots. Paper didn't crash and forget things. It was a decent day up there above the ocean, with a high thin overcast and enough breeze to give the water a bit of chop.

What Loren was looking for was a destroyer or frigate, a gray warship. He wanted to torpedo it, then leave the gulf and head around Florida for the Atlantic. First, he thought, put the fear in them. No, first you must find a target. The good news was that any submarine or surface warship amid the rigs was as acoustically deaf as he was.

Always look on the bright side, Loren told himself. *Be optimistic. That's one of the rules for successful people*. And we are highly successful people, looking for a place to get a little more of it.

He gave orders to Ada Fuentes on the helm. He wished he knew more about drilling rigs: he wondered if they were stabilized with underwater cables that fanned out from the surface to the seabed. Stay between them, he told himself. Don't get near one.

He looked again at the chart. *Texas* was off Louisiana's southwestern coast and proceeding into deeper water on a course just a bit east of south. Over a thousand feet of water below the keel. If he didn't find a surface warship by the time he reached the southern tip of the area, he thought he should swing more westerly to get into the main channel to Houston and Galveston.

He went back to the monitor. He was looking southwest, almost on the right beam, when something airborne passed quickly from left to right. He tried to focus the image, pan out, and catch it. If it was a patrol plane, they were in trouble. But it had been so small. A chopper servicing rigs?

Whatever it was, it was gone now. Off to the northwest.

"What was that?" Jugs Aranado asked. She was behind him, watching over his shoulder.

"I don't know."

"Play it back and freeze-frame it."

"You do it. You're better at this."

He got out of the chair, and she sat and began manipulating the controls. In fifteen seconds she had it on the screen.

"Tomahawk."

Loren Snyder looked at the chart and gave Fuentes a new course to steer, one twenty degrees to the right of her current course. "Let's kick it up to about twelve knots, see if we can close on this guy. I'll keep you away from the rigs. George, those rigs should stand out like sore thumbs on the sonar."

"They do, but there is so much noise in the water…"

"We're very shallow for twelve knots," Fuentes objected. She was worried that an aircraft or satellite scanning the surface with radar or in optical wavelengths might detect the wake.

The problem, Snyder knew, was that the surface ship, if that was what shot the Tomahawk, could simply run away from a sub cruising slowly. Snyder wanted to put a fish into a destroyer or frigate, and to do it he was going to have to take some chances. On the other hand, if a sub had fired the missile, going in there at twelve knots was asking to be smacked, although Snyder doubted an attack sub would be shooting missiles in water this noisy.

"Twelve knots," he said.

Five minutes later Snyder saw another Tomahawk fly past, just a little to the right, or west, of the sub, on a reciprocal course. It was low, no more than a hundred feet above the ocean. This one seemed to come from almost dead ahead.

He picked up the ICS mike and keyed it. "Folks, I think we should all take our general quarters stations. We have a ship ahead, surface or subsurface, that is punching off Tomahawks heading for Texas. I intend to try and torpedo it."

Loren lowered the photonics mast and told Ranta to listen carefully. To give the hydrophones a little better angle, he turned another twenty degrees to the west. A half hour later, he had Fuentes go a little deeper and slow to ten knots.

Now Ranta heard the destroyer, or thought he did. It was just a low, deep throb amid the cacophony, one of the echoes bouncing off the bottom. There it was again! Three-three-five degrees, relative. Twenty-five degrees left of the bow.

"There are two destroyers out there," George Ranta announced. "Both at slow speed, probably launching missiles."

"Retract the photonics mast," Loren Snyder said, and to Ada Fuentes on the helm he added, "Take us down to two hundred fifty feet. Maybe the acoustics are better down there."

The first Tomahawks from the navy's salvo slammed into power plants in the Houston area and knocked out the grid.

JR Hays and Elvin Gentry thought this moment might come, so they had some planes on alert, with the pilots sitting in cockpits. Four planes on alert at Lackland in San Antonio were scrambled and fanned out to the east to look for cruise missiles inbound. They stayed relatively low so their radar would be more effective against the missiles with tiny radar cross-sections, a choice that gave them a high fuel burn.

The fighter pilots were forbidden to cross the coastline. Neither general wished to risk those precious airplanes in attacks on destroyers, which were very capable of defending themselves.

There wasn't much else they could do. Except give a heads-up to Jack Hays, who had spent a long half hour with Billy Rob Smith, the Texas emergency coordinator. Billy Rob had been busy borrowing National Guard emergency generators and wiring them into nursing homes and hospitals that didn't have their own. He had even signed a contract with a machine shop in Bryan, Texas, that normally made custom oil-field equipment. Now the fifty machinists employed there were busy manufacturing emergency generators. It would be a week or two before the first ones were ready to be installed, but as Billy Rob told Jack Hays, it was the best he could do. Every generator he could buy, borrow, or steal was being positioned and wired up.

Jack Hays gave him a slap on the back and told him, "Good work!"

★

The acoustics were indeed better at two hundred fifty feet. Ranta found a cluster of rigs ten degrees to port, and found both destroyers. One was dead ahead, the other ten degrees starboard. They were heading northwest, toward Galveston.

To get the range to the target, Ada Fuentes turned the boat, which was trimmed up and doing about ten knots. After a few minutes, plotting the bearing change, the range was resolved at ten miles to the port target, ten and a half to the starboard one. The targets were moving from left to right, but this would be a fairly simple shot for the Mk-48 torpedoes. They had active sonar seekers and trailed a fiber optic cable behind them, which would allow the submarine crew to ensure they were heading toward the proper targets. If the cables didn't break. If they did, the pump-jet torpedoes would continue on course at fifty-five knots searching for their targets on passive sonar based on the internal logic of their onboard computers, which were programmed by Jugs Aranado. At the very last moment the torpedoes' sensors would go active, ping. Nineteen feet long, twenty-one inches in diameter, the weapon would run under the target and a proximity fuse would trigger its 650-pound warhead. The explosion would break the target ship's back. Time to cover the ten nautical miles to target—eleven minutes.

"Flood Tubes One and Two," Snyder ordered. Jugs Aranado was on the torpedo control console, programming each torpedo. She worked her way through the checklist quickly.

"Torpedoes ready, Captain," Jugs sang out.

"Fire One," Snyder said, and Jugs checked the panel, saw that all lights were green, and pushed the fire button on Tube One. The boat bobbed slightly as the torpedo was ejected by compressed air. On the sonar, Ranta said, "It's running."

"Fire Two." Another little bob as the boat reacted to the loss of the weight of the torpedo and the rush of incoming water to replace it.

"Close outer doors," Snyder ordered.

Now the data from the torpedoes began coming in. Number One was running almost straight, so the chances of the fiber optic cable breaking were small. Number Two turned to a course to intercept the second destroyer. Both were soon up to fifty-five knots, rising from the depths to just under the surface. Both were now armed, but they weren't pinging from their seeker heads.

Jugs Aranado was watching their track, waiting. She didn't want to activate their seeker heads until the last possible moment, because the active pinging would be plainly audible to the destroyers' sonar operators. Amazingly, the propulsion system, a pump jet, was very quiet, and so the targets of the torpedoes might not hear them until they were very close. Too close. Especially in these noisy waters.

Aboard USS *Harlan Jones* the cry "Torpedo incoming!" from the sonarman in the Combat Control Center galvanized the watch. They knew *Texas* might be in the area, but had relied upon the noise from the drilling rigs to shield them from attack. Obviously they had been detected and fired upon. The sonar operator had picked up the telltale sound of the pump-jet engines in the torpedoes. He didn't know how close the torpedo was. Actually, it was less than a mile away, approaching at fifty-five knots.

The tactical action officer, the TAO, a lieutenant commander, ordered decoys fired and used the squawk box to notify the bridge. "Torpedo inbound starboard side."

On the bridge, the captain didn't waste a second. He shouted, "All ahead flank. Full right rudder. Give me a ninety-degree turn to starboard."

A destroyer is a large ship, and accelerating it takes time, time the captain didn't have. He was only making eight knots to give the Tomahawk missiles a stable platform to launch from. Now, even with full right rudder, it would take time to turn the ship, and time was what he didn't have. Still, he could feel the four turbines answer the engine telegraph. The ship seemed to squat as the twin screws bit deep into the water and her bow slowly began to swing.

Aboard *Texas*, the sound of the destroyer's screws was a signal to George Ranta. "Port target is accelerating."

"Take her down to a thousand feet," Loren Snyder ordered. Ada Fuentes repeated the order and pushed the control yoke forward to use the planes to help drive her down as Jugs was busy on the panel flooding tanks. "Give me twenty knots." Fuentes pushed the throttle forward.

"Twenty knots, aye."

"Launch the decoys," Snyder ordered. Jugs pushed the buttons and the sound of the decoys being launched could be faintly heard; the panel showed four were launched. Decoys were noise- and bubble-makers, which hopefully would attract any ASROC missiles the destroyer might launch. ASROC, an antisubmarine rocket-propelled torpedo, was launched from a vertical tube. The rocket engine carried the Mk-46 torpedo well away from the ship, where it would plunge into the sea and begin searching for a submarine. The noise of the decoys would attract an acoustic seeker, and the bubbles would create a return for an active, pinging sonar.

"The fiber optic wires are going to break," Snyder told Jugs. "Go active on the torpedoes."

In *Harlan Jones*' Combat Control Center, the TAO plotted the probable launching position of the submarine and instructed the man on the ASROC panel where to put the missiles. The TAO decided to launch four. One would hit six miles up the bearing of the torpedo, another at eight, another at ten, and the last one at twelve. Once they were in the water, they would circle and search with active sonar for the submarine.

Then the TAO remembered the oil-production platforms. There was a cluster of them, six or seven, ten degrees right of the bearing line. Would they attract the ASROCs? She shrugged the possibility away and ordered four missiles fired.

But time was up! The torpedo ran under the hull of *Harlan Jones* in front of the bridge and exploded. Water being essentially incompressible, the explosion blew a large hole in the bottom of the ship, breaking the keel, and water began rushing in. The ship shook from the hammer blow.

"All stop," the captain ordered, which was merely a term that meant the adjustable-pitch screws were to be brought to fine pitch so the ship wouldn't drive headlong into the ocean and increase the possibility of bulkheads giving way. She began drifting to a stop, which would take a while.

Meanwhile the ASROC launchers spit out four missiles, which roared along the bearing the torpedo had followed.

The crew of *Harlan Jones* began trying to save their ship. Fifteen *Harlan Jones* crewmen were dead. Others would probably die if the watertight bulkheads inside the ship weren't shored up against the sea fighting to invade the vessel. *Harlan Jones* had fired thirty-three of the fifty Tomahawks she had been ordered to launch.

★

The second destroyer, USS *O'Hare*, also heard the pinging of the incoming Mk-48 torpedo, and like her sister ship, turned into it so as to present as narrow a profile as possible. She fired her ASROCs up the bearing line of the incoming ship-killer. She had fired off two when the Mk-48 from *Texas* went under her bow and exploded. The explosion literally cut the ship in half, severed the bow from the ship twenty feet aft of the sonar dome. She wasn't going at flank speed, or the sea would have blown out every internal bulkhead and doomed her. As it was, she lost speed as several watertight bulkheads buckled under the pressure and she began going down at the head. The captain let her drift to a halt.

Both destroyers had been at General Quarters when torpedoed, with all watertight hatches dogged down, so the damage was not as extensive as it could have been. Aboard *O'Hare*, as in *Jones*, the fight to save the ship began immediately. *O'Hare* had launched thirty of the fifty Tomahawks she had been ordered to launch.

Aboard *Texas*, George Ranta and the control room crew heard the whumps of the torpedoes exploding. Snyder had the sound on the loudspeaker. A moment later, they heard the splashes of the antisubmarine torpedoes launched from *O'Hare*, followed by the sound of the ASROCs fired by *Harlan Jones* hitting the water.

Loren Snyder looked at the computerized plot. The cluster of oil platforms were to his port side, perhaps two miles away, so he told Ada Fuentes to turn in that direction. Perhaps the sound of the platforms, at least one of which was drilling a well, would attract the torpedoes searching for his boat.

He glanced at the depth meter, which read seven hundred feet. They were still going down.

He had hoped the torpedoes he had fired would catch the destroyers flat-footed, but apparently the crews were well-trained and alert, just in case. Snyder and his small band of fools might well have run flat out of luck.

Rose-Marie McGarrity's F-16 was over Galveston when her radar showed a low target running fast to the northwest; it had to be a Tomahawk.

She rolled her fighter and plunged down, pulling Gs and getting her nose well in front of the missile on a course to intercept. Down through a layer of clouds, down into the gray day underneath, closing on the blip that had to be a cruise missile. It was doing about five hundred knots. Due to the angle at which she was intercepting, she didn't need her afterburner. Yet. She flipped switches, arming the Sidewinders. If she could get a lock-on....

Intercepting at a forty-five-degree angle, still diving into the hot, humid turbulent summer air, Rose-Marie McGarrity found that visibility underneath the goo was no more than four or five miles. She doubted that she would see the missile. This air was like thin soup and she was bouncing in turbulence. She checked to ensure her radar altimeter was set at two hundred feet: it would give her an audible warning if she got within two hundred feet of the surface of the earth.

Then she heard a tone from the Sidewinder, indicating it was locked on a heat source. She was down to five hundred feet above the ground, doing about Mach .9. The target was dead ahead, crossing slowly from right to left.

With the tone in her ears, she punched off a Sidewinder, a heat-seeker. It left the rail with a blast of fire and shot forward into the haze almost too fast for the eye to follow.

McGarrity was looking through the heads-up display, the HUD, at the target symbol, when she saw the flash. The Sidewinder had scored a kill.

Instantly she was off the juice and soaring upward and right, to point her radar out to sea, just in case.

And, by golly, here came another one. Four or five hundred feet above the earth, scorching along to the northwest. McGarrity got that one with a Sidewinder too. Elation flooded her. This fighter pilot gig was hot shit! Again she soared up and turned southeast, toward the sea.

Two minutes later, she found a third Tomahawk on radar, this one going almost north. Catching it meant a chase, so she engaged the burner and let her fighter accelerate as it again went down toward Mother Earth. She didn't see the Tomahawk until she was about four miles from it—it was a little thing, only visible because the radar told her exactly where to look. She kept the juice on, coming in from an angle, nose well in front to bounce it by sliding up behind it. Gun selected. She kept the missile just below the visible horizon, because to dip below it was to risk flying into the ground. Flying this fast this close to the planet was sublime, a sensory overload.

She was only a mile from it, flying at just above two hundred feet on a course to intercept, closing at Mach 1.2, when she saw something out of the left corner of her eye. Even as the object registered as a radio tower, she hit one of the supporting cables with her left wing.

At that speed, about 1,300 feet per second, the steel cable sliced halfway through the wing as if it were cheese; the spar in the left wing broke and the wing separated from the racing F-16.

There was just no time to react. In a tiny fraction of a second the F-16 rolled hard left, the nose dropped, and the fighter smacked into the ground inverted. The fireball rolled along the land for a thousand yards, dribbling pieces of airplane and Rose-Marie McGarrity. Two houses and one barn caught fire. Smoke mixed with the thick, humid haze.

No one spoke in the control room of *Texas*. They knew that passive antisubmarine torpedoes were hunting them. And the pundits said the age of robots was still in the future!

"Put out some more decoys," Loren Snyder said. Jugs Aranado went to the control panel and launched four.

"Where's the bottom?" Loren asked.

"Two thousand feet down."

"Take us to fifteen hundred," he said to Ada Fuentes.

The sub continued its descent as water poured into the ballast tanks. Snyder was worried. *Virginia*-class submarines were the quietest ever made, and the antisubmarine torpedoes weren't designed to find subs this quiet. But...

The tension mounted. They could be dead in a moment. Each breath could be their last, each heartbeat.

"Do you hear the torpedoes?" Loren asked George Ranta.

"Too much noise," he whispered. "I hear pinging but I can't get a direction."

Boom. The explosion rocked the boat. One of the torpedoes had found a decoy.

And another boom.

"More pinging," Ranta said.

Where had the other torpedoes gone?

"We've got to turn," Ada said. "That production platform is dead ahead."

"Right ninety degrees." The boat was still going down. Fourteen hundred feet and sinking.

But they were still alive.

They heard two more explosions. Well away.

"The torpedoes went for a platform," Ranta said.

A wave of relief swept over the little crew of *Texas*.

"There are more of them out there," Ranta said. "I can hear at least one. Maybe circling." They turned the boat toward the noise and waited. Finally the noise from the torpedo's engine faded.

Snyder said to Fuentes and Aranado, "Go back up, so we can use the photonics mast." To Ranta he said, "You must keep us clear of those platforms."

"I can hear them."

So they rose slowly from the depths. When the photonics mast was raised, it revealed the injured destroyers lying dead in the water at least six miles to the west. The damaged production platform still stood, but no doubt the crew on it was on their radio reporting the torpedoed destroyers and the torpedoes that struck the platform. And trying desperately to prevent a major oil spill.

Loren Snyder was exhausted. He'd slept six hours in three days. "Let's get the hell out of the gulf," he said. "Jugs, lay a course for the Straits of Florida. When we are clear of these platforms, take us back down to a thousand feet so the P-3s can't find us. I'm going to sleep."

He staggered along to the tiny captain's cabin and collapsed into the bunk.

Fifty-five of the sixty-three Tomahawk cruise missiles launched by USS *O'Hare* and *Harlan Jones* actually impacted Texas power plants. The resulting explosions took seventeen power plants off the grid instantly. Subsequent inspections revealed that at least nine of them could be repaired, and they began producing electricity, at least at a reduced level, within a week or two. The remaining eight were damaged beyond salvage.

The Texas government kept the amount of damage a closely held secret, although within a day or two satellite reconnaissance would allow analysts in Washington to make reasonably accurate assessments.

No doubt more Tomahawks were in Texas' future.

A few minutes before three that Friday afternoon, six Secret Service agents climbed from an SUV in front of the main entrance of the Pentagon and went inside. They were escorted to the E-Ring, where they arrested Admiral Sugar Ray, the army chief of staff, and the air force chief of staff. They put all three men in handcuffs and took them to the ground level of the building and into the interior courtyard. The sun was shining and the temperature was already in the low nineties.

Each man was handcuffed to a small tree with his hands behind his back. Admiral Ray knew what was coming. He cursed himself for waiting so long. *We should have done it yesterday*, he thought bitterly.

The senior agent drew his weapon and shot each of them in the head. Sugar Ray just happened to be last. "Rot in Hell," Ray told the agent, who then pulled the trigger.

The agents left the bodies handcuffed to the trees, walked back through the Pentagon, past those horrified officers and enlisted who had actually managed to get to work today, and out the main entrance to their waiting car.

Al Grantham was worried. He had visions of squads of armed troops coming into the White House and arresting the president and everyone around him, taking them to some dungeon and chaining them to the wall. Shooting three senior officers at the Pentagon was an in-your-face insult the armed services couldn't ignore.

He broached the subject to the president, who sneered. "They'll do nothing," he said. "They are bureaucrats, paper-pushers, and they achieved their high ranks by not making waves." The president lit a cigarette and puffed on it contentedly. "We have nothing to fear from the generals. They have taken orders since their first day in uniform. Nothing in their experience has prepared them for the day when their superiors might use violence to make them behave."

"They aren't cowards."

"Oh," said Soetoro with a hint of derision in his voice, "but they are. They believe in nothing but the holy flag, keeping the boss happy, and collecting their pensions in the good by and by. The man who believes in something and will use any means to get it will leave them at a loss."

Grantham's face reflected his doubt.

"Relax," Barry Soetoro said. "Whatever they are, they are not gamblers. When have you ever known one of them to take a risk?"

TWENTY-SIX

★

A couple of days after our first visit, Armanti Hall and I decided to call on Angelica Price to deliver a deer haunch. A little fresh meat always goes well, we thought, and maybe we could trade for some fresh potatoes and beans.

We were in civvies and wearing our web belts that morning, and each of us had an M4 beside us in the cab of Armanti's pickup. There weren't many vehicles on the roads, but the pickups we passed were piled high with firewood and one was hauling a steer. I wondered if it was stolen.

We followed the little ribbon of asphalt into the hills. When Angelica Price's house came into view, we saw three cars parked nearby. One looked as if it were about eight years old, the other two were show-room new. The new cars didn't have license plates.

We coasted on by for about fifty yards, then Armanti stopped and I got out with my M4. "I'll go look the cars over. How about you snuggling up against the bank there and give me cover if I need it."

"Notice that there are only two cows in the pasture now?"

I hadn't, but a quick scan showed he was correct.

I strolled back with the M4 under my arm, just in case. The new cars weren't locked. One had 170 miles on it, the other 180. The older car, a gray Toyota, wore a Maryland license plate.

"Hey, man!" A black guy with a rifle was walking toward me from the house. At a glance, the rifle looked like Angelica Price's old lever action.

"Get away from them cars!"

I was partially shielded by the front end of the old one, and I retreated one step to get a little more metal between us. I snicked the safety off the M4.

"Where's Mrs. Price?"

"Never heard of her."

"This is her house." I was scanning on both sides. I could see someone at the window of the house watching, and the window was open. If there were anyone to the right or left in the pasture or garden, I didn't see him.

"You mean that old white woman? She's out in the chicken coop, man. Gave us some shit, she did."

"She dead?"

"Not yet. If you don't get the fuck outta here, you—"

That's when I swung the M4 up and fired a burst at his legs. He went down hard and lost the rifle.

Someone fired from the house. I heard the bullet smack into the car. The report sounded like a pistol to me. The distance was about sixty yards, and whoever fired wasn't a good pistol shot.

I couched down, used the car hood for a rest, and put a burst into the window. Silence followed.

On my right, I could see Armanti removing two AT4s from the back of his pickup. Apparently sneaking up on the house and taking a chance on getting shot didn't appeal to him, either. I hoped the thug lying in the yard had told the truth about Mrs. Price.

Armanti ran up the road, using the embankment of a drainage ditch as cover.

To keep their heads down, I fired another burst through the window.

The guy lying in the yard was moaning, holding on to his left thigh. I could see blood at this distance, about twenty yards. Looked like a bullet had clipped an artery.

I moved aft along my mobile fortress, with just the top of my head showing. Armanti was about a hundred yards away now, looking back at me. I gave him a thumbs-up.

He stood. He had one of the AT4 tubes on his right shoulder. Five seconds, six, then the exhaust blast behind him raised a cloud of crap from the road.

He had fired at the base of the chimney of the house, which was probably the only thing hard enough to trigger the detonator of the armor-piercing missile warhead.

The windows blew out, flame gushed forth, and the roof rose a few feet, then crashed down. In seconds the house was on fire.

I began a bent-over trot toward the house. Looked at the guy lying in the yard with blood pumping between his fingers.

"Help me, man," he pleaded.

I grabbed the pistol in his waistband and left him there.

The house was blazing nicely. No one in the yard or garden. One of the exterior walls of the house was tilting out, falling slowly. I glanced through the open door into the fire. Anyone in there was too far gone to save, even if I wanted to be a hero, which I didn't. Near the garden was a hole with a fire smoldering. Looked like a barbecue pit. Pieces of cowhide and half a carcass were lying near it.

I went on around to the chicken coop, the M4 ready to go. Only one chicken was in sight.

Mrs. Price was lying on the hay in the shed. She had been smacked in the side of the head with a pistol several times; one of the blows had laid open her scalp. Now her gray hair was matted with blood.

Beside her were a dead white man and an unconscious white woman. Sparks from the house were causing the hay to smoke. I stepped on the hot spots, and pulled the two women and the dead man out of the shed.

"Mrs. Price. Mrs. Price, it's Tommy Carmellini. We were by to see you a couple of days ago. Remember?"

Armanti walked up, looking grim. "The one in the front yard is still alive."

"Find out who these people were," I said. He trotted off.

I went through the dead man's pockets. His driver's license in his wallet, which was empty of cash, said his name was Lincoln B. Greenwood, of Clarksville, Maryland.

Mrs. Price was stirring. She was a tough one.

"They killed him for the fun of it," she said. "He refused to beg. That's his wife, Anne." Only her left eye tracked. "They got here an hour before the others showed up."

"Mrs. Price, I'm going to carry you to the pickup. Then I'll come back for Mrs. Greenwood. We've got to get you two ladies to a doctor."

She couldn't have weighed more than ninety pounds. After I deposited her in the truck, I stopped by where Armanti was squatting beside the wounded man.

"He says they're from Baltimore," Armanti told me. "Four guys and a whore. Stole the new cars from a dealer and hit the road. Nothing to eat in Baltimore. Stopped here because they were about out of gas."

Blood was still pumping from that hole in the guy's leg. He had three or four other holes in his legs, and the right leg was obviously broken, but the one high in his left thigh was a real bleeder. His jeans were sodden. He was lying back on the grass and had relaxed his hold on his thigh.

"Let me have the keys to your truck. Got to get two women to a doctor. I'll be back for you after a while."

Armanti handed me the keys from his pocket. "This one's gonna be gone soon."

"They pistol-whipped the women and killed the man driving the gray sedan," I told him. "Don't forget Mrs. Price's rifle."

I went on to the chicken coop, picked up Anne Greenwood, who had been struck at least twice recently. She also had an old welt across her face. I carried her to the pickup. The wreckage of the house was completely aflame when I drove off.

★

Dr. Proudfoot was in at the clinic in Greenbank. I carried Anne Greenwood in first. The doctor was attending to his nurse, who had been whacked on the head.

"Got two women for you, Doctor. They've both been pistol-whipped. This is Mrs. Greenwood."

"Just like my nurse. An hour ago. We were held up at gunpoint by a gang of pill-billies looking for drugs. We didn't have any painkillers, but they took every drug I had."

I carried Mrs. Greenwood into the examining room and put her on a gurney. Went back to the truck and brought Angelica Price in. I put her on a gurney in the second examining room.

"My God," the doctor said. "I know Mrs. Price. Why on earth?"

"Baltimore thugs. They were after her food. Have you called the law?"

"No phone. They wouldn't have come, anyway. Everyone is busy getting robbed or robbing the neighbors. It's anarchy. Maybe the lawmen are home taking care of their families. I would be if I were one of them."

He finished bandaging the nurse and sent her home. Then he spoke to Mrs. Price. "Can you hear me, Angelica?"

"Yes, Doctor."

"I want you to just lie here quietly and let me look at Mrs. Greenwood. Will you do that?"

"Yes."

I sat holding Mrs. Price's hand while Proudfoot worked on Mrs. Greenwood.

"Pills," she said bitterly. "The hollow trash is on meth and OxyContin. Surprised they aren't robbing drugstores."

"No doubt they are," I said. "This little clinic looked too good to pass up, I suspect."

"Thanks for coming by, Tommy," she said.

"We've got to stop meeting like this."

Twenty minutes passed before the doctor returned. "Mrs. Greenwood is in a deep coma. She needs to be in a hospital, but the one nearest here is closed."

"What can you do for her?"

"Pray."

He began examining Mrs. Price. "You have a concussion too, Angelica. I'm going to clean up that cut on your scalp and stitch it up, but that's about all I can do. You should be in a hospital too, but since there isn't one around, you need to stay in bed. You're going to have a terrible headache. We'll pray for you too."

"I don't think much of prayer," Angelica Price told him. "I've been praying every night that Barry Soetoro would wake up dead, but apparently God hasn't taken him yet."

I went out to the pickup while Dr. Proudfoot worked. Clouds were building over the mountains to the west.

I changed magazines in the M4 and examined the pistol I had taken off the bleeder. A 9-mm, and the magazine was full. God only knows where the bastard got it, but I would have bet a thousand to one he didn't buy it. I decided to give it to the doctor. We were getting a nice collection of weapons, but no matter how hard you try, you can only shoot one at a time.

Another guy pulled up in an old truck. His son was in the right seat, shot once above the heart. I helped him carry the boy inside. He was maybe fifteen. People were stealing the cows, the man said, and the boy put up a fight.

"It's like trying to stop an avalanche," the old man said. Tears were running down his weathered cheeks.

I emptied my wallet for the doctor, who tried to wave the money away. "Got nothing to spend it on," he said.

"It won't always be like this," I said, with more conviction than I felt. I told him I would be back tomorrow to check on Mrs. Greenwood, and carried Angelica Price out to the truck. I got the deer haunch from the pickup that I had intended to give Mrs. Price and gave it to the doctor instead.

I took her to the CIA safe house and made the introductions.

After Sarah had Mrs. Price in bed, I made sure Yocke and Molina were standing by the machine guns in the pits and drove down to the guard shack where Travis Clay and Willie the Wire were playing gin. "Big-city punks are out, hillbillies are hunting drugs, and scared people are looking for food. All of them are armed. You guys better cowboy up and be ready."

Willie was appalled. He wanted to argue, but I told him, "It's us or them, Willie. If you want to keep on living, you'd better be willing to shoot."

Mrs. Price's house was down to smoking boards when I got back. The bleeder was dead, and Armanti Hall had dragged him around the house and put him beside Lincoln Greenwood.

There were four corpses in the remains of the house, burned beyond recognition. The boards were still hot and smoking, and we didn't have body bags, so we left them there.

We buried Greenwood and the bleeder up on the hill in the Price family plot. Before we tossed the bleeder in the hole, I checked his pockets. He had a nice roll of bills on him.

"You can't take it with you when you go," Armanti Hall said with a sigh.

Some of the bills were blood-soaked. I peeled them off and tossed them in the hole. "He can take these," I said, and handed the rest to Armanti. "Grab his feet."

We tossed him in, then went down the hill to the garden gate for the man lying there. He stunk to high heaven. Each of us grabbed a foot; we dragged him up the hill and dumped him in on top of the bleeder.

I heaved my cookies before we got the holes filled up.

As we walked down the hill for the last time, Armanti said, "I don't want to live in Barry Soetoro's new empire. I'm thinking of going to Texas."

The taste of vomit was strong in my mouth and the smell of death in my nose. "Maybe I'll go with you," I said.

He had picked some potatoes and green beans from Mrs. Price's garden while he waited for me, and had them in five-gallon buckets. We loaded the buckets into the truck and headed up the road to find a place to turn around.

On the way back by Mrs. Price's, before we got there, a pickup pulled up below the three cars in the parking area and three white males got out. The oldest one had a rifle. He aimed it at one of the cows in the pasture and pulled the trigger. The cow staggered a few feet, then went down. As the younger males, apparently teenage boys, climbed the fence, the guy with the rifle turned to face our stopped pickup. He held the rifle in both hands and looked at us defiantly.

"Protecting his kill," Armanti muttered. "I could drop the bastard before he gets a shot off."

"To what purpose?" I asked, and put the truck in motion.

We drove on by. The shooter never took his eyes off us.

"This place is like fucking Syria," Armanti remarked.

I didn't argue.

The evening after the Tomahawk strikes, Jack Hays held a press conference at an "undisclosed location," which was the bottom floor of an underground parking garage in Austin, which fortunately was still on the electrical grid. Three print reporters were there, and two local television reporters, whose cameramen were set up with lights and sound and all the bits and pieces, including a set with a podium for the president of Texas and folding chairs the reporters.

Jack Hays started by reading a statement about the progress of the government in converting a state in the United States to a standalone nation. Much had been accomplished by the legislature, which was in session twelve hours a day, seven days a week. A new currency had been approved and a Texas Border Patrol and Customs Service established. The tax department was expanded and statutes passed adopting federal tax rates for the new nation.

"Everything has to be done at once," Jack Hays said, "and we are up to our elbows in it. Inevitably there will be glitches, but we will try in good faith to correct any mistakes and injustices, if everyone will help us find them."

The first question was, "Mr. President, what can you tell us about last night's missile strikes in the Houston area?"

"The missiles were launched from at least two United States Navy surface ships, both of which were subsequently damaged by an attack from a Texas naval vessel. We know that much because crews on nearby oil-production platforms radioed what they had seen to their companies, who passed it to news media. We are doing our best to get power restored in the Houston area. We understand that at this time of year, loss of electrical power in that area is a humanitarian crisis."

After a half hour of answering questions about the measures the legislature had passed and was considering, Hays said, "One more question and we'll call it an evening." Three hands went up and he pointed to a reporter from the *Wall Street Journal.*

She asked, "Under what circumstances would Texas consider rejoining the United States?"

"Under the old Constitution?" Jack Hays asked.

"Yes."

"I can't think of any," Hays said curtly. He had learned long ago that the best tactic for a politician was to just answer the question asked or evade it. In the silence that followed that short sentence, he reconsidered his answer. Texans deserved to know his thinking, and if they didn't like it, they could say so.

As he tried to decide what to say, the reporter followed up with the question, "What if it was no questions asked, all forgiven?"

"I'm certainly not going to engage in international diplomacy via your newspaper," he said tartly.

"Even if President Soetoro were removed from office?"

"My answer stands."

"You mean, sir, there is no peaceful way to restore the Union?"

Jack Hays weighed his answer as the cameras scrutinized his face and the reporters watched.

"The old nation was seriously divided," he said, "with political power split between large urban populations and the people in the heartland. Even Texas has some of that. Some of the policies that the elected politicians in Houston wish to follow have been resoundingly rejected by the rest of the state's residents. In a free nation there will always be the push and pull of conflicting views, conflicting desires, conflicting interests. Yet in my judgment, in the old nation the system had broken down, irreparably, and that is why Barry Soetoro chose to become a dictator, to force his political vision on people who rejected it repeatedly at the polls and in the Congress.

"Be that as it may, the reality is that if the people of Texas wish to continue to enjoy the rights granted by the old Constitution, such as free speech, freedom of religion, freedom of the press, the right to own a gun, the sovereign right to control our borders, the right to be ruled by elected representatives and not be dictated to by the executive or the courts or bureaucracies . . . if Texans want those things, they need to be an independent nation."

Jack Hays paused, gathering his thoughts. "Our parting from the United States has not been amicable. Barry Soetoro is raining Tomahawk cruise missiles on the people of Texas. If he wants Texas back in the Union, I would tell him what the citizens of Gonzales, Texas, told Mexican army Colonel Ugartechea in 1835 when he demanded return of a cannon. If you want it, 'come and take it.'"

TWENTY-SEVEN

★

The interview with the Texas president Jack Hays was broadcast via satellite to those stations and networks still broadcasting in an America with limited electrical assets. It also was soon on the internet. Yet it was on clandestine radio stations that it was picked up by the refugees hidden in the CIA safe farm in the Allegheny Mountains.

I was there when it was played on the recorder that Friday night to the assembled audience in the cabin on the mountainside. I had spent the evening worrying about what would happen when we were discovered, which was bound to happen in the near future. I inspected the machine-gun pits, strategically located around a kill zone in front of the house where any vehicles would have to come to a stop, and inspected each and every rifle and pistol and AT4. I was a worried man, and tired of waiting.

Sarah Houston watched me fret and said nothing. Perhaps she was becoming fatalistic. It would be a miracle if any of us got out of this mess alive. I wondered if she was resigned to the inevitable.

Yet she was at my side when the tape played, and Jack Hays' clear, confident baritone voice spoke of the problems of the United States and the future of Texas. I watched Jake Grafton's face—the man should have been a poker master in Vegas—and the much more expressive faces of Sal Molina and Jack Yocke. And, I confess, cynic that I was, I wondered how all this squared with the White House plotting that Grafton had overheard. I had quizzed Sarah about that—she said she had listened to little of it. Grafton kept her too busy with other things. But, she said, Jake Grafton had listened. By the hour. Night after night. He knew!

He knew what?

When the tape was over, Sal Molina spoke first. "When Puerto Rico and Illinois melt down, America has two choices. We can let those two go bankrupt and default on their bonds, or the federal government can take over their debts. If the latter, the states as we know them are doomed: They will cease to exist as sovereign entities. The federal government—actually the executive—will be the ruler of America, able to dictate the smallest decisions, the minutiae of American life, dictate how it will be for his allies and his enemies, of whom he has a great many."

Yocke snorted. "It will never happen," he declared.

Molina merely gave him a derisive glance, stood, and went up the stairs to bed. Yocke piddled and diddled, looked out the window a bit, then followed Molina upstairs.

Grafton and I were the only two left in the room. I decided to brace him. "How long are we going to hide here?"

He looked at me with two raised eyebrows. "Are you getting impatient?"

"Yes, sir."

He nodded, readjusted his fanny without wincing, and sipped at a cup of cold coffee that rested on the stand beside him. After all his years in the navy, it seemed that he was impervious to caffeine.

"The whole country is going to hell," I said, "and I feel like a tit on a boar sitting around here. I'm ready to shoot somebody."

"I thought you did that earlier today."

"It wasn't enough. I want to shoot some of those Soetoro sons of bitches, the assholes who decided to rule America and everyone in it. I want to kill those bastards for what they did to my country."

He grunted.

"We can't just sit here! What about your wife? Your daughter and her husband? What about *America*?"

He smiled at me, which drove my blood pressure up another ten points. "Tommy, there is a time for everything. This pot has to simmer before the country is ready to throw Soetoro out. We're almost there, I suspect, but not quite. Another day or two, then we'll hit the road. We'll have lots of help."

"Oh," I said, less than enthusiastically. "And where the hell are we going?" I wanted to be sure the old fart had a plan.

"Why, to Washington of course."

"And this help? Like who?"

"We'll pick them up on the way."

"You hope!"

Grafton looked at me askance. "You don't really believe in the American people, do you?"

"I've killed too many of 'em." He didn't say anything, so I added, "They voted for Soetoro twice. They've sat on their collective thumbs watching the bastard pervert the Constitution, lie like a dog, and poison race relations, and they haven't done anything about it other than elect some gutless Republicans who refuse to stand up to Soetoro. The American people don't seem to give a damn about their country or the future that their kids are going to have to live in. Americans just *don't care* anymore. Naw, I don't think much of the American people. I wish I'd gotten out years ago."

When I wound down he cocked his head and looked me in the eyes as he said, "These are the descendants of the people who hacked out homes in the wilderness. They fought Indians, the British, the Mexicans, and each other. Over a half million Americans died in the Civil War. They peopled a continent and built a nation. They helped win two wars in Europe and defeated Japan. They fought in Vietnam to help a poor people resist communism. They've done their best to fight terrorism and help people in the third world get a leg up. You grossly underestimate them.

"True, they voted for Soetoro, and a lot of them did it because they naively thought Soetoro would be *good* for race relations in America, and they thought that was a larger good. This race thing...," he shook his head, "...people want America to include everybody. Martin Luther King left a huge legacy, and America wants his vision, wants an American to be judged by his character rather than the color of his skin. *That* is the society we want to live in, but we're not there yet. Our first black president got into office not because of his character or his politics, but because he's half-black—or in the parlance of today, black. He gets away with pissing on the Constitution because he's black. He gets away with lying because he's black. He gets away with poisoning race relations because he's black. Even the liberals on the Supreme Court have given him pass after pass."

Grafton sighed. "His time has run out. The American people have gotten a good look at Soetoro this past week, and I don't think they like what they saw. I thank my stars that I'm not Barry Soetoro. He won't like his future."

I wanted to believe him, but I didn't. For once I did the smart thing: I kept my mouth shut.

"Help me to bed," Jake Grafton said.

As I hoisted him, my resolve melted. I asked, "Do you really think Joe Six-Pack and the missus will shoot at Soetoro's thugs?"

"This republic is their heritage," he said. "If they don't value it enough to fight for it, a great many men have wasted their lives fighting for them."

The next morning, Saturday, the first day of the three-day Labor Day weekend, the radio gave us the news that seven more states—Kansas, Nebraska, South and North Dakota, Wyoming, Idaho, and New Mexico—had declared their independence. Georgia had tried to, but federal paramilitary police broke up the legislature and arrested half the politicians. In South Carolina, a gun battle had broken out in the statehouse and at least ten people had died.

The governor of New Mexico read a statement to the press after the Declaration of Independence was read. "The proud citizens of New Mexico will never escape poverty unless the flood of illegal immigrants from Mexico and Central America is drastically curtailed. New Mexicans are being robbed of the American dream, the dream that by hard work and thrift they can improve their lot in life and provide a better life for their children. We have taken a stand here tonight. Let history be our judge."

"The liberals are going down hard," Jake Grafton remarked.

"You knew they wouldn't go easy," Sal Molina shot back.

"Yes. I did know that," Grafton replied, glancing at Molina's face. I was watching him. No doubt that is why he kept his mouth so firmly shut about Soetoro's plans, which he had overheard on Sarah Houston's White House bugging operation. I wondered what Molina's reaction would be when he learned—if he ever did—that Grafton had been listening to all the White House bullshit and plotting for the last six months, including Molina's.

That Saturday was the day the Mexican army invaded Southern California. Maybe the Mexicans thought they could carve off a chunk for themselves, or maybe the troops were funded by the drug cartels that wanted their own country.

As the day wore on, we heard that the Marines at Camp Pendleton were fighting back. All up and down the west coast, U.S. military units raced south to engage. Two carriers left San Diego and began launching strikes against the invading troops and fighting to maintain air superiority.

When I had had all of the news I could stand, I went out onto the porch, carrying my M4. Sarah joined me and we climbed the hill and sat under a tree. A breeze whispered in the pines, and we sat for so long and so quietly that a doe and her two fawns eventually wandered by.

When they were out of sight, she whispered, "Life goes on."

"With or without us," I said.

Ten or so minutes later an airplane broke the silence, flying low, just above the trees. A piston-engine plane. Then I got a glimpse of it through the forest canopy. A tail-dragger. A little Cessna by the look of it. It circled the safe house twice, and the pilot probably got a look at the trucks, even though they were parked under the trees.

I was up and running, searching for a hole in the canopy so I could track the plane, which was still humming pleasantly. The sound was fading though. Then and I saw it in the distance, to the south, apparently circling to land on the grass runway in the valley.

"Come on," I shouted at Sarah. We trotted down the hill, jumped into a pickup, and raced down the road toward the valley.

The little plane was sitting by the hangar when we arrived. It looked like a Cessna 170, all polished aluminum. I took the carbine as I got out of the truck. A man was helping a woman and two small boys. I didn't see any weapons on them.

"Hey," I said as I walked up.

"Hello. Is this your place?"

"It's private property, but I don't own it."

"The thugs from Philly are looting and burning houses in our neighborhood. We got to the airport and I got my plane. I didn't know where to go, and when I saw this runway, I said, 'Guess we'll try our luck here.'" He had been eyeing my carbine and the pistol on my web belt. Then his eyes shifted to Sarah, who walked by us over to the woman.

"My name's Johnson. That's my wife," he told me. "We had to get out. I think thugs killed the woman next door and left her body in the house when they burned it down."

We opened the hangar and shoved his plane in tail-first, chocked it, and closed the doors. I loaded everyone in the truck and took them to the safe house.

Jake Grafton was sitting in an easy chair in the main room. He perked right up when I told him about the plane. He skipped the social pleasantries with Johnson. "How much fuel is in it?"

"Both tanks are about half full."

"Tommy, go back to the hangar and see if there is any avgas there."

As I left, Grafton was asking Johnson about bridges and roadblocks he might have seen from the air. *Maybe this will galvanize Grafton*, I thought. *Get him moving.* God, I was tired of sitting doing nothing while America went back to the stone age.

A plane would be a good thing to have if we could keep it fueled. Our own air force. I opened a panel of the sliding hangar door and went inside. And Lady Luck smiled. I found a fifty-five-gallon plastic drum full of fuel in the hangar. The drum had a hand-crank pump mounted on top and a hose. I was maneuvering the drum under the left wing when I heard a pickup truck drive up. I figured it was Armanti and I needed him to crank the pump while I stood on the ladder with the hose.

I turned. Two scraggly faced locals in filthy jeans and T-shirts stood at the door of the hangar and had me covered with scoped deer rifles. Both were grinning at me with yellow teeth.

"Well, well, well! By God, we heard it and here it is," said one of them.

"Just shuck that pistol, asshole, and maybe we won't shoot you," said the other.

I pulled out the Kimber and tossed it in the dirt.

"Look the plane over, Benny. You, get over here against the wall." He waggled the barrel of his rifle and I went.

The one called Benny picked up my shooter, examined it, and tucked it into his pants. The other kept his rifle pointed at my belt buckle while Benny opened the door to the plane and looked around inside.

"Jearl, that kid is gettin' away!" A call from outside. So there were more of them out there.

Jearl must have been the stalwart guarding me, because he forgot me and ran back to the open panel in the door. "Hey!" Jearl went dashing out of sight, shouting, "Get off your asses and catch her!"

I grabbed a heavy wrench off the shelf and stuck it up my sleeve. Benny strolled over from the plane, pulling my Kimber from his waistband. He had a big wad of snuff under his lower lip. "You're a big one, ain't you?"

"Your mom know you boys are out causing trouble?" I asked.

"Man, the country has gone to hell. We can be just as bad as we wanna be and ain't nobody to say we can't."

"And how bad is that?"

I heard the sound of another truck. So did Benny, and he turned his head to his right toward the door. I let the wrench slide down into my hand; as he turned back toward me I hit him in the jaw with it with everything I had, right on top of his snuff wad. The blow put him down hard and I was all over him. Got my pistol and his rifle. He was only partially conscious. His jaw was obviously broken. Blood, saliva, and brown tobacco juice dribbled from his open mouth.

The rifle was some cheap piece of Walmart crap with a plastic stock, but it had brass in the chamber when I pulled the bolt back for a peek.

I stepped to the left edge of the hangar door and looked around. Jearl was on the runway, about fifty yards from me, pulling a girl about nine or ten years old along by the arm. There were two men in the back of their pickup, and they had rifles pointed at Armanti, who was stepping from his truck with his hands up.

I braced the rifle against the door and shot the man on the right in the bed of the truck. Worked the bolt. The other one was quick as a cat. He spun toward me, leveled his rifle, and fired. Something burned my neck and my shot went wild. I worked the bolt again and got on him, but he was already going down. Armanti had shot him in the back.

Jearl, the guy in the meadow, held the girl against him with his left hand and pointed his rifle toward me with his right. I didn't figure he could even hit the hangar with that rifle shooting one-handed from the waist. I rested the rifle against the edge of the hangar door again and looked through the scope. Steadied the crosshairs on Jearl's head and squeezed one off. He went over backward.

I walked out for a look. The bullet had taken his head clean off. Above his neck only his lower jaw remained.

The girl was sobbing. I picked her up and walked back to the hangar. Armanti was standing, pistol in hand, over the guy I had tamed with a wrench. The guy was coming around.

"You want me to finish him?" Armanti asked me.

"Be as bad as you wanna be," I told him flippantly.

"Who is this kid?" Armanti asked Benny, who was now moaning and writhing in the dirt.

Benny mumbled something, holding his mouth. Armanti kicked him, and he squirmed and moaned louder.

"I asked you a question, Jack," Armanti said, "and if you don't tell it to me straight, things could get really iffy for you. Hold your jaw together and answer me! Who is she?"

With a supreme effort, holding his jaw with both hands, Benny said, "Some kid we picked up. Jearl was porkin' her."

"Where's her folks?"

"Jearl killed 'em."

I didn't even see it coming. Bang. The pistol in Armanti's hand went off, and the guy lying in the dirt was instantly dead with a 9-mm bullet through his head.

Armanti Hall holstered his pistol and came over to me, looked at the girl's face streaked with dirt and tears. "It's gonna be all right," he said softly.

"Take her up to the house," I said, "then come back and help me fuel this plane."

He carried the child out to his truck, and I got busy tossing bodies into the back of the junky pickup they had arrived in. The corpses had almost stopped oozing blood, but I got some blood and brains on my shirt anyway. I figured the stuff would wash off. The key was still in the ignition of the truck, so I didn't have to go through their pockets.

My neck burned like fire and I could feel blood trickling down into my shirt. Another fucking scar! Welcome to the revolution.

TWENTY-EIGHT

★

The CH-47s dropped Colonel Kevin Crislip and his troops of the 10th Special Forces Group at six bridges across the Canadian River in the Texas panhandle, five highway bridges and one railroad bridge. The Canadian was not much of a river, merely a wet, sandy depression in that cap-rock country, but knocking the railroad bridge down would prevent any trains from using the railroad until it was replaced. The destruction of the five highway bridges across the Canadian would severely inconvenience truckers, who would have to go east to the main body of Oklahoma or west to New Mexico to find an alternate route south.

Colonel Crislip thought this whole mission a bad joke, political revenge on the Texas politicians who had embarrassed Barry Soetoro, but General Seuss and his staff had been trading messages with the Pentagon, so here the Green Berets were, blowing up bridges in the panhandle, each demolition team delivered by helicopter. Crislip consoled himself with the thought that these demolition jobs were good training, if nothing else.

Each bridge had one demolition team assigned and it was delivered by a Chinook, which moved safely away from the bridge after off-loading the team, their explosives, and a few guards. Colonel Crislip accompanied the team blowing the bridge north of Borger. He stood in the warm Texas night listening to crickets and inhaling the faint aroma of cow manure drifting on the breeze while the team worked. Crislip sent the guards up the highway on either side of the bridge to stop traffic.

There wasn't much. A semi came from the north fifteen minutes after they arrived and was waved on through. Five minutes later a pickup full of Mexicans who had been drinking came from the direction of Borger. They were going back to the ranch, they said, so the guard waved them across the bridge. They went by Crislip saluting and shouting and laughing. Although the Mexicans could see the helo parked in a nearby pasture, they couldn't see the soldiers working under the bridge, so they certainly couldn't warn anyone that the bridge was soon to be destroyed.

The colonel had never actually demolished a real bridge before; he went down the riverbank and stood underneath, looking up, ten feet, with a flashlight to see where his troops put the charges. They seemed to know what to do and how to do it.

They were planting C-4 charges, which the experts at Fort Carson had assured the colonel were quite enough to put the bridge in the sand of the Canadian River, if, the experts said, they were placed properly.

Always the big *if*, Crislip fumed. So if any bridge remained standing after its charge was detonated, his troops would take the blame. Wonderful!

He climbed back up the bank and was standing beside the highway listening to the crickets and savoring that stockyard smell when a battered old pickup coming from the north was stopped by the guard. Crislip walked over, just in time to hear his soldier tell the driver to turn around and go home. There were two other people in the truck's cab, Crislip saw, two women.

"Let him across the bridge if he wants to go," the colonel told the guard as he walked up.

The driver, who looked to be in his fifties and was wearing a ratty ball cap, asked, "Who is the head man here?"

"I am," Crislip said. "Colonel Kevin Crislip, United States Army."

"I live just a little west of here, and we saw you people come in on that helicopter after dark and we been watching you. What the hell is going on?"

The dashboard lights let Crislip see the other passengers, one a woman about the driver's age and the other a teenage girl. "That's none of your business, sir. What's your name, anyway?"

"Zeke Lipscomb, buddy. And telling me to mind my own business ain't the way we do things here in Texas."

"Mr. Lipscomb, this is army business. Cross the bridge or go home."

"I'll cross." He put the truck in motion, drove it a hundred yards and stopped right in the middle of the bridge. He killed the headlights, parked the truck, and he and the two women got out.

Crislip strode toward them. The guard was going to accompany him, but Crislip growled for him to stay put.

"I told you to drive across," he said to Mr. Lipscomb, who had a female on each side of him.

"Well, I didn't. And I ain't a gonna. We kinda think you soldiers are up to no good, and we're not going to let you get away with it."

Crislip sighed.

The older woman, presumably Mrs. Lipscomb, spoke up. "You federal troops got no damn business in Texas, Colonel, and you know it. We done declared ourselves a separate nation."

Crislip looked back at the guard. There was just a sliver of moon and enough starlight to see him clearly, standing there in the road looking this way, no doubt wondering what the colonel was going to do about this stubborn rancher.

"Mr. Lipscomb and Mrs. Lipscomb—" he looked at the girl. "What's your name?"

"Ruby."

"And Ms. Ruby Lipscomb. I am here obeying the orders of my superior officers, and the men with me are obeying my orders. We are doing our duty. Now I am asking you nicely to please get in your truck and drive on into Borger or return to your home."

"You're gonna blow up this bridge, ain't ya?" Lipscomb said, scrutinizing Crislip's face.

"Yes, we are."

"Well, we ain't goin' anywhere. We use this bridge to get back and forth to town, and so do our neighbors. Our tax dollars built this bridge, and we ain't gonna let a bunch of Soetoro's soldier boys blow it up. You people get in your helicopter and get the hell outta here."

"There are ten of us, Mr. Lipscomb, and we're all armed."

"I ain't packin'. My wife and daughter ain't packin'. But if we have to go home and get our rifles and start shootin', we will. You people ain't blowin' up this bridge without a fight...and that's my final word."

Crislip walked over to the guardrail on the edge of the bridge and looked down. The soldiers in the riverbed had finished placing the charges under the bridge and were unrolling det cord.

He turned around and found Lipscomb beside him.

"You people must be idiots," Lipscomb said. "Blowin' a bridge in the middle of the Texas panhandle ain't no way to win friends. You think that'll make us submit?" He spat onto the pavement. "When they hear about this glorious military raid in Austin, no doubt they'll decide to drag Texas back to Soetoro's slimy embrace, kiss his shitty ass, and beg for forgiveness."

Crislip tried to decide what to do.

"Meanwhile the folks who live around here ain't got no bridge, thanks to the United States Army and Barry Soetoro."

The colonel examined his options. He could have his soldiers drag these three people off this bridge and blow it. Or he could tell the Lipscombs to go get their rifles and blow it while they were gone. Or...

He took a deep breath of that foul stink of cow shit. "How the hell do you stand the smell?" he asked Lipscomb.

Lipscomb sniffed the air. "Oh, the cows. You get used to it."

Kevin Crislip grew up in Des Moines, son of a lawyer. His mother's father had been a farmer, growing corn on three sections of land every summer. Kevin had loved his visits to his grandparents' farm. There he learned to drive a tractor, shoot a rifle—learned what hard work was.

After four years at West Point and twenty-three years in the army, four deployments in two wars, here he was standing in the darkness on a bridge in the middle of nowhere breathing that pure Texas smell, arguing with a rancher who really didn't deserve to lose his bridge to make Barry Soetoro happy.

The colonel made his decision. He leaned over the guardrail of the bridge. "Lieutenant," he called.

"Yes, sir."

"There's been a change of plans. Remove the charges from under the bridge, and let's go back to Colorado."

"Ahh..."

"Do it," the colonel said.

"Yes, sir."

And that is what they did. The three Lipscombs were still standing in the middle of the bridge when the twin-rotor helicopter lifted off with all the soldiers aboard.

With the electricity off in much of east Texas, the prison, its power provided by emergency generators, seemed an oasis of light that Saturday evening. Although it was only six and darkness was several hours away, the institution's floodlights were all lit. That was an irony that didn't escape the seven armed men in National Guard camo uniforms who pulled up to the main gate in two Humvees with fresh Lone Star flag insignia painted on the doors. Behind them was a National Guard bus that contained another ten soldiers, also sporting newly painted Lone Star flags.

"It's after visiting hours," the bored gate guard said. The officer in charge, a colonel, displayed a letter. He passed it through the window to the guard, who picked up a telephone on his desk and made a call.

From his right front seat in the Humvee, the colonel had a good view of the star-shaped building, the tiny barred windows, the guard towers, and the double-chain-link fence topped by concertina wire that encircled the entire facility. Popular legend had it that there had never been an escape from the prison, and the colonel could see why.

After a few minutes, the guard said, "I'm going to open the gate and you drive in and park by the stairs. Someone will be down shortly to escort you."

That is how it went. Ten minutes later the colonel, whose name was embroidered on his left chest, and a captain were sitting in the warden's office. The warden was eating from a heaping plate on his desk, apparently his supper.

The colonel passed the warden the letter, which was on the stationery of the governor, now president, of Texas. The warden dropped his eyes to the signature. Jack Hays.

The warden, Arlen Kirkpatrick, was forty or so pounds overweight, was balding, and had prominent jowls. Kirkpatrick picked up a bite of fried chicken with his fingers as he started to read. He read in silence. In the document, President Hays summarily relieved him, thanked him for his past service, and appointed Colonel Ezekiel Holly in his place. Warden Kirkpatrick was told to report to the Bureau of Corrections as soon as possible to be reassigned or, if he wished, placed on the retired list.

He read the letter quickly, abandoned his dinner, then read it again much slower.

He dropped the two sheets of paper on the desk and looked at the colonel. "What did I do to earn this honor?"

"Obviously, the president is putting the military in charge of the prisons for the time being. He said he intends to see that you are reassigned to another prison when the crisis is past."

Kirkpatrick shook his head in amazement. "Colonel Holly, someone has lost their senses. Soldiers aren't trained to run prisons. Our inmates are some of the worst in the system. Only a fool would send you here."

"You are entitled to your opinion."

Kirkpatrick picked up the letter and read aloud, "The Republic can no longer afford the past level of outlay on prisons.... Having full faith and confidence in Colonel Ezekiel Holly, I have ordered him to assess the prison population at your facility and recommend which prisoners should be released early."

The warden stared at Holly. "Does this mean..."

"Indeed, there may be some early releases," Colonel Holly said with a curt nod. "Texas is fighting for its life and must save dollars wherever it can. The president thought extraordinary measures were necessary."

"I must verify this with the president," the warden said.

"Certainly."

"But I cannot. The electricity is out and the telephones are dead."

Colonel Holly's face was impassive.

"I will not admit you to the prison proper until I can verify this with President Hays."

"Just how do you propose to do that?" Holly asked softly.

"Well, wait until power is restored, I suppose."

"Mr. Kirkpatrick. I have sixteen armed soldiers with me. Do I have to bring these troops in here and forcibly remove you from this office?"

"Now see here—"

"If that is what I need to do, please excuse me." Colonel Holly stood. "I must be about it. I have my orders."

"Sit, Colonel, sit. Please." Arlen Kirkpatrick knew when he was beaten. He pushed his unfinished dinner out of the way. "What can I do to help?"

"Bring your senior staffers in, tell them you have been relieved, and go home."

"Only the night guards are here. We are finishing the dinner hour, then the prisoners will be locked down for the night."

"That will do."

"What do you intend to do, Colonel?"

"That isn't your problem. As I said, I have my orders. I suggest you make a copy of that letter, keep the original, and let me have the copy."

Arlen Kirkpatrick rose from behind his desk, made the copy on a machine in the outer office, called in the senior people on the night shift, and introduced Holly. The warden shook hands all around, the guards wished him well, and then he departed, leaving his half-eaten dinner on the desk.

Holly called for the records. His armed staff found seats in the outer office while the night shift, mostly guards, carried in the records in alphabetical order.

Holly read for several hours as darkness fell and made notes. He sent the captain and the senior NCO, a staff sergeant, to ensure the prisoners were indeed locked in their cells. Then he sat in the warden's office and watched the security monitor high on the wall shift automatically around the security doors and corridors. About midnight, the guards were called in. "Gentlemen, we are sending all of you home for the evening."

"You can't do that," one of the guards said curtly. "Regulations require—"

"The military is now in charge of this facility. With the prisoners locked up, I have enough men to see that they remain behind bars through the night. Report tomorrow at your usual shift time."

The guards didn't want to go, but Ezekiel Holly looked stern and every inch a senior military officer used to being obeyed. They went by the armory, turned in their weapons, which were locked up, and filed to the courtyard in front of the prison for their cars. One of the soldiers closed the gate behind them. Soldiers replaced guards at key checkpoints throughout the prison.

The colonel nodded at the security monitor. "Get all the tapes, or if the feed goes on a computer, the hard drive."

When that was done, the colonel led a half-dozen soldiers, all that remained after the guard positions within the prison and at the gate were manned, to the security checkpoint outside Cell Block A. When they got there, the colonel consulted a list he had made from examining the files.

"James Abbott," the colonel said. "Bring him here." Two soldiers left their weapons on the desk and went through the checkpoint. Another manned the panel that opened the cell doors in the block.

In a few minutes, Abbott appeared. He was a pasty-faced man of medium height with a prominent spare tire. His hands were cuffed into a wide leather belt that encircled his waist, and he had cuffs on his ankles that were held together with about fifteen inches of chain. He had lively eyes and a semipermanent smile upon his lips. One of the Texas Guard soldiers that had accompanied Holly to the prison stood behind him.

"Mr. Abbott, according to your file, you were convicted of raping and murdering four girls. The Texas Rangers believed you raped and murdered at least six other girls over a period of nine years, but you refused to admit the crimes or tell where the bodies were buried."

Abbott said nothing, merely looked from face to face with nervous eyes, wearing that smirk.

"You were sentenced to life in prison without parole."

The smirk didn't change.

"Do you want to tell us now how many other young women you murdered?"

"You're shitting me, right?"

In the silence that followed, Ezekiel Holly looked at his list. When he looked up, Abbott had said nothing and was still wearing that semi-permanent smirk.

Holly nodded at two of the guards who were still wearing sidearms.

The soldiers grasped Abbott, one on each arm, and started leading him to the corridor that led to the courtyard one story below.

"Hey," Abbott said, trying to resist. "Where are you taking me?" That is when he really looked at the face of the soldier on his left side. "I know you," he shrieked. "You are the brother of—"

He refused to walk, so the soldiers dragged him along, supporting his weight.

A minute later a young man was brought in, also wearing shackles and manacles.

"Jason Brodski. Apparently you opened fire with an assault rifle in a movie theater and killed a dozen people and wounded thirty-three more. Your attorneys argued that you were insane, and the jury rejected that defense. They convicted you but couldn't agree on the death penalty, so you were sentenced to life without parole. Is that correct?"

A sneer crossed Brodski's lips. He was a slightly built white man with a mop of unruly black hair and pimples. "Yeah," he said.

"Mr. Brodski, the world has turned. The Republic of Texas is not going to force taxpayers to pay for your maintenance and medical care, nor for the guards to watch you. You will be executed tonight."

"What the fuck! You can't do that! Goddamn, I know my rights. I want my lawyer. I—"

Holly nodded to the two armed soldiers near Brodski, who grabbed his upper arms and removed him through the open security door along the corridor. The smell of feces was in the air. Holly glanced down the corridor and saw a dark stain spreading on the seat of Brodski's pants.

The next prisoner was standing in front of Holly when the muffled sound of a shot could be heard through the window overlooking the interior basketball court.

"What was that?" the prisoner, a Latino, asked nervously. "What the fuck is going on here?" He had a thick accent, glowered, and shifted from foot to foot.

"Alfredo Mendez, citizen of Mexico. Apparently you were an assassin for a Mexican drug syndicate, and you were convicted of murdering six men with an automatic weapon as they sat in a Del Rio beer joint."

Mendez merely glared. "What the hell is this, anyway?"

Another muffled shot could be heard from the basketball court.

Alfredo Mendez looked around wildly as the first two soldiers returned carrying the empty shackles and manacles. They handed them to the unarmed soldiers and grabbed Mendez.

"*Madre de Dios*! No! I can pay. My *patron* swore—"

The soldiers took Mendez down the corridor, still swearing and shouting.

The next man was a hulking black with scars on his face and tattoos on his knuckles and forehead. He had apparently been spending a lot of time in the weight room, because he was heavily bulked up.

"James Elvin Dallas," Colonel Holly said. He looked Dallas straight in the eyes as he recited, "You were convicted of raping three women. Then, while in prison, you beat a man to death, apparently because he refused to be your butt-boy. It is thought you killed another with a homemade shiv, but you were never charged due to lack of evidence."

"So?"

"Did you ever wonder what became of your victims?" Holly's eyes scrutinized Dallas' face.

Dallas' eyes were roaming, measuring the men in the room.

Another shot was heard from the courtyard.

James Elvin Dallas went nuts. He lunged sideways and tried for the rifle on the table. Four of the soldiers tried to subdue him. That task was only accomplished when one of the soldiers struck him repeatedly on the head with a rifle butt. As Dallas lay immobilized upon the floor, Holly pulled his service pistol and, from a distance of one foot, shot him between the eyes. Brains and blood splattered across the concrete floor.

"Take him to the courtyard," Holly ordered, "and shoot him again."

The next prisoner was large and sloppy, with greasy, curly black hair springing from his head and his chest. He had a full beard too—something that had been banned in Texas until last year. "Muzzaffan Mehsud. You were convicted of throwing acid in your wife's face because she went shopping without your permission. You were sentenced to twenty years."

The man spat at Holly, who merely nodded to the soldiers. They took Mehsud away as he shouted, over and over, "*Allahu Akbar.*"

After three more men were removed from Cell Block A, the colonel led his soldiers to Cell Block B.

"Francisco Colon, you are a serial rapist. At least six girls, none older than fourteen."

"You fuck! I know my rights. You can't revisit a sentence."

"Did you ever wonder what happened to the girls you raped?"

"Everyone heard the shots from the courtyard. You can't get away with this."

"One of the girls, Judy Martinez, committed suicide six months ago. She had been in psychiatric care for four years. Apparently she could never come to grips with the fact that animals like you roam the streets. Her father paid ten thousand dollars to hear that you were dead."

"Fuck you!" Colon lowered his head and launched himself at Holly. He didn't get there. The men on either side dropped him on his face on the concrete floor, smashing his nose and releasing a torrent of blood. Semiconscious from the impact, he was carried to the courtyard.

The next man was a white man, medium-sized, with a full head of hair. He could even be called handsome. He was calm. "We heard shots. Are you executing people?"

"Robert Winston Carrington. You were convicted of running a Ponzi scheme that took in over twelve million dollars, most of which you squandered to pay for an extravagant lifestyle."

Carrington glanced at the bloodstain on the floor from Colon's nose, then his eyes came back to Holly. "I didn't kill anybody," he said.

"Did it ever occur to you," Ezekiel Holly said conversationally, "that prisons exist for two reasons? The first of course is to keep the guilty in, and the second is to keep the victims out."

"They were all greedy bastards and got what they deserved."

"As we all shall, rest assured. Two of your victims committed suicide. Many were reduced to penury after a lifetime of work because they believed in you, trusted you. We are here tonight as surrogates for your victims."

Holly nodded at the soldiers, and they took Robert Winston Carrington away. He walked with his head high. Maybe, thought Colonel Holly, he doesn't believe he will really be executed. Or, perhaps, he doesn't care.

Three minutes later another shot was heard.

When Colonel Holly and his soldiers left the prison at three that morning, thirty-two corpses were laid out side by side on the prison basketball court, where they were found by the day shift.

Warden Arlen Kirkpatrick was summoned, and he sent a man to Austin. When the man returned two days later, he reported that no one at the Bureau of Prisons, in the governor's office, or at Texas Guard headquarters had ever heard of Ezekiel Holly. The governor's signature on the letter was a forgery.

Perhaps fingerprints might have identified Colonel Holly, but all the other soldiers wore tactical gloves. When the Texas Rangers finally sent a man around to hunt for prints, more than a week had passed and the task was hopeless.

TWENTY-NINE

★

"We leave tomorrow," Jake Grafton said on Sunday morning.

Boy, that was good news to me!

Sarah Houston was carrying the little girl around, everywhere, and gave me The Look every time she passed me, as if it were my fault the kid got raped. She didn't even say anything about my neck wound. Mrs. Johnson was a nurse and bandaged me up after she had smeared some sort of antiseptic on it. My neck was so sore I couldn't turn my head.

Willie Varner said, "Goddamn, Tommy. You keep lettin' these sons of bitches shoot at you. It's just a matter of time, dude."

"Hey, Willie, I—"

"Don't want to hear it. I done tol' ya. Just a matter of time. Ain't goin' to cry at your funeral, Tommy. Sarah might, or Mizz Grafton, but I ain't a gonna. See you in Hell, dude, and we'll catch up then."

"I can hardly wait. Thanks, asshole."

"You're welcome."

I was fed up to here. I broke out the two sniper rifles from FEMA's Walmart stash and took them down to the meadow. Put a target out at two hundred yards—measured with one of the laser rangefinders the military had thoughtfully included in the box—and laid down by the hangar. Used a box of MREs as a rest and commenced shooting. The rifles were .308 caliber, actual designation 7.62x51 NATO, and we had plenty of ammo. I played with them a while and got them zeroed. Just in case.

I am not a sniper: I am not good enough with a rifle, and I don't have the patience for it. However, the concept of whacking bad guys from beyond the effective range of their weapons strongly appeals to me. I have no sporting instinct whatsoever and am a disciple of W. C. Fields: Never give a sucker an even break, and its corollary, do it unto others before they do it unto you.

When I got back to the safe house, the sun was down. In the twilight everyone was sitting around outside eating venison that I had shot, Molina and Yocke had butchered, and Jake Grafton had cooked on the outdoor fire. Burned on the outside, pink in the middle. Everyone but me complimented him on his outdoor culinary skills. To accompany the venison we also had Mrs. Price's green beans and baked potatoes with margarine and ketchup, for those so inclined. With the smell of wood smoke in the delightful evening air and plenty of good, wholesome food, some of the folks around the fire looked like they were dumping some stress. The meal was filling and a nice change from MREs, but I wasn't ready to sing Kumbaya.

I figured that there was a lot of shooting and dying coming up in the days ahead. Going to Washington to clean up the government wasn't on my bucket list.

But what the hell! A man can only die once. That's a good thing, by the way. We've all gotta go sometime, and, truth be told, the sooner you check out, the more shit you miss. That's the gospel according to Reverend Carmellini. Amen.

The girl spent the evening sitting by Sarah Houston. Armanti was sitting with Mrs. Price. The Johnsons were huddled together, the parents taking care of the kids. Yocke and Molina sat engaged in earnest conversation, solving the nation's problems, probably. The warriors kept by themselves, although they had included Willie Varner in their little group. They liked Willie's brand of pessimism, I suspected: I certainly did.

After the fire died down to glowing coals, Sarah Houston picked up the kid and carried her into the house. I waited a moment, then tagged along. I found them upstairs in the bedroom we had been using, and the door was open a crack. I eavesdropped. It's one of my failings. But, to paraphrase that great American philosopher Yogi Berra, you can learn a lot by listening.

"My name is Sarah too," the girl said.

"We have a lot in common," Sarah Houston said warmly.

"I saw that man shoot my parents. He was really mean. He hurt me terrible down there. Then Mister Tommy shot him and his whole head came off. After what he did to me, I was glad." I knew that Mrs. Johnson, the nurse, gave the kid a vaginal exam and had to do some stitches, after she had numbed her.

"I suppose so," Sarah Houston said. "Tommy is a good man. Was your father a good man?"

"Oh yes. He wasn't tall, and he was sort of heavy, not a bit like Mister Tommy. But he loved me very much. So did Mommy."

After a bit I heard Sarah Houston say, "I am sure you will miss them very much."

"Mommy and Daddy loved me."

"I am sure they did."

"I like Mister Armanti too. He's a real nice man. Sort of like a bear."

The two sat in silence for a while, then the big Sarah said, "You and I are going to sleep right here. If you have a nightmare, you wake me up. Will you do that?"

"Daddy always read me a book before bed."

"I don't have any books. Maybe I can tell you a story, after you get in bed."

Five minutes later Sarah began, "Once upon a time..."

A half hour later, Sarah came out. I was sitting on the top of the stairs. She sat down beside me.

"That kid has been through a hell of a lot."

"I guess."

"She's in denial right now. Sooner or later the implications of the murder of her parents, rape, all that is going to hit her hard. She is only eight years old and she saw all that mayhem."

"God help her," I murmured.

"You can sleep on the couch downstairs."

"Okay."

"Oh, Tommy. What a disaster...for all of us."

"Yes."

I put my arm around her. After a while she said, "I'm staying here when you leave tomorrow. Someone has to take care of this child."

"Okay."

"Will you come back? Afterward?"

"You can bet your life on it."

Sunday evening two Muslim male refugees from Syria, ages nineteen and twenty, raped a thirteen-year-old black girl in St. Louis. She screamed and they beat her. Despite the perilous state of law enforcement in St. Louis after a week of rioting in the black neighborhoods, the police apprehended the pair. They were taken to a police lockup.

That night a crowd of almost eight hundred people, mostly black, surrounded the police station. These were not ghetto dwellers, but middle-class suburbanites, and many were armed. They held the police at gunpoint and removed the two rapists from the cells. The two were taken outside and hanged by their necks from a nearby tree with ropes some members of the crowd had thoughtfully brought along.

Then the crowd, now containing about 1,500 people, walked in a body to the downtown mosque that the imam had made infamous by preaching jihad from the pulpit; the mosque, incidentally, where the two rapists had worshiped. The crowd found the cleric cowering in a closet in a nearby house, dragged him outside, and hanged him too. The mosque was set on fire.

While the imam dangled and strangled, a few people in the crowd fired some shots in the air and shouted catcalls, but mainly the crowd was quiet. Some police officers sat on the hoods of their cruisers, watching and smoking. An intrepid television cameraman filmed the holy man swinging in the wind for broadcast whenever. An hour or so later, the crowd began to dissipate and trudge away into the night.

Amazingly, the energy seemed to go out of the rioters in other sections of town, many of whom actually went home. For the first time since Barry Soetoro declared martial law, the hours from midnight to dawn on Labor Day were quiet in St. Louis.

At nine o'clock that Labor Day morning, a convoy of two companies of Marines from Quantico arrived at the Pentagon. A colonel was there to meet the company commanders, both captains. After a short conversation, the troops set up machine guns inside sandbagged positions at the entrances to the Pentagon, other Marines were sent to guard the Metro station downstairs (even though it wasn't running) and to guard the entrances to the parking lots. They set up a bivouac on an empty section of the vast parking lot on the western side of the massive building, a lot that looked relatively empty because, despite the crisis engulfing the nation, many of the civilians had Labor Day off.

The chairman of the Joint Chiefs, General Martin Wynette, knew nothing about the Marines' arrival. He was upstairs in his office on the E-Ring going over readiness reports from the U.S. armed forces around the world, with special attention to those units in the United States. The United States armed forces were in full mutiny, he said to his staff after a quick perusal of the reports. People in uniform willing to fight for Barry Soetoro against Americans were a rare commodity. The only bright spot was the Marines in Southern California, who had strapped on the Mexican military as though they were God's gift to starving men. At last, an enemy to shoot at. The crews of the navy's two carriers now cruising off the coast of San Diego were apparently happy as pigs in slop launching strikes at the Mexican invaders. They had achieved complete control of the air, left Mexican armor burned-out wrecks, destroyed Mexican staging areas on the American side of the border, and flown support missions for the Marines. It was a proverbial turkey shoot.

The rioting Mexicans in the slums of LA weren't the military's problem. What the civil authorities were going to do about them was up to Barry Soetoro and the politicians in LA and Sacramento who wanted those Hispanic votes more than they wanted salvation. If they wanted salvation, which was doubtful.

Martin Wynette was trying to figure out what he was going to tell the president and his disciples when he went over to the White House to brief them at eleven o'clock when a group of flag officers led by CNO Admiral Cart McKiernan came into his office unannounced and closed the door. The commandant of the Marine Corps was there, as well as the deputy chiefs of staff of the army and air force. The four officers stood in front of the desk looking down on Wynette.

"Marty," said the commandant, Morton Runyon, "tell us why you threw Sugar Ray, Jack Williams (the army chief of staff), and Harry Miller (the air force chief) to the wolves."

Wynette stood up. "You don't know what you are talking about."

"We've talked to Major General Stout, who was there at the White House with you. Remember?"

"Now, listen, people. Someone told Soetoro that a coup was being planned over here in the Pentagon. He already knew. What could I say?"

"He didn't know shit, Marty. Schanck tried a shot in the dark and you spilled your guts. You pulled the trigger on Sugar, Jack, and Harry."

"Well, Jesus, they *were* planning a coup! Talking about it, anyway. For Christ's sake, he's the *commander-in-chief.* He's the *president*!"

"And you took an oath *to support and defend the Constitution of the United States.* Soetoro has become a dictator. He's ripped up the Constitution."

"These are perilous times," Wynette explained. "The president has a right to do whatever is required to maintain the government. You know that."

"He doesn't have the right to convert the country into a dictatorship," Cart McKiernan said, and made an angry gesture. "But we aren't here to debate politics. This has gone too damned far. Three senior officers were executed without a trial in the courtyard downstairs. This isn't Nazi Germany or Soviet Russia. Get your head out of your ass, Marty."

Wynette sank into his chair and his gaze went from face to face.

"What do you want of me?" he said softly.

The CNO, who was in short-sleeve summer whites, nodded to the commandant, who was in greens. He lifted his blouse and pulled out a pistol. "This is yours, Marty. I stopped by your quarters and your wife let me in. I got this from the desk in your study."

Martin Wynette stared at the faces. "I'm not going to shoot myself, if that is what you are implying."

"We'll call Mrs. Ray. What is her name? Naomi, I think. Maybe she'll do it for you. Or Barry Soetoro can send his goons over to do you in the courtyard."

Wynette said nothing. He was sweating and licking his lips.

Morton Runyon walked around the desk and fooled around with the pistol. Then, quick as a flash, as Wynette looked at the other officers, he put it to the right side of Wynette's head and pulled the trigger. Blood, tissue, and little pieces of skull spurted out the other side. Wynette slumped in the chair.

Runyon picked up Wynette's dead hand, put it around the pistol, got fingerprints all over it, then dropped the gun on the floor.

"Damn," said Cart McKiernan. "I think he shot himself. Get the staff in here for the bad news."

★

Jake Grafton sat everyone down after breakfast and announced that Mr. and Mrs. Johnson and their children were staying at the safe house, along with Mrs. Price and the young Sarah. "Armanti, would you be willing to stay here with them and keep an eye on things?"

"Yes, sir," Armanti Hall said.

"I'm staying too," Sarah Houston announced.

"No, you're not," Jake Grafton said, eyeing her. "Too much is at stake."

Sarah looked at me, then shrugged.

"Uh, Admiral," said Willie Varner. "Maybe I could stay too. I ain't much of a shooter and all, and—"

"We may need your lock skills," Grafton said crisply. "Tommy, load the trucks. Leave what you can for the people who are staying, and let

Armanti keep whatever weapons he might need. Pistols for all the adults who want one."

"What about the plane?" I asked.

"I'll fly it. Mr. Johnson has given me his permission and the ignition key. Take me down to the hangar and let's get it out."

We pulled the plane from the hangar, spun it around, and I helped Grafton in. He wasn't spry and obviously had some discomfort, but he seemed able to move without pain.

He looked over a sectional chart that Johnson had used to get here, and said, "You get everything loaded up. I'll be back in about an hour."

He started the engine, taxied down to the far end of the runway, swung the plane around, and ran the engine up to a pleasant hum. I looked at the sky: clear above, hazy, only a couple of knots from the north, just enough to stir the wind sock a little. The morning dew hadn't yet burned off in the sunny places, so people and the plane left tracks in the grass. If you didn't know any better you'd think it was just another late summer day in paradise.

After a moment the Cessna accelerated down the runway with its tail-wheel off the ground and got airborne. It flew away to the north, climbing slowly. The plane got smaller and smaller and more indistinct, then it merged into the haze and the sound of the engine faded completely away.

The guys and I loaded the trucks. Willie the Wire did some bitching. "Hell, he don't need me to open locks when he's got you."

"The only place you know how to rustle grub is in a grocery store," I said. "You eat too much to leave you here."

"We get back to Washington, dude, there ain't gonna be no grocery stores. Not ones with anythin' in them to eat, anyway. Did you think of that?"

"No liquor stores or beer joints either," Armanti offered. "Gonna be like Baghdad or Damascus. Nice of you to share the pain, Willie."

Willie Varner said a crude phrase.

"Look on the bright side," I suggested, just to buck him up. "It couldn't be as bad as the sewers of Cairo. Did I ever tell you about the month I—"

"You too, Carmellini."

Sarah Houston and I got to spend a few minutes with young Sarah before we left. The girl was sobbing, finally letting her emotions out, which was a good thing. The Sarahs put their foreheads together and hugged. Finally Sarah kissed the kid and said, "I'll be back."

On the way down the hill, I told her, "You're optimistic."

"Live every day until you die," she retorted. Then she touched the pistol butt in its holster on her web belt. I doubt if she even realized she did it.

"You're taking your computer along, I see."

"Yes."

"When do you suppose you'll get a chance to use it?"

"You never know."

When Grafton landed, he said the roads were clear to the airport in Elkins, which looked deserted. "Before we go, run me down to that clinic."

"Okay."

In Greenbank Dr. Proudfoot didn't seem surprised when Grafton and I walked through his door. He and Grafton shook hands.

"Could we have a little talk in your office?" Grafton asked him.

While they were talking, I went into the room where Mrs. Greenwood was. She was still in a coma. The nurse and I chatted.

After about fifteen minutes, Grafton and the doctor came back. "Dr. Proudfoot is going with us. He needs to run up to his house for some things, and he'll join us at the hangar."

Back at the hangar, Grafton spread out the sectional chart and our one roadmap on the hood of my pickup, and Travis, Willis Coffee, and I studied them.

"If there are rebels around," Grafton said, "I suspect we will find them at Camp Dawson, where FEMA had their concentration camp. I want to fly up to Elkins, wait for you there, and then we'll fuel the plane if we can and I'll fly up to Dawson and look around. If it's safe, we can all go."

"Why Dawson?" Travis asked.

"A National Guard base figures to have an armory. People with deer rifles are guerillas. To turn them into an army you need machine guns, mortars, and artillery, if you can find some."

Right then I began to suspect that Grafton wasn't leveling with us. Maybe everyone else thought he was, but I was no virgin. I had worked with him too many times in the past. I kicked myself for not cornering him several days ago and getting the lowdown. If anything happened to Jake Grafton, Sarah and I and all these other fools were going to be up the proverbial creek without a paddle. Too late to brace him now, though.

Grafton got back in the plane and we climbed into the trucks. The doc and Sarah rode with me. As we rolled along he wanted to talk about Jake Grafton. He was obviously star-struck and called him "Admiral" in every sentence, finishing with, "You didn't tell me he was a retired admiral."

"I didn't think it mattered."

"Or director of the CIA. Why didn't you say so?"

"Because I didn't want you telling anyone anything." I turned my head and locked my eyes on him.

Dr. Proudfoot got uncomfortable and shifted his eyes to the road ahead. "Well, I'm glad he asked me to go along. It's a great honor."

I thought he should talk to Willie Varner about that, but I kept my mouth shut and drove. Sarah just sat looking out the window.

The JCS staff was shocked by the suicide of General Martin Wynette. Still, everyone knew he had been under tremendous pressure from the White House, and after the deputy chairman and the army and air force chiefs of staff were summarily executed by Secret Service personnel, his personal choice to end his own life was understandable, if tragic. While his remains were being carried away to a freezer in the cafeteria, to wait for a better day for his funeral and burial, the four surviving heads of their services met in a conference room behind locked doors.

"Gentlemen," Cart McKiernan said, "we have some critical decisions to make, and not much time to make them. We must announce Wynette's demise, and no doubt the White House will have a serious reaction to the news. Either Soetoro will send people over here to take over the Pentagon, or he will think this is the start of a putsch. Your thoughts, please."

The army deputy chief Franklin Rodriquez said, "I think it would be a terrible precedent if the armed forces were involved in decapitating a president or in assisting a popular uprising to overthrow him. Or in assisting in keeping a hated president in office in the face of a revolution. In my opinion, the best thing for America is for the armed forces to remain neutral."

"As if we could," Morton Runyon scoffed. "We're already up to our necks in this."

The acting air force chief of staff, Erhard "Bud" Weiss, said, "We can't win, gentlemen. If we fight for or against Soetoro the people will never trust us again. We must let the American people sort this out."

Rodriquez tapped his chest. "This isn't the uniform of Barry Soetoro's army; it's the uniform of the United States Army. There's a big difference. And this afternoon the order is going out to every army commander: we're not arresting civilians anymore, and we're releasing the political prisoners from every army-run camp."

The Marine commandant's gaze went from face to face. "Well, that's a start, but I think we should go over to the White House, drag Soetoro and his staff out into the Rose Garden, and execute them. That prick is a traitor! He violated his oath to uphold the Constitution. He ordered officers murdered without trial. He deserves a bullet. I volunteer to take a company of Marines across the river and personally deliver one between that bastard's eyes."

"You're wrong, Mort," Bud Weiss said. "The military *must* remain neutral. We must publicly announce it. Confine all our forces to base. Defend ourselves, yes. But not take sides. California is a different story. Southern California has been invaded by the Mexican Army. It's our job to defend America and shove them back."

"What about defending America from Soetoro?" grumbled the Marine Corps commandant.

Cart McKiernan took his time before he spoke. "Mort, you know damn well we can't lead a revolution. But that said, I'm going to start carrying a pistol, and if I ever come face to face with Soetoro, I'm going to exercise my rights as a free American and shoot him dead. Now let's get the staff in here and get orders drafted. All offensive operations against Texas and other states are to stop immediately. All forces in the United States are confined to base except in Southern California. Bud, you are going to have to use the air force to supply our forces in SoCal. The navy will cooperate fully. Are we in agreement?"

"You understand that if we wash our hands of the Soetoro administration, Barry Soetoro is doomed," Franklin Rodriquez remarked.

"That's up to the American people," McKiernan shot back. "Our problem is to preserve the American armed forces to defend future generations of Americans from foreign threats. I repeat, are we agreed?"

They were. They opened the door and the staff trooped in for orders.

The news that General Martin L. Wynette, chairman of the Joint Chiefs, had committed suicide in his office was merely a footnote to the press release issued by the Pentagon. Henceforth, the release announced, United States armed forces would take no part in or play any role in the political problems the country was enduring. All offensive operations were canceled, all troops confined to base, all ships ordered into port, and all airplanes grounded. Except, however, in Southern California, where United States forces were actively engaged in armed combat with invading forces from Mexico. The statement went further: "Unless the Republic of Mexico desires a wider war with the United States, it will recall its troops from United States soil immediately. If all Mexican forces are not back across the international border within twenty-four hours, United States forces will attack Mexican forces wherever they can be found."

"Those Pentagon bastards just revolted against the government and issued an ultimatum to the government of Mexico!" Al Grantham roared as he read the press release. "What in hell is going on over there?"

He found out within two minutes. An icy Cart McKiernan told Grantham on the scrambled telephone, "You people at the White House are on your own, Grantham. We won't obey your orders and we won't fight rebel forces. We will defend the Pentagon and armed forces bases worldwide, and kick the shit out of Mexico if they don't wise up fast."

"This is mutiny, McKiernan. Treason. You know the penalty for treason."

"Label it anything you like."

"Are you demanding that President Soetoro resign?"

"I don't think anyone on this side of the Potomac gives a flying fuck what Barry Soetoro does or doesn't do. Please tell him I said so." And Admiral Cart McKiernan hung up on Al Grantham.

THIRTY

★

We were sitting in our pickups in the parking lot of the little one-story brick office building at the Elkins airport when Jake Grafton landed in the Cessna tail-dragger and taxied up. He shut down, got out of the plane, and came strolling over. It looked to me as if his ribs weren't hurting him too badly; his stride was almost normal.

Willis Coffee and Travis Clay had gone up the road to the main entrance of the airport and were settled in there behind trees, just in case.

Except for the two on guard duty, we gathered around Grafton. "Okay," he said. "The road to Dawson is open. I'll take Yocke with me in the plane. The rest of you drive on up there. There is a roadblock about five miles from the southern entrance, but they know you're coming and will let you through. Any questions?"

"Yeah," Jack Yocke said angrily. "Just what the hell is going on?"

"We're joining the revolutionary army," Jake Grafton said calmly, as if that were as plain as the nose on his face.

"Did you land there?"

"No. I talked to them via radio. Tommy," he said, "keep yours handy. Call me on one-twenty-two point nine if you have any trouble. I'll be listening on that freq."

"But who's there?" Yocke asked, his puzzlement evident.

"We'll find out when we get there."

He walked back to his plane with Yocke trailing along. The admiral climbed in, and in less than twenty seconds the prop began turning, a little cloud of black smoke puffed from the exhaust, then the prop spun up to a blur as the engine settled into a nice idle. He swung the tail of the bird with a little blast of power and began taxiing for takeoff.

Sarah and I were sitting in the front seats of the truck, Dr. Proudfoot in the back, when the Cessna lifted off and turned northward.

"Well," Sarah said with a sigh, "let's go to the war."

"You knew all about this, didn't you?" I growled.

She glanced at me and smiled. "*He is Jake Grafton*, Tommy. You, of all people, should have known that he'd be a mile ahead of Barry Soetoro on the best day Soetoro ever had."

I couldn't think of a thing to say. We picked up Willis and Travis at the airport entrance and headed up the asphalt ribbon through the mountains for Camp Dawson.

On the way I fiddled with the radio. Got a station with a seductive female on the mike who said her name was Dixie Cotton. She read the latest news releases from Washington, including one from the Pentagon that said they would no longer fight Americans, on whichever side of the political spectrum, and the ultimatum to Mexico. I wondered if that threat would frighten the Mexicans.

I found myself rubbing my sore neck and, to take my mind off it, kept playing with the radio. I finally got a station that identified itself as being in Kingwood, West Virginia, which I knew was just a mile or two up the road from Camp Dawson. "Guess the folks up there have their power back," I said brightly.

Sarah just grunted.

"Hey, electricity means commodes flush. Don't knock it."

The announcer was telling people in the Kingwood area which stores were open, where they could buy food and fuel. The senior center was open, she said, and would feed anyone who was hungry.

Maybe America was starting to get back to normal. I rubbed my sore neck some more.

★

A reporter came crashing into the governor's office in the parking garage under the Austin hotel with the Pentagon press release, which his newspaper had downloaded off the satellite. An aide took it into Jack Hays, who was in a meeting with bankers, college professors, and Dallas Federal Reserve officials. The subject of the meeting was the new Texas currency. As one of the Fed's bankers, now working for the Republic of Texas, held forth on the value of money, Hays read the press release.

Hays held up his hand, which silenced the moneymen. He read the press release aloud, all of it, including the ultimatum to Mexico.

The bankers cheered. "We've won!"

"If this is true," Jack Hays muttered, too softly for anyone to hear.

He sent an aide to find his cousin JR.

The bankers were leaving when JR came in, so they all had to tell him the news and shake hands and congratulate him. "Best general since Sam Houston," one of them told JR, who looked a little stunned.

With the door closed, JR read the press release. "Is this true?" he asked Jack.

"I don't know," Jack Hays said, shrugging. "But the implications are vast. Either Soetoro wants a political peace, or the U.S. armed forces have mutinied against him."

"Hadn't we better find out which it is?"

"We'll find out soon enough. If Soetoro wants a settlement, we'll be hearing from them. In the meantime, let's stop all offensive military operations until we know more."

"What about that attack boat, *Texas*?" JR asked.

"You know where she is, what she's doing?"

"Hell, no. Loren Snyder and a handful of volunteers took her to sea. Apparently they torpedoed two destroyers busy squirting off Tomahawks at our power plants, but there have been no more ships torpedoed nor has the U.S. Navy shot any more Tomahawks."

"Do we have any way to contact them?" Jack Hays asked.

"I certainly don't. I think all we can do is rely on Loren Snyder's good sense and hope for the best."

"Could you call the Pentagon and talk about this?"

"I can send them a message through the National Guard message system."

"If they try to locate and attack that submarine, your Mr. Snyder might well fight back."

"Might? Of course he will. But let's not get our knickers in a twist. Loren can take care of himself. I'll pass along a heads-up to the Pentagon, however."

President Hays leaned forward. "I've got another project for you too. Texas has roughly a billion dollars in gold on deposit in a vault in a New York bank, the Bank of Manhattan. I want you to make a withdrawal and bring that gold back to Texas. All the bankers say that backing the new Texas dollar with gold will give it instant credibility. That's their prescription for the next few years. After that, they want the Texas dollar to float so the money supply isn't linked to the price of gold, which is nothing but a commodity. We'll see how that goes, but a gold standard does sound like a place to start."

"How much does a billion dollars' worth of gold weigh?" JR asked.

Jack Hays said, "The treasurer's office said a pound or two less than forty tons. Actually, it's probably worth a lot more than a billion dollars since Soetoro shut down the markets and gave investors worldwide the jitters. In the past, state government sort of ignored the gold. It's like oil under the southeast forty or Grandma's diamond ring—no one gave it a thought. They simply talk about a billion dollars' worth of gold. However, it's there and it's ours, and now we need it."

JR whistled. "New York City," he said thoughtfully. "Forty tons."

"Ingots, I guess," Jack said. "I hope it isn't in wafers in boxes or some such thing." He grinned. "I've got a feeling that the sooner we get that gold to Texas, the better. If Soetoro knew we were coming for it, we wouldn't get it without some kind of political settlement. And there isn't going to be a political settlement between Texas and the United States with Barry Soetoro in the White House."

"I'll need some kind of paper from the treasurer, and maybe a letter from you. You know how bankers are. They'll want to paper their ass."

Jack Hays frowned. "They aren't going to turn loose of that gold without Washington's say-so even if you have a letter from Jesus. Take some guns."

"Oh, we will," JR said with a disarming smile. "Rest assured, we won't forget to pack those. But give me a letter from the treasurer and one from you."

Jack called in a secretary and dictated one. While she typed it, he called the treasurer and told him what was wanted. "He'll send it over to the Guard this afternoon," he told JR.

When he left with Jack's letter in hand, JR went to the Texas State Library and Archives building on Brazos Street. He asked to see the head librarian and told him what he wanted. Twenty minutes later he left with a copy of a letter from the White House in his hand, one congratulating some scout for achieving the rank of eagle. That kid's parents knew somebody, he thought.

His next stop was a printer at the Texas Department of Public Safety. He asked to see the head printer, and after introducing himself, presented him with the copy of the White House letter to the Eagle Scout. "I need at least four sheets of a nice white bond with the president of the United States' seal on it. Exactly like this, identical."

"Whoa. On whose say-so?"

"Mine. Or we can get the president's, or Colonel Tenney's. Whom do you want?"

"This isn't going to be used for a forgery, is it?"

"Perish the thought."

The man sighed and asked, "When do you want it?"

"Well, I have to go see Colonel Tenney upstairs. That should take no more than an hour. I'll pick it up when I finish."

"An absolute rush job will take about a week. Every office in government wants new stationery now that we're a republic again. We have—"

"One hour, or I go get Colonel Tenney and bring him here to talk to you."

The man frowned at the letter with distaste, as if JR had been using it for toilet paper, then at JR Hays. "You're serious?"

"As a heart attack."

"Who the hell are you?"

"I told you. Major General Hays, commanding the Texas Guard."

"Never heard of you. When the Guard wants something, they always send a sergeant, a gal named Dooley." He waved the letter. "But okay. One hour." Then he wheeled and marched away from the counter.

JR went upstairs to see Colonel Frank Tenney and explained the problem. "Maybe the vault will be open when we get there, but probably not. Maybe they'll open it for me, but maybe not. More than likely I'll have to help myself. I need some expert advice about how to get into a gold bullion vault."

"Forget it," Tenney said. "It can't be done. There is no way in the world to get into either of the big gold vaults in New York. Texas' gold is in the Bank of Manhattan, which has a helluva vault. But the biggest gold repository on earth, bigger than Fort Knox or the Bank of England gold vaults, is under the New York Federal Reserve Bank. They have at least five thousand tons of gold there, and it's guarded by a private army."

"Explosives?"

"Two Mosler vaults were in banks in Hiroshima when we dropped the bomb there. The banks were obliterated, but the vaults were intact. In 1957 the air force set off a thirty-seven-kiloton bomb near a vault, and it remained intact. JR, you ain't going in one of those things unless they let you in. And the chances of them doing that are essentially microscopic. Go back and tell your cousin Jack that it can't be done."

"That's probably good advice," JR acknowledged. He said good-bye and went to the Texas Treasury Department, where he had a private interview with the treasurer of the Republic. The man was prematurely bald and wore a suit and tie even though the building wasn't air-conditioned. All the juice from the emergency generator was being used to run lights and computers.

They discussed Texas' gold reserve, how many ounces and so forth.

"So where is Texas' gold?" JR Hays asked.

"Bank of Manhattan."

"Have you ever visited the facility, looked at the gold?"

"Oh yes. Impressive vault. The bank installed it when people started speculating in bullion ten or fifteen years ago. They didn't want to store the stuff at home or in a suburban safe deposit box, so the bank got into the business of storing gold for a fee. Modern facility, great vault, as secure as any vault on earth. We put about half a billion dollars of the state's funds into gold, and they stored it for us. Our gold has essentially doubled in value, so it's worth about a billion, or was until the current political difficulty arose. Probably worth twice that now."

"Good investment."

The treasurer nodded and looked pleased.

"What about the New York Federal Reserve's vault?"

"I got a tour once," the bureaucrat acknowledged. "Didn't get into the vault, of course, since they never let humans inside. The gold is moved on trolleys by remote control. Robots stack the ingots and load and offload the trolleys."

"I've heard they have a private army guarding the vault."

The treasurer nodded. "Yes, indeed. Most of what I know about the vault I picked up in casual conversation from the assistant treasurer, who used to work at the Bank of Manhattan. He wanted to get back to Texas so I hired him. Guy named Chuy Medina."

"May I talk to him?"

"Sure. Great guy. You'll like Chuy. I talked to the governor about the gold, but why are you interested in it?"

"Oh, that gold has to come back to Texas someday. We thought we should ask some questions."

"Sure."

Chuy Medina was of medium height, about fifty years of age, from McAllen, Texas, and had spent fifteen years at the Bank of Manhattan. Left two years ago when he scored a job at the Texas treasurer's office.

"Tell me about the Bank of Manhattan," JR prompted. "They have about forty tons of Texas gold, and I have been ordered to make a withdrawal."

Medina laughed. "That's a joke, right?"

"Perhaps."

"This is like some weird plot from *Mission: Impossible*. There ain't no way, man. No way at all."

"Talk to me," JR Hays said with a smile. "Convince me."

★

The FEMA concentration camp guard towers on the edge of Camp Dawson were empty when we rolled by and went between the guards at the main gate. Several of the guards were wearing old army shirts, but most were in jeans and T-shirts. They were armed to the teeth and looked to me like they knew precisely what they were doing. This might be amateur hour, but there was some military discipline and brains guiding the amateurs. There wasn't a FEMA uniform in sight.

The place was as crowded as a state fair, but without the animals. I estimated I could see over a thousand people, all adults, most in civilian clothes, all armed and doing army stuff, like working on weapons, loading trucks, and doing calisthenics. Cars were parked in rows, men wearing pistols directed us to a parking place, and a girl who looked as if she had ditched her classes in high school that afternoon escorted us toward the headquarters building, not the one in the concentration camp, but the main National Guard building. I could hear rifles popping, no doubt over at the shooting range. And a buzzing overhead. I looked up and saw a Predator drone taking off with a Hellfire under each wing.

I glanced over my shoulder and got a good gander at Sal Molina's face. The man was stunned. Almost stupefied. Obviously Grafton hadn't been whispering to him, either. If he had been doing any whispering, I supposed it was to Sarah Houston, who looked as if she were trooping up to the director's office to be given another twenty-hour-a-day assignment.

Willie Varner was looking around wide-eyed. He had been clueless too. Willis and Travis were almost as surprised as the Wire.

I confess, I was a bit pissed at Grafton. I would have bet the ranch that *he* wasn't surprised, that he well knew what we would find here. Why hadn't the spook bastard confided in me? Need-to-know and all that spy shit, I suppose.

They confiscated all cell phones as we came through the front door, and put a sticky on each one with the owner's name. Then they patted us down.

We ended up in the back of a conference room standing against the wall, all of us, including Dr. Proudfoot. Grafton was sitting at a table right up front, and that *Washington Post* weenie Jack Yocke was sitting beside him as if he were number two in the chain of command. Three big bananas, all in their fifties, were standing in front of a map that covered a blackboard, I suppose, taking turns briefing Grafton. They had started a few minutes ago, and they didn't bother starting over for us. Another dozen or so people, perhaps half of them women, all wearing pistols, were in the chairs behind Grafton and Yocke and in front of us. One was a congressman I recognized from television, Jerry Marquart.

"So our plan is to have First Corps..." Yep, I thought, these are army dudes. "...proceed east on I-Sixty-Eight to Cumberland and Hagerstown. Second Corps will go east on U.S. Route Fifty to Winchester and then to Leesburg and into the District along that route. All this is subject to change if we hit opposition or find bridges have been blown. We'll be close enough together on parallel routes that we can mass if necessary. Keep the drones up and looking, use our Special Forces veterans as scouts, and take whatever comes."

Grafton had a few questions, then asked to see the Pentagon's press release again. He read it carefully, then laid it on the table in front of him and said, "This is too good to be true."

"It could be disinformation, deception," the head dog agreed. "We don't have their crypto codes, but from all the plain-language traffic we are hearing, perhaps there is some truth in it."

"What plain-language traffic?"

"FEMA and Homeland. They are complaining bitterly that Soetoro has betrayed them."

"Even if we get into a firefight with that crowd, that doesn't mean the Pentagon's press release is inaccurate. It may only mean that the paramilitary boys are taking orders directly from the White House. If we see army troops, however, we'll know this is a pretty little lie."

"Yes, sir."

They chewed the rag about trucks, ammo, food, weapons, and all of that for another half hour, then I ducked out to find a restroom. There was toilet paper in there and the commode flushed. Life was looking up.

When I got back, the conference had broken up, the rebel officers were leaving, and only our little crowd remained. Everyone had taken seats around the conference table so they could talk to Admiral Grafton, who looked at Willie and said, “Please escort Dr. Proudfoot to the hospital. They may need his services. Is that all right with you, Doctor?”

It was, and the two of them left.

Jack Yocke jumped right in before the door shut behind them. “This rebel enclave didn’t just happen, Grafton. Someone made it happen and you knew all about it.”

“I made it happen,” Grafton said, looking around and taking in faces. “Sarah and I knew several months before Soetoro declared martial law that he was going to do it. We knew he was waiting for an incident that would justify martial law. The terrorists obliged. I have spent my adult life in the military and intelligence business. I talked to people I knew I could trust, told them Soetoro’s intentions, and asked for their help.”

“How did you know Soetoro was going to seize power? Did Molina tell you?”

“Sal, do you want to answer Yocke?”

“No,” Molina said. He had to force the word out, and it came out unnaturally loud.

“But you knew Soetoro’s plans,” Jack Yocke persisted, staring at the president’s man.

“I’m not going to—”

Grafton spoke, which cut off Molina. “Sarah.”

She was seated at the end of the table. She had her computer out of its case and was fiddling with the keyboard. “I bugged the White House,” she said, “at Admiral Grafton’s order. We used every electronic device in the White House as a listening device, including computers and cell phones.”

Molina turned ashen.

“Including yours, Mr. Molina, and President Soetoro’s.”

Molina gaped at her. The way she said it, matter-of-factly, as if she were making a report to her boss, made it impossible to disbelieve her. Then Sarah pushed a button.

The president's voice came from the speaker, quite plain. "Martial law will give us the opportunity to remake America the way it should be, take charge of industries and banks, tax the rich, redistribute income, give full citizenship to illegals, take power from the states, and rule from Washington. We'll make America into a progressive socialist country that all of us will be proud to live in, and, incidentally, we'll make a good start on saving the planet."

Molina's voice: "It won't work, Mr. President. The majority of Americans will never approve. Revolutions from the top down never work. You can't take the American people where they don't want to go."

Sarah pushed a key and the sound stopped. She hit a few more and closed the computer.

In the silence that followed, Molina turned his attention to Jake Grafton, who had his eyes on him.

Jack Yocke broke the silence with a question aimed at Sarah. "What have you done to that file?"

"The background noises have been digitally suppressed so the speakers' voices are clearer. That's it."

He grunted and faced Jake Grafton. "You knew that they were waiting. For a terrorist incident? Did they arrange those incidents?"

Grafton turned those gray eyes on the reporter. "They let those people into the country, lied about the vetting they would receive. They played for a terrorist incident, or incidents, and they got them. Considering who they were letting into the country, it would have been a miracle if there weren't any terror strikes."

"You could have stopped it. Hundreds of innocent people were killed. Obviously you didn't stop it."

"And just how do you think I should have accomplished that feat?"

"You sacrificed those people."

Grafton's face didn't even twitch.

"You are a ruthless man, Admiral," Yocke said softly.

"I think this has gone quite far enough," the admiral said. "Jack, go find someone to interview. You might start with Congressman Jerry Marquart. I am sure he has quite a story to tell." His eyes moved to Molina. "You stay," he said.

Yocke stomped out with little grace. That's the free press for you. When the door to the room was once again closed, Grafton said, "I think it is time for a confession from you, Sal. Not one in the hearing of the *Washington Post*, but here before me and Sarah and these men who risked their lives to drag us out of that concentration camp a few hundred yards away."

Molina seemed to have shriveled and aged ten years. He tried to compose himself, but it was a lost effort.

"Let me start your confession for you," Jake Grafton said. "You were never Barry Soetoro's advisor—you were his controller. Your boss is Anton Hunt, the billionaire left-wing financier. He created Barry Soetoro, and you were there to tell him what to do, to make him obey Anton Hunt, so he could make more billions and create the kind of world he thought we all should live in."

Molina licked his lips. "I—"

Grafton smacked the table a healthy lick with his palm. It sounded like a pistol shot. "I'll do the talking. You even suggested that Soetoro arrest me as one of the conspirators in the fake plot to take over the government. You argued that spies are easy to blame, and people would automatically give credence to any story of nefarious activities at the CIA. When you reported Soetoro's plans to Anton Hunt, he was horrified. He hadn't signed on to a communist dictatorship.

"He thought Soetoro was a black man of modest intelligence with a good gift of gab who would be grateful for all Hunt had done to lift him to the highest place in America and make him the most powerful man in the world. He thought he could control Barry Soetoro because he had written evidence of all he had done for him: a fake birth certificate, passport applications removed from the State Department, bribes to get him into school, bribes to conceal his academic records, all of it. He thought the evidence would ruin Soetoro if it ever came out, but the evidence was a two-edged sword. Soetoro knew the evidence would also take down Anton Hunt, so Hunt didn't dare to ever reveal it."

Molina licked his lips and wiped a sheen of perspiration from his forehead.

"But somewhere along the line," Grafton continued, "Hunt began to realize that he had no control over Soetoro, but the reverse was true. Soetoro controlled *him*. Perhaps the revelation occurred when Soetoro demanded Hunt fund demonstrators to protest racial injustice, demonstrations designed to drive a wedge between white and black America. Or perhaps the light dawned for Hunt when Soetoro sacrificed an ambassador and several Marines to the Taliban. Perhaps you can tell us, Sal. When did Hunt see the evil in Soetoro?"

Sal Molina was staring at the tabletop.

"Certainly both of you were in no doubt when Soetoro plotted martial law and suspension of the Constitution. You knew then, didn't you, Sal?"

Silence.

"*Answer me*!" Grafton roared.

"Yes."

"One of the most amazing things I heard on Sarah's eavesdropping program was Soetoro telling you that Hunt thought he had a nigger slave in the White House, and the nigger had made a slave of him. And he made a slave of you, the slave driver. Do you remember that? Remember his laughter?"

"He's a monster," Molina whispered. "He loathes white people. He wants to rule a nonwhite America. He's willing to ignite a race war, burn America, and rule in the ashes."

"And you didn't think it would work." That wasn't a question, but a statement.

"I didn't," Molina said.

"You argued, unsuccessfully, and only managed to convince him you were disloyal and a danger, so he sent you to the gulag."

Grafton leaned back in his seat, his eyes fixed on Molina. "You were lucky that sadist Sluggo Sweatt decided to have his fun with me before he got to you, because Soetoro wanted you dead. But Soetoro gave Sweatt his priorities. First the scapegoat, then the traitor."

"You don't know that," Sal Molina whispered.

"I deduce it. I thought it was a stroke of luck that FEMA brought me to the concentration camp here at Dawson, because that is where we—my friends and I—agreed to rendezvous two weeks after Soetoro declared martial law. Then Sweatt began his program of forcing a confession. The irony is, I was and am guilty of a conspiracy to remove the president of the United States from power, which was Sweatt's accusation. I thought it likely he would beat me to death.

"Not that my death would have made any difference. If I weren't here, the others still would be. There are two thousand five hundred men and women here at Camp Dawson, and they are committed to the hilt. It's victory or death for them. If they don't kill Soetoro, he will kill them. They understand that."

Grafton smacked the table again. "Yocke accused me of being ruthless. I *am*. The life of the United States is at stake. If I had thought it could be done, I would have shot Soetoro myself." He pointed his finger at Molina. "If I thought your death would move Soetoro one inch away from the White House, make an iota of difference, I would shoot you myself, here and now. Do you understand?"

Molina bit his lip.

Grafton smacked the table again, and the map fell off the blackboard. "Answer me!" he roared.

"Yes."

"Consider yourself a prisoner. If you try to escape, you will be shot." He turned to Travis. "Lock him in one of those cells in the concentration camp. See that he is guarded twenty-four hours a day and arrange to have him fed."

"Yes, sir." Travis Clay grabbed Molina's arm, hoisting him from the chair in which he sat. I pulled out my .45.

"Get rid of the web belt," I told Molina. "Take it off." He was wearing a pistol.

He reached down, released the buckle, and let the belt fall on the floor.

"Your leather belt too," Grafton said. "We'll save you for a firing squad."

The belt came off and went onto the floor.

Molina could barely walk, so Travis almost dragged him.

THIRTY-ONE

★

"You could have confided in me," I told Grafton.

He looked surprised. "I told Sarah to tell you about the eavesdropping scheme. Did she tell you?"

"Well, yes, but not about all this other stuff."

"Tommy, you have a good brain between those ears and you had better start using it."

You would think that after all these years around Grafton I would know how to keep my mouth shut. One of these days I am going to get that trick down.

"The local radio station is back on the air," Sarah told the boss. That female could read minds. "I don't know if the power is on or if they are using a generator."

"Okay," Grafton said. "Tommy, take Sarah over there. She is going to put some of that stuff from the White House on the air. She has winnowed it down to about sixty hours. Convince the radio staff to do it, and then set up an ambush around the station and transmission tower. Use Travis and Willis Coffee. Take whatever weapons you need. If the military is still in the game, they'll take the tower out with a Hellfire or commandos. If it's FEMA or Homeland, expect a few truckloads of thugs. Don't take any prisoners—we don't have anywhere to keep them. The beds in the concentration camp are being used as barracks."

"Yes, sir."

"Sarah, you know what to do."

"This will set off an explosion in the White House," she said flatly.

"I hope. Infuriated, frightened men don't think very well. Go."

Sarah repacked her computer and we left, with Willis Coffee trailing along behind. We picked up Travis ten minutes later and took my stolen FEMA pickup truck.

★

Downtown Kingwood was a typical American small town, in my opinion. A Walmart on the edge of town had pretty much turned the old downtown into a wasteland of vacant stores interspersed with insurance agencies, lawyers' offices, gift and craft shops. All of them looked closed, and there were no parked cars.

The radio station's offices were in one of the old storefronts on the east side of the street in the middle of the block. The transmission tower was obviously offsite, probably on a nearby hill. I parked right in front, and Sarah and I strolled in while Willis and Travis, each with an M4 in their hands, walked to the adjacent corners.

The lady at the front desk was still on the right side of forty and had a cute hairdo and a ready smile. She even had on a plastic name tag: "Sue."

"Good afternoon," she said brightly. The studio was right behind her, visible through a double-pane window. A woman was in there talking into a boom mike, and a young guy in a ponytail was fielding telephone calls. We could hear the station feed over a hidden loudspeaker system, background noise. Above the window was a large clock with a sweep second hand.

"Are you with the government?"

"Not anymore. We were federal employees and left under a cloud." I smiled.

"Really!" she said, her eyes widening.

I confided in a low voice, "I stole our truck." Then I introduced Sarah and myself.

The desk lady stared. I continued smoothly, as if stealing a government vehicle needs no explanation. "How long has the power been back on?"

"Since yesterday morning. We got back on the air as quickly as we could."

"Don't you have an emergency generator?"

"We ran out of gas for it. The station manager is down waiting in line at the filling station to fill some cans now." With only a little prompting from us, she chattered on. The station was licensed at one thousand watts, sunrise to sunset. The transmitter was outside town on Mount Morgan, named after a local farmer who leased the site to the station. "He's such a nice gentleman," she added.

"We should probably wait for the manager," Sarah said, glancing at me. "When do you expect him back?"

"In a little while, certainly, unless the line is too long or the filling station runs out of gasoline. We close the office here at five." It was ten till. "And go off the air at..." she glanced at her calendar. "... seven thirty-two."

There was a hallway that looked as if it went all the way through the building, and a door at the end of it. The door opened and a portly man of medium height with a fringe of gray hair around a white pate came bustling through it. He opened the door to the studio and went in. In less than a minute, he came out. He addressed Sue. "I got the last of the gas at Plunkett's. I just told Jan. She'll put it on the air immediately."

"These folks want to talk to you," Sue told him. She said his name, Howard Shinaberry. He glanced at us, at our web belts and holsters, and waited.

"Sarah Houston," I said, nodding at my companion, "and I'm Tommy Carmellini. Sarah wants to talk to you in your office."

He shrugged and led the way down the hall to another door. Sarah followed with her computer case.

I smiled at Sue, then walked down the hallway and went out back. There was an alley and a parking lot. Three cars and an old Chevy pickup were parked there. I surveyed the alley. All I could see was a cat wandering around and a bunch of garbage cans. The gas cans were in the back of the truck, so I unloaded them and put them in the hallway.

I closed the alley door and waited by the front desk with Sue. "Does Mr. Shinaberry own the station?"

"Oh, no. He's just the manager. Three doctors own it."

"Local doctors?"

"They live in Maryland, Bethesda I think."

Sue chattered on. She was a local and had worked at the station for five years come November. She liked it. She met such interesting people. "Do you have an ad you want us to air?"

"Something like that," I replied.

She got busy locking the cash register and putting things away. Five o'clock came and went.

"If you want to go home, that's all right," I said. "I'll tell Mr. Shinaberry."

"I'll just wait, in case he has something else for me to do." She was obviously getting nervous. I didn't blame her. I gave her my best innocent smile that had melted a thousand hearts.

At nine after five, Mr. Shinaberry and Sarah came from the office out to the front desk. She paused beside me and said, "He doesn't want to do it."

"Our license is up for renewal in three months," Shinaberry explained. "That stuff on that computer is dynamite. The FCC—"

I went out the front door to the sidewalk and gave Travis Clay the Hi sign. He came walking back, his M4 cradled in his arms. We went back into the radio station together.

Shinaberry was explaining to Sarah why the owners would fire him if the file on the computer were put out on the air. "I know the president's voice, and it certainly sounds like him, but if the file is fake, airing it would be libel, and if it's real I can't imagine how that recording was obtained legally—"

"You know about the rebels down at Camp Dawson?" I asked as I rubbed my sore neck. I realized I was doing it and stopped.

"The general in charge—at least he said he was a general—was in here and asked us not to mention all the people there over the air. And we haven't. Haven't said a peep about Camp Dawson. I gave our staff strict instructions."

"This gentleman is Travis Clay. Travis, take Mr. Shinaberry over to Dawson and let him talk to Jake Grafton. Use Mr. Shinaberry's truck. It's out back."

"Now, see here—" Shinaberry protested.

Travis put his hand on the guy's shoulder and smiled. "Don't be difficult," he said. "You can drive."

After they left, I suggested to Sue that it was time for her to go home. "We'll lock up when we leave, after Mr. Shinaberry gets back."

She was obviously relieved. She grabbed her purse without saying good-bye, trotted down the hallway, and closed the alley door behind her.

"It's all yours," I said to Sarah. "Send Jan out and get that guy in the ponytail to show you how the equipment works."

Sarah took her computer and went into the studio. After ten minutes the announcer lady came out, frowned at me, and left via the alley door too. Ponytail was busy with a thumb drive Sarah had given him. Then Sarah got on the mike.

"We are going to air segments of a recording that was made at the White House over the previous six months. Not all of it, but segments. The voices you will hear are those of President Soetoro, his staff, and other public officials. There are about sixty hours of recorded material, a small fraction of the whole, and this station will be on the air day and night until the entire sixty hours has played, then we will run it again. Josh, let it rip."

And he did.

Barry Soetoro's voice came over the loudspeaker. Three minutes later the telephone rang. I answered it with the station's call letters.

A man's voice: "Where in the hell did you guys get that tape?"

"How does it sound?" I asked.

"Holy shit! President Soetoro said that?"

"He did."

"Jesus Christ!"

"He didn't have anything to do with it," I told him and put the phone back in its cradle. It rang again. I figured that we were going to get a lot of calls, so I unplugged the phone. I looked into the studio and saw that Sarah was doing the same thing to the phone in there. I could hear the phone ringing in the manager's office, so I walked down and unplugged that one too.

★

Tobe Baha, the Secret Service sniper, was having dinner that evening at his hotel on Congress Avenue in Austin. It was a nice hotel, perfect for expense-account executives and rich oilmen bringing their wives or girlfriends to see the bright lights of the big city. Tobe thought his odd hours would bring less notice here and he would have to answer fewer well-meaning questions than he would have at some cheap motel on the interstate where guests rarely stayed more than a night or two.

So he was studying the menu and contemplating ordering a steak when three men entered the dining room, looked around, and seeing him, walked purposefully toward his table. They were in civilian clothes wearing sports coats, and from the slight bulges he could see that they were packing pistols in their armpits. After years in the Secret Service, he could spot an armed man at fifty yards.

The man in front seated himself on Tobe's left and put an iPad on the table. The other two took the remaining chairs.

"Good evening, Mr. Baha," the man on his left said. He was the older of the three, in his mid-fifties, with salt-and-pepper hair getting thin on top. "I'm Colonel Frank Tenney. I'm the head of the Texas Department of Public Safety. These gentlemen are colleagues of mine."

Tobe tried to hide his surprise, and did fairly well, he thought. He was registered at this hotel under a false name, so the use of his real name put him on notice.

"Are you carrying this evening?" Tenney asked, just making conversation.

Tobe tried to look surprised. "Of course not."

Tenney just nodded. The waitress came over, delivered Tobe's Scotch on the rocks, passed out menus to the new arrivals, and inquired about drinks. The lawmen all ordered iced tea.

"I have some video on my iPad I'd like to show you," Tenney said, then picked up the tablet and began playing with it. In a few seconds, he placed it so Tobe could see it.

The screen began showing aerial shots. Tobe Baha instantly knew what he was looking at: drone surveillance video. And there he was, in the van, parking it, getting out, looking around, strolling the street. Then there were shots of Tobe up on roofs, using the laser rangefinder, back on the street, driving through the city, going into stores and public places...

After three or so minutes, Tenney picked up the iPad and shut it off. He put it on his left.

Tenney smiled at Baha. The waitress came back with the drinks. Tenney told her that they would not be staying for dinner. She looked at Tobe, who told her, "Later."

When she had moved off, Tenney said, "We were surprised when you showed up in Austin, since Texas is no longer a part of the United States and Barry Soetoro isn't planning a visit, at least to the best of my knowledge."

Tobe picked up the Scotch and sipped it. His hand was steady, and he hoped that the colonel noticed that. If he did, he gave no sign.

"We thought that perhaps you were here to use your sniper skills on someone in Austin. Of course, we haven't yet seen you with your rifle. No doubt it is somewhere in Austin, and if necessary we could arrest you and search and find it. It will probably have your fingerprints on it and so forth. But President Hays thought that an arrest and trial would not be good for future relations between Texas and the United States."

Colonel Tenney leaned toward Tobe Baha. He was speaking softly, and his eyes were impossible to avoid. "I also thought about disappearing you. That would solve any diplomatic problems, and the justice system wouldn't have the expense of fooling with you. Do you understand?"

Those eyes boring into his made evasion impossible. "Yes," Tobe said.

"That's good. We're tying up a lot of people flying these drones and keeping tabs on you, and enough is enough. So I stopped by this evening to let you know. If a sniper fires a shot anywhere in Austin and you're still around, we'll come for you. You will be killed resisting arrest and be buried somewhere in west Texas in an unmarked grave. Have I made myself clear?"

"Yes."

"Barry Soetoro or your Secret Service colleagues may decide that you have lived long enough, so you may want to rethink your return to the States. Be that as it may, you may reside in Texas as long as you never again show your face in Austin. If someone fires a rifle in Austin and you are around after this evening, you are a walking dead man."

Tenney stood and picked up his iPad. "Just a friendly warning. You can pay for our tea."

He and his colleagues walked out of the restaurant.

Tobe Baha drained his Scotch. He glanced at the menu, decided he wasn't hungry, and ordered another drink.

About ten after six, Travis Clay came through the alley door of the radio station with four buffed-up guys. "Grafton sent Mr. Shinaberry home. The sheriff and city police chief were there and we won't have any trouble with them."

"Patriots are they?"

"With twenty-five hundred armed people at Dawson, they saw the light, whether they are patriots or Soetoro loyalists." He gestured to the other men. "Grafton thought we could use more help."

"Get Willis in here."

The ex-soldiers, for that is what they were, stood listening to the radio feed on the loudspeakers, shaking their heads. One of them muttered, "That son of a bitch."

I briefed the troops. Two of them at each end of the alley. I sent Willis across the street and asked him to put an M240 machine gun on the roof of the old bank building on the corner; the false brick front would give him a little protection. Travis was to be on the roof on the other corner with another M240. These were belt-fed guns that fired the 7.62x51 NATO cartridges. I would have our third machine gun, an M249 that was fed by a belt of 5.56x45 NATO cartridges, inside here on the counter. "Lots of grenades and AT4s. We'll make the street in front our killing zone."

Everyone trooped out to the FEMA truck, where Willis passed out weapons and ammo. We carried some MREs into the station, and I drove the truck around back and backed in up to the alley door. We carried stuff in. I brought in two boxes of ammo for my machine gun, an M4 carbine, a dozen grenades, and a couple of AT4s.

I was feeding a belt of ammo into the M249 when Josh came out. He looked at the weapons and ammo and at me. "Where did you people get that recording?"

"What did Sarah tell you?"

"That a little bird gave it to her."

"There you are."

"I'm getting the hell outta here," he said, and marched for the alley door. I heard his old ride fire up. Josh needed new mufflers. Then it went away down the alley.

After a while Sarah came out. "It's all automatic," she said. "I don't need to sit there and watch it."

"Want some dinner?"

She gave me The Look.

"I put some MREs in the break room. There's a microwave. I'd like meatloaf, some potatoes, and corn."

"Yes, General," she said, and marched away.

As I dug into my gourmet repast—Sarah could do MREs, let me tell you—individual cars and pickups, each full of people, kept creeping down the street and looking into the radio station. Finally I wised up and turned off the lights in the office.

It was after nine o'clock and Soetoro was plotting with Al Grantham and Sulana Schanck on how they would turn off the power and blame it on the right-wing constitutionalists, when a van pulling an army generator drifted to a stop at the curb outside. The van had a big, flexible aerial mounted on the rear bumper.

I cradled the M4 and waited. A woman walked around the van, tried the door to the station, found it unlocked, and came in. I could see a guy still in the van.

The woman looked at the machine gun, the grenades on the counter, and me. "I'm Dixie Cotton," she said. She couldn't have been a day over thirty, with a sexy bedroom voice and a figure to match. She was wearing tight jeans and a T-shirt that revealed everything she had, which was a lot.

"Tommy Carmellini."

Sarah came from the hallway. I introduced the two.

"I've heard of you," Sarah said. "Aren't you 'The Mouth of the South'?"

"It's been said," she admitted modestly. It sure had. She had a talk show on an Atlanta radio station and thrived on controversy, which she created by trashing everyone who disagreed with her, which was practically everybody.

"I thought Soetoro had FEMA lock you up as a dangerous subversive. How did you get out?"

"A doctor certified that I was crazy and some of my friends paid a few bribes, so they turned me loose."

"Could I get a certification like that?" I asked hopefully.

"So where did you people get that recording?"

"You know the old story: if I told you I'd have to kill you," I said deadpan.

"Bullshit," she said dismissively. "Is it real?"

"Of course."

"I run a mobile pirate radio station these days, during the current difficulty, while my station in Atlanta is up to its armpits in federal censors. I'd like a copy of that recording. I'll cruise Washington and broadcast it."

"They'll kill you if they catch you," I told her, "tits, mouth, and all."

"Not the way I work it, they won't. They've been trying for four days and haven't caught me yet."

"You're living on borrowed time."

"That's my lookout."

"Sarah, what do you think?"

She shrugged. "Can you use thumb drives?"

"Sure."

"Let's make you some." And Sarah led her into the studio.

Cars and pickups crept by at random intervals all evening. The locals were getting an earful and they were curious.

About midnight, an army truck pulled up outside and soldiers piled out of the back. Jake Grafton climbed down from the cab, carefully, and led the soldiers, six of them, inside. The soldiers were in full combat gear, with helmets, weapons, and body armor. Grafton was wearing a camo shirt and trousers. Willie Varner was the only one in civilian duds, and he was carrying an M4.

Grafton introduced the soldiers. Two army officers and four senior sergeants, all with combat experience. "They came to Dawson with General Netherton," he explained. "Where do you want them?"

"On the roofs on this side of the street," I said to them. "The street is the kill zone. Don't let any of the bad guys get into this office."

We talked about frequencies, because they all had handheld radios, and they trooped out.

"FEMA and Homeland have at least a dozen people on the way," he said. "They're on the clear-voice radio. Soetoro is raving mad."

I told him about Dixie Cotton. "She's nuts," I added. "Literally and figuratively. Certified even. They'll execute her."

"That's her problem," Jake Grafton said. He looked around. "Break out those windows. You want the glass on the sidewalk, not flying around in here."

"I'm worried about the radio tower, which is out on some knoll called Mount Morgan."

"We have it covered," he said. He glanced at the machine gun on the counter. "Is that where you want it?"

"I doubt if they'll be stupid enough to drive up in front of the joint, but if they do…"

"A man can always hope," he said.

"You could ambush these dudes on the way into town," I pointed out.

"It'll take most of the night to get ambushes set up. We'll whack the second wave. You deal with the first bunch."

"If they get a bullet into the equipment in the studio we are well and truly fucked," I remarked.

"Make sure they don't."

I almost said something I would probably have regretted later, but I managed to stifle myself.

"What are you doing here?" I asked Willie.

"I'm your bodyguard."

As if I needed something else to worry about.

"You had dinner?"

"Oh, yeah. They're good feeders over at that camp."

"You should have joined the army when you were a kid."

"Maybe you're right."

Grafton, Sarah, and I chatted for a bit, the admiral shook Sarah's hand and mine, then went back out and climbed into the army truck, which got under way in a cloud of diesel exhaust.

"There goes the next president of the United States," Sarah said.

"Not after Jack Yocke gets through with him," I replied.

"Screw Jack Yocke," Sarah said.

Sarah went into the break room, which had a cot, and sacked out. I broke out the office windows, as Grafton had suggested.

Willie was in a talkative mood. He carefully laid his M4 on the counter. "Nice shooter," he said with feeling.

"You know which end the bullet comes out of?"

"The little tiny round end with the asshole. I shot that thing this evenin' at the range and the guy in charge said I was a natural-born marksman."

"Was coming over here your idea?"

"Yeah. I was sittin' beside Grafton participatin' in a high strategy session when a radio dude came runnin' in and told him all about these Soetoro dudes coming to shut this radio station down. I volunteered to come help. Knowin' you, I figured you'd need all the help you could get."

That must have been the first time in his life Willie ever volunteered for anything but beer. "It's good to see you, shipmate. You can stay in here with me, but why don't you lay down in the corner and try to catch some Zs."

He did so, after bitching about how hard the floor was and having to use his jacket for a pillow. "Turn off that damn radio noise out here," he said. "I've had enuffa Soetoro to last me a lifetime."

"I thought you were a Soetoro voter."

"Don't remind me."

I cranked the volume of the speaker to zero and settled down to wait. Willie and Sarah were sound asleep when I went into the break room at one a.m. and made a pot of coffee. While it dripped through, I went in to the studio and put on the earphones. The prez was talking about his enemies. I put the earphones down and went back to the break room for a cup. Nothing but that white powdered stuff for creamer, so I silently cussed the Maryland doctors and drank it black.

Waiting was hard. I went out and surveyed the street. Two or three truckloads of them—we would kill them right there.

Waiting has never been my long suit. I must have been at the head of the line for good looks and natural charm; when I got to patience there wasn't much left—I only got a teaspoon full, if that.

I found myself rubbing my sore neck again. The doctors at Camp Dawson had put more antiseptic on it and a sticky bandage. The muscles were still stiff.

I wondered about Willie, why he was here. A warrior he wasn't. Growing up in the Washington ghetto and a couple of stretches in the pen had taught him to stay out of the line of fire and keep his head down. Willie was a survivor. That was one of the reasons I liked him. When I had had my fill of agency operators full of bullshit and testosterone, I could visit Willie at the lock shop and come back down to earth.

Musing along those lines, my handheld squawked. The voice was Travis Clay's. "We have a truck two blocks north, and someone standing beside it looking the situation over with binoculars."

"Okay."

I nudged Willie with my foot. He came right awake.

"Uh-oh," Willis Coffee said. "I hear helicopters.... Coming this way. Getting louder."

Damn!

It was beginning to look like the bleeding wasn't going to be one-sided at our little party.

I walked to the busted window and listened. I could hear the choppers now, definitely coming this way. If these were paramilitary thugs, from FEMA or Homeland or the IRS or wherever, they were catching on fast. If they were military, oh boy.

"Trucks are moving, at least three. Guys walking along beside them. All armed. Looks like FEMA uniforms."

The choppers were above us somewhere.

"*They stopped in the wrong block*! They're in the next block north."

"Choppers overhead. Two Blackhawks. Guys rappelling down onto the roofs on the east side of the street. But they're in the wrong block too."

I keyed the mike on my hand-held. "Machine gunners, take out the choppers. Everyone else, hit 'em."

And the world split apart. The hammering of heavy machine guns rolled up and down the street. I grabbed an AT4, fired it up, and stepped right through the empty window onto the sidewalk. The lead truck was in the middle of the next block. Perfect. I didn't waste time and got the round off within three seconds. It went right into the engine compartment and exploded. Pieces of the truck went flying everywhere.

Bullets were whanging off the concrete sidewalk and brick facade, so I dived right back through the window socket with the empty tube in my hands.

The sound of combat rose to a roar.

Those soldiers—I saw uniforms and helmets—would quickly figure out there was no radio station in that block and be heading this way if the guys on our roofs didn't manage to keep them pinned.

Then I heard a chopper crash. The explosion was tremendous. The other one was trying to get away, it sounded like.

I grabbed two grenades, pulled the pins, and went over to the window. Risked a quick squint. Guys coming down both sides of the street, shooting up at the roofs. I threw one as far as I could across the street at an angle, then leaned out and tossed the other left-handed up the street.

Willie was hunkered down in the corner, trying to see up the street through the empty window socket.

"Shoot low," I shouted. "Ricochet the bullets off the walls over there."

He began squirting bursts.

"More, more," I urged.

I became aware that Sarah was behind me, and she handed me a couple more grenades. I sent them down the street, and the explosions were gratifying.

This went on for what seemed like an hour, but couldn't have been more than a couple of minutes, if that. Willie changed magazines twice.

"Keep your goddamn head down," I told him when he kept bobbing up to squirt off a burst.

I glimpsed a grenade flying into the street in front of our position. "Down! Grenade!"

It went off and showered the office with shrapnel. I looked at the studio window, which was grazed but intact.

Then I realized the shooting was tapering off. Another burst or two, and a deafening silence descended.

"Willis? Travis?"

"The survivors are running for the trucks," Willis shouted into his radio. "Don't let 'em get away!"

About that time the alley door crashed open. Willie Varner spun on his knee, a very athletic move, and fired a burst from the hip. Then another burst that emptied his weapon.

I was there with my M4, waiting, so I cranked my head to see. Two soldiers in uniform down.

With the carbine at the ready, I went down the hallway. One was still alive, a black kid. The other was seriously dead. From the streetlight in the alley I could see the patches on their shoulders. New Jersey National Guard.

Willie was there, kneeling, checking on the wounded man. The guy looked at Willie, gurgled something, then his eyes froze and he stopped breathing.

Willie dropped his weapon and put his hands over his face.

"Hey, man," I said. "It was them or us."

Sarah put her hand on his shoulder.

"If you had waited another half second to shoot," I told Willie, "you'd be the one lying dead."

Willie straightened up, left his weapon right where it lay, and walked out the alley door and turned right, away from the fight.

"Let him go, Tommy," Sarah said.

"I just hope there are no more bad guys out there."

"Let's check on the broadcasting equipment."

The radio came to life. It was Willis Coffee. "There was a fire fight over west of town, about where that radio tower should be. Maybe they tried to take it too."

One of our guys was dead and three more wounded. The soldiers who lay on the floor in the hallway had apparently come south down the alley and gunned the two good guys on guard at the north entrance, then kicked in our door.

Among the attackers on the ground there were nineteen bodies and eight wounded. The rest had gone north running or riding the surviving trucks.

"If they had stopped in the right block, we'd have gotten them all," Travis Clay said. And they would have destroyed the radio broadcast equipment, I thought, but I managed to bite it off before it came out. "And we have one prisoner, a FEMA guy who surrendered. His name tag says his name is Lambert. What do you want me to do with the wounded and this guy?"

"Put all the wounded on trucks and take them out to the camp. Maybe the doctors can save them."

"Our guys already left. Grafton said no prisoners."

"I'm giving the damned orders. Take all the wounded out to the base. And bring that prisoner over here. I want to look at him."

Three minutes later Travis had him standing in the radio studio with a plastic tie around his wrists. Yep, it was Zag Lambert, whom I had met in Colorado a lifetime or two ago. He was even porkier than he had been in Colorado, with a truly awesome gut jutting out above his belt. I doubted if he had seen his dick in the last ten years unless he used a mirror. It was a wonder he could even reach it. He didn't look as feisty now as he had in Colorado.

"Take him to Grafton," I told Travis. "After they interrogate him, lock him up with Sal Molina. Don't feed him for a few days. Maybe a week. Water only. He needs to lose some weight. His wife will thank us."

"Yo. Come on, fatso." And he led Lambert away.

"New Jersey National Guard," I told Grafton when he called on the radio a few minutes later. "FEMA guys in trucks and two Jersey guard helicopters with grunts who rappelled down. Travis is bringing you a prisoner to interrogate, Zag Lambert, the guy who ran Jade Helm 16."

"Good work, Tommy," he said. "We'll send some people to relieve you when the sun comes up, and you, Sarah, and Willie can get some sleep."

"Yeah." I didn't mention that Willie had bugged out. I figured that I would run into him at Dawson in the chow hall. At least, I hoped so.

One of the choppers had crashed on a baseball diamond, and the other went into a block of old houses a quarter mile away. There were no survivors from the Blackhawks. Someone said six or eight civilians were killed in the crash into the houses; no one knew for sure. The smoke was still rising from the fire at dawn.

Thus ended the battle of Kingwood. Maybe someday they'll put up a commemorative plaque.

I just hoped that somewhere people were listening to the radio.

THIRTY-TWO

★

JR Hays had four C-17s lined up, fueled, and ready to go. Aboard them were twelve trucks, three apiece. For now, the trucks were loaded with ammo, welding torches, and C-4 explosive. On the trip back, they'd be loaded with gold. He had selected and briefed his men—all one hundred of them. They were dressed in U.S. Army combat gear that would have passed the inspection of any sergeant major. The men had been briefed to shoot only in self-defense. He meant this to be a bloodless adventure.

JR had confirmed, in three satellite calls with the Pentagon, that the United States armed forces were in a state of armed truce and officially neutral in the war between the United States and Texas, and he had letters in his pockets, all forgeries on good paper with appropriate letterheads affirming that he was Lieutenant General Robert Been, United States Army, with written orders from the president of the United States, Barry Soetoro, and the secretary of the Treasury to transport the gold in the Bank of Manhattan to the New York Federal Reserve Bank for safekeeping until the current political crisis had passed. To further his ruse, he had five Texas Rangers, three men and two women, in civvies carrying FBI pistols and credentials, which Colonel Tenney had confiscated from agents in Austin. Chuy Medina had told him the bank had at least a hundred tons of gold on deposit. JR hoped to take every ounce.

★

Sarah and I went to the big head honchos' meeting in the conference room of the headquarters building on Tuesday night after dinner. The place was packed, standing room only.

There were four generals: Jose Martinez, an active-duty two-star who either took leave or deserted (he wasn't telling); Mort Considine, a retired brigadier; Lee Netherton, a retired three-star; and Jerry Marquart, a congressman if Congress ever got back in session. Jake Grafton was the general commanding, by the unanimous vote of the four, and he presided.

The big news was that radio stations along the East Coast had received duplicate thumb drives of Sarah's recordings from Dixie Cotton; and Dixie herself was making a splash as she flitted through Washington, Baltimore, Philadelphia, and New York, broadcasting on her mobile radio. FEMA and Homeland were after her, but I figured they would drop the chase soon enough—news of the recordings had already gone nationwide, and the rumor was that even FEMA and Homeland were now having doubts about Soetoro.

Within twenty-four hours of the first Kingwood broadcast, more than a thousand people joined our little army—veterans, truck drivers, steel workers, mechanics, carpenters, dentists, students, housewives, eccentrics, whackos, and no doubt some true psychopaths, all angry about Soetoro's violation of their "rights" and the "Constitution." Many brought their own firearms.

The generals fretted about the willingness and ability of civilian volunteers to follow orders. As usual, Grafton cut to the chase. "We've got to keep control of our troops or we are nothing but a mob. Let's agree right here, right now, that anyone caught robbing, stealing, raping, or murdering noncombatants will be summarily executed on the spot. Anyone accused of these crimes but not caught in the act will be court-martialed as soon as possible with the accuser and any witnesses testifying. If found guilty, he or she will be executed immediately. That will be General Order Number One."

Further orders followed swiftly. Jose Martinez, with Mort Considine as his deputy commander, would take the units designated as the First

Army, or our northern army, to Washington via I-68. Lee Netherton, with Jerry Marquart as his deputy, would lead the units organized into the Second Army, or our southern army, to Washington via Leesburg. Grafton would fly the Cessna, our only observation plane, and keep in touch with the columns via radio. Predators would scan the ground for bad guys and ambushes.

Then they got into logistics. The generals told their staff officers to stay but ordered the rest of us to get busy.

Thinking that good advice, I wandered out with Sarah and asked, "Wanta get laid?"

She stopped and did a double take, then said, "Why, Mr. Romantic, I thought you would never ask. You must be overwhelmed by my feminine charms." She held up a palm. "Don't explain. I would rather keep my illusions."

"Wise woman," I acknowledged.

"Where do you plan to conduct our tryst? The barracks is full of people playing poker, shooting craps, and listening to Barry Soetoro on the radio, and I'm not doing it in a pickup truck, period."

"I was thinking of walking a little way up into the woods and finding a leafy glade that we could remember fondly all our days."

"You animal! Lead on." She placed her hand in mine.

Apparently some other couples had similar ideas, so we had to go a bit further uphill into the woods than I wanted. It was so dark we tripped over tree roots twice.

When we thought we had a private spot free from brush and snakes, we sank to the ground. "Ooh," she said as she ran her hand around, "moss covered with sticks and stones and spiders. I've always dreamed of getting laid on a bed of moss, our very own private bower of carnality."

"I'll bet," I said, and got busy brushing the debris off the moss.

★

Hours later gently pattering raindrops woke us. The night was as black as the inside of a coal mine but a lot noisier, what with drops loudly whacking leaves, which were beginning to drip on us. Sarah and I hurriedly put on our clothes and threaded our way through the trees downhill toward the barely visible lights of the camp.

When we got back to our barracks we were a little damp, so we hung our trousers and shirts and web belts on the posts at the end of the bunk and both of us crawled under my blanket. When I woke up, it was dawn and Sarah was still sound asleep in my arms.

Other people were stirring, but they studiously ignored us.

Jake Grafton came thumping in. I pretended to be asleep. He shook my shoulder anyway and said, "Come on, Tommy. See you at the plane in fifteen minutes."

"Yessir."

Grafton was adding a quart of oil to the Cessna's engine when I came walking up. I put my M4 carbine and a little bag of extra loaded magazines and a dozen grenades in the plane. The sun was trying to come up under a high overcast. The earth smelled of late summer, pungent, fertile, and hinting of fall. The temperature was in the fifties so my sweatshirt felt good. Truly, we had a marvelous piece of the planet.

I stood there inhaling it all and watching the sun fire the tops of the trees as Grafton finished his preflight. I could hear the PA system squawking, wakening the troops. I had been hesitant to wake Sarah so I didn't kiss her good-bye; now I wished I had.

"You ready?" he asked.

"I suppose."

We got aboard and put on seat belts and headsets, and he fired up the engine. It caught on the first crank, and the prop spun into a blur with a nice little roar, blasting the morning dew from the windscreen. I checked the fuel gauges on the butts of both wings: we were full.

There was no wind, so after waiting a moment for the engine to warm and doing a short run-up and mag check, we were rolling down the runway. The tail came up and in less time than it takes to tell, we were airborne. Out over the camp and the trees, climbing into that morning sky between the low green mountains, then turning eastward into the morning sun.

He gave me a brief on the ICS. "We'll check the roads the two columns are going to take, then we're going to Washington."

"I thought we were the eyes of the army?"

"For a little while. Then we have places to go, things to do, people to see."

"Right."

"It's a great morning to fly," he said. That was Jake Grafton. He was wearing a little smile.

After an hour in the air, he reported on his handheld to the generals. No ambushes were evident. We did find a couple of campsites in the woods, but apparently the people there were refugees from the cities. Fires were giving off smoke, and we saw no evidence of heavy weapons. Our scouts would see the smoke and be forewarned.

Then Grafton set a course to the east. No low clouds, excellent visibility, so he climbed to four thousand feet. Soon Leesburg came into view, and a few moments later the long runways at Dulles airport.

The C-17 Globemasters landed one after the other at LaGuardia airport in Brooklyn. There were no flight plans, of course, since the FAA was out of action because the power was out, but these were air force planes on official business, so they landed and that was that.

The ground controller parked the four giant cargo planes on the cargo ramp, appropriately enough, and the loadmasters and their soldier passengers got busy off-loading the trucks. Also on the trucks were little cargo donkeys driven by gasoline engines, just in case.

The caravan got itself arranged, the soldiers got their weapons and got into cabs and on the backs of the trucks, two armed guards were posted at each plane, and the fliers stayed with their steeds. The rest of the hardy band of adventurers set off through the wilderness of Brooklyn toward Manhattan.

The place reminded JR Hays of Baghdad. Trash was everywhere, windows were broken out, and knots of idle young men congregated on corners, looking like packs of feral dogs. Few women could be seen, and those that were, were always walking with several men. Carcasses of burned-out cars sat pushed to the side of the street. Other cars had been stripped of wheels and even doors.

None of the stoplights worked, which didn't matter because there was little traffic, probably because there was little or no fuel available, so the caravan rolled steadily at twenty-five miles an hour onto the main thoroughfares that led to the bridge into Manhattan.

He looked at his watch. At least this Wednesday, the seventh of September, there weren't a couple million commuters and an endless stream of over-the-road tractor-trailers and local trucks fighting to get into Manhattan. The roads were essentially empty, with pieces of cars strewn randomly that the army trucks had to drive around. Wrecks were abandoned against the median barriers. It looked to JR as if Barry Soetoro had finally managed to choke America, and it was dying.

It was ten minutes before nine. His convoy would arrive at the bank a few minutes after the hour. He straightened his uniform, the dress uniform of a lieutenant general in the United States Army. He had given himself a promotion. He had used his own ribbons on his left breast, which was a dazzling collection for a twenty-year light colonel, but rather sparse for a three-star. JR doubted that the bankers had met many three-stars in full regalia.

As the truck rumbled along, he sat in the right seat on the lead truck praying that the Bank of Manhattan was going to be open today. If it weren't, this trip would be nothing but two airplane rides and a short jaunt on abandoned highways and streets.

From the right seat of the Cessna buzzing over suburban Virginia, I didn't see any airliners in the air, but I saw a bunch parked around the terminals at Dulles. Every gate was full and the ramps were crowded.

We flew on. The Washington Monument rose like a finger ahead of us. Grafton flew toward it. What a view that was, with the Potomac winding into town, the Lincoln Memorial, the Capitol Building, the White House, the Jefferson Memorial, and the long slash of the Mall.

I was nervous. I figured someone might decide to take a pot shot at us with anti-aircraft artillery or a surface-to-air missile, but apparently not. The streets looked almost deserted, yet the Mall and area around the White House certainly weren't. People everywhere, a sea of people.

Grafton swung the airplane to fly around the White House counterclockwise, with the good view on his side. But I could see plenty. Uniformed police and cops in riot gear were arranged outside the fence that encircled the executive mansion. They faced a sea of people, ten, perhaps twenty thousand flooding toward the White House. It was the damnedest sight I ever saw.

Books have been written about what was going on in the White House that morning of the seventh day of September, about how the president and his advisors and staunchest legislative allies weighed options and tried to figure out what to do next. At the risk of stating what you already know, I will summarize by telling you that Barry Soetoro was in denial, according to later accounts, and so were Al Grantham and Sulana Schanck. They raved about the treason of the military, demanded summary executions.

The vice president thought the mob outside could be handled by the Secret Service and police riot squads, augmented if necessary by fire trucks with high-pressure nozzles. He urged calm and assured everyone who would listen that America's progressives and people of color would ignore the crap spewing over the radio (and now some television stations), and support their president with their lives, if necessary. According to an account written by a senator, a delegation from Capitol Hill tried to warn the president that the fury of the American people was real and widespread, and had been dismissed as traitors for their pains.

Of all that drama Grafton and I were blissfully ignorant. After Grafton had made two complete circles, he leveled the wings and aimed the plane across the river toward the Pentagon, that massive stone structure between the Potomac and Reagan National Airport.

Grafton circled the Pentagon, eyeing the vast parking lot. On his second circuit, I had a good view of armed soldiers, machine-gun nests, military vehicles, and tents. We were only a few hundred feet above the parking lot by then, but no one started shooting.

Grafton swung out and began a straight-in to the parking lot. There were light poles here and there, but most of it was empty. He pulled up on the bar between the seats, which put in half flaps, then pulled again for full flaps and we were on final doing about seventy miles per hour. He plunked that thing in a three-point landing within twenty feet of the edge, just clearing some power wires, avoided all the light poles, and slowed to a taxi. Then he braked to a stop and pulled the mixture knob out. The prop swung to a stop as a Humvee came rushing up.

Grafton killed the mags and master switch and we got out. Two soldiers jumped from the vehicle with guns in hand. Optimist that I am, I left my M4 and bag of grenades in the plane.

"My name is Jake Grafton. I want to see the CNO or army chief of staff, if they are around."

"Sir, you aren't supposed to land here."

"Right. Now get on the radio and find out if Admiral McKiernan has the time to see Jake Grafton."

Fifteen minutes later we were in some kind of situation room still wearing our sidearms. At least they weren't going to arrest us on the spot, I thought, which was a relief.

Grafton shook hands all around—the room was full of admirals and generals—enough brass to make a few dozen monkeys. He was even courteous enough to introduce me, although all I got from the heavies were nods, then they ignored me. They all knew him and were obviously happy to see him. The commandant whacked him on his back so hard I worried about his ribs, but Grafton didn't wince.

"Was that you we saw flying around the White House a few minutes ago?" someone asked, and Grafton admitted it was.

"The FAA will mail you a flight violation."

On a console were three large screens showing the mob surrounding the White House. It only took me a moment to figure out that these pictures were the datalink video from drones. A large map of downtown Washington covered one wall. It was held there with masking tape, so it hadn't been there long.

I watched the video while Grafton chatted and the brass nodded at the screens and shook their heads. "He's going down before long," one general said.

Everyone seated themselves in chairs and Grafton got right to it. "Is it true that the military is no longer taking sides in this civil war?"

"That's right," Bud Weiss, the air force general, said. "We're America's armed forces, not Barry Soetoro's."

Jake Grafton nodded. "I had hoped that you would see it that way."

Cart McKiernan explained, "Marty Wynette committed suicide in his office two days ago. This war against Texas and Soetoro's enemies had gone far enough, so we decided the best course for the military was to remain neutral."

Fifteen minutes later I thought I had the picture. The military was devoting its efforts to pushing Mexican forces out of California. A very unhappy Barry Soetoro was hunkered down at the White House fulminating and making big noises, but so far he had left the Pentagon, and the Marines surrounding it, alone—probably because he had nothing to bother them with.

"What does Jack Hays down in Austin say about all of this?"

"I talked to him earlier today on the radio," the army general, Frank Rodriquez said. "He says if we leave Texas alone, Texas forces will leave our troops and military installations alone. I guess you could call it a truce."

Grafton gratefully accepted a cup of coffee from an aide. He sipped it and told the brass, "There are a bunch of folks, about three thousand, but the number is growing by the hour, heading this way from Camp Dawson in West Virginia. They'll probably be here tomorrow."

"Who is in charge of this group?"

"I guess I am," Grafton said with a smile. "We intend to enter the White House and arrest Soetoro, if we can get there before that mob beats us to it. His days are almost over."

"Then what?" some general asked.

"We need to get the United States up and running again. Get the power turned on nationwide, get water flowing through the pipes, and restore public order.

They weren't yet ready to talk about tomorrow. "What do you know about this White House recording that is all over the radio dial? We think three or four stations are broadcasting it." General Weiss said that and he gestured at the video screens. "That is what has them stirred up. The big problem is that that mob is made up of people who hate Soetoro and people who think he is the risen Christ and is being viciously slandered. We have people down there reporting on what's happening. That thing may turn into a battle royal between the two groups right there in Lafayette Park, a bloody riot."

Grafton replied, "I authorized secret electronic monitoring of the White House about six months ago. We used an Israeli program to turn all their cell phones, computers, and surveillance equipment into listening devices. The signals were gathered by the White House Wi-Fi system, encrypted, and sent to us. My tech staff" (that was only Sarah Houston, by the way—she was going to smile when I related this remark to her) "waded through hundreds of hours of conversation, but edited our take down to the pithiest sixty hours. That is what the radio stations are broadcasting."

Rodriquez whistled. "That stuff is dynamite." He jumped right to the key point. "So you knew Soetoro was planning to declare martial law for weeks before he did it?"

Grafton merely nodded.

"How many weeks?"

"Two months," Grafton said.

As they digested that revelation, General Runyon said, "You should have told us."

Grafton made a face. "There is always the question of whether clandestine recordings are genuine, and that cannot be answered to a certainty by listening to them. Even if you concluded that I was as honest as Diogenes, what would you have done after you listened? The American people needed to *see* the reality of a dictator in the White House, not listen to him scheming. *Now* they have seen and believe and most are ready to listen. The die-hards, a minority, are convinced the recordings are a plot to slander the saint; nothing on God's green earth will make them change their minds."

The military brass sat and looked at each other. "He's right, you know," Cart McKiernan said. No one wanted to argue. All eyes went to Grafton.

Grafton took another sip of coffee. "You made the right decision when you pulled your troops to the sidelines. The American people need to solve this problem. And I think they're about to."

That was the moment when I knew my country had a future. Jake Grafton talked about the rebuilding mission ahead, and the Pentagon generals and admirals listened carefully to every word.

I slipped out of the office, closed the door behind me, and asked the aides in the reception area how to get to the men's room. A major escorted me, and when I had lightened the load, I asked if there was food available. There was. The major and I had a delightful late breakfast of scrambled eggs, sausage, fried potatoes, and toast with real butter.

I was in an expansive mood. The major wanted to talk about the splash the Soetoro White House conversations were making. I wasn't about to tell him that was a Sarah Houston/Jake Grafton production, so I just listened. When he had expressed his and his colleagues' stupefied amazement, he segued to the subject of the rebels coming to town. I told him what I knew, which wasn't much.

"Who is leading the rebels?"

"Admiral Grafton, the officer who flew me here. I think you lead a rebel army by moral suasion. That's Jake Grafton. I used to work for him but I quit. Now I do what he asks or tells me to do because he's Jake Grafton and I'm me."

"What's going to happen to Soetoro?"

"I haven't the faintest idea," I said. "If Grafton has an idea, he hasn't shared it with me. I doubt if he does. He's sorta playing the melody by ear. May I have another cup of coffee?"

We both went and filled our cups. Seated again, the major said confidentially, "The betting in my shop is that Soetoro will fly to Iran and ask for asylum."

"Maybe the ayatollahs will put him to work in a bomb factory," I suggested.

"I don't think he's going to get rich making speeches," the major declared.

"Probably not," I agreed and finished the coffee.

THIRTY-THREE

★

JR Hays' convoy arrived at the Bank of Manhattan. He walked across the plaza, accompanied by his five fake FBI agents and two officers armed with M4 carbines. He pushed on the revolving door.

To the vast relief of JR Hays, the door wasn't locked. In seconds they were inside and crossing the lobby, which actually had a good crowd of civilians lined up facing only three tellers. JR strode over to the receptionist and announced he was here to see the president of the bank.

"Mr. Gottlieb?"

"If you please."

"I don't know if he is available just now. I'll check."

She made a call and read his rank and name tag into the telephone. With the instrument in her hand, she asked, "May I tell him what this matter is about?"

"Government business," JR said curtly and directed his gaze around, as if he were a bit peeved to be kept waiting. The two soldiers in combat gear, Colonel Adam Holt and Lieutenant Colonel Charley Grayson, adjusted their helmets and fingered their carbines, which looked black and ominous and very out of place in this marble temple to capitalism. People eyed the soldiers, who didn't seem at all self-conscious.

"If you will follow me, gentlemen. . . ." The receptionist opened a short door and admitted them behind the counter, then led the way to a bank of elevators. They were lifted up, up, up.

The president's office was in the executive suite. They were shown to a conference room, one with a long, polished mahogany desk and portraits on the walls of past bankers who had presumably gone on to an honorable retirement and whatever was awaiting them after that.

JR and his men cooled their heels for four minutes by JR's watch when the door opened and a man in his fifties bustled in. He was wearing a rumpled shirt and slacks and carrying his shoes in his hand.

He proved he was a top-notch executive by going straight for JR, whose silver stars gleamed on each shoulder. "I apologize, General," he said, "but since the power has been off I have been sleeping at the office."

JR looked the president up and down and gave a quick, tight smile. He stuck out his hand. "Lieutenant General Been, sir."

"I'm Abraham Gottlieb."

JR introduced the two soldiers in combat gear and the FBI agents, who whipped out their credentials.

"The army and the FBI," Gottlieb said, merely glancing at the credentials. The agents put them away and JR tried not to relax. None of the photos on the credentials matched the faces of the people holding them. That was one of the little hurdles he had to clear, and he was over.

"Let's sit down," JR said to Gottlieb. He reached into his tunic and pulled out two letters and handed them to the banker. One was a letter on White House stationery to Lieutenant General Robert Been, United States Army, ordering him to proceed with whatever troops he thought appropriate to the Bank of Manhattan and transport the gold in the bank's vault to the New York Federal Reserve Bank for safekeeping. The other letter was on Treasury Department stationery and was addressed to Mr. Gottlieb. The secretary of the Treasury regretted the necessity of moving the bank's gold, but threats from mobs and various unnamed rebel forces required that the gold in bank vaults in New York be moved to one central location where it could be guarded by the army.

Gottlieb seemed to shrink. He wiped his forehead and read both letters again while the lieutenant general reached into his tunic and brought out another sheet of paper. "Your copy of the president's letter, sir. I need to keep the original. If you don't mind."

The banker surrendered the document without a murmur. "I never thought it would come to this," he said, and swabbed his brow again. "I'll have to verify these letters of course, and if they are genuine, you may have the gold. Unfortunately most of our staff aren't in the bank today, although the vault is open so our customers can withdraw gold."

"Just how do you propose to verify these letters?" JR snapped.

"Well..." Gottlieb tried to compose himself. "The telephone system, internet, and telex are down, so I suppose I'll have to send a bank officer to the New York Fed to see the chairman there. He should have received similar documents."

This was the make or break moment. JR looked at the banker, overweight, with fleshy features, measuring him. "Mr. Gottlieb, as you know, the president has declared martial law. The army is running America now, subject to the president's orders. As far as you are concerned, *I am the army. I own New York and everyone in it.*"

"Yes, sir, but we have our procedures, which the SEC and banking authorities require us to—"

"*Mr.* Gottlieb, my troops are now surrounding the Fed—your messenger would not get through. You have just read the president's and secretary of the Treasury's orders, and I am obeying them. If I run into any difficulties, these agents of the FBI are authorized to arrest you and your staff." JR simply stared at the banker, daring him to open his mouth. As briefed, the senior woman removed a set of handcuffs from her purse, and Gottlieb's eyes went to them. Obviously he knew that people on Barry Soctoro's shit list were being hustled off to concentration camps.

"We are not going to be delayed by disloyal people, Mr. Gottlieb," JR intoned, as if he were talking to a buck private who had his shoes on the wrong feet. He stood, signaling he was through talking. "Now call down to your lobby and tell the head cashier to stop passing out gold. All of it is going to the Fed. When the army has it in our trucks, I'll give you a receipt for every ounce."

Without waiting for a response from the banker, JR turned to the colonels and said, "Gentlemen, let's get at it."

He turned back to Gottlieb. "If you wish to put on your shoes, sir, you may come to the vault and help supervise my troops, and ensure the receipt is properly prepared."

The banker slammed his feet into his shoes.

JR spoke to his FBI agents. "It looks as if your services aren't needed today."

"We'll stay, just in case," the senior woman said and slid her handcuffs back into her purse.

JR Hays made sure his missive from Barry Soetoro was safely in his pocket. The letter from the Treasury secretary lay on the polished mahogany where Gottlieb had left it. Maybe, JR thought, he should frame the president's letter and a copy of the one from Treasury. They were great pieces of work, signed by the best forger in the Texas prison system.

He strode out of the conference room, looking every inch a man in complete command, the general from central casting.

★

When I got back upstairs after brunch, my escort found that the brass had moved from a situation room to an office on the E-Ring. They were huddling behind closed doors. I asked one of the outer-office types if Grafton was in there, and informed he was, headed for the door.

"You can't go in there unless they send for you," I was told.

I smiled to show I could forgive a social faux pas. "I'm Grafton's official biographer. He wants me there unless Mother Nature shrieks for my attention. It's just one of his peccadilloes." I opened the door, slipped in and closed the door behind me.

Grafton glanced my way but continued talking. I dropped into an empty chair near the door.

Grafton said, "As I see it, our first priority must be getting people out of Soetoro's concentration camps. Then, in no particular order, we must get electrical power, telephone, and internet service restored nationwide; get police and firefighters back on the streets and highways; and tackle the humanitarian problems this mess has caused. I would bet there are forgotten and abandoned elderly, sick, and addicts tucked away in odd corners dying of malnutrition and dehydration. In other words, we must get the nation moving again."

"What about the states that declared their independence?" the blue-suiter, Bud Weiss, asked.

"It wasn't just Barry Soetoro who caused this mess," Grafton replied, "it was a vast overreach by the federal government, by which I mean the executive, judiciary, congress, and bureaucracies."

"That's not our business."

"It's our business if we're rebuilding this country. Frankly, gentlemen, if we're going to restore the United States of America, we need a constitutional convention to decide if we really want the federal government to rule America, or if we even want a federal system. I don't know the answer, but I know that without a political settlement to resolve lots of festering issues, this nation will fracture into several nations."

"You're saying we need a new constitution," Cart McKiernan murmured with his chin down, looking at Grafton over the top of his glasses.

"The states are going to have to figure that out," Grafton said with a gesture of irritation. "The military needs to stabilize the country and get it running again so the politicians can ruminate and negotiate without the house burning down around them."

Grafton stood up and started shaking hands. "Gentlemen, I want to thank you for your time this morning. This is our country. Soetoro won't be here long. The sooner he's gone, the better."

General Rodriquez said, "Still think we should call the White House and offer to fly him out of the country?"

When I heard that my eyebrows went up toward my hairline.

"Yes," Jake Grafton said. "Tell him the military won't protect him. In my opinion America will be better off going forward if people don't have his blood on their hands, but—" He raised his hands in a shrug. Then he said his good-byes. I opened the door and followed him out.

Fifteen minutes later, when we were in the Cessna and he was taxiing around the parking lot to find a lane for takeoff, I asked Grafton why he recommended flying Soetoro into exile.

"None of the leaders at Dawson can control our little army, and that's only one of at least eight or ten armed mobs marching on Washington. They'll kill Soetoro if they get their hands on him. If they do, his supporters will try to make him a martyr. A lot of people still think he's the black messiah, beset by evil enemies on all sides."

"Think he'll go?"

"No, but it's worth a try."

A minute later we were airborne and climbing over the Potomac for the White House. Maybe it was my imagination, but the crowd outside seemed larger. As we crossed the Mall, we could see people walking toward the mansion, like an incoming tide.

I looked away from the scene below. There was a house fire somewhere up to the northeast, and the plume was rising and drifting on the wind. I wondered if the fire department was on the job. Grafton finally leveled his wings heading west and added power to climb.

The flagship of the Texas Navy, the attack submarine *Texas*, was fifty miles east of Cape May, New Jersey, running at three knots when Loren Snyder poked the telescoping photonics masts—*Texas* had two of them—above the surface. In less than a minute, the video from the mast confirmed what the sonar was telling the crew, that there were no surface ships of any kind within their visible horizon.

Five days had passed since the combat with the destroyers among the oil rigs offshore of Louisiana. *Texas* had transited the Florida Straits and headed north. Snyder had it in his mind that if he torpedoed a couple of container ships in the approaches to New York and Newark, he could probably shut down those ports for a while. Days of cruising deep and listening via sonar for ships and submarines had been unproductive. The ocean seemed extraordinarily empty.

"Maybe the war is over," Jugs Aranado suggested.

"We should hope," Snyder said, but just in case, he decided to listen to East Coast radio stations to see what he could learn.

The AM band was remarkably quiet, but there were a few stations on the air. He channel surfed, looking for a news show. What he found was a station broadcasting the White House eavesdropping show. Barry Soetoro's voice sounded in his ears. The fidelity was quite good, and he could readily understand the conversations. They were talking about declaring martial law and arresting subversives.

As he listened on a headset, Snyder wondered what he was listening to. Gradually the idea dawned that someone had recorded a White House conversation weeks ago, perhaps months.

Thirty minutes later he was sure. They were talking about the upcoming Republican nominating convention. *This had to be recorded in late July or early August*!

He flipped a switch to put the audio on the loudspeaker in the control room.

Jugs was there, and Ada Fuentes was on the helm.

The two women sat, startled at first, then mesmerized.

"How did this get on the radio?" Fuentes asked, dumbfounded. What she was hearing just didn't compute.

When the scene was over, an announcer came on. "You were listening to President Soetoro and his advisors, Al Grantham and Sulana Schanck. Now for the next scene."

Snyder reached for the dial and turned it. He found a news station. The announcer was interviewing a Long Island congressman. "We have fifteen hundred people assembling at the Meadowlands parking lot. Tomorrow we will begin our march on Washington. Food has been donated from the local food bank and some local farmers. Anyone who wishes to join us should do so today. Bring your own weapon and ammunition and whatever camping gear you think you will need. Bring whatever food you can."

"What will you and your 'army' do in Washington?"

"We are going to drag Soetoro from the White House and hang him."

"And you are sure the military won't interfere?"

"They said they wouldn't—you have been reading their press release every hour on the hour. They're fighting Mexico, not Americans. We're taking them at their word. If they want a fight, however, we'll give it to them."

Snyder looked at Jugs. "What do you think?"

"Holy Christ!"

He lowered the photonics masts and told Ada to speed up to arrive off the Narrows at dusk. He suggested she descend to two hundred feet, and as Jugs flooded tanks, she did.

Stabilized at that depth, they discussed what they had heard.

"Let's go home," Ada suggested.

Jugs didn't say anything, merely scrutinized Loren Snyder's face.

He had to make a decision, so he did. "We'll take a look at New York Harbor and listen again this evening, with everyone not on duty in the control room. We'll let everyone have his say, and I'll make a decision then."

Things began to go wrong pretty quickly when JR Hays saw the Bank of Manhattan's vault. It had a massive circular door that weighed about twenty-five tons, Gottlieb said proudly. The ingots were stacked in the vault and almost filled it. Around the walls on shelves and in drawers were the packs of small wafers, small bars called kilobars, Krugerrands, and other gold holdings, all labeled with owner's names. The sight of all that gold was awe-inspiring, the wealth of nations.

The bank had precisely two electric forklifts and four dollies to move the gold ingots, but they weren't set up for speed. Each bar had a serial number, and two men were busy writing down the number on each bar. JR put a stop to that. "The gold is going to the Fed," he said. "You already have the numbers."

"Can you guarantee that all the bars will arrive in good condition?" Gottlieb demanded.

"Sure as shootin'," JR said, and told him to watch and simply count bars.

Colonel Holt took him aside and said, "I figure it will take two days to empty this vault, if nothing breaks."

"How long to load up fifty tons? Can we get that accomplished today?"

"Maybe."

"Make it happen. Get soldiers down here to help carry the ingots out by hand. Fifty tons is our goal. I'll tell Gottlieb we'll be back for the rest tomorrow."

"Yes, sir."

With the help of a dozen soldiers who were soon sweating profusely, the work speeded up. The soldiers grabbed an ingot in each hand and carried it to the elevator while Gottlieb and another bank officer counted them. For the receipt, of course.

JR tried to stay calm. Fifty tons would be a good haul. *Be satisfied with that*, he told himself.

He had been there an hour when one of the officers came to the vault holding a handheld radio. "Just talked to the airport," he said. "Some FAA guy came around. He stayed ten minutes and left."

"Keep me advised," JR said, and watched the gold being loaded onto dollies. He was learning a lot about gold ingots. The standard bars in the vault were Good Delivery bars, each with a serial number. They weighed 12.4 kilograms each, contained 400 troy ounces, or 438.9 ounces. That translated to about 27.5 pounds each.

He did some figuring in his head. Fifty tons was one hundred thousand pounds, which equals about 3,600 bars, more or less.

They weren't going to get it done using dollies or a dozen soldiers. He had Colonel Holt assemble a conga line of thirty soldiers, and they passed gold bars from hand to hand into the elevator, and when it held a couple of hundred, sent it up to be off-loaded into a truck while more were stacked at the entrance. The work went faster.

The men ate MREs in shifts at midday and took a five-minute potty break in shifts. The pile of gold shrank slowly.

We should have brought some dollies, JR thought. Well, one can't think of everything. He found himself glancing at his watch every few minutes. The minute hand crawled.

Our flight back to Dawson was uneventful. The weather was benign, a typical September day in the eastern United States. We watched for ambushes and found none. We did see our columns snaking along. They had made almost a hundred miles since we saw them in the early morning. We saw another convoy of trucks and cars heading west from Baltimore, approaching Frederick, about fifty miles behind our northern army column. This convoy wasn't ours.

Grafton circled the convoy, low enough that we could see flags with Soetoro's image on them (a sort of Che Guevara T-shirt look) fluttering from car and truck aerials. Then we headed for Dawson.

I decided to deliver myself of an opinion. "The problem with democracy," I told Grafton on the ICS, "is that fools elect fools."

He snorted. "And the problem with hereditary kings is that too often you get the pampered, coddled village idiot running the country."

"Life is tough," I told him.

The National Guard camp near Kingwood was almost deserted. We taxied up and shut down in the precise spot where we had manned the plane hours before.

I chocked the plane and tied it down after Grafton went off to find whoever was manning the radios. I got busy fueling the plane. An army portable generator supplied the power to pump the avgas.

As I finished I noticed some metal blossomed out on the left wing. I climbed off the ladder and took a look. There was a bullet hole in the wing, about six feet in from the port wingtip. A bullet had gone in the bottom of the wing and out the top. A .30 caliber, from the look of it. And neither Grafton nor I had felt a thing. Someone we flew over today was unhappy with us, with life, maybe with the world.

After I got the fueling hose put away and the generator secured, I looked the airplane over carefully for any more punctures, didn't find any, and then strolled away carrying my M4. I found Sarah with Grafton in the headquarters building by the radios.

He was on the horn to General Martinez. "I'll meet you at first light at the Hagerstown airport. I suspect you are going to meet that bunch coming from Baltimore tomorrow mid-morning between Hagerstown and Frederick. I want to be with you."

"Roger. I'll meet you there."

Sarah looked at me and I looked at her. She didn't say anything, and I couldn't think of anything except, "Want to go see if we can find something to eat?"

She did, so with a nod to Grafton, we left. He got busy talking to the southern column.

"Seen the Wire around?" I asked.

"Not hide nor hair."

I wondered where in the world that fool was. Giving him a weapon the other night in Kingwood was a bad mistake. He wasn't any part of a warrior, which was why I liked him. I was worried. It was a tough world out there these days, and he wasn't a tough man.

The Bank of Manhattan's president, Abe Gottlieb, wanted to know if the Fed was waiting for the gold. "Of course," JR said. "I have troops there. They'll stay open until we arrive and if necessary will work all night getting it into their vault."

"Ah, the army!"

"Indeed."

"How do you know that a few soldiers won't steal some bars?"

That sally drew a frosty stare from the general. Gottlieb said he needed something to eat, and wandered away.

JR was upstairs in the bank when the power came back on in Manhattan. He knew it was on because the outside telephone lines began ringing. The receptionist smiled broadly, shouted to the other tellers, and answered the phone.

Uh-oh.

JR looked around for Gottlieb. Two FBI agents were with him, and he signaled to one of them, who jogged over.

"Power's on, phones are up," said JR. "We've got to move. Close the doors, round up the staff—all of them including Gottlieb—and put them in a conference room upstairs. Confiscate all cell phones and remove the regular phones from the room. Get cracking."

"Yes, sir."

JR went back to the vault. Soldiers were passing bars along at a good clip. "How many ingots have you loaded?" he asked Holt.

"By my count, about two thousand." JR looked at his watch. It was almost one o'clock.

"Sixteen hundred to go. Get the bank employees out of here and give them to the FBI agents. Get more troops down here."

"Yes, sir."

JR went along encouraging his soldiers. "Come on, men. You can do it. We're over half way there."

He went up on the street and checked the trucks. As soon as a truck had four hundred bars in it, a new truck was pulled into position. Armed soldiers were stationed around the trucks, and they kept the curious moving on. Not all of them, of course, since the sight of all that gold stopped people in their tracks.

Three policemen had been enlisted to help keep the crowd moving along the sidewalks. As JR watched, another police car pulled up and a captain in uniform came over. He had scrambled eggs on his hat. He saluted JR, who returned it.

"We got no notice of this move."

"We can handle it. We figured you had enough troubles as it was."

The cop took off his hat and wiped the sweat from his hair, then put it back on. "We sure do, General. We sure do. But with the electricity back on, maybe things will start returning to normal."

"We can only hope."

He pointed to JR's combat infantryman's badge on his chest. "I got one of those," the captain said. "The Gulf War, Desert Storm."

"Thank you for your service," JR replied.

"Yeah. Got out and joined the police. Probably should have stayed in the army. It was a great experience, but I wanted to come home to New York. You know, you're the first general I ever talked to."

"Well, you're my first police captain. I hope we never meet professionally."

The cop grinned. "You're pretty young too."

"Good whiskey," JR confided. "Never drink the cheap stuff."

The captain held up his hand and adjusted the earpiece in his ear. He rogered the transmission, then said to JR, "Gotta go. Got some dead people in an apartment house. Someone just found them. Been dead a few days."

They shook hands, and the captain trotted over to his cruiser and jumped in. The driver hit the lights and siren, and away the cruiser went up the street, howling madly.

Everyone has problems, JR thought, and got back to attending to his.

Texas poked her photonics masts up as she approached the narrows. Loren could see the Verrazano Bridge across the narrows, and he saw ships. Lots of ships, none of them going anywhere.

"Water is pretty shallow, Captain," Jugs said.

"Surface," Loren said. "I'll go up to the bridge. I want to see what's in the harbor. Listen to the radio and brief me over the sound-powered phone."

So *Texas* rose from the depths and her sail broke water. Loren opened hatches and was soon standing on the small bridge. He plugged in a sound-powered headset and talked to Jugs.

Giving heading commands, he went around ships that were anchored and under the bridge. Not much traffic on it, he noted, and he used his binoculars to examine the freighters and tankers anchored in the lower harbor, waiting for pier space.

He saw no navy ships. Not a one. Maybe there was a submarine outside the narrows, but maybe not. Maybe peace had broken out all over. The sky was empty of airplanes, even helicopters.

Staying at ten knots, Loren took the boat around Liberty Island. "Jugs, come up here."

In about a minute she was standing beside him, gazing at Lady Liberty, the ships, and the Manhattan skyline.

After a bit she said, "It's time to go home, Lorrie."

"I think so too," he said, and put his elbows on the rail in front of him and breathed deep of the tangy, salty air. "Why don't you go below and send the others up here for a look, one by one."

"Aye-aye, sir," she said, and went down the ladder.

Loren used the sound-powered phone to order a turn back toward the narrows. George Ranta came topside, looked and laughed and pounded Loren on the back, then went below and sent up Mouse.

Two hours later, safely back through the narrows and with good water under the keel, *Texas* slipped beneath the waves. In the control room, Jugs briefed him on what she had heard on the radio. The power was back on in New York. The Pentagon was adamant that the military was not taking sides in the Soetoro administration's squabble with the states. People were being released from concentration camps in droves. Politicians were lining up at radio and television stations to be interviewed.

Maybe America—and Texas—will make it after all, Loren thought, and gave orders for the voyage back to Galveston.

★

It was four in the afternoon when the 3,600th gold ingot was laid in a truck and the tailgate closed. The bank's personnel were locked upstairs in conference rooms, and the fake FBI agents had put the fear of God in them.

Five minutes later the last of the soldiers and Texas Rangers were aboard the trucks and they were rolling. The traffic signals were working again, although the streets were still almost devoid of traffic. The trucks didn't stop for lights—they simply drove on through.

At LaGuardia the planes were sitting with their ramps down when the trucks rolled up, and the loadmasters used hand signals to guide the drivers into the cavernous bays of the C-17s. Every soldier helped with the tie-down chains, then the loadmasters checked everything as the ramps came up and the planes started taxiing.

When they were airborne, a sergeant passed out bottles of water and MREs to the troops. JR went up to the front of the plane and came back with an open packing case. He walked down the line of soldiers sitting beside the trucks passing out bottles of champagne. "You guys have to share. We only brought a case for each plane."

Corks popped and happy smiles broke out.

JR went up to the flight deck and sat down in the jump seat. *By God, we did it*, he thought. *Fifty tons of gold*!

THIRTY-FOUR

★

A riot in the streets in front of the White House and in Lafayette Park broke out between supporters and opponents of Barry Soetoro that evening. The melee quickly got out of control, so the police called for fire trucks with water cannons, which were waiting a half-mile away. And they fired tear gas grenades.

The mob wavered under the gas, but it was the fire trucks that finally dispersed the crowd. A dozen people were dead, either beaten to death or trampled, and several hundred injured.

While the tear gas wafted into the White House, the survivors of the battle surged through the streets smashing out store windows, looting, and overturning cars and setting them on fire.

In the White House, loyalists gathered around Barry Soetoro and urged him to accept the Pentagon's offer of a plane to take him into exile.

"Their price is a letter of resignation," Soetoro said, "and I am not going to resign this office. It would be a betrayal of all those people who believe in me." His chin quivered. "I am America's hope, the hope of all people everywhere to build a just society and save the planet. That is my destiny."

Sulana Schanck believed. "You are the hope of the *world*! And the world will come to your rescue. These racist pigs *will not prevail*!"

Amid the coughing and fervid pledges of loyalty, the realization sank in that they couldn't stay in the White House. The mob would return. And when it did…

They took the tunnel to the Executive Office Building across the street, and from there went to the basement, where their staff had a fleet of cars waiting. Not everyone got into the cars, of course. Most of the senators and representatives decided not to go. One said later that he knew when Soetoro's car pulled away that he would never see Barry Soetoro again.

The standoff between the crowds and the police and Secret Service guarding the executive mansion ended at about midnight. A crowd of almost two hundred people, mostly men, came walking out of a side street on the west side of the grounds. With them was a large tow truck, one used to rescue tractor-trailer rigs. Leading them was a black man in the uniform of a captain of the D.C. police. They came straight to the west gate, where four D.C. police in riot gear stood guard. Behind the gate, which was closed, were a half-dozen federal police, also in riot gear. Accompanying the crowd was a television reporter and her cameraman.

The police captain, who was unarmed, walked up to the cops, who knew him. "Guys, we are going to open that gate and go through it. You have two choices: you can shoot me or get out of the way while we pull the gate down."

"What the hell do you think you're doing, Captain?"

"I've joined the rebels. It is time to stop the bloodshed over Barry Soetoro. We're going in."

One of the cops fingered his radio. While he was doing that, the captain gestured to the tow truck, which moved up to within six feet of the gate. Men carrying chains went around the cops and ran the chains around the gate and hooked them to the massive bumper hooks of the truck. Then the helpers got out of the way and the truck backed up with its audible warning beeping madly.

The federal cops backed away from the gate with their weapons at the ready. One of them was already on his radio.

That was when the senior cop on duty, a sergeant, staring at the captain whom he had served under for more than a dozen years, gestured to his mates. "Get out of the way, fellows. The captain is pulling it down."

The captain nodded once, and the tow truck engine revved and the driver popped the clutch. The slack came out of the chains and the gate came off its hinges and went skidding as the truck backed across the street, blocking it.

The captain strode up the now-open drive and said to the federal police. "Shoot me or get out of the way."

They looked at the crowd surging forward, the television camera catching it all, and moved aside. The crowd surged onto the lawn and made for the White House. The television reporter and police captain walked, but many of the men in the crowd—it was almost exclusively male—ran ahead.

In fifteen minutes the police captain and television reporter learned to their satisfaction that the president was not in the mansion. Only a few servants remained. Not a single staffer or aide or politician could be found.

As the crowd surged through the first family's quarters and the Oval Office grabbing souvenirs and vandalizing furniture, the reporter and cameraman went trotting out the way they had entered. They had footage that they needed to get on the air fast. The reporter could smell a Pulitzer.

Grafton and I were off the ground Thursday morning when the sky was black as coal and the morning star was just ooching up over the horizon. He climbed to 4,500 feet and headed straight for Hagerstown. The little plane didn't have a nav aid or GPS, so Grafton took a squint at the sectional chart, decided on a course, and hi-de-ho, here we go. As we flew along, I communed with Venus. Like most people, I rarely visit with the morning star. Praying that we wouldn't make this a habit, I gazed with wonder at the sprite. The night faded, and almost as if God had taken a hand, at the proper time the Hagerstown airport appeared in the dawn haze.

The northern army was camped on the airport grass. It was a sea of military vehicles; a few APCs; several howitzers; lots of trucks, generators, tents, portable kitchens; and several thousand people, about half in uniform. Pickup trucks and cars were parked in rows.

"Wow," I said.

"That's only about half the troops," Grafton said. "The rest are camped at the fair ground, and a lot of the veterans are on picket duty. Martinez thinks he has about five thousand people now."

We landed and parked near the control tower. General Martinez was there to meet Grafton. They went over to Martinez' ride, a pickup, and conferred while I chocked the Cessna and tied it down. I looked to see if we had collected any more bullet holes. Not yet today.

I faced into the dawn, surveyed the encampment, and took a leak. I gave thanks that I hadn't chosen the military as a career; the hours are terrible. Zipped up and yawned. Okay, I was ready.

I strolled over to the meeting of the general staff at the pickup truck.

"General Martinez says Soetoro isn't in the White House. Civilians got in last night and found he had skedaddled."

"Terrific," I said, yawning again. "If the Pentagon didn't fly him to some third world paradise, this will be like looking for Elvis."

"Oh," Jake Grafton said with a gleam in his eye, "I have a feeling he's close. Like up at Camp David." He pointed to the east. "Just twenty miles that way, on the other side of that low mountain."

I turned and looked east at the mountain bulging against the dawn sky. Actually, it sort of figured that Barry Soetoro might run to earth in that rustic presidential getaway, which was designed for defense by Secret Service and federal police. Local crackers couldn't get within five miles of the place without alarms going off. If I were going to hide out for a while and had the federal government to pay the help, chefs included, Camp David would be high on my list.

"Maybe so," I said to Grafton.

"Indeed," he said, "maybe so."

He turned back to General Martinez, so I walked around the pickup truck to see if it had any dings. It looked clean. After this mess was over, maybe I could make an offer on one that FEMA didn't need anymore. I had decided that I needed a truck. My old Benz convertible was cool, but a truck had more possibilities for a man of my métier.

Grafton and Martinez gabbled on their handhelds a while, then Grafton motioned toward the Cessna. He shook hands with Martinez and conferred some more while I untied the plane and stowed the chocks. I climbed into the right seat and put on my belt and headset. Arranged my little bag of grenades behind me so I could reach them easily and made sure my M4 on the backseat was loaded and handy. I wished I had a flak vest to sit on, but I didn't.

Finally Grafton strode over, jumped into the left seat, and cranked the engine. With it at idle he put on his seat belt and headset. "Martinez will get the Predators up. They are flying them out of Dawson, so until they get here we are the eyes of the army."

"Roger eyes."

"We need to find out what happened to that column of people coming from Baltimore along the interstate and see what's happening at Camp David."

"The feds will likely shoot at us if we go swanning over in this crate."

"Then we'll know, won't we?"

The asshole! It was on the tip of my tongue to tell him that if he had an ounce of sense he'd send a Predator over David, but not-a-minute-to-waste Grafton had made his decision and he wouldn't change it. How come I always get stuck with the heroes?

Both our side windows opened on hinges at the top to a limit of about three inches. I checked mine. It was a bit too small for me to push a grenade through the opening. Not to worry, I could always open the door against the slipstream and drop them like eagle shit on the multitudes below. Maybe they would be inspired to keep their heads down. I reached behind me and got a couple, which I put in my lap.

Twenty minutes later we realized that the interstate east all the way to Frederick was essentially empty. That column of Soetoro volunteers had to be somewhere, but where?

Grafton turned toward Camp David. He was only about a thousand feet above the trees. Plumes of smoke rose from the forest, formed a thin cloud in the still air, and pointed the way to Camp David. Lots of fires down there, so there were probably lots of people.

And sure enough, we found them. Grafton got looks through the trees at people camping, then he dropped lower and we saw vehicles by the dozens, mainly trucks. Saw the presidential buildings surrounded by lawns and stately mature trees, and many people on those lawns. Most of the people I saw had rifles. Then a few of them pointed their weapons skyward and I saw flashes against the dark of the forest floor.

"They're shooting at us," I told Grafton.

"We're leaving," he said, and headed west over the low mountain.

When we were clear, he got on the radio to Martinez. "Many people around Camp David. I think you need to check it out. The man may be there."

"Wilco."

We landed at Hagerstown and I tied the plane down after inspecting it again for bullet holes. The shooters all missed. Maybe this was going to be a lucky day for me. Sarah Houston drove up in our stolen FEMA pickup, the one that had my money in it, along with spare weapons, AT4s, and my sniper rifles. I was ready for a real war.

She was wearing jeans, a green army T-shirt, and a web belt with her pistol holster attached. Her hair was pulled back in a ponytail. "You're looking great this morning, lady," I told her.

"Have you heard that Soetoro left the White House sometime yesterday?"

"I have."

"The Pentagon said he refused an offer of a flight into exile."

"Probably no one would accept him. He'd want to take Mickey with him, and that's a deal killer."

Sarah sighed and looked at the sky and army and mountains. "I'll be glad when this is over," she said. She flipped a hand at the ad hoc army, now getting ready to move. "The officers say that the former soldiers and guard troopers and veterans follow orders. The civilians are here on a toot. They don't do what they're told unless they feel like it. They were up drinking and partying all night. Some of them didn't get an hour's sleep."

"My prediction is they're going to get shot at today," I said. "Some of them will run like rabbits. Don't get caught behind them or you'll get run over."

I jumped in the driver's seat of the truck, Sarah climbed in beside me, and we went looking for Grafton, who would be at headquarters if we could find it.

Turned out HQ was in the airport office building. Outside, I ran into Willis Coffee. "How goes the war?" I asked.

He looked disgusted. "Two accidental shootings last night. Civilians! One dead, one injured. Amateur hour."

"We'll see if Soetoro's army can whittle them down today. They're at Camp David, just over that little mountain to the east. The man himself may be there, so Grafton will probably have us humping hard to surround the place so he can't sneak out."

"Fine with me," Willis said. "Let's pop him and get on with the program."

"You'd shoot him?"

"That son? In a New York minute. *Vaya con Dios*, asshole, and bang!"

"Where's Travis?"

He gestured vaguely. "Scouting somewhere. Martinez sent him out before dawn."

"Good luck today," I said, and Sarah and I went inside the building.

Grafton was conferring with Generals Martinez and Considine. I listened in and gathered that they wanted to surround Camp David as quickly as possible. Trucks full of troops and the APCs would get on the highway and go around to the east as fast as they could. Another load of troops and APCs would go around to the north. The civilians would be pointed east and told to hike over the mountain, with some professionals along to ensure they didn't get lost in the woods.

When the meeting broke up, Grafton said he was riding with me. "Which column are we going with?"

"The civilians, through the woods."

My face must have fallen, because he said, "There're a couple of dirt roads. We'll take the pickup. If we do this right, the people at Camp

David will think the mob coming through the woods is the main assault and leave the front door open for the pros."

I wondered if he was having a senior moment. "If they aren't stupid," I suggested tactfully, "they might think the main assault is coming through the front gate."

"Didn't you see them when we flew over this morning, Tommy? The pros are dug in to defend the front gate and perimeter fence. They're well dug in, with at least two machine-gun nests and a couple of artillery pieces that I saw. Our troops out front will set up ambushes a couple of miles from the front gate, and the defenders won't even see them or know that they are there. With a little bit of luck, if the civilian volunteers coming through the woods can make enough noise, Soetoro will flush and boogey out the front and we'll bag him."

So he intended to capture the president of the United States. "What are you going to do with him when you have him?" I asked.

"Lock him up and let the new government worry about him. A significant percentage of Americans still think he's God's other son. We have got to bring people together, not drive them apart. The next government can have a trial, send him to Switzerland or Kenya, whatever floats their boat. And we can start putting America back together again."

"What about all these civilian volunteers? They're undisciplined, don't know tactics, are poorly armed, won't obey orders—they don't know shit about combat. They'll panic and get shot in droves."

"We're rebuilding a nation here, Tommy. It takes blood to create legends and myths. These people want to fight for their country. We'll let 'em."

That was the Jake Grafton I knew, one hard man. God help all these civilians.

There must have been three or four thousand of them, armed with everything from shotguns and deer rifles to black civilian versions of the M16. Lots of pistols. It seemed a quarter of them carried pistols and nothing else. I was appalled. If you were within pistol range of the enemy, you were too damned close.

Trucks passed out water bottles, and cases of water were tossed in the beds of our pickups. For all those people, it was not enough. A lot of them were going to get seriously thirsty, even though the temperature was only seventy degrees. I suspected many would pass out from heat exhaustion, especially those who were overweight. Today they had a mountain to climb and a fight on the other side ahead of them. It was at least fifteen miles, I suspected, to the Camp David perimeter fence, and most of it uphill. The crest of the mountain was about a thousand feet in elevation above us.

Looking them over, I thought the average age might be around forty. Everyone who claimed he was a U.S. Army or Marine veteran or retiree had already been winnowed out, given a uniform and a military rifle, and those folks were in trucks and APCs, going to fight the Secret Service and Federal Security police on the other side of the mountain. These were people who claimed no military experience, which meant they knew nothing of tactics or how to handle military weapons and hardware. They probably had minimum experience obeying orders, our modern world being what it is.

And yet…it was the men over forty who interested me. Many were apparently construction workers or farmers, wearing bib overalls or work trousers and leather boots. Lean and tanned, they carried their rifles like they knew how to use them and had a rucksack or backpack over their shoulders with water, rations, and ammo. Lots of ball caps; some of them were my very favorite, John Deere. I had no doubt most of these guys could walk me into the ground.

Then there were the outdoor types, men and women, also lean, wearing walking shoes with shorts and logoed T-shirts. They all had backpacks, some of them with the logos of purveyors of outdoor gear. Many wore floppy sun hats with strings that hung under their chins. A few even had bicyclists' water bags over their shoulders. They carried their rifles or shotguns as if they were unsure how to do it.

And then there was everyone else. A few were teenagers, but many looked to me like they were professionals or middle managers, some pudgy, some downright overweight, wearing jeans and everything else you could imagine. Their T-shirts were from colleges, high schools, and state parks. At least a third of these folks looked as if a walk across a large parking lot would wear them out. I would have bet some of the women were soccer moms.

Black, white, brown, Asians, with ancestors from all over the globe, they looked like America to me.

At least three thousand of these volunteers gathered around the spot where the first dirt road left the pavement. They had walked over two miles through suburban Hagerstown to get there. It was getting on toward ten o'clock.

With General Considine beside him, Grafton stood in the bed of the truck and shouted for them to gather around. They did. He raised his voice, and I swear, I think everyone in that mob heard him. Grafton in full cry was a primal force.

"We're going up this road to the top of that mountain and will hit the Camp David perimeter fence on the other side. It's a good hike up there, and you need to keep up. Don't fire your weapons until we make contact with the enemy. Obey your officers and stay together. No straggling. When you tell your grandkids about this someday, you'll want to be able to say you were there at the finish, there when the dictator was captured and a new America was born. Keep your head down and shoot low. Let's go." And he waved his arm up the road.

There was a fork a mile or so up the road, and he had stationed guardsmen there to divide the civilians, sending half on one road, half on the other. Travis Clay had reconnoitered both, he told Sarah and me, and both roads led to a bald spot on the mountain crest; the Camp David perimeter fence was just beyond that. "Considine will take the north fork and I'll take the south. We expect to meet most of Soetoro's volunteers at the bald crest," Grafton told us as we watched our crowd trudge up the road. "That's the fight that will flush Soetoro, I hope, and Martinez will bag him on the other side of the mountain."

"If he's there," I said. "For all we know he may be in Hawaii playing golf."

"If he is, he swam over," Grafton shot back. "Tommy, you drive. Follow that howitzer. The guardsmen with their mortars will follow you."

THIRTY-FIVE

★

The trek up the mountain was the most frustrating experience I have ever had. We averaged two miles every hour. I would move the truck ahead a couple of hundred yards and shut off the engine to save fuel.

The western side of that mountain, the crest of which ran generally north and south, was a mix of pastures and woodlots with farm houses and ramshackle barns thrown in, and here and there a mobile home surrounded by the owner's junk collection. Rotting tractors, curious cows staring at us over fences, abandoned pickups manufactured during the Truman administration, stray dogs, yards full of weeds, fences covered with poison ivy, it was rural America in late summer in all its glory.

The fat people had it worst. They began dropping out, just sitting down. Some of the skinny people put their weapons in the truck and on the army trucks behind us carrying mortars, MREs, and water, just to lighten the load. People trudged and trudged up the edge of our road, raising clouds of dust.

Grafton sat in the rear seat and was on the handheld radio constantly. He gave Sarah and me updates on the southern army. They were through Leesburg and had collected another two or more thousand civilians, who were walking and driving cars and pickups and vans. Everyone seemed to want to go to Washington. Our ambushers, Martinez' bunch, were in position blocking the roads into and out of Camp David.

The power was back on in eastern Virginia and Maryland, and television and radio reporters were giving their audiences the blow by blow. Dixie Cotton was with the army marching through Leesburg, heading for the eastern Virginia suburbs, and she was on the air and on fire, urging all loyal Americans to join with the army of volunteers on its way to liberate Washington.

It was nearly one o'clock when I saw Travis Clay standing beside the road. I stopped beside him.

"This is like herding cats," he said. "Got any water?"

"In the bed. Help yourself."

When he had guzzled a bottle and had another bottle in his hand, he came back to the driver's door. "You going to sit there riding along in your limo, or are you going to help?"

"I'm an officer. Rank has its privileges."

"I'm going to write a letter to your mother. 'Tommy doesn't play well with other children.'"

I told Sarah to drive the truck and got out with my M4.

I helped Travis and Willis herd the troops up the road. Every little bit a shot would echo around. The wannabe warriors got bored and shot into a tree or a deer or whatever. I saw a guy with a shotgun drop a crow that was flying over.

"Save your ammunition," I admonished the trekkers. "You're going to need every damn bullet before the day is over. And for God's sake, don't shoot the cows: they don't vote, don't have guns, and can't shoot back, so it isn't sporting." Some listened, some didn't.

We came upon a farm where the lady of the house had gone all out. Apparently she knew the column was hiking up the road, so she had a folding table set up by the gate and she and her daughters, both early teens, were pouring good well water for anyone who wanted a drink. And serving homemade cookies.

"Thank you, ma'am," I said as I helped myself to an oatmeal raisin cookie and filled up my water bottle. "How'd you know this mob was coming?"

"Your scouts came up the hill at dawn this morning, and I met them coming back. They said a lot of people would be along."

So I sipped water and munched my cookie as the troops did the same, then we moved along while other people crowded the table. Everyone had a good word to say to the lady and her daughters, and she had a good word for everyone. America walking by your door, on a dirt road that leads nowhere in particular. It was a strange experience.

Two miles farther up the road, I found a woman sitting with her shoes and socks off, looking at broken blisters, now leaking blood. A double-barrel shotgun lay beside her. "Are you going to be able to keep going?" I asked.

She looked to me to be in her fifties. She cocked her head to eye me, squinting against the sun. "I'll make it, Jack," she said.

"My name's Tommy Carmellini."

"Betty Connelly."

She took a pair of dry socks from her backpack. "My daughter died in that parochial school in Arlington Heights a couple of weeks ago. She was a teacher. One of those jihadists Soetoro let into the country shot her in the face. I'll get up this mountain if I have to crawl it."

While she put her shoes and socks back on, I inspected her shotgun, an elegant old side-by-side. I opened the breech and extracted one of the shells. Number six birdshot, perfect for pheasants. I put the shell back in, snapped the breech closed, checked the safety, and put her on the tailgate of our truck. Gave her a bottle of water and her shotgun. "You ride there until we get on top," I told her.

She nodded and brushed the hair back out of her eyes. "Thanks," she said. I just hoped she didn't get shot.

After two hours, I got back in the truck. Although the temp was only seventy-five degrees, according to the truck's thermometer, I was hot and sweaty, and so was everyone hiking up that low mountain to get to whatever fate awaited us. I guess I was a little nervous, right along with everyone else.

Somehow, someway, we made it up the grade. The dirt road got worse and worse the higher we went, until it was just a rutted road full of dried-up mud-holes. No farms up here, just woods. I glanced at the truck's odometer. It had driven fourteen miles to cover the twelve miles direct distance to the edge of the bald.

Grafton had received radio messages from the Predator crew long before. Soetoro's army was on the crest of the mountain, and at least three hundred yards of cow pasture lay between the forest on the top of the western slope and the naked crest.

It was four o'clock by my watch when I first sighted the bald. Sarah was at the wheel of the truck, so I got out and started directing our tired volunteers into the woods. I estimated we had lost at least half through straggling and heat exhaustion, but that was just a guess.

"Get the troops spread out," Grafton told me. "Link up with the people on the other road and stay in the woods. Have the mortarmen take their weapons out there a ways for max coverage."

Already the people on the crest were popping away at us. The bullets pattered on the trees and leaves like rain, but if they hit anyone, I didn't see him or her go down. With all the dust and engine noise and gunfire all afternoon from our crowd as they climbed the mountain, there was no possibility of surprise. Not that Grafton wanted surprise.

Our troops retrieved their weapons from the vehicles and went scurrying out through the woods as the distant firing and pattering of bullets encouraged them on. The howitzer was turned and set up in the road. The truck pulling it had already run over the cattle gate, flattening it. A three-strand barbed-wire fence on ancient, half-rotted posts ran away on both sides of the gate. The artillery officer, a captain, came over to confer with Grafton. "Not yet," the admiral said.

I went into the woods, trying to show the civilians how to take advantage of cover, advising them not to fire their weapons, but to wait. Some of the fools huddled down behind a bush or sapling that wouldn't stop a BB, so I moved them to rocks and behind big trees. Inevitably a few of them began banging away at the distant crest, wasting ammo; they probably had no idea how far their bullets would drop at that distance. Some were shooting into the air at a thirty-degree angle; maybe they were trying to hit Camp David.

One guy was walking around like it was Sunday afternoon in the park, shouting to his fellow warriors, "Hang tough. We'll kick the shit out of those stupid sons of bitches."

"Get down, you idiot," I told him.

He looked at me with distain and struck a pose. "At this distance, they can't hit—"

Whap! There is no sound on earth like that of a bullet striking a living body.

I heard the sound and saw the hole appear in the side of his head. Blood began leaking out. He swayed like an old oak in a storm, his eyes fixed on infinity, dead on his feet. He fell beside me.

He had a nice rifle, an old 1903 Springfield with a four-power scope. I laid it across his chest and moved on, shouting, "You morons get behind something solid and stay down! Save your ammo!"

After twenty minutes of that, when I had positioned the men and women who had made the climb on the left side of the road, I went back to the pickup.

"Get out your sniper rifle, Tommy, and look at the people on the crest," Grafton said. "When the action starts, shoot anyone who looks as if he is directing troops." That was always the advice to snipers: kill the officers.

"Yo," I said and got out the best rifle, deployed the bipod, filled my pockets with cartridges, and set up using a pile of dirt that some snow scraper had deposited there in past years.

I lased the crest. Three hundred fifteen yards, give or take.

"Start shooting, Tommy," Jake Grafton said.

I picked out some fool who was standing up looking this way with binoculars and let him have it. After the recoil, I didn't see him. I scared or hit him.

I had fired ten shots when Grafton said, "Do you have a machine gun in the truck?"

"Yes."

"Put it up there and get ready."

I had no more than gotten the bipod deployed and the belt in it when the howitzer began firing at a high angle. I saw the shells popping on the crest. Then the mortars opened up, dropping their shells along the crest too.

This is it, I thought. They'll break for the woods behind them and we'll charge up there to take the crest.

Grafton was running to the left, telling everyone who would listen that we were going to charge the crest, but to stop there. In all likelihood, the people on the crest would retreat to the woods on the other side and be waiting for our bunch to charge them.

But...

I was astounded when the enemy on the crest stood up and began running downhill toward us. They charged, at least two thousand of them, screaming at the top of their lungs and firing wildly. They were dedicated Soetoro fanatics, not professionals.

I hunkered down over the M249 and began firing bursts. They went down in handfuls. To my right and left the woods came alive as the civilian volunteers let loose with everything they had, shotguns, rifles, and pistols.

The charge broke halfway to the trees. The ground was carpeted with people when, suddenly, the survivors began running back up the hill en masse, some of them carrying and dragging wounded people.

I shot the whole belt at them as the howitzer banged away to my left and the mortarmen dropped their shells among the survivors. Then the artillery shells that had been popping viciously moved their aim point and I no longer saw the shells land. They were obviously shooting to land their shells on the back side of the ridge.

All along our line a shout went up and people who thought they didn't have another erg of energy left in them left the trees in a trot, charging up that hill. That's when my admiration of the American volunteer went through the roof. By God, they had guts.

They swarmed up that hill.

Sarah motioned to me, so I grabbed the machine gun and belt and got in the back. She put the truck in motion and I hung on. I wanted to change the belt in the machine gun but with the uneven ground tossing the truck around, there was no way. I grabbed my M4 and squirted a burst at any of the enemy who paused in flight to shoot at people charging up the hill.

When we made the crest, it was empty. The enemy was running down the other side. Sarah stopped the truck. I dumped the carbine and grabbed a belt of ammo and slapped it in the M249 as bullets snapped around the truck. People running, guns blazing: it was the damnedest battle I have been in yet, like something from an American Civil War movie, blues versus grays. I dismounted, set up the gun, and shot at the retreating people dashing into the trees on the east side of the bald.

"Hose the tree line," Grafton shouted. He was outside the truck, crouching, watching everything. "They may have an ambush there." Out of the corner of my eye, I saw him run over to the howitzer crew and point. In seconds the artillery shells began falling just back of the treeline: explosions, clouds of dirt, trees falling. The mortarmen came up to the crest in the pickups that they had used to transport their tubes, recoil plates, and ammo. After taking a moment to get set up again, they began lofting shells into the woods below.

To my amazement, our guys who had scaled the crest stopped for only a moment to get their breath, then set off running downhill for the trees.

I finished the belt and got another into the gun, which was getting damned hot.

Grafton jumped into the truck and Sarah raced it downhill. I sprayed lead, then grabbed the gun and followed them.

She stopped forty feet from the edge of the trees. I threw my machine gun in the bed and picked up my M4.

Willis Coffee came running up. Grafton shouted at him, "Get some AT4s and shoot them into the trees."

"We've got about a dozen."

"Get them running for Camp David."

Willis did as he was told. Stood in the bed and launched the rockets as fast as he could.

When our troops were no longer in sight, Willis got down. Our guys and gals had gone into the trees. They had literally jerked the old fence posts out of the ground rather than climb over or through the barbed wire.

Grafton, Sarah, and Willis each got an M4, and we trotted toward the trees. We hadn't taken five steps when Willis grunted and fell. I stopped and went back to check on him. He had taken a bullet in the chest. He looked at me and said, "Tell my wife..."

"What?" I demanded. "Tell her what?"

But he was dead. I realized then that I really didn't know Willis Coffee very well. And I would never know him better. "God bless you," I whispered, and ran on toward the trees.

Dead and wounded lay everywhere. We disarmed the wounded and kept going. Our troops were in front of us, driving the enemy toward the perimeter fence somewhere in the woods ahead.

When we hit the fence, it was down. Who tore it down I never learned. It was down when we got there and that was the reality of it. We kept going.

Somehow in the woods amid the smoke and bodies, we lost Grafton. He must have run on ahead. I was too old a dog for loping through the woods when people could be hiding behind any tree praying for a good shot at their pursuers. Ahead I could hear the cacophony of gunfire. Bodies lay every which way, a lot of them shot in the back. The wounded were groaning. The rocky forest floor looked like hell's half acre.

A moment later I saw the first body that had been scalped. The head was a bloody mess and the hair was gone. At the time I thought, maybe shrapnel did that.

I kept going, and soon found another. Scalped.

A hundred yards later, I met an unarmed man wandering amid the shattered trees and rocks. He had long hair, at least on the fringes; his scalp had been cut and torn off. The top of his head and his face were masses of blood.

I stopped him, forced him to lie down. "Whoa. What the hell happened?"

"A shell hit near me. I was out for a bit, and when I woke up some guy was ripping the top of my head off. He had a big knife. He left me there."

"Lie still. The medics will be along after a bit."

"Help me, mister! For God's sake!" He clutched at me but I drew back and scanned the woods.

"Lie still," I repeated. "Your war is over."

I picked up the pace. I had covered maybe two hundred yards when I came upon a big tattooed guy with a long knife and a black rifle. He had a bag on a strap over his shoulder. I could see hair protruding from it. He was bending over a figure on the ground, a woman in shorts with long blond hair, and he had his knife out. She had an arm up, trying to fend him off. "For God's sake," she screamed. He grabbed a handful of hair, lifted her head a little, and jabbed the knife into her scalp.

"Stop," I roared. He turned toward me and I shot him.

I ran toward him as he went down. The woman on the ground looked at me stunned, then she was dead, as if someone had turned a switch. He had her scalp half off.

He was still alive. He looked at me with the strangest expression. I kicked his rifle away.

Then a shot rang out. He took the bullet in the head. I turned and saw Sarah Houston standing there with her carbine at her shoulder.

She shot into him three or four more times, turned, and began walking downhill, east toward Camp David and the rolling racket of gunfire.

The woman on the ground was wearing a Penn T-shirt—University of Pennsylvania—now soaked with blood from a mortal wound caused by a large shard of a tree that was still sticking two feet out of her chest. She had bled a lot before the scalper got to her. Blood, almost black, was everywhere. She and the scalper lay in it.

The sun was already behind the bald crest above me, leaving the woods in dark shadow. Below on the slope, Sarah threaded her way through trees still standing and those blasted by shellfire, around downed trees, limbs, and rocky outcrops, and disappeared from view. I got myself in motion, following along.

Grafton must have passed these wounded people on his trot down the hill, sore ribs and all, trying to get to Camp David before the mob killed Soetoro. He was a man on a mission.

I wasn't. I didn't give a damn what happened to Barry Soetoro.

★

It got dark as I went through the woods. There was just enough moon and starlight to allow me to see trees and rocks except under dense foliage, when I had to literally feel my way along. I wished I had some night-vision goggles, but I didn't. And of course, neither did anyone else. I only tripped and fell four times.

After a while I got glimpses of fires burning around the presidential enclave. I moved carefully, the M4 at the ready. I came out of the trees and walked along a graveled path toward the biggest of the fires. People were everywhere, and all of them were armed. I figured they were our guys, and was sure when I saw fifty or sixty people sitting on the ground wearing white plastic ties around their wrists. There must have been a thousand people in the lawn and flower beds, most of them shouting like fiends.

Near the front door of what I took to be the main building or lodge, I saw Grafton and some of the people from the camp this morning confronting a knot of men and women in business attire. They had to be Secret Service. Barry and Mickey Soetoro were not in sight. I went around the corner of the house away from the group. The house, or lodge, was a two story. Looking around and concluding I was unobserved, I leaped for the bottom of a balcony. Got my hands on the concrete floor of the thing and pulled myself up with every muscle screaming about all the exercise I hadn't been getting.

Checking over my shoulder, I decided I still didn't have an audience, so went up like I was climbing a rope. Hooked an ankle over the top of the rail and voila, I was in. The door, unlocked, led to a bedroom. The lights were on inside and it was empty.

I closed the balcony door and stood listening with my pistol in my hand as I scanned the room. Actually, it was the sitting room of a suite. The crowd noise outside was now only a murmur. First I checked the bedroom, which was dark and empty. So was the bathroom.

The interior door of the sitting room opened into a hallway. I could hear voices from my left. That was the way I wanted to go, but only after I checked these other suites, for there appeared to be four of them off this hallway. When I went toward the voices, I wanted to know that there was no one behind me. The second suite I checked was empty of people, but the bed and bathroom had obviously been used.

In the third suite I found the body. It was lying beside the wet bar, as if it had fallen off a bar stool. The remnants of several drinks were on the bar. His throat was cut and he had done a lot of bleeding. I tried not to step in the blood, but to get a look at the face to see if I could recognize it. Yep. Al Grantham, the chief of staff.

Whoever cut his throat knew exactly how to do it. It looked like just one vicious swipe had severed the carotid arteries and his windpipe. Apparently done from behind. Unconsciousness had followed within a second or two as blood pressure in the victim's brain dropped toward zero.

I reached and touched his hand. It was still supple, although just beginning to cool off. He hadn't been dead long, not more than a few minutes. The blood was red and sticky.

I found that the palm of my hand on my pistol was sweaty. I dried it on my jeans and checked to make sure the suite was indeed empty of living people. A surprise by a knife fighter of that caliber was something to be avoided.

The hallway still empty, I tried the door of the fourth suite. Sucked it up and went in fast with the pistol ready. No one there.

Back down the hallway, gliding along beside the wall, listening intently. The voices got louder as I moved.

I could see that the wall I was against turned into a railing, and the hallway became a balcony leading to a stairway down into a great room. I got down on the floor, and after crawling, inched the top of my head around the edge of the wall and peeked between it and the first balcony upright.

There in the main room below, no more than fifteen feet from me, were Barry and Mickey Soetoro...and Sulana Schanck and a male aide I didn't recognize, talking to a couple of Secret Service types carrying M4s. Vice President Rhodes was there, the veep from central casting, with the superbly barbered white hair and square chin, in a gray suit that fit perfectly. Two other people were facing the agents: I couldn't see their faces and didn't know who they were. Rhodes' aides or politicians, no doubt, and true believers to the core.

"...There are at least a thousand of them, Mr. President. Perhaps twice that. They have the buildings surrounded and have complete control. We have six people left. The rebels can come into this building anytime they decide to walk over us and do it."

"Have you called for reinforcements? Assistance? Whatever you call it?"

"Yes. No one answers our radio transmissions, and no one is picking up the scrambled landlines."

"You're going to have to talk to Grafton," the veep said to the prez.

"I am not going to surrender," Soetoro declared. I thought I could detect a slight tremor in his voice, but it may have been only the acoustics. "Where are our supporters? Where are the liberal armies that were going to preserve order and support the federal government against the reactionaries? *Where are they*?"

I thought that his loyal supporters lying dead or maimed on the mountainside or sitting outside with their hands shackled by plastic ties were beyond caring how much they had disappointed ol' Barry.

Which of these people killed Al Grantham with a knife, and why? If you were going to do it, why not years ago? Truthfully, his mother should have done it way back when she realized what a twisted, diseased monster she had foisted upon the world, but that was water under the bridge, until today.

Of course, the knife artist could be somewhere else in the building, not down below. I glanced back down the hallway, a bit nervously, I suppose, to ensure that it was still empty. I certainly didn't want that dude within twenty yards of me.

Meanwhile they were jabbering away just below me. Everyone talking at once. Just beyond the door was a seriously unhappy crowd, or if you were inside looking out, an angry armed mob. These people in the lodge had no idea what fate awaited them. Jake Grafton didn't know either. Not only did I not know, I didn't give a damn.

I became aware that Sulana Schanck was having a serious private conversation with Barry Soetoro, just a few steps away from the others. No one else was apparently paying attention to what was being said, and they were talking too low for me to eavesdrop, even though my hearing is excellent. I tried to read lips and body language. She was adamant and he was resisting.

Whatever fate awaited these two, it would probably be worse for Soetoro. Schanck was merely a bit player. Or so I thought.

Then, in a twinkling of an eye, I found out how wrong I was. Sulana Schanck pulled a large knife from her sleeve and with one vicious backhand sliced Soetoro's throat from ear to ear. Blood geysered forth, showering Schanck, as the president sank toward the floor.

I scrambled to my knees and pointed my pistol, but I was too late. She spun like a ballet dancer, took one bound, and used the knife on the veep's neck, with similar results. John Rhodes went down in a welter of blood.

One of the Secret Service agents beat me to the trigger. He put a burst in Sulana Schanck's chest, hammering her to the floor.

"Drop it," I shouted. I had the Kimber .45 at arm's length pointed right at his head. If he tried to swing that carbine in my direction he was going to die.

"Drop the weapons," I roared again. Both carbines hit the floor.

The outside door swung open and a man appeared there with a pistol in his hand. I shouted, "You in the door. Get Admiral Grafton and send him in here *now*!"

Down below, Mickey had freaked. The aides and pols were fluttering around uselessly, staring horrified at the corpses of Barry Soetoro and his vice president. There was nothing anyone on earth could do for them. Sulana Schanck hadn't twitched since she hit the floor. Maybe she was in Paradise now or shaking hands with Muhammad in Hell.

To my eternal relief, Jake Grafton and General Considine walked into the room accompanied by four guys carrying weapons.

I sat down on the floor and holstered my shooter.

About two hours later the bodies of the president, vice president, chief of staff, and chief political advisor were carried out of the house and placed on a stack of firewood in the middle of a grassy area. The crowd had raided the presidential woodpile. They piled the bodies on that rick of wood, poured a couple of gallons of gasoline on them, and set them afire.

The National Guard had arrived by then and the volunteers had stopped shooting their guns into the air. The prisoners were loaded on trucks and driven away. I didn't ask where they were being taken.

A huge silent crowd encircled the fire. As I watched, the woman from the hike up the mountain, Betty Connelly, stepped from the crowd, leveled her shotgun into the fire, and fired twice.

Then she turned and walked away.

Grafton and Considine came over to where I was standing.

"Tell me what happened in there, Tommy."

So I told it, from climbing the balcony, to finding Grantham's corpse, to watching the Soetoro party trying to decide what to do...to Schanck's unexpected knife work.

"So you didn't hear what she and the president said?"

"No, sir. It looked like she was urging him to do something that he didn't want to do. Maybe she wouldn't take no for an answer."

"Workplace violence," General Considine remarked flippantly.

They had a few more questions, but I had no more answers.

"ISIS or Al Qaeda will claim they got him," Grafton said gloomily.

"Soetoro is the one who chose Sulana Schanck to sit beside him and whisper in his ear," Considine remarked. "The true believers are going to have to swallow that, Jake, whether they want to or not."

"*Et tu, Brute*," Grafton muttered.

I scored a flashlight off a soldier on the water truck and went looking for Sarah. Meanwhile she found Grafton. The funeral pyre was burning steadily now. The admiral had a handheld radio up to his ear, so I gave him the Hi sign and he acknowledged. With the fire illuminating a thousand faces, Sarah and I turned our backs to it and plunged into the darkness.

It was a five-mile hike through the woods, all uphill, and we came out on the bald about a half-mile north of the pickup. A sliver moon was hanging in the sky and the stars were out. This old earth just keeps on turning. Walking toward the truck, I asked her, "How are you feeling?"

She didn't reply.

"If that truck isn't hors de combat, I thought we might head west."

She didn't say anything.

"You got the keys to the truck?" I asked.

"I left them in the ignition."

Oh boy.

That half-mile hike through the grass in the moonlight, with corpses lying on the ground in a random pattern, was one of the memories I will carry with me all my days. There were at least two army trucks out there, lights ablaze, looking for wounded. The whole scene was surreal. The dead didn't even whisper.

We passed a young woman wandering along, trying in the moon and starlight to see the faces of the dead. She didn't have a weapon. Maybe she never did, or threw hers away or lost it. She didn't speak to us, so we passed her and kept hiking. I wondered which side of the fight she had been on, then decided that really didn't matter.

It was a little after midnight when we got to the truck. The keys were dangling from their slot. Is this a great country or what? All four tires had air. The windshield had taken at least three bullets and was in bad shape. One of the bullets had gone through the windshield and out the rear window. Fortunately Sarah had been lying on the seat at the time, protected by the motor and lots of metal, so she wasn't tagged. One of the truck's headlights was shot out. Some of the sheet metal had holes or gouge marks from bullets, and the radio aerial was missing, shot off. I opened the hood and examined the radiator and hoses with the flashlight. No visible leaks. Maybe the antifreeze all ran out. I looked at the ground under the engine, which was dry. We were good to go.

About a hundred yards to the south was an army truck with every light on. I walked over and saw a white cross painted on the side. Dr. Proudfoot was there, and he said the medics were out looking for wounded.

"We found some guy who had been scalped," he said. "Hell of a wound. He's a professor from some little college in New England. I sedated him."

"Is he going to make it?"

"Probably, if infections don't kill him."

I shook Proudfoot's hand and walked back to my stolen FEMA truck. Sarah was already in the passenger seat, buckled up.

"Idaho," Sarah said.

"Idaho," I agreed.

I fired up the motor. The lone headlight bravely stabbed the darkness.

THIRTY-SIX

★

We spent what was left of the night at Camp Dawson, which was manned by a skeleton crew of guardsmen. I gave them the machine gun and extra ammo and three AT4s that Willis hadn't managed to shoot. After lunch, we hit the road.

In a little town in Ohio I found a glass repair shop that was open. They replaced the windshield, rear window, and headlight. The head man wanted to talk, so I told him about the battle for Camp David.

When I finished he said, "I have been really worried about America for years, and martial law was my worst nightmare come true. I think the socialists and left-wing radicals want to change America into a nation my kids won't want to live in. It seems like they don't know the basics of economics, don't believe in work, don't believe that a person should earn and keep the fruits of their labor. They'll run America into the ground, then what?"

"Maybe now the future will be better," Sarah said.

"Then there is terrorism, all those Muslims admitted willy nilly," he said. "I can only hope and pray."

The power was back on in Ohio and Indiana, so we spent a night in a chain motel that was open. We ate a free breakfast at the bar off the lobby, which consisted of cornflakes and milk. I asked about the milk, and was told cows keep giving it regardless.

Filling stations were open again, and before the tank in the truck was empty, we found one with fuel to pump. Life was looking up.

In Illinois a state trooper took offense because I was driving at eighty miles an hour when the speed limit was sixty-five. He pulled us over.

"I told you to slow down," Sarah said primly as the trooper walked up.

"You with the government?" he asked, looking us over. The pickup had federal government plates, although it lacked logos on the doors. Sarah and I were still wearing our web belts and pistols. The trooper was a big black man with hair going gray at the tips. For a man who spent most of his working life sitting behind a wheel, he was reasonably trim and fit.

"Ah, no," I admitted. "We quit. We were with the CIA."

"Spies, huh?"

"I stole the truck," I said brightly, "from FEMA."

"Those assholes? No shit! You got ID?"

I dug out my wallet and passed him my CIA Langley pass.

He looked it over and passed it back. "What you got in the cooler in the bed?"

"A six-pack. Filling station back in Indiana had some. Want one?"

"Man, I haven't had a beer since Soetoro declared martial law. Yeah, I'd like one."

We got out and opened the cooler, and all three of us took a beer.

"If you have a camera in your cruiser, they might get unhappy seeing you with a beer," I said.

"Camera's broken. Piss on 'em." He popped the top on his can and took a swig. "Ahh! Tell me about the bullet holes in your ride."

So we sat on the tailgate of the truck and sipped beer while I told him about the attack on Camp David. As I talked and he asked questions of Sarah and me, he visibly relaxed. He believed us. If he only knew how good a liar I was, he would have been more suspicious, but ignorance is bliss, so they say. And for a change I stuck strictly to the truth.

When he finished asking questions about the death of Barry Soetoro, the trooper, whose name was Davis, waxed philosophical. "Soetoro made life a living hell for us cops, made us targets, turned people against us, and stirred up racial hatred we sure as hell didn't need. Sure, there are a few bad cops, the same as there are bad dentists, doctors, CEOs, and plumbers, but all these body cameras and shit, and the constant second-guessing of cops who put their lives on the line—that's bullshit. That bastard Soetoro killed a lot of people by making criminals feel free, taking their side, and giving carte blanche to illegal aliens with criminal records. He destroyed a lot of trust, especially with law enforcement. And you know, without the rule of law, we don't have a civilization. It's that simple."

I'd seen enough to know that.

He stood and dusted off his trouser seat. "You two slow it down, huh?"

"Yes, sir."

Davis got into his cruiser and drove away. We put all three empties in the cooler and got our chariot under way, heading west.

I didn't want to read newspapers or watch television or listen to radio. I had had enough of the world's troubles. Sarah and I chatted and watched the countryside pass by and the road unwind endlessly before us. Although traffic was light, things were getting back to normal. We saw tanker trucks sitting in filling stations, food trucks rolling the highways, trucks hauling cattle and hay, and farmers in the fields running combines. Trains went by on tracks that paralleled the highway. Here and there construction crews were back at work on road and bridge projects. Jets were flying again, so contrails streaked the blue sky.

Yet even political hermits like Sarah and me found the political crisis impossible to avoid. Every diner or bar we went into had televisions going full blast. The generals in the Pentagon had asked Jake Grafton to get an interim civilian government up and running and to hold elections in every state that wanted to remain in the old Union. Texas was independent and intended to stay that way, President Jack Hays said. The commentators were still aghast, and delighted, at the effrontery of the Texas military in stealing—or "replevying," Jack Hays' word—fifty tons of gold. At the quoted market price that morning—$2,132 an ounce—the metal was worth $3.4 billion. Jack Hays assured an interviewer that

Texas would return any excess after Texas' claims against the federal government were settled by negotiation.

In California, the Mexican Army had been driven out, but Mexican gangs and their radical supporters were now engaged in a civil war against everyone else. They had supported the Mexican Army, and now were fighting for an independent Mexican Southern California they planned to call Aztlan. They were being crushed, but Southern California, and Los Angeles in particular, would never be the same again. Television cameras lingered lovingly on columns of smoke rising over the LA basin.

In Mexico, another civil war had broken out. The reasons seemed to be manifold: the flood of illegals back to Mexico, Texas closing the border, the failed invasion of California (some said at the behest of the drug lords), and massive unemployment. The good news was that without the United States as a safety valve, Mexico was finally going to have to come to grips with poverty, monopoly, corruption, and lack of opportunity for most of the people who lived within its borders.

The violent death of Barry Soetoro had, as Jake Grafton feared, transformed him into a cultural icon among certain groups. His sins were forgotten in the pathos of his demise. Bogus eyewitness accounts aired between newscasts. Mickey Soetoro publicly and loudly blamed "white people." A waitress at a truck stop told us that Oprah was in tears for her entire show. All this despite the fact that the conversations Sarah captured in the White House in which Soetoro plotted to become a dictator were still airing on some radio stations.

We had been on the road for four days when we rolled into Idaho. We examined the brochures at a visitor's center and signed up for a float trip down the Salmon, the River of No Return. That took six wonderful days under a September sky. The nights were spent camping on a beach, and the days riding the river with a guide who paddled occasionally while Sarah and I fished the riffles and rapids for steelhead going upriver to spawn. We actually caught several good ones, which we immediately released back into the river.

The whole experience was magical. The canyon was wild and glorious, the eternal river flowing through rapids and down long, languid stretches, then through more rapids. We saw mule deer and coveys of chukar. Eventually we ended up on the Snake and spent a day drifting with the current to the pullout. People along the banks of the Snake on farms and in yards waved to us.

Sarah and I were laughing and smiling when the experience was over. America was still here, still glorious.

After another week of driving through the mountains, we ended up in Idaho Falls. That evening we finally turned on the television to a news channel and began catching up.

A constitutional convention had been announced. Jake Grafton was on television with the leaders of the House and Senate asking the governors of states both in and out of the Union to send delegates. He finished with this statement: "I think a great many people feel that the constitutional mandate for separation of powers between the three branches of government, and between the states and the federal government, got badly warped through the years. We hope a convention can fix that, especially by putting more teeth into the Tenth Amendment."

Grafton continued, "The judges decided the interstate commerce, due process, and some other clauses were loopholes big enough to swallow the states and give the federal government control of every aspect of American life. That control was not exercised by Congress, an institution totally inadequate for the task, but by unelected, unaccountable bureaucrats, sometimes controlled by the executive but often controlled by no one at all. That has to change. I don't know what devices the convention delegates will come up with to harness the Cheshire Cat, but they can try or fail or surrender, as they choose.

"The delegates may also choose to revise our democratic institutions to make them more efficient and responsive to the electorate.

"What is not on the table are the basic civil rights we Americans as a free people enjoy. We are seeking new ways to preserve those rights, not diminish them.

"If the delegations do their jobs well, we will have added safeguards to preserve liberty, the rights of the states, and the freedom of the people. It is my hope that the states that have declared their independence will return to the family of states that we call the United States, a family that has provided shelter and livelihoods for a free people for over two centuries, and I believe, with tweaking, can shelter us and our descendants for many more.

"May God bless a restored and reunited America."

After the speech a commentator appeared on camera. I stared. Yes, it was Jack Yocke, clean-shaven, with a haircut, wearing a suit and tie. He was now the network's expert on all things Grafton.

Jack Hays was next.

"Texas is getting its act together," he said. "We are in talks with Oklahoma, New Mexico, and Arizona to form some kind of federation. How that will work out, I don't know, but I am encouraged. The illegals who don't speak English and have no job skills are going back to Mexico; we have about two thousand families a day moving to Texas to find jobs, families that do speak English and have trades and job skills to support themselves and make positive contributions to the economy and tax base. We are reforming the education system, training Americans, and putting them to work. Texas has a bright future."

When we turned off the television in the wee hours of the morning, Sarah asked, "So what are we going to do with our lives?"

"I don't know," I replied, truthfully.

"We can't keep doing nothing."

"I know."

"I want to go home," she said.

The following day we pointed the truck east. The highways were more crowded, almost back to normal, I thought, and every filling station and truck stop had gas and lots of customers.

Four days later we rolled into West Virginia and stopped by the safe house near Greenbank. Dr. Proudfoot was there making a house call. Mrs. Price sat on the porch with a jacket around her shoulders and a blanket over her legs enjoying the fall colors, which I thought were near their peak. Little Sarah threw herself at Big Sarah, and Armanti Hall shook my hand until I had to jerk my appendage out to save it.

"I thought you were boogying off to Texas," I said, flexing my fingers.

"Gonna stay here and rebuild Mrs. Price's house. Then the three of us are going to live in it."

"Got enough money for lumber, toilets, and pipes?"

"I have a little saved up," he said, looking down his nose at me. "Need a loan?"

"Ah, right now, no. But if in the uncertain and unpredictable future I unexpectedly find myself in a fiscal hole, I know where to find you."

"Right up the road. We should be in by spring."

"It's great to have friends."

"So they say."

We drove on to Washington and stopped in front of the lock shop. We went in, and there sat Willie the Wire Varner.

"Where the hell you been?" he demanded. "I thought you two were dead."

"Still kicking," I said. "What happened to you after the battle of Kingwood?"

He said he had hitchhiked back to Washington. "I'm no warrior," he declared defensively. "Ain't got it in me."

This was the Willie Varner I knew and liked.

We were catching up, telling him of our adventures and listening to him describe his odyssey back to Washington, when my cell phone rang.

I looked at the caller ID—Jake Grafton—and answered it. "Hey."

"Tommy, where are you?"

"In Washington."

"Good. Come see me tomorrow. I need you."

"See you where?"

"Callie and I are bunking at the White House temporarily."

"Okay."

"I want you to go to Europe. Some of the Middle East refugees flooding in there turned out to be jihadists, which seemed to surprise the Europeans. Maybe you can help keep us advised of what's going on."

"See you tomorrow."

I hung up.

Sarah looked at me and raised her eyebrows.

"Jake Grafton," I said. "He wants me to go to Europe."

"It's about time," she said, and smiled.